ROUTE 66
THE LAST MILE

TO MOM AND DAD

THE AUTHOR

     Mike Clarke was born in a hospital in 1953, at least that's the story his mother is sticking to. Upon graduating from the University of Toronto, at St. George, with a degree in Geopolitics he started work as an engineering inspector on civil engineering projects because Henry Kissinger has the only job in

Geopolitics and he wasn't going to wait around until Henry died to apply for it. He drives a 1961 Thunderbird, writes books and drinks Metaxa.

He's also the author of "The Learning Curve" which will be available in the fall of Nov 2014; go to clarkeae35.blogspot.ca, for details.

TABLE OF CONTENTS

INTRODUCTION

The Oxford American Dictionary describes a highway as follows:
1.   A public road.
2.   A main route by land, sea or air.

The engineering description for a highway is as follows:

Before the work begins, the constructor center line is staked out, usually at fifty-foot stations. After the initial lane is placed, additional stakes may be set for other lanes or the forms may be set by leveling one with a line level. The amount of stakeout done for highway construction depends on the value and importance of the work. (1)

In reality, a highway is a ribbon of asphalt, concrete and rock built up layer upon layer. A layer is put down, compacted, and another is put down, until finally, concrete or asphalt is put down. Lastly, lines are painted and a highway is created.

A high way begins life as so many tons of sand, gravel, and topping. After that, it evolves into a machine that converts dreams into memories. The present is nothing more than wheels on pavement. Many lives pass over a highway. Some are converted to memories, some are changed, and tragically, some die with their owners. Whatever, the case, a dream must reach its destination. It is the role of a highway to ensure it happens.

This story is about a dream that was never finished. It's the story of two men who started down the road with a destination. Their journey was never completed. The road is still waiting. It can wait a long time, but it cannot wait an eternity. A dream fulfilled, memories completed, this road has waited long enough. They will be called back to finish what they started on Route 66.

1 Seelye Elwyn E. Field Practice, Data Book for
Civil Engineers Vol 3,
John Wiley London. 1947

CHAPTER 1
SADDLE RIVER

In America, money rolls down hill and
Saddle River occupied a lot of space at the bottom of
the hill. If you lived at the end of Saddle River Road,
you were up to your neck in it. Anyway, that was the
way the good citizens of the State of New Jersey saw
it. Fortunately, there were only three houses at the
end of Saddle River Road.

The good citizens of New Jersey would
also tell you that there are two types of money a
person can have. Anyone looking at the three houses
on Saddle River Road could tell that the house on the
left is definitely new money. The BMW and Volvo
are obvious signs of a young couple with far too
much disposable income. He's an arbitrage trader,
she's a lawyer.

The house on the right is definitely old
money. There's a very expensive Rolls Royce sitting
out front. The house has only one occupant, the
daughter of a very wealthy industrial magnate. The

daughter had inherited the whole ball of wax and had added a considerable amount of wax to the ball.

The house in the middle is neither new money nor old. It's more like money that got tossed into a corner and forgotten. To be precise, the owner simply doesn't know what to do with the stuff. There is a car in the driveway. It's difficult to ascertain the make and age because it's badly damaged.

This particular house has two occupants. One's feeling violently ill and the other could care less. The one feeling badly is, in fact, suffering from a hangover. Not one of those friendly you have been naughty dull ache type of hangovers. This is a violent, God-Almighty--I've-done-something-horrific-but-I can-not-remember-what type of hangover. The kind of hangover reserved for mass murderers and the criminally insane. The owner of this particular hangover is Todd Stiles and he'd decided to take the coward's way out. He instructed the other occupant of the house to go find a gun. He instructed the other occupant to come back with it and shoot him, thereby putting Todd out of his misery. The other occupant of the house, whose name is Al Johnson, informed Todd that there were many occasions when he would have been more than happy to grant him his wish. However, on this particular occasion, he would prefer watching him roll around in agony.

Todd was on his own this time. He rolled over and saw the glass of orange juice Al had left on the night table. Todd's brain told him to go to the bathroom and throw up. The problem was he couldn't get to the bathroom standing up. When he sat up, his brain tried to sneak out of his head through the back of his eyeballs.

It took about four minutes, but Todd did manage to make it to the floor. From there, he had to get up on all fours, another two minutes. His journey was delayed when he discovered he was headed for the closest instead of the bedroom door. Things looked a lot different down here at floor level. He wondered for a brief, fleeting moment, how his pet beagle managed to get anywhere in life. Fortunately, the bedroom door was ajar and he could pull it open with his hand, without having to reach up and turn the knob. Al watched the one-man parade pass him in the hallway. When the weird float dressed up in a terry towel bathrobe had passed, he continued down the hall without so much as batting an eye.

Todd made it to the toilet but the hangover said "no, not yet! I want to torture you some more." He decided to lay there and let it have its way with him. It took an hour, but he finally made it to the height of the sink. Things got really scary when he made it to the mirror. It was a very grim picture. Sticking out his tongue was an all-time low, was that fur? The mirror responded by cracking violently into several hundred pieces. Tod's brain stopped torturing him for a brief, amazing moment. that was a really terrific trick, he thought to himself. His brain agreed, and then got back to the business of crucifying him for the night before. Al Johnson, besides being a butler, handyman, valet or whatever he needed to be called at any particular time, was also a terrific practical joker. The mirror was one of his favorites. Todd stumbled to the window, and then decided against it. Barfing out the bathroom window was a bit too tacky, even for him.

He lay down in front of the toilet. If he had to blow chow, at least he wouldn't have to travel far. On the other hand, if he died, that was all right too. No problem. Elvis punched his ticket in the bathroom. Todd decided to take a nap. He woke to find Al staring down at him. For a horrible, brief moment, he thought he was in heaven and God was really Al Johnson. Even worse, he was in hell, and Al was a man who really enjoyed his work.

"Was I supposed to be somewhere today?"

Al smiled. You're supposed to be in L.A. at 1:00 p.m. for a directors meeting."

"What time is it?

"6:30 in the evening."

"I'm late, aren't I?"

"I told David you were in a car crash."

Todd looked horrified'

"Don't worry, he promised to be home in time for the funeral."

Al stepped over Todd's remains and examined his own teeth in what was left of the mirror. "You're booked you on the 8:30 flight. You'll get in late, but you can sleep on the plane. The meeting has been rescheduled for tomorrow morning.

Forty-five minutes later, a more or less functional Todd Stiles was, more or less, dressed and ready to go to the airport. He stopped at the bedroom mirror and looked at his reflection the mirror remained intact this time.

In the last thirty-plus years, he had traded in his unemployed, blond; beach boy looks for a fifty-three-year-old man with a paunch. Still, it had been a good thirty years. He landed in California in 1965, and decided to go back to school for a degree in electrical engineering. It was either that or Vietnam.

When he got out of school, he wandered around for seven months looking for work. In his spare time, he designed circuit boards for ham radio buffs. It didn't make him rich, but it did keep him in beer. One day, a twelve-year-old kid showed up at his door, wanting to know if Todd would make him a circuit board that could add, subtract, multiply, and divide. Todd told him it would be a lot easier to just buy one. The kid said he couldn't afford one. Todd asked the kid what made him think he could afford Todd. The kid replied that he figured that Todd was broke and would take whatever he could get. Todd told him he'd see what he could do.

The kid's final request was that he wanted it small enough to fit into his pocket. Todd thought that was pretty funny. What the kid ended up with was a desk top calculator with eighteen different mathematical functions. It was actually fairly impressive. However, the idea of a calculator in a pocket continued to rattle around in the back of Todd's mind.

Todd went back to the drawing board trying to figure out how to compress the whole system down to something the size of a cigarette package. As it turned out, the discovery of the first integrated circuit didn't occur in an advanced ATT lab in New Jersey. It happened in the back of Todd Stiles fridge. He'd left a block of cheese back there on some wrinkled tin foil. The fridge hadn't been working for a couple of days and the cheese had gone bad and soft. When he was moving and the fridge needed to be cleaned out, he found the cheese had sagged and that the foil had left marks which looked like an electrical circuit. An hour later, he was out buying wax and solder. He discovered that by making an imprint of a circuit in the wax, then filling it with melted solder, he could make a circuit. Within a week and with the help of a good microscope and jeweler's tools, he'd created a circuit on a piece of silicon the size of a dime. Next stop was the patent office.

Todd took his patented integrated circuit to the advanced ATT lab and sold it to the telephone company for a lot of money. Like his father, Todd was very good at making money. Unlike his father, Todd was able to hang onto it.

Todd took his new-found fortune, set up a computer circuit company, and made one hell of a pile of money. His personal assets were crowding $150 million, by his mid- thirties. He had it all: a beautiful and loving wife and two great kids, David and Jan.

In 1987, it all started to fall apart. Not the business, just his life. His wife Marcie developed Multiple Sclerosis. At first, she would drop things and give him a funny puzzled look. Within two months, she couldn't walk. It was all downhill from there. She just up and disintegrated right in front of him. Marcie was gone in a year, mercifully, but Todd never got over it completely. A year later the kids were gone. David went West after university to take over the business from Todd, although Todd kept control. David added to his father's already wealthy status.

His daughter, Jan, was finishing law school and would soon be articling. Of the two, he was closer to David. Jan was about as compassionate and caring as a rock. Even Marcie had felt Jan's cold exterior. She had neither the time nor the patience for the trappings of being feminine. At Marcie's funeral, Jan had gone through the motions of saying and doing the right things. But there was nothing behind her words or actions. When it was over, Jan immediately left for school. Todd hadn't heard from her in over a year.

Except for Al, who had shown up at his door two years ago and announced that he was applying for the butler's job, Todd had been alone for the last five years.

Todd stuck out his tongue. No doubt about it, this was one tough mirror. Al appeared at the door and nodded his approval. "Welcome back to the land of the living."

He pulled down an eyelid and a mild wave of nausea rolled over him. "More like the living dead."

"Your bags are waiting downstairs."

"I'll be along in a minute."

Taking a brief glance at Marcie's picture on the night table, he turned and went out the door. He was surprised to see a cab waiting for him in front of the house.

"Where's my car?"

Al pointed to the left. Lying parallel to the garage were the remains of his car, brand new and barely a month old. The car was way beyond write off and into the realm of mauled. The cab driver, who had gotten out of his cab to help with the bags, walked around the wreck and looked carefully in a window. He gave a low whistle, and shook his head in amazement.

The car had met its terrible end while being driven through the cement wall separating Todd's money from the old money next door. The car succeeded in passing through the wall, but at a terrible price.

Todd walked over to the wall and looked through the hole. Not a pretty sight. His brand new car had done some serious damage to his neighbor's landscaping.

He turned to Al, who had a horrible, wicked grin on his face. "You're going to tell me how all this happened, aren't you?"

Al nodded silently.

"I'm not going to enjoy this, am I?"

Al nodded again, silently.

Todd's neighbor was Amanda Tewksbury. Her money went way, way, back and apparently, so did the wall Todd had put a hole in with his car. Amanda believed in all the rules about money and class. It belonged to the chosen few and people who had money should behave like they had money. Todd thought she was a stuck up old fart. From the first day that he and Marcie moved in next door, Amanda took an immediate and active dislike to Todd; however, she liked Marcie. Things had gotten worse between the two of them since Marcie had passed away. Ironically, Todd and Amanda had the same age and birthday, but that's all they had in common.

Al proceeded to describe the previous night, which had, in fact, started around noon. Todd had confronted Al about a run in he'd had with Amanda four days ago which he'd just heard about from the Yuppie neighbors an hour before.

The Yuppies had stopped by Todd's to ask him to join them for a barbecue. What they encountered was Amanda Tewksbury, at Todd's door, demanding to know why Al hadn't trimmed the tree at the wall. Its leaves were falling into her $12,000 rose garden. Amanda then proceeded to tell Al how her people felt about his people. If his kind wanted to come into this neighborhood, they'd have to learn their place. As she left the porch, she made it clear there was nothing wrong with a good, old-fashioned lynching. The Yuppies were visibly uncomfortable when they had to repeat Amanda's exact words. Amanda didn't get an invitation to the barbecue.

Todd was royally pissed off. He not only respected Al, although he never said it to him, he'd also had begun to consider Al a friend.

"Why the hell didn't you tell me about this?"

Al looked right at Todd when he spoke. "It didn't concern you. It's between Amanda and me."

Todd shook his head. "When it happens on my property, it concerns me."

"You're never going to understand. You are always going to be here and I'm always going to be black."

Al was right. Todd would never understand what victims of prejudice really felt. He raised his hands in surrender. "Next time, if there is a problem, let me know, and maybe I can help."

Al nodded. "Understood."

If a barbecue had been scheduled on that particular day, Al and Amanda were the briquettes. The lighter fluid showed up at 1:30 in the form of Bert Buntmayer. Bert, or Fat Freddy as he was often called, was a corporate lawyer who'd decided to become a stock broker. In his words, he could make a shit load of money without having to do any real work. He was right. Bert was a brilliant stock trader but a wreck at everything else. He was fat, sweaty, and unkempt. His wife left him because it was "either her or a bath!" Bert promised to write when he had a chance. His kids had disowned him, despite his money. His million dollar condo in Central Park looked and, more importantly, smelled like a landfill site on the inside. He was currently up on morality charges. The police caught him relieving himself in the fountain in front of the Securities Exchange Commission,...it was a number two."

Al announced that Bert was at the front door and continued to announce Bert's arrival as he proceeded through the house. Todd caught up with him when he got to the bar.

"Todd, old buddy, let us repair to the club!"
Normally, Todd was fairly cautious around Bert.Things tended to get out-of- hand pretty quickly when he was around.

"Hell of a plan, Fred. Let us be off!"
So much for caution.

The Sherman Oaks Golf Club was very exclusive, a tough course designed by Arnold Palmer, and most members golfed in the low 90's. Bert, or Fat F,... Freddy as the members called him, saw the place as an enormous backyard to party in. Todd had not been to a Club Christmas party in four years after Bert, aka Santa Claus, decided to do a swan dive off the pool table and onto the club pro's wife. Bert continued to insist that he would've made it if the eggnog bowl hadn't got in the way.

"Fred, you're in the president's parking spot, again."

"Tough noogies! I spent 40 g's in this place last year! The old fart can park someplace else.

"No doubt about it, thought Todd. This day was seriously out of control."

Todd and Bert spent most of the afternoon at the bar looking for the perfect Rusty Nail. Todd figured they found it around 4:00 p.m. The Club president told Fred to move his car around five, Fred told him to go have sex with himself, *not his exact words*. The president told Fred that his membership would be brought up at the next meeting. Fred told the president that if he was suspended or expelled, the bar would go broke, and they would have to close it. The president went and parked someplace else.

Around 6:00 p.m., Todd and Bert decided that the club didn't offer the kind of plus excitement that the evening required and went looking for live entertainment? They ended up in a bar way past the wrong side of the tracks.

Sometime during the ninth stripper's act, Todd realized that he hadn't had sex in three years. He decided that he should go home and have sex. The problem was that there was no one at home to have sex with. Todd's memory was not very clear at his point, but stripper number twelve looked a lot like Amanda Tewksbury. Actually, he didn't think she looked that bad. Somehow, or other, he decided that if could not have sex at his house, he would just have to have it at Amanda's. Since he didn't think she would approve of him having sex with someone else at her house, he would just have to have sex with Amanda.

The cab driver dropped a thoroughly plastered Todd Stiles in front of his house at 1:30 in the morning. In fact, he could barely stand. If the Cabbie had helped him to the door, nothing would have happened. *Good Karma!* Unfortunately, in the process of looking for his house keys, he found the keys to his car instead. Despite the fact that his brain was almost totally disabled, he managed to make the connection between his car keys, the now infamous wall, and sex with Amanda. *Bad Karma*! It took him about twenty minutes to get the key in the lock and open the door, but eventually he figured it out, the door wasn't locked. Todd's motor skills had begun to fail badly by the time he figured out how to get behind the wheel. His arms and legs had seemed to develop a life of their own. He was down to his last working brain cell, as he was putting on his seat belt. On the other hand, his desire to really do it to Amanda had increased dramatically.

He turned the ignition. It needed yet another key! More fumbling, wrong key, fumble some more. It seemed as though every time he tried to sort them out, the keys would multiply, wrong key again. Fumble some more. Maybe blink a bit to get the eyes focused. The eyelids are out of sync. We will just have to scrunch the whole face. Right key but it is upside down. One more time and we have finally got it right.

Todd held the key down for a full two minutes, just to make sure the engine was running. Finding the right gear was a bit tricky. Todd had to back the car into the side of the house, in order to figure out which gear he was in. He looked out the window. The place needed painting, anyway. Reverse was obviously the wrong direction. Just to be on the safe side, he pulled the shift lever all way down. Yes- Sir, you can't go wrong with the old low gear. Lots of motoring power there!"

He got a good grip on the steering wheel and jammed the accelerator to the floor. There was a few seconds of roaring, as the tires tore up the grass and then a violent screech as the wheels got a purchase on the curb. The car took off like a bat-out-of -hell. It was at least sixty feet from where the car was sitting to the wall. Todd and the car were moving at an impressive forty-seven-miles-per-hour, when they arrived at the wall.

It was, in a word, spectacular, and in no small sense, a miracle. Driving a car into a cement wall at over forty-miles-per-hour is usually fatal. In this case, however, the wall was very weak at the point of impact. The center of the wall had long since washed out, leaving only a hard mortar shell.

The quiet gentile southern atmosphere of the Tewksbury estate was shattered by the smoking and rumbling remains of Todd's car and its inebriated occupant. I'm coming for you, Amanda! Yes, indeedy, we are going to have sex tonight! Todd stomped on the gas. Amanda's rose garden died a final, violent, and horrible death under a two-ton rotor tiller.

Amanda awoke at the sound of the crash. She reached her bedroom window to find an unbelievable scene of destruction. Her beloved wall destroyed, her beautiful garden violated, and the massacre was continuing right before her eyes.

Todd did a couple of donuts in front of the house just for effect, and a couple more just trying to get the car stopped. He leaned out the window of the rose killer mobile. Amanda, are you up there? It's your love machine coming for you...baby. I can hear the bed springs rumbling from here!"

Righteous indignation didn't exactly describe Amanda's feelings when she saw the carnage, nor did vexation or annoyance. It was at this point that she displayed a command of the four-letter word which is unsurpassed to this day. To put it simply, she brought the house down. For a full minute, everyone, including the police who had just arrived at the request of Amanda's butler and the yuppie neighbors, were transfixed by the shrieking apparition in the second story window. It was an incredible sight.

Todd's last and only active brain cell correctly realized that it was being reduced to second billing. Acting out of self-preservation, he stomped on the gas and steered the car back through the wall. Todd's body was merely along for the ride. The officers in the first car patrol car on the scene immediately got back in their car and went after Todd, through the wall.   Amanda went berserk. Her wrath fell on the officers of the second patrol car still remaining in her driveway. Officers

Turner and Collins, or Toodey and Muldoon to their colleagues because they were assigned to Unit 54, had only been on duty an hour. I wonder if we should arrest her for talking like that.

Collins shook his head. "She's on her own property and she can say anything she wants."

Turner persisted. "Yes, but listen to her. She's being awfully rude to people." He wondered aloud where a woman would learn that kind of language.

Collins was clear on the issue. "Nope. We got a call about a lunatic in a car, not one in a house."

Amanda looked down from her window and pointed at Collins. Her wrath was upon him. "You sausage sucking jigaboo, stop playing with your fucking pork sword, get your fucking hands out of fucking your pockets, and go arrest that fucking asshole. When you are done, come back here and fucking dance for me!"

Collins. "I'm-going-up-there-and-arrest-that BITCH!

Turner. "Wow!"

It was a hell of a fight. It took them twenty minutes to put the cuffs on Amanda, and drag her, kicking and screaming out of the house. At the front door she got her feet up on the door sill. "Shit man,...you got to get her feet off!"

"I can't get her legs down,...she's like a wrinkly thigh master!"

Getting her in the car was like stuffing an angry badger into a suitcase.

"Damn, her negliger is hanging out."

"It's called negligee, Turner."

"Still don't look right."

Collins got a can of red spray paint out of the car the police used to mark accident lines on the road. "See. Now it looks like one of those wide-load flags."

"Yeah, but we don't have a wide load."

"By the time she's done kicking out the trunk walls, we'll be a wide load."

When they got to the station, they didn't even try putting her in holding while they wrote up the charges. They just left her in the car. Turner was convinced that if they let her out, she'd kill someone. Things were not going any better on the other side of the wall. A small crowd had gathered on Todd's lawn. Nobody was going near Amanda's place.

Unlike Collins and Turner, officers Masters and Johnson had an hour left on their shift. They wanted a statement from Todd. Todd wanted to go sleep in the bushes. After twenty minutes, Johnson wanted to take out his gun and shoot Todd. His partner said he couldn't do that because there were too many witnesses.

"Sir, you have to give us a statement, or we're going to be here all night. Officer Masters pleaded.

Todd relented. "I just wanted to give Amanda a jolly good fucking!"

Masters looked at his partner and then back at Todd. "That's it. That's all you have to say?"

Todd gave Masters a "Two Thumbs Up." His duty done, he slid down the fender of the car and passed out in the driveway.

The cab driver was leaning on the hood of his car with his head in his hands, totally engrossed in Al's recounting of what went on the previous night. "Man! You did all that in one night? You rich guys really know to party."

Even Todd was in awe. "I must be in serious trouble."

Al looked around at the carnage. "Well, the police have laid charges of disturbing the peace, destruct Ion of private property, trespassing, drunk and disorderly conduct, and driving under the influence. He pointed at the cab. The police have your license, but only for twenty-four hours, because you were on private property."

Todd looked relieved. "It could have been worse."

Al smiled, "And now, for the bad news. Amanda is going to sue you right to hell when she finally gets out of jail."

Todd flinched. "She's still in custody?"

"I'm posting bail and bringing her home this evening.

Todd looked at Al hard. "Why?"

"She doesn't keep any money in the house, because she doesn't trust the housekeeper, and the police want their car back. It shouldn't be a problem getting her out."

Al opened the door of the cab and pushed Todd in. He tossed the bags in the other door. He leaned in the window. "I'll have everything straightened out by the time you get back."

Todd nodded. Al seemed to have different personalities for different circumstances. This was the professional Al, the one who got things done. Over the years, Todd had come to realize that Al was one of the most competent people he'd ever known.

"You didn't answer my question, Al. "Why?"

As the cabbie pulled his car out of the driveway, he looked at Todd through the rear view mirror. "He's a good man."

Todd nodded and leaned back in the seat. "He's a good man."

The nausea was gone and exhaustion was beginning to set in. Todd resisted the urge to sleep. There would be plenty of time on the plane. Rolling down the window, he let the warm evening air flow into the cab. Watching the neighborhood roll by, he wondered why people spent so much time and money on their property. Whole lives spent acquiring a few square yards of real estate and for what? It all seemed so pointless.

As the cab turned on to the turnpike and headed for New York, he began to feel detached from life. Money tended to do that to people. Meals were cooked for him, cabs arranged, flights book. The more of it you had, the less control you had.

Thirty long minutes later, the cab was at the airport and the driver was taking his luggage off the back seat. That'll be $40.00, Sir. Mind if I ask you a question?"

"No."

"How much money do you have to have to pull off a stunt like that?"

"About 300 million."

The driver whistled.

Todd shook his head. "It won't get you a cab in Camden at 3:00 in the morning."

The driver nodded in agreement.

Todd breathed a sigh of relief as he entered the airport. It was empty. That didn't change the fact that the United Airlines counter was at the far end of the terminal. At JFK, that meant a long walk. There had to be an easier way to get from one end to the other, he thought.

The next step was to check in. Unfortunately, the process was delayed due to the woman in front of him. He wondered if he could fall asleep in the line-up and someone would carry him onto the plane. Nope.

The woman was very pregnant and because of her condition, she needed a seat at the partition, because she would not be able to get up if there was seat in front of her. Despite the fact that she had a reserved seat, the flight was overbooked. The reservation agent politely, with many teeth and smiles, informed the pregnant woman that she could upgrade to first class or wait until a morning flight. The pregnant woman politely responded with no teeth or smiles, that she could not afford first class and that she was in no condition to wait anywhere.

Todd decided to move the process along. "What's the problem here?"

"The airline overbooked the flight and gave my seat away."

"How about I buy you a first class ticket? Todd inquired.

The woman thought he was crazy. "Do you have any idea how much that costs?"

Todd handed his credit card to the ticket agent. "Get her a first class ticket at the partition and a limo to wherever she wants to go at the other end." He nodded politely as the pregnant woman thanked him ten times. He then told her to get out of the way so that he could get his boarding pass.

He turned to the Sky Cap that had pushed him and his luggage to the check-in. "To the air machine, Jonathan, and mind the bumps."

Todd, more or less, sleep-walked through security and on to the plane. He'd gotten a good window seat near the back of the plane and had the row to himself, which was way better than first class. With his body finally at rest, he could start using his badly abused brain. Yesterday felt like a hundred years ago. For the first time in a day, he wondered if Bert made it home. The familiar thunder of the engines finally came. As the jet climbed into the dusk, he could see the Interstate below. There was a single white car on it. It reminded him of a scene from that movie. What was it they used to say? "Where were you in 62?"

Twenty minutes out of LAX, the first officer of United Airlines 1212 stowed his pre-landing checklist. "Checklist complete, Sir."

The Captain nodded. "LAX is reporting wind gusts on 18 at 30 knots."

"Right down the center line of the runway, Sir."

The Captain made some minor adjustments to the DC 10's trim.   "We'll reset again at the outer marker."

The first officer checked the glide slope indicator and looked out the window. The runway was perfectly centered in the window. "Instrument Landing System contact confirmed. We've got the middle marker."

"Middle marker confirmed. We are above the glide slope and 20 knots fast, Sir."

The Captain acknowledged his first officer.

"We are coming in high and hot, Sir."

The Captain again acknowledged his first officer.

The first officer took one more look at his instruments and looked over at his surprisingly calm Captain, before getting a good grip on the arm rests of his seat. Then, under his breath, so the Cockpit Voice Recorder would not pick up his voice, he whispered. "This is going to leave a mark on the runway."

The pilot pasted the DC10 onto the runway hard enough to wake Todd up with a jolt. As he walked off the plane, the stewardess gave him the obligatory smile that said, "I hope you enjoyed the flight and now I'm going up to the cockpit and choke the living shit out of the pilot for that landing. Todd took small comfort in the fact everyone else on the plane looked as bad as he felt. Tired and dirty. The airport did not look any better. Airports always looked shabby when they were empty. He looked around for David, but couldn't see him. He decided to do what he did best in airports. Walk from one end to the other. There were no Skycaps available to push him in a cart.

He was at a duty free shop looking at book with a catchy title, *"Bar-tending for the visually impaired"*, when David caught up with him.

"Dad, what are you doing here? You should be up at the turnstiles."

It took Todd a few minutes for his mouth to go into gear. "David, why are you dressed like that?"

"Dressed like what?"

"It's 11:30 at night and you're standing in LAX wearing a $1200.00 suit."

"It's business Dad. I was working late."

"What kind of business requires a suit like that at this hour?"

"Dad, this is L.A. Anyone who is going anywhere out here has to maintain an image."

Todd looked at the Skycap waiting behind David for some kind of understanding. The man just shook his head and rolled his eyes.

Todd paid the Skycap and shook his hand. "Where did you park?"

"The car is in the R1 lot."

"Do you think you could find a spot a little farther out? That's a ten minute walk."

"The company pays a lot of money for a corporate parking space in R1. Beside that's why I had the Skycap."

The air was surprisingly clean and cool. Unfortunately, there was no view to go with it. Asphalt and concrete can take the fun out of being anywhere, particularly when it goes on forever. Todd was looking hard for another Skycap by the time they reached the car. "What kind of car is this? Todd wanted to know.

It was an impressive piece of work. Low, wide and it looked expensive. Even when it was standing still, it looked fast.

"It's a Mercedes Benz Dad."

For a brief moment, Todd wondered how well it would hold up if it was driven through a cement wall. "This must have cost you a lot of money. Are you sure you can afford it?"

David smiled. "You should know, you sign the checks."

Todd didn't have answer for that one.

As they headed for the city, Todd wanted to roll down the window.   People in L.A. did not roll down windows. The car was also annoyingly quiet. The kind of silence just before a symphony starts, which would be a bad time for a roaring good fart.

"Want to get something to eat, Dad?"

Todd shook his head. "No, I need to get some sleep."

As they pulled up in front of the hotel, David tried to give his Dad a rundown on the next day's schedule. Todd waved him off. "I'll be in the office at 9:00. The meeting can wait. I want to look around and tour the plant."

David began to protest, but Todd cut him off. "I know there's a lot business to discuss, but the employees make the place run. It won't kill us to put them first in the order of business."

David raised his hands in resignation. "Ok, Ok, but I'm going to fax the agenda to the hotel, so you can review it before you get to work."

Todd smiled. "I can live with that." He pulled his luggage out of the back seat ignoring the waiting valet and his cart. He also impressed the doorman holding open the door, by walking through the opposite door.

David got out of the car and tipped the valet and doorman. "My old man knows how to make money, but he sure doesn't know how to spend it."

The front desk clerk watched Todd as he crossed the lobby. The clerk tried to make his face smile. The best he could manage was a grimace that said, "you're that awful man who comes here and makes my life a wide-awake nightmare. You are the guest from hell!"

"Good evening, Mr. Stiles. We have already checked you in."

"Where's Eddy? Eddy, the bellhop."

The front desk clerk scrunched up his face in the mistaken belief that he could scare Todd out of the hotel. "Eddy, sir?"

Todd scrunched up his face on the assumption this was some new L.A. fad. "Eddy the bellhop, the fellow who looks after things for me when I stay here."

A face appeared in the clerk's mind. "Are you referring to Edward Gluck sir? He comes on duty at 7:00 am."

"That's him. Send him up to my room when he gets into work. I have some things I need him to look after for me."

"I'll see to it."

The bellhop gave up trying to get his hands on Todd's luggage, so he could carry it by time they got to the elevator.

The Beverly Wilshire, Hotel was a class act, right down to the marble in the bath tubs. It was the hotel he stayed in every time he came out to the West Coast. Actually, it was the hotel David booked him into every time he came out to the West Coast,... Todd hated The Beverly Wilshire.

There was a knock on his door at precisely 7:00 a.m. When Todd opened it, the man holding his fax didn't look like Eddy Gluck. He looked like the hotel manager.

He handed Todd the fax. Good morning, "Mr. Stiles. I trust you slept well?"

Todd nodded silently. The manager was not seeing him at his best.

"I understand you will need some errands taken care of?"

Todd nodded silently. So far, so good, the manager thought.

"Mr. Jeppeson will be looking after you during your stay."

Todd shook his head silently. "Oh, God!"

"Sir, Mr. Jeppeson is one of our most senior staff and very reliable."

Todd leaned forward and placed a large nasty chunk of morning breath on the hotel manager's lapel. The carnation he was wearing died horribly. "I want Eddy Gluck up here in five minutes. If he isn't up here in five minutes, I will come down to the lobby in my underwear and breathe on everyone who comes in the front door."

Edward Gluck was at Todd's door in less than three minutes.

Todd had stumbled on Eddie Gluck a year before when his shoes went out to be shined and never returned. While the hotel was trying to locate his missing footwear, there was a knock at the door. Eddy, the bellhop, had found Todd's room key still in the lock. Todd decided to resolve the missing shoe problem. He handed Eddy a hundred dollars and instructed him to purchase a new pair of shoes. Todd assumed Eddy would go to the hotel clothing store and purchase a new pair of Florsheim's. Eddy got in his car, drove to the nearest Zellers, and bought a pair of very comfortable, $19.00 black loafers. Eddy, the shoes and $80.00 change were back at Todd's door thirty-five minutes later.

Todd, the shoes and his change were long gone by the time the hotel manager was knocking at his door with $180.00 Florsheim's from the hotel store to replace the one's the hotel had lost. Todd never forgot the shoes or Eddy.

Todd handed Eddy a list as soon as he stepped in the door. The first things on the list were not going to go over well at the hotel manager.

1.   Check out of the hotel.
2.   Cancel the hotel limo, get a rental car
3.   Check into Holiday Inn near the plant.

"Got any vacation time Eddy?"

"I've a week accumulated so far." Eddy replied.

"Go take it now and I will pay your salary."

Eddy had plans for that holiday time. On the other hand, double-time salary for a week would go a long way in paying for college tuition. "No problem Sir."

Eddy and the car were waiting outside the Beverly Hills Wilshire sixty minutes later. Sandwiched between a Rolls Royce and the hotel limo, it didn't exactly match the decor.

"What's this, Eddy?'

"It's your car, Sir."

"You're sure about that?"

"Yes sir, Mr. Stiles. I rented it personally."

"No, are you sure it is a car? In fact, it looked a lot like the car he'd left parked in his driveway, except for the rust. Maybe this was what it would look like in fifteen years.

"I'm sorry, Mr. Stiles. It was the best I could do. I don't have a credit card."

Todd felt badly. Eddy was doing his best on his own dime and he'd stepped on him.

"Eddy, I'm sorry. I'll make sure you are reimbursed."

As he tossed his luggage in the back seat, he could see a distinct kink in the limos front bumper. The paint marks matched the rust on the bumper of his rented 1966 Chevy Impala.

As Eddy eased the Impala out from between the two cars, Todd looked out the window and down as the Chevy's door cheerfully roughed up the back end of the Rolls Royce. Todd turned, looked at Eddy and grinned.   "You did great, Eddy, this car will do just fine."

As Eddy and Todd were pulling out of the Beverly Hills Wilshire hotel parking lot, David's secretary was calling the front desk to inform Todd that David would be picking him up in twenty minutes. The manager informed her that Todd had checked out. She politely informed the manager to bill the company account. The manager went on to inform her that account or no account, Mr. Stiles, behavior was not up to the standards of the Beverly Wilshire. The manager's words were doomed to wander the phone system forever. She had long since hung up.

She dialed Todd's office number.

"Mr. Stile's office."

"They're at it, again."

Todd's secretary did not need an explanation. "Where is he?'

"I don't know. He checked out of the hotel. Put the meeting on hold until 1:30 this afternoon."

"They are going to be severely pissed off!"

"We are dealing with crazy people here. All bets are off and just to make it interesting, turn off the air conditioning and wait an hour before telling anyone about the delay." Todd was oblivious to the trail of chaos following him down the Santa Monica Freeway.

The car seemed to trigger old memories. No, they were more like images! He was going somewhere, wasn't he? He was on a two-lane blacktop. It was a new road. It had that look of shiny asphalt shoulders that were clean, straight and flat. The sky was an uninterrupted blue right down to the horizon. The road went on forever right out to the point where the road and sky met. He was headed someplace, a destination, but he couldn't remember where.

"Where am I supposed to be going?

"Sir?"

Todd started. He was back in the Chevy.

"I was just thinking out loud, Eddy."

David had discovered that his father had checked out of the Beverly Wilshire about the same time that Todd was phoning his office to tell David that he was at the Holiday Inn. "Mr. Stiles. David left to pick you up forty minutes ago." David's secretary was used to playing go-between with father and son. She was using her you two are playing games again and starting to piss me off, voice. "I'll sort it out, Mr. Stiles. Just let me know what hotel you are staying at for the next hour. She hung up a second after he gave her the name and location of the hotel. David's secretary had a very low tolerance for crazy people. Todd had the terrible feeling that he ran the company in name only. His voice was doomed to wander the phone circuits forever along with the manager of the Beverly Wilshire.

David, meanwhile, was sitting in the manager's office at the Wilshire. He wanted to be someplace, maybe an island. Yes, without phones, hotels, or his father--particularly his father. He had just gotten off the phone with his secretary. He was going to need his hearing checked. It seems my father has decided to find lodging elsewhere."

"I am sorry to hear that. We value our association with CTI and will always consider Mr. Stiles a special member of our family here at the Beverly Wilshire, said the manager's mouth. The manager's mind was cheerfully burning Todd on a stake in front of the Beverly Wilshire. As David shook his hand to leave, he noticed that the manager's carnation needed to be replaced. The hotel clerk at the Holiday Inn fared considerably better. He did not have a carnation.

Todd opened the door to his room and tossed his bags in the door without even looking. "What's the matter, Eddie?"

"Aren't you going to check the room?"

"No, why do you ask?"

"Well, don't people usually have a look at their room when they check in?"

"Would you check a garbage bin before sleeping in it?"

The question surprised him. "No Sir, of course not."

"Neither did I, the last time I slept in one."

Eddie shook his head as they walked out to the car. It was going to be a long, long week.

In the half hour drive to the CTI plant, Eddie began to notice a change in Todd Stiles. The erratic crazy was replaced by a no-nonsense, goal-directed professional who kept the conversation direct and to the point.

"Eddie, take the second entrance and stop at the gate. Do exactly what the guard asks, nothing more, and nothing less."

"Can't we drive right straight through? I mean, Sir, you are the boss."

"Eddie, the man is paid to enforce security, not to break it."

As the car pulled up to the gate, a very large and very tough looking man stepped out of the guard house. The creases in his uniform were so sharp, you could shave with them.

"Your passes please.." Todd handed his ID card to the guard.

"Can I have your pass, Sir?" Eddie kept both hands on the wheel and wished the guard would hurry up and hit him so that he could start screaming.

Todd leaned over and spoke to the guard. "This man is not an employee. He is working for me, personally, while in I am here."

"I cannot admit him without authorization from someone on duty."

Todd nodded. "I understand. Contact CEO David Stile's office and they will authorize."

The guard asked for and got Eddie's ID. He disappeared into the guard house.

"Mr. Stiles, I don't mind waiting outside.

Todd patted him on the shoulder. "Relax Eddie, you're doing fine."

The guard returned five minutes later. He leaned in the window and took a good hard look at Eddie and compared it to his Eddie's driver's license photo. He handed him a visitor pass and told him where he could and could not go. He also told Eddie that he wanted the visitor's pass back at the end of the visit, and that he would be really annoyed if it wasn't returned.

He walked around the car and took a hard look at Todd and repeated the same perusal of credentials. When he was satisfied, he opened the gate. Eddie was shaking so badly, he could barely drive.

Twenty minutes into Todd's tour of the CTI plant and halfway through the conversation he was having with a plant engineer, Eddie had given up trying to understand anything. He looked into the clean room at the people dressed in funny white suits. He wondered, briefly, what would happen if someone sneezed in there.

The conversation was interrupted by the David's arrival. "Dad, we've got a board room full of really pissed off computer executives."

An exasperated Todd stopped his conversation and turned to his son. "David, relax they can wait a bit longer."

"Dad, we've got a roomful of engineers and computer executives with no air conditioning."

"Think of the boardroom as a sauna full of crazy people in suits. Relax. What's wrong with the air conditioning?"

"Our secretaries had it turned off for maintenance."
Todd looked at the plant engineer who shook his head and shrugged.

"Dad, we've got Dr. Caroline Beta Carlyle sitting in a roomful of pissed off engineers and executives without air conditioning.

A look of panic crossed Todd's face, and stayed there. "Now would be a good time to start that meeting."

Not having specific instructions, Eddie followed along, trying to get someone to tell him what was happening. He finally got David's attention. "What's going on?"

"It's a project meeting. We have them every two months. All the representatives from the different companies, such as contractors and the government if they are involved meet to check progress and deal with problems when they arise. In this case, however, we are running late and overheating. By the way, who are you?"

"My name is Eddie Gluck. Mr. Stiles hired me to help out with things while he is here."

David held his hand. "I'm his son, David Stiles, pleasure to meet you."

Eddie shook his hand. David took note of the fact that Eddie had a firm hand shake. "You're looking after my Dad? It sucks to be you!"

Eddie laughed. "Yeah, something like that."

David nodded over his shoulder. "C'mon, let's get this show on the road."

When David and Eddie arrived at the boardroom, David went in and Eddie took a seat in the hall. Eddie picked up a magazine and waited for the guard at the gate to come and arrest him. He managed to get past the cover when he looked up and saw Todd looking down at him. "What are you doing, Eddie?"

"I was just waiting here until your meeting was over, Mr. Stiles."

"I am not paying you to sit in the hall and read magazines. You're here to learn. Come on, let's go in."

"In there?" Eddie was shocked.

Todd pointed to the door. "In there."

"Gentlemen, Dr. Carlyle, I'd like to introduce you to Edward Gluck. He's an associate of mine; he will be sitting in on this meeting as an observer. Todd steered him to a chair next to an IBM executive whose suit cost more than Eddie made in a month.

Todd took a seat at the end of the table. "I would like to thank all of you for coming and apologize for the delay. The minutes will show that this is meeting 34 for project ERF 404."

In the following three days, Todd attended six more meetings involving different projects and one final meeting regarding some issues with ERF 404. Eddie, although overwhelmed with what he saw and heard, completed all the assignments that Todd gave to him. On the last day, as they drove to the plant, Todd asked him what he planned to do when he finished college.

"To tell the truth, Mr. Stiles, I'm not sure what I want to do. I've been so busy saving money for college; I haven't had time to think about what I'll do when I get there. There was an awkward pause. When he resumed, there was genuine embarrassment in his voice. "My grades aren't very good. I barely made it into State."

Fifteen minutes later they were, once again, at the boardroom door.

"Eddie, why don't you sit this one out, you've earned it. Besides, this one will just be with Dr. Carlyle, and even I find her scary."

Eddie nodded. "Thanks, sir."

Todd pulled open the door. Except for the distant sound of air in the ducts, there was no sound. For a brief moment, until a movement near the window caught his eye, the room definitely appeared empty. Leaving her notes and briefcase on the table, Dr. Carlyle had turned her chair around and pulled it over to the window, apparently lost in thought, if you could call it thinking. Computation would be a better term for it. To say she was an enigma would be an understatement. Carlyle was reputedly one, if not, the brightest mind of the century. She possessed a doctorate in Nuclear Engineering, but went into computer design. The Beachler-Carlyle Corporation built the most advanced computers in the world, including the first functional autonomous goal seeking logic circuit. Computer pundits dubbed it the HAL 9000. Arthur C. Clarke briefly came out of retirement to administer the Turing Test, which is a five minute conversation with someone on the phone to determine if it is a machine or person. There was dead silence in the room when it passed the test.

Carlyle's physical appearance often defied description, 6'3", long skirts and square wire-rimmed glasses; she had a genetic flaw that left her with brown hair in the front and grey in the back. She looked like a nun who couldn't decide which century to live in. Someone, who had the temerity and too much alcohol, to asked her about it. She looked down at the inquisitor and responded that she preferred the year 1890 because the cost of living was lower."

"Has Mr. Gluck decided not to join us?"

Todd wondered how she knew how many people were in the room when she hadn't turned to look. "I thought he should sit this one out. He's had a busy week."

She responded without turning away from the window. "I would like him to join us. I have no doubt he can assist us with the project. Besides, if he hopes to improve his grades, he won't do it sitting in the hall reading magazines."

The meeting lasted over four hours. Dusk was beginning to set as Eddie and Todd crossed the parking lot. David was waiting at his car to take Todd to the airport. "Hi dad. It looks like you have had a long day."

'Todd smile. We both have."

"We had better get going. Your plane leaves at 8:30.

"David, would you mind if I had Eddie drive me to the airport?"

David shrugged. "No problem. I have an appointment and I could use the time to get ready. He held out his hand to Eddie.

"It was nice meeting you, Mr. Stiles."

"It's David and the pleasure was all mine."

Todd had a wicked look on his face. "Oh, by the way, can we use your car?"

David was horrified. Al had given him an accurate and frightening account of Todd's last road trip. "Don't worry, Eddie will be driving. Todd opened the door and started pushing him in.

"Mr. Stiles. I don't think . . . ."

Todd cut him off in a soothing voice. "Don't worry, David can use our car!"

He grabbed David's keys and dumped the Chevy's keys into his hand.

Before he could organize his brain enough to realize that his father had, once again, pulled a fast one on him, David's car was through the gate and rapidly disappearing in traffic.

David walked over to Eddie's rental car. Two questions went through his mind simultaneously. Was his father's weird sense of humor genetic, and where was he going to find another Mercedes at 7:30 at night?

"Mr. Stiles. I really shouldn't be driving this car!"

Todd laughed. It's a bit late for that now. Don't worry, just take it back to the plant and pick up your car. Trust me; it will still be there when you get back. Eddie and Todd were at the airport forty minutes later.

As Todd finished unloading his bags out of the trunk of the car, he looked up at the sky. It was a beautiful night. "Eddie, I can't thank you enough for your help."

"All I did was drive you a round and run a few errands. "

Todd reached in to his pocket and pulled out an envelope. "Here's your paycheck. When you decide what you're plans are I'd like you to give me a call. The number is on the envelope."

As they shook hands, Eddie wished him a safe trip home.
Todd walked to the check-in, because the sky cap refused to push him on the cart, he noticed an advertisement for *American Graffiti*. It was having another revival. What was it they used to say? Where were you in 62?"
As he took his seat on the plane, he wondered where he was going. The ticket said New York but a voice in the back of his mind said, "Wanna make a bet? "

The pilot definitely knew where Todd was going. Up. A former Vietnam pilot with one month to go before mandatory retirement, the pilot had decided to push the envelope. His first officer was a little worried.

"Sir, we are at VR. We need to rotate."

"Not yet."

"Sir!"

He yanked the nose up 10 degrees pushed the throttles out to 110 percent and pulled the nose up another 10 degrees hard. The passengers were getting one hell of a ride. The pilot had to yell over the sound of the engines. "Is this a great country or what?"

The Todd Stiles that returned to New Jersey was in far better shape than the one that left. Al stopped at the bathroom door and waited; there was no weird terry cloth float. His boss had been home for at least sixteen hours and nothing bizarre had happened. He finally found him in the kitchen trying to convince the coffee maker to give him a single cup of coffee. The machine had been in the house for three years, and it still hadn't produced an ounce of hot black liquid. Todd had named it Amanda.

"I didn't hear you come in last night. Usually, your arrival is accompanied by the sound of bending steel and shattering concrete."

Todd laughed. "That's because the cab driver would not let me drive."

They shook hands. "Did everything go all right in L.A?"

Not directly answering the question, Todd asked his own. "Did David call?"

Al nodded. "He wanted to know if you had been arrested when you got back to New York."

"Am I going to be?"

"No, but you are still in trouble."

"Amanda?"

"She is going to sue you right to Mars and back! But don't worry. I got your license reinstated and paid your fines so you can get out of town without taking half of the state police with you."

"How did you manage to do that?"

"I sold your wheels."

Todd looked puzzled. "How much did you get for it?"

Al raised his eyebrows. "About $300,000.00 dollars."

"*$300.000.00!*" Todd mouthed the words.

"How did you manage to get that much money for a wreck?"

Al smiled evilly. "I didn't say I sold your car. I said I sold your wheels."

"The ones in your garage, you had five cars."

Todd tried to remember when he bought that many cars. "I had five cars?"

"Not any more. Now you only have one. 1.5, if you count the Amanda mobile."

"Why didn't you sell that one, too?"

It's out in the driveway. Why don't you go have look at it?"

Todd walked out to the driveway and, there it was, just like the day he first got it. "I don't believe it."

Al walked over to the car and ran a hand along the quarter panel.   "A lot of people can drive a car like this, and have their name on the registration, but it can only have one owner."

"Thanks for hanging on to it, Al.

"It was an easy decision."

Todd looked at him. "How so?"

Al frowned briefly trying to put words to thoughts. "My guess is that the last time you drove this thing, you were headed somewhere, but you didn't get to where you were going."

Todd rolled over and looked at the alarm clock. It said 2:30 in the morning. He rolled back and put his hands behind his head. In the darkness, he could hear the tree outside the window creaking in the breeze. He got out of bed and wandered around the house for a few minutes before ending up in the kitchen. He wasn't hungry, but he must have come down here for a reason. A flash of gold caught his eye, scotch! He took the bottle down from the shelf and looked at the label. It was very good whiskey. It was Al's bottle. He liked to have a drink after work on Friday evening. Todd got a glass poured out a mouthful and put the bottle back.

He took his drink and went out onto the patio. The only light was coming from the pool. He found an old patio chair and sat down. He couldn't remember the last time he had been back here, and the pool, had he ever been in it? The quiet allowed a lifetime of memories to come rushing in. The places he had been, things he had done. It was like watching a tape rewind at high speed. Occasionally, he would wince as he saw, or remembered, something he regretted.

The images in his mind slowed to a crawl and stopped. He was standing in the middle of a road. His head involuntary jerked to see if anything was coming from behind. It was definitely a new road; clean, straight lines right out to the horizon. He could almost feel the heat coming off the pavement. This looked really familiar. Was this road in L.A.?

Suddenly, he remembered he was day-dreaming about this road, when Eddie was driving him someplace. He got up and looked out over the yard. He suddenly realized that if he didn't do something now, he'd spend the rest of his life here, looking at this. He looked down at his glass, picked it up, and drank the whiskey. It felt good as it burned its way down. Back in the kitchen, he washed the glass and put it back in the cupboard.

"Where was that old suitcase I used to have own?" It took a while, but he found it in the storage locker.

Packing is an art and Todd used to be pretty good at it thirty-five-years ago. Now, it was slow going. He hated to admit it, but with Al looking after all the small details, he had become pretty much retarded when it came to looking after himself. He took stuff out because he could not close the case, rearranged things, and then caught himself putting the things he took out back in again. He finally threw everything out and tried to remember what he put in a bag when he was in his twenties. He looked at the contents. "Is that it?"

"I must have had more than a few shirts pants, wind breaker, and a few changes of underwear and socks." He closed the case, lifted it off the bed, and stopped. Marcie . . . .

He sat down on the edge of the bed next to the suitcase. Todd reached over and lifted her picture off the night stand. The memories rushed in. What would she think, what would she say to him?

"She'd tell you it was time to go." Al was standing in the door.
Todd looked at the picture for a long time before putting it back. "I never told you how much I loved her. Even now it still hurts."

"You didn't have to." Al picked up the suitcase off the bed. "It's time."

Out in the driveway, the car stood out in the darkness like a bright red star. "Did you polish it?"

Al took the keys from Todd walked to the trunk and opened it. He stopped and smiled. Some items had been in the trunk for years. He rearranged some things, put in the suitcase, and closed the lid.

"Nope, but you have to admit it does look good." Al handed him the keys and offered his hand.

"I can't thank you enough for this, Al."

"Pleasure was all mine."
"I haven't got a clue where I'm going.
Al smiled and opened the door for him.

Todd started the car and checked the gauges as the engine came up to speed. The tach came to 500 rpm and held steady.

"You do know where you're going."
Todd looked up at Al. "Back the way I came?"

Al followed the car out to the gate and watched the tail lights as they disappeared into the night. He could feel the wind change as he looked up at the night sky.

CHAPTER 2
MURDOCH

"Adversity is hard on a man. But for everyone who can handle prosperity there are a hundred who can handle adversity."

--- Thomas Carlyle

Orchard Valley Wyoming, unlike Saddle River New Jersey, did not have any hills for money to run down. No hill, no money, the occupants of the Westland trailer park were definitely aware of this. While not exactly poor, they were not exactly swimming in the stuff, either. A more accurate description would be tired, overworked, and seriously middle class. On the plus side, while the park residents were not afraid of a drink, they did not, as far as anyone could recall, trash their gardens and knock down cement walls with their cars.

There was a phone booth outside the gate. From the booth, a caller would have a clear view of the highway in either direction. The bench next to the phone was old and weathered by wind, rain, and sand.

There was a man in the phone booth. Although he looked like he had lived in the trailer park all his life, he was, in fact, just visiting.

Robert Murdoch, Buzz to his friends, and there few of them these days. At fifty-plus years of age, he was still in good shape. It was still possible to see remnants of his youth because he still went down to the gym to box three times a week.

He was born in New York and grew up in Hell's Kitchen in the 1950's. It was a tough neighborhood, a tough time. A young man had to grow up fast. It did not take him long to figure out that the asphalt of those streets could suck the life out of someone quick, and before you knew it, you were an old man. The day he moved out of the Kitchen, the only things he took with him were two shirts, his Dad's pocket watch and a coin. He found a place near the Battery. On the first night he walked up to the park, looked out over the river, and took a deep breath. He'd never smelled air so clean. Murdoch never looked back, knocked around the country for four years, finally ending up in Buffalo in 1965. It was time to find a job.

He started driving a cab for the Able Atlantic Cab Company; it didn't pay well, but it put bread on the table. Able Atlantic Cab was described by some of its competitors and all of its customers as an "asylum on wheels." The joke on the streets was "Do you want a cab or do you want Able?" The first thing he noticed when he walked into the manager's office to apply for a work was that the door was missing, and the second thing was the cab parked next to his desk.

The interview lasted for fifteen minutes and except for the fact that the radiator had begun to smoke, it went pretty well. The manager concluded the interview by telling Buzz that he had the job and was pleased to have him on the team. "See the dispatcher. turn left and down the hall, he'll get you set up."

Approaching the dispatcher's office, he could hear what sounded like a man who had gone totally berserk. When he got to the office, Buzz discovered that the lunatic was, in fact, in the dispatcher's office; even worse, the lunatic was the dispatcher. The office had an inner and outer space divided by a glass wall. The secretary in the outer office politely asked the nature of his visit, as the lunatic inside screamed obscenities into a two way radio.

"I was told to report here. I'm the new driver."

She smiled. "I don't think Mr. Peepers is available at the moment."

Mr. Peepers had climbed up on his desk and was trying to stomp his desk blotter to death.

The look on Buzz's face prompted her to answer the question he wanted to ask. "Don't worry, he's fine. He always gets a little annoyed when he talks to #12 on the radio. Why don't you come back at 6:00 p.m? He's usually calmed down by then." She stuck out her hand. "By the way, welcome to the Club." There was a loud crash as Peeper's two-way radio exited his office through the glass of his window.

Buzz returned to meet a much calmer Wally Peepers. A fire plug of a man with a short fuse and salty language, he did not suffer fools easily. He had been a career marine forced out at mandatory retirement. In his mind, the world was a chaotic mess, but he was sure he would get it squared away, eventually.

After what Buzz saw that afternoon, he was going to have to do it without a radio. "You're on the night shift, 12:00 p.m. to 8:00 a.m., starting tonight." That was the entire conversation.

He went home and got some sleep, arriving back at Able Atlantic around 11:30. The entrance to the driver's lounge was at the back of the building and for good reason. The lounge was a bomb shelter after a bomb had gone off, in it. Walking around and over debris, most of it impossible to identify, he made his way to the coffee machine. Something under a newspaper made a soft squishing sound. He raised his foot and looked down. It was *The New York Times*. He was briefly impressed, but decided that it would be safer if he kept moving. As he sat down at the table and leafed through a magazine, he heard what he thought was snoring. He put the magazine down and looked around the room. It was empty.

At 12:05, five of the night shift drivers arrived. Al Bannister, the oldest, and like Peepers, was a veteran. He had been with the company the longest. Dave Gillespie was an out-of-work chemical engineer with a Ph.D. He was fired from his last job because his lab blew up after he poured unused Sulphuric acid down the drain. There was a cleaner in the lab next door who'd dumped her unused caustic floor cleaner full of nitrates down her drain. Sulphuric acid and nitrates don't like each other very much and got into a fight in the pipes. They fired Gillespie because PhD's are a dime a dozen, and she was a really good cleaner.

Louis Rankin, a recent immigrant from Jamaica, was studying at Stony Brook University to be a teacher. Gary Spunkmeister, who possessed no academic credentials or any credentials of any kind, was a complete psychopath who liked to drive fast on the sidewalk. Spunkmeister had the only cab in the northern hemisphere with a crate engine and flame decals on the hood. He had a habit of picking up fares that were not even looking for a cab. Doug Flatt was the owner's son, a nice guy, a bit slow, with a really bad memory. On occasion, Doug would pick up a fare and half way to his destination, forget where was he was going. Dave and Al looked after Doug when he was having problems.

The sixth driver was Number 12. He had started on the night shift eleven months ago on November 11th and never returned. He didn't disappear. If he had, that would have made things a lot easier. He just refused to complete his shift. After eleven months, he was still out on the night shift picking up fares. The company was aware of this because the car hadn't returned and Number 12 hadn't picked up his pay checks, which Able Atlantic was legally required to issue.

The dispatcher was aware of Number 12's absence, because every night, he could hear the screams of passengers on the radio, who were trapped in a cab with a driver who hadn't had a bath in nearly a year and neither, apparently, had the car. Number 12 had removed the door handles on the rear doors, so the unfortunate fare could not leap out of the car in desperation while it was moving. The reason Number 12 was put on the night shift was because he picked up a fare at the *Piggly Wiggly* and proceeded to tie the poor woman's six grocery bags to the bumper of the car, and drag them the ten blocks to her address. Somebody should have seen it coming.

After a few minutes of introductions and idle conversation, they got up to, as Louis liked to call driving, squash asphalt. Buzz stopped at the door.

"Is there something wrong? Al asked.

He looked back into the room. "It's that damned snoring, where's it coming from anyway?"

Bannister grinned. "We've never been able to find out. He's been in there for years and no one has been able to find him. We think it's one of the mechanics who got walled up when they renovated after the last fire."

Buzz shook his head. "The last fire, you make it sound like a regular occurrence?"

Bannister grinned. "Once a month, for insurance purposes, you understand?"

Buzz eased himself past Al, slowly. Just for insurance purposes--you understand? "You know, you guys do a lot of weird here?"

Bannister's grin got even bigger. "I like you, Murdoch. You're going to fit right in here!"

Ten minutes later, the night shift was parked at Weird Walt's Swine and Dine. A badly run-down dump of a diner, frequented by cab drivers and the criminally insane, sometimes one and the same. No one ever ate there, and the only person reported to have done so, according to a rumor, probably started by the owner, died a slow painful death. What people did consume at Walt's was coffee, literally hundreds of gallons of it. Yellow Cab was there during the day shift, Checkers 3:00 to midnight, and Able Atlantic starting at 12:10.

The police drank as much coffee as the Cabbies, but they didn't have a set schedule. Most of the time, they were at Walt's when there was a shift overlap between companies. They got free coffee for breaking up fights. Able Atlantic's night shift arrived at Walt's at precisely 12:11 to start work.

"Who's buying coffee tonight?"

"Buzz is."

"Hey, c'mon, that's not fair!

"Why not Doug?"

"Give the man a chance to make some money before we rip him off."

"Hey, that's not fair. I don't make enough to be ripped off, either!"

"Your Dad owns the company!"

Doug looked at Dave with confusion. "He owns the Able Atlantic Cab Company?"

Buzz checked his pockets for change. "No worries, gentleman, I got it covered." As he walked back to his cab, he found the rest of the night shift sitting in the car. He leaned in the window. "Is there something I should know about you guys?

Bannister leered out the window. "Get in; you're going to enjoy this."

Buzz got behind the wheel and his coffee cup joined two others on the dash. The silence was broken by a quiet cough from the back seat. Someone asked what time it was. Louis looked at his watch. It was 12:29.

Bannister spoke to Buzz in a hushed voice. "Start the engine and just let it idle. We're not going anywhere." He looked at his watch. Buzz had been with the company for almost an hour and still had not completed his first mile.

The radio crackled briefly, and someone whispered, "Here we go."

"Get out the book, Rankin. It's your turn to drive."

Buzz looked over the back seat. How are you going to do that? You are in the back seat."

Louis smiled. "Trust me. I can reach the pedals from here."

Peeper's voice erupted from the radio. "4 call dispatch!"

Nobody moved to pick up the microphone. "4 call dispatch!" Nobody moved.

"God damn it all to fucking hell 4, pick up the freaking mike and answer me!"

Everybody in the car went nuts. "Man, is it going to be a great night or what? No slow burn, just a kaboom!"

Bannister reverentially pulled the mike off the radio and handed it over the back seat to Spunkmeister. Louis held the up the driver's city route book and pointed out to Gary where he, in theory, was supposed to be. He nodded in approval when he saw the location. He slowly squeezed the mike button, cutting off Peepers, just as he was beginning to speak at the other end. The radio screeched and groaned in protest. "4 here, Chief, I'm at the corner of 12th and Sycamore." The radio was silent when Gary let go of the button.

For a brief moment, Buzz thought the radio was actually trying to convey the confusion on the face of the man on the other end. "How could you get all the way across town so fast?"

"I took a short cut. You can ask Number 6. I just passed him at 13th Street.

The radio voice immediately went after Dave Gillespie.
"6 call dispatch."

Gary handed the mike to him. Gillespie stuck a big wad of paper in his mouth, making him virtually unintelligible. "Wumba thwix thweif."

Peepers was clearly becoming agitated. "What the hell is wrong with your radio?"

"Nothwing thweif. Gillespie took the wad out of his mouth.

, did you see fourteen at 12th and Sycamore?"

"Sure did, Chief."

"Ok, fine, and your transmission has cleared up."

Gillespie stuck the paper back in his mouth." Thwanx thweif."

"Aw crap, now it's started again!" Peepers' agitation had been cranked up another notch.

Everybody took a turn torturing Peepers over the radio. When Buzz's turn came, he wasted no time getting into the act.

"What's you location, Murdoch?"

"I'm at Weird Walt's."

"What the hell are you doing there?" The radio demanded to know.

"Just picking up a coffee to take on the road, and I'm just pulling out of the lot heading east on Bleeker. He revved up the engine for effect.

They patted Buzz on the back. "That was nicely done, rookie."

The sound of an enormous fart erupted from the radio.

?"Peepers, are you there? This is the anti-Christ calling from hell."   The voice was followed by a maniacal laugh that would have scared the skin off of Vincent Price.

Buzz pointed at the radio. "What was that?"

Bannister shook his head in awe. "12."

"You freaking maniac. You get your ass in here. Your shift is finished."

"No."

"Whadda you mean, no? You've been out there for eleven months without a bath!"

"Have so."

"Have not!

12 giggled. "Yes I have. I drove through Bernie's' car wash with the windows down. I've even got a witness."

A voice in the background pleaded, "Please let me out."

They could hear Peepers gagging on the other end of the radio and then the sound of him going off the deep end, again, followed by the sound of broken glass caused by a flying radio.

It was two in the morning by the time Buzz was finally on the road. His ribs hurt from laughing. His first fare was a good one. A woman leaving a party needed to go across town. The ride was a full twenty-five minutes, with 12 and Peepers punching each other out over the radio. At first, the woman was horrified at the language. She asked him to turn the radio off. He told her that he couldn't do that.

She agreed to have the radio turned down. Five minutes later, curiosity got the better of her. "You know, I guess it would okay if you turned it up a little bit."

"Hey Peepers. I've been doing the rug nasty with your wife. You gotta buy better Scotch. That varnish remover you got doesn't exactly light up her switch board, and man, she needs all the plugs in to get her lights blinking, know what I mean? Snort!"

Buzz's fare leaned over the front seat and screamed at the radio.   "You're a scumbag, 12. I hope you get leprosy and die! Sorry, I guess I got a little carried away."

He looked at her and then at the radio. "He seems to have that effect on people."

By the time they arrived at the destination, she was alternately cheering and condemning the participants. It was a bizarre trip, but a really good tip.

He had been at Able Atlantic four months when he picked up the fare from hell. The man had seen a lot of hard living, most of which was still attached to his shirt. The fare wanted to go to a part of town where people lived hard and off their shirts. The destination was, not surprisingly, a bar. More precisely, it was a more like a burned out building with a bar sign on it. Buzz wanted eight dollars for the fare. The man told him to go fuck himself and got out of the cab.

As he walked away, he completed the sentence with "Asshole." Buzz assumed that was his tip. Well, eight bucks was eight bucks, and Buzz knew that he would have to go after him to collect. He also knew the man was a biker. He was in a biker bar and the bar was in a part of town full of bikers. If Buzz got into trouble and he could get to the radio, the rest of the shift would come after him, but that could be a long wait in a brawl. Still, eight bucks was eight bucks. Buzz stopped at the door. Directly overhead was an extremely bright halogen light. The bar would be dark. He would be at a disadvantage in the ten or fifteen seconds it would take for his eyes to adjust. He reached down and picked up a two-by-four conveniently leaning against the wall. It had a nail in it. Buzz had to admire these guys, they thought of everything.

A strong swing broke the lamp off at the wall. It would take more than a new bulb to fix it. He took a full minute to let his eyes adjust. With the light gone, the place was already starting to look better.

Buzz put his right hand on the door knob, his left hand on the frame. He stepped into the door, almost to the point of touching it with his shoulder. He turned the knob slowly until he was sure it was open. He waited a full four seconds and then swung it open, hard and fast. The guy behind the door took it full in the face. It would be at least a week before the swelling went down enough for him to see again.

He stepped over the doorman and walked over to the bar where Mr. Fuck You was having a drink. "You owe me eight bucks."

When Mr. You turned around, Buzz had to admit he didn't get any better looking close up.

"How about I cut your head off and feed it to my dog?" The guy's breath wasn't much better either.

Out of the corner of his eye, Buzz could see the guy reaching behind him for something. It would be a knife and he would know how to use it. Buzz didn't wait for it to make an appearance. Buzz grabbed him by the shirt and pulled him off balance. Mr. You took his eyes off Buzz and looked down at the hand on his shirt, big mistake. When he looked up, the first and only thing he saw was a fist. Buzz delivered five fast straight arm blows to the face.

The first one broke off three upper front teeth, the second one, and the bridge of his nose. The last three were for effect. He could've broken an eye socket or worse, but the guy was already out of it. That's the way it's done in the Kitchen. If the guy was still able to throw a punch after that, you had a fight on your hands.

Buzz threw the biker over the bar and pulled out his wallet. The smallest he had was a ten. The bartender handed him the change with a nod of approval. He could see the man had a baseball bat in his hand. The message was clear, "If you need help getting to the door, all you have to do is ask."

"Your door lamp is burned out."

"No shit!" The bartender chuckled and gave everyone in the bar the look that said "Clear passage."

Buzz found Louis and Gary waiting for him in the parking lot. "How did you guys know I was here?"

"One of the Checker guys saw you headed this way with the fare from hell and gave us a call. The rest of the crew is on the way. We may be competition but we look after our own. You okay?"

Buzz nodded. "No problem. How about we meet at Walt's?"

Louis smiled. "We're already there."

It was not long after, that Buzz realized it was time to move on. After all, you can't spend the rest of your life driving a cab.

On his last night, the night shift threw a party for him. The fact that it was on the night shift was irrelevant. The fact that Peepers was off that night was not. It was a great night. Everyone showed, including the day and evening shifts. By midnight, the dispatcher hadn't dispatched a single cab; neither had Yellow or Checkers, because their cars were also at the party.   Even 12 made an appearance. He drove through the lot at forty-miles-per-hour, and tossed an empty liquor bottle with a picture of Peepers' wife in it through his office window. Around two in the morning, a search party was formed to locate the mad snorer. They never found him. On the plus side, there was new door way between the lounge and the garage.

Buzz's first day of unemployment was blunted by one hell of a hangover. He wasn't really up and functioning till the day after and even then, it was touch and go.

The first problem with being unemployed, as he quickly discovered, was being unemployed, and the second was being unemployed in Buffalo. There wasn't anything wrong with the place; it just didn't have a lot of excitement going for it.

In addition, he did not have any formal training except for high school equivalence. There were lots of jobs but he didn't fight his way out of the Kitchen so he could spend the rest of his life in a dead end job. A week later, he found a job at a warehouse. The pay was a lot better and there was room for advancement, provided someone died.

After a month, he began eating his lunch on the loading dock. The lunch room was a windowless hole in the basement and the restaurant across the street served food that did not belong to any known food group. He bought what he needed from the local grocer and brown- bagged it.

As he ate lunch, he watched the new building across the street being constructed. It wasn't going up in any kind of a hurry and it didn't take a rocket scientist to realize that things wouldn't be speeding up any time soon.

A crowd had gathered around a crane that had decided to take a nap on a pickup truck. There was also a considerable amount of screaming and yelling going on. Buzz could hear a fork lift starting up. It was time to get back to work.

At 5:00 p.m., the crane was still sitting on the truck. The bus would not be along for twenty-five minutes, so he decided to go have a look for himself. There was a man wearing a hardhat standing beside the crane. He seemed to be trying to move the crane by sheer force of will. The crane was having none of that and had no intention of responding to any force of anything.

"You don't have enough bricks."

Gus Whithers turned on the guy behind him, ready to blister him with a lot of four-letter words. He kept them to himself when he got a look at the man. Whithers was good at two things--people and building. He knew construction and the kind of people you needed to get the job done. "My problem right now, fella, is this crane. You got any ideas how to get it upright?"

Buzz walked around the crane looking at it from different angles. He did a mental calculation of the length of the boom. The crane was leaning at about a thirty-degree angle. He'd seen the bulldozer sitting next to the construction shack. He doubted it would be able to move the crane the way it was. His bus was coming. "Take the boom off and remove the fuel and oil. If you can lighten it by a couple of tons, your dozer should be able to pull it up right."

"How many bricks did you think I'm short?"

"8745, two pallets to complete the north wall to the bond course above the lintel."

Gus waved and muttered that he was one brick short of a load. That was Tuesday.

On Friday morning, Buzz was in the back of the warehouse looking for a load of limburger cheese, which incredibly, had gotten lost. He could hear someone yelling his name. It sounded like the forklift operator. It took a while, but he finally caught up with Buzz. "I was calling for you.

"How come you didn't answer?"

Buzz kept looking at some labels behind some crates with a flashlight. "Would it have mattered? By the way, where's the forklift?"

"It's broken down, again. There's some guy out on the loading dock that wants to see you. I don't know who he is, but he wants to talk to you really bad.

Buzz stood up and dusted himself off. "Okay."

The driver yelled after him. "What're you looking for, anyway?"

"Limburger cheese."

The driver winced.

"It's been missing for a couple of weeks."

A look of genuine terror climbed up the driver's face and decided to stay there. He looked around him, fully expecting the cheese to leap out from behind something and devour him. "Hey, wait for me. I'll go with you!"

Buzz took a deep breath as he stepped out of the warehouse. The last time he felt air like that he was on a highway heading west almost a hundred years ago; at least, that's what it felt like.

"Hey, you remember me?"

"Sure, you're the guy working on the building across the street." He'd noticed that the crane had given up on the truck and was sulking next to a pile of sand.

"Gus Whithers, this is my masonry foreman, Ted Davos. He tells me how many bricks he needs. I get them, and he makes me a wall. Last week he told me he needed 27,695 bricks to complete the building. He completed the north wall his morning. How many bricks did you need?"

"8,745" the man said quietly.

Whithers' eyes glared at Buzz from between his mustache and hard hat. Buzz just shrugged. "I don't hear a lot of conversation going on here, so I'm going to help you two fellows out. I've been coming up short on quantities, particularly bricks. Someone has a story to tell and we're going to stand here till I hear one. Maybe you can start by telling me how you could figure out that quantity the way you did."

Buzz rubbed the bridge of his nose. "It was a game we used to play when we were kids. We'd look at building and count the bricks. The guy who computed the number fast enough won. The trick is knowing the depth of the mortar and size of the brick. Once you figured it out, the counting was easy. Some of the faster guys could add up a four story building, all sides, in a minute and a half. We really used to enjoy pissing off the bricklayers by telling them how much they were off."

"I wanna see the both of you in my office."

Buzz objected. "I have work to do here."

That did not impress Whithers a damn bit. "I'm not going to say it twice."

Buzz turned to his supervisor, who was standing behind him with a smirk on his face. "Sure, go ahead. We can spare you for a while and we all want to know how it comes out."

Whithers seemed to get bigger as he got closer to his trailer. When they got inside, he took up a position behind his desk. Murdoch and the very uncomfortable foreman were standing in front, like a couple of errant schoolboys. "I'm still not hearing any noise here. Someone is going tell me why I keep coming up short on quantities. How about it Ted? This is the third time this month I've had to re-order. I'm beginning to think you've forgotten how to count."

Ted responded in frustration. "You know how it works. You order bricks until you're finished."

"How about you?"

Buzz shrugged. "I've got no interest in this one way or the other."

Gus hollered for the woman in the next room. "Molly, get in here."

A head appeared in the door. "What's up, Dad?

"Get your hard hat and work clothes, and find Walt. I want the two of you to count up all of the bricks in the walls and what's in the yard."

"You're joking, right?"

"Do I look like I'm joking?"

"Christ Dad, that could take days.

Gus leaned over his desk. "You don't have days!"

The head disappeared.

I'm going to find out many bricks I've actually got. Until I do, I don't want to see either of you around here until I call you. Get out of my office."

The head from the day before was waiting on the loading dock for Buzz at 7:00 in the morning. "Gus wants to see you."

Buzz was starting to get frustrated." Look, I have a job over here, not over there."

She just shook her head. "You know, if I come back without you, he's just going to come over here again, and the result is going to be the same."

Buzz went and talked to his boss who wasn't impressed. In his words, he wanted to know exactly who Buzz was working for, and if it was for the guy across the street, why he was paying his salary. He gave Buzz a half hour to get the problem sorted out. As they walked over to the constructions site, the head, whose name was Molly, asked him what he did at the warehouse. He told her he counted bricks.

Whithers was waiting with Ted and Walt in the yard. When Buzz and Molly arrived, he turned and walked over to the corner of the building without saying a word. He leaned back and looked up at the back wall. He yelled at Buzz. "How many bricks have I got?"

Buzz frowned. "You mean how many in the building?"

Whithers shook his head. "Count everything on the walls and on the pallets."

Buzz went to the pallets first, down the front of the building, and then, he disappeared around the corner.

Ted rubbed his eyes. "This is nuts, Gus. A guy just can't walk around a building and count up bricks like that. What's this supposed to prove?"

Gus stared back at Ted. "We'll know when he gets back."

As Buzz appeared from behind the building, Ted turned to Gus. "We've worked together for eighteen years. Why are you doing this?"

His plea fell on deaf ears. Ted knew it was a waste of time. Once Gus got something into his head, he wouldn't let go of it until he got what he wanted.

"How many bricks are out there?"

6.149."

Ted burst out laughing and relaxed. "That's crap. My invoices say 7440."

Gus turned to Molly and Walt. How many are there?"

Molly and Walt looked at each other. You believe that?"

Walt just shook his head. It took an entire day to work that out."

Gus was being ignored and he didn't like it. "How many bricks?" He roared.

"6,148."

Buzz smiled. "6,149. There's one on his desk. He's using it as a paperweight."

Gus turned to Ted. "You're fired!"

"What the hell are you talking about Gus? You can't fire me just because a brick count doesn't work out; just the wastage alone could add up to that."

"You've got four minutes to get off my site or I'll kill you right where you stand."

Ted smirked. "You got squat, Whithers. This is a union shop and I run the local. If the brick layers don't work, you got no building, and I decide when and where they work."

Gus pushed him out of the way, hard, and walked to his truck.

Molly whispered under her breath to Walt. "You had better stay out of this. It's going to get ugly."

Walt gently put a hand on her shoulder. "You'd better come with me."

She shook her head. "Take Buzz. I'll try and calm him down."

Walt tapped Buzz on the shoulder. "You and I had better go to the trailer."

Buzz nodded. "Okay, sure."

Gus reached his truck, yanked open the door, reached behind the seat, and pulled out the biggest shotgun Buzz had ever seen. It was a modified pump action Remington twelve-gauge with a lengthened barrel and choke. It was over four-feet long. Chromed, with a hand carved stock, it was an incredible piece of hardware.

Gus walked over to Ted's car, jacked a shell into the chamber, pointed it at the back door of the car, and pulled the trigger. The gun roared. A fist-sized hole appeared in the door. It was like a small bomb had gone off the inside of the car. Steel and glass from the door and seat upholstery exploded all over the interior. Gus jacked another shell into the gun, pointed it at the quarter panel, and fired again. The explosion blew the trunk open, expelling the contents onto the ground.

Gus reached into the trunk and pulled out a brick. He walked over to the group. Everyone was so impressed with his marksmanship that no one had moved. He dropped the brick at Ted's feet. "What part of fired are you having trouble with?"

"You crazy bastard, I'll break you! I'll be back here in an hour with the rep and we are going to shut you down. You've just screwed with a union. You're never going to get manpower in this town again. If you use scabs, we'll burn you out!"

As Ted walked away, Molly reached over and gently took the gun away from Gus. "We need to work on those people skills, Dad."

Walt turned at the sound of footsteps. The bricklayers had come down off the scaffolding and were heading off the site. One of them broke away and walked over to him. "Mind if I use your phone? I am going to make some calls and get this straightened out."

Gus was surprised. 'Aren't you wildcatting?"

"Don't sweat it. We'll put on a show, solidarity and all that crap. We'll be back in the morning. We've been trying to get rid of that asshole, he's been ripping off dues for years and we've never been able to catch him at it. Our bargaining unit wouldn't budge till we could prove it. This should be the one that does it. We got him cold, or rather, you did. Our people will be around tomorrow. Just make like the humble contractor trying to make a living. I'll take care of the rest. By the time we're done, they'll bury Ted along with his union card."

Halfway to the trailer, he stopped and looked at Gus. "By the way, do us a favor and don't bring the bazooka."

Gus acknowledged with a wave. He looked at Molly and shrugged.   "I'm out of shells, anyway."

She just shook her head. "Thank God for that!"

Walt looked around. "Where's Buzz?"

They turned to see him starting back across the street, to the warehouse.

Gus started after him. "Where the hell are you going?"

Buzz stopped and yelled. "I'm going back to work."

"You're already at work!" Gus retorted.

"What are you talking about? I don't know anything about construction."

"We'll teach you what you need to know. I need a foreman, and you're hired."

Buzz shook his head. "Thanks for the offer, but I am making $2.50 an hour over there. That's pretty good coin."

"I'll pay you six dollars an hour if you get out of the street."

Six bucks an hour was tough to argue with. Besides, if he was run down by a car, Buzz was sure he didn't have enough money for a decent burial.

The next day, Walt introduced Buzz to the art of bricklaying. His philosophy was simple; you have to start from the ground up, or in Buzz's case, the brick up.

Buzz scratched the back of his head. "That doesn't sound too difficult. A dog could do that."

Walt smiled and wiggled his eyebrows. "We'll see."

The man sitting in front of Gus's desk was the head of the union local. Ron Blatz looked like a union rep was supposed to look, tough and mean. He had worked his way up the union ladder, the hard way. Opponents were bullied and intimidated. If they didn't back down, they were beaten or worse. He was thoroughly pissed off. Gus Whithers wasn't behaving the way he wanted him to. "What the hell is that Goddamn noise?"

Gus sat expressionless behind his desk as another round of barking burst in the window of the trailer, "Barking."

Blatz was an hour older, well passed pissed off, and really tired of barking. "Whithers, you have screwed with the wrong guy. If I were you, I would watch your back. You're going to find a bullet in it."

Gus didn't even give him a chance to finish. He stepped up to Blatz and slammed the car door he was opening. His voice was barely above a whisper. "You arrogant pile of crap, you haven't got the balls! You're a bully and a coward and everyone knows it and the only thing smaller than your dick is your brains. So I am going to make this real easy for you to understand.

If I smell your stink within a mile of here, if anything happens to my property, this site or the men on it, if any harm comes to my daughter, if she so much as sees you on the street, I will come after you. I will find you and I will kill you. It won't matter where you are or the time of day, at home in your bed, at church, in your car, restaurant: it will make no difference. I will kill you. By the time I am done, they will bury everything but your head, because that I am going to blow right off your shoulders."

Gus turned and walked away. By the time he was halfway to the building, his mind had moved on to something else. That damned barking. It was getting louder by the minute. The bricklayers were obviously giving Buzz a thoroughly bad time.

He figured Murdoch would be fed up by now, so he decided to cool things down. As he turned the corner and looked up, it was pretty clear that Buzz had a lot to learn about bricklaying. He'd just completed a course that was a bit straighter than a dog's hind leg. Two men were following behind him making repairs, and a third was showing him what he was doing wrong. There was barking. Buzz looked over the scaffold and gave Gus a wave to indicate that everything was all right.

Gus just shook his head and walked back to his trailer. He stopped and turned back to the building. It was an incredible site. Murdoch was playing a perfect straight man to three guys pretending to be chickens. One guy was scratching his armpits and the other two were making arm pit farts, and there was barking. Murdoch had only been on the site a day, but he was having an impact. For the first time in weeks, his crews were making progress and having fun doing it. Murdoch gave Gus thumbs up and turned back to work.

That's when the sensation hit him--a road, a long straight highway going right out to the horizon. Gus knew that he and Buzz would travel that road together for a short time. Gus also knew that Buzz's journey would take him to a destination far beyond the horizon, to a place that Gus could never hope to see. He turned and walked back to his trailer. That afternoon, the police arrived. They had a complaint about someone abusing dogs but all they found was barking bricklayers. They went away because they didn't want barking bricklayers hanging around their jail.

Buzz learned fast. In a couple of weeks, he could lay a course of bricks as straight and as fast as anyone on the site. In the months to follow, he learned concrete, steel, form work, electrical, plumbing, and all the in-between work that goes into the construction of any structure. As the months turned into a year and then two, Gus began to loosen his grip on the reins.

Gus looked out the window of his trailer. The scenery was different, a new site, a new building. It was a little larger and more complex but pretty much the same as all the others. These buildings were the bread and butter of his company.

Out on the site, he could see Buzz and Walt going over a detail on the plans. They had gotten on well and were producing good work, which was important. Walt was only a few years younger than Gus. But with Gus looking towards retirement, it was only fair that he have a shot at running the show. But Walt had shown a lot of class and stepped aside to let Buzz run things. He had walked every single mile with Gus, even when things got really tough.

Gus had a secret that even Molly didn't know about. He had a brilliant business mind. Beginning in his late teens, Gus had been investing his money and investing well. Gus, Molly, and Walt were going to be very well looked after.

Buzz stepped into the trailer, pausing to knock some dirt off his boots. Molly did not look up, as she waved to him when he walked past her into

Gus's office. He had some drawings to show Gus. "So, what are your intentions towards my daughter?"

Buzz didn't have an answer to that one. Molly looked around the corner of the door, also at a loss for words. Gus just stood behind his desk and stared at the both of them. Buzz turned and looked at her, as if he had suddenly come out of a trance and discovered her standing in front of him. In the two years they had known each other, neither had given a thought about the other, except that Buzz worked outside and Molly worked inside. She tugged at his shirt sleeve. How about dinner tonight?"

Buzz shrugged. "How about Wongs?"

She nodded. "Fair enough."

Buzz had to admit she had an incredible figure. He remembered watching her checking the laces in her boots, which was a total waste of time, considering nature had really over done the top of Molly. He didn't get around to the reason he'd come in to see Gus until the next day. Buzz had plans, big plans.

"I've got problems with this."

"What's the matter, Gus? We can do this."

Gus pinched the bridge his nose. "To begin, we are going to need ten times the men and equipment we've got out there, and if you haven't noticed, we are in Buffalo and this thing happens to be in Florida."

"Gus, we can build this thing."

He shook his head in frustration. Buzz, I can't even tell what this thing is, and look at the road that leads to it or rather away from it, The thing doesn't even go anywhere and the compaction specs are ridiculous. What kind of weight requires that kind of compression?

Buzz nodded.

"How heavy are we talking here?"

"About 1.5 million pounds."

It was the only time Buzz would ever see surprise on Gus's face. "What kind of a vehicle weighs 5000 tons?"

Two weeks later Gus, Buzz, and the government project manager were staring out over the Florida panhandle. Gus looked down at the photo in his hand. "You guys really think you can build this thing?"

The manager nodded. "It's happening now. We're going to put it together and then we're going to go to the moon with it. You don't have to bid for the whole project. You can break it up and go for the road, or the building, or both. It's your call."

Buzz looked at Gus. "What do you think?"

Gus handed the photo to Buzz." It's your call."

"We can do it all."

Gus looked over at the manager. "Deal the cards. We're in."

The manager had a big smile on his face. "I'll get the bidding paperwork and specs together for you. How about you and I make some history?"

Gus's ability to bid successfully on contracts was as good as his ability to invest. When his trailer showed up strapped to the back of a flat deck trailer, the looks on the faces of the Florida contractors, local trades, and NASA representatives said it all. They were used to shiny and new, not old and dented.

In three years, Molly, Gus, Walt, and Buzz watched the first Saturn Five leave the launch pad they helped build. There'd also been changes for them as well. Buzz and Molly were married and had a family on the way. Gus, while still owner of the company, was more a consultant than a boss. Walt had made arrangements to retire on a beach far, far away when the project was done. They were very good years for all of them.

Buzz hung up the phone and stepped out of the booth. He looked west up the highway. The sun had just set and the sky had turned the color of Indigo. He hadn't seen a road that straight in a very long time. The urge to travel briefly came over him. It was triggered by a memory of a highway. He couldn't tell if it was an old or a new memory. It was just there. As fast as it came, it was gone, and he was back in the present.

He turned and walked back into the trailer park to wait for the last member of his family to die.

Buzz and Molly had three children and for eighteen years, life was constantly heading upwards.

In fact, it was incredible how far they had come. With Gus's and Walt's help, Buzz had learned the construction business very rapidly and in a short ten years, had turned a small company and fortune into very large ones. After fifteen years, they could have retired and never worked again.

More importantly, Buzz and Molly discovered how much two people could love each other. It was a great marriage. When they did fight with each other, it was over principles and issues, with the understanding that even principles took a back seat to love and family. Buzz taught Molly how to fight and not to back down. Molly taught Buzz when to stop. They were great parents and their children reflected that.

Things began to fall apart when their son Alan, an Air Force reserve pilot, was killed in a plane crash. From the day he could stand, Alan was pointing at the sky and never looked back. Buzz was away on business and Molly had to drive to the airfield for Alan's first flying lesson. Molly got white knuckles standing on a thick carpet and it showed when they were standing at the flight desk getting Alan ready.

A man joined them at the counter to arrange for an aircraft for a flight to Nevada. He offered to buy Molly a coffee and have a chat while Alan was outside getting a pre-flight briefing.

"I'm not due in Nevada till this evening. I'd be happy to take you son up on his first flight."

Molly felt comfortable with the man and agreed. "You're a pilot?"

He smiled. "I have some experience instructing."

As Molly watched the man walk out to meet Alan at his airplane, she hoped to God that he would never ask his mother to go for a ride. "The man who is going up with my son, what did he say his name was?"

"Yeager, Ma'am. Your son is getting his first flying lesson from Chuck Yeager."

In six short years, Alan was a Captain flying with the Air National Guard. He was departing Grand Forks AFB, North Dakota in an F4. The Phantom had a fire in the Number 2 engine during rotation. It went off the end of the runway at 190 knots and exploded. Eight months later, Buzz came home to find the police waiting for him in his driveway. Molly and his youngest daughter, Ann, had been killed in a car crash. A truck had gone through a guard rail and hit them head on. The police had spent their entire shift with a man who had lost almost his entire family in a year and half. The burden for that terrible time fell to Buzz's oldest daughter Andrea. She had her father's stubborn streak and while they loved each other deeply, they rarely saw eye-to-eye on anything. In fact, when things were getting a little dull in the little house in the bush, as she used to call it, although it was actually a very large estate in Connecticut she would go out of her way to provoke him.

On one occasion, she had put on a halter top, a total waste of material considering she had inherited her mother's figure, and walked right past her father at breakfast heading for the door.

Buzz coughed up a mouthful of Cheerios and roared. "Don't let me catch you going out that door dressed like that!"

"You couldn't catch your own reflection, Lardo!"

She then did a perfect imitation of Buzz looking in the mirror and tugging at his waist. He was concerned that he was putting on a few pounds. Andrea, who'd him doing it, wasn't above a little blackmail, and she never missed an opportunity to remind him. The fact that he'd never been in better shape didn't make any difference. The chase was on.

Andrea had even left the front door open so she could get out faster. When she went through the door, she yanked it shut behind her to slow her dad down.

As the voices receded in the distance, Molly, Ann, and Alan, who had been at the table during the dust up, didn't even bother to look up.

Alan raised the corn flakes halfway to his mouth and then stopped. "Do you think Dad will catch her?"

Molly's voice came from behind the newspaper she was reading. "Who cares?"

When Andrea graduated from MIT with a degree in chemical engineering, Buzz was the proudest father on the planet. He took it hard when she moved to New Mexico with a guy named Stu, who had a son from a previous marriage. Buzz objected and fought with her, but it was a battle he knew he couldn't win.

Andrea's last words to him before she got in the car were soft. "I know you're angry, but just don't stop loving me!" Buzz held her tight for as long as he could, and then opened the door. He only saw her once after that, at Molly's and Ann's funeral. She didn't tell him she had cancer.

Buzz took a deep breath before stepping through the trailer door. It always amazed him how neat and clean it was. Ken and Jessie, Stu's parents, wouldn't have it any other way.

Ken once told Buzz, after a couple of beers, that Andrea was the child they wish they had. Their son Stu had, despite their best efforts, been a total failure. Buzz felt Ken and Jessie were being hard on themselves, and that it took a long time for Ken to see it that way.

Buzz and Ken didn't see eye to eye on anything, from the day they first met, until Andrea started to get sick. Buzz hated them for taking his last daughter away from him. Ken saw Buzz as arrogant and rich.

They had accepted Andrea as their own. Andrea came to love them and their grandson, despite the fact that Stu had abandoned them both and left her with a mountain of debt.

When the day came to call Buzz about Andrea, Jessie told Ken it was his job to do it. He objected, saying that he had no use for the man and wouldn't know how to say it. She told him to talk to Buzz, as one father to another.

That was six months ago and Buzz hadn't left her side. Jessie made it clear that Buzz was to stay with them, because he was as much a part of the family as Andrea was.

Ken didn't look up from the eggs he was cooking. You ok?"

"I just needed to check with the office. They seem to be getting along fine without me."

"You could have used the phone here."

Buzz eased himself into a chair. "I just needed a walk."

Ken nodded, understanding, and motioned to the table as he put down two plates. "Jessie's on her way back from the hospital. I'll stay here with her tonight so you can have some time alone with Andrea."

"Thanks, I appreciate it."

Jessic came in just as Buzz got up to go to the table. Her eyes said it all. She went right to the bedroom without saying a word. Ken looked down the hall to the closed door. "You'd better get to the hospital."

Twenty minutes later, he was in the hallway outside Andrea's room. Her doctor was waiting for him. "Mr. Murdoch, I'm glad you're here. We called, but you were already on your way. We've tried to make her as comfortable as possible. She's been asking for you."

Andrea couldn't move her head because the drugs had almost immobilized her. But when he walked in, she managed to smile at him.

"How do I look, Dad?"

"You look beautiful, sweet heart." He took her hand and kissed her forehead. She smiled, again, to let him know that she could still feel his touch.

Her voice was now barely a whisper. "Are you going to be ok?"

He nodded, fighting back the tears.

"I know you will. I had a dream about you."

He frowned, not knowing what to say.

"Dad, I'm sorry for the grief I caused you and mom. If I had known it was going to like this . . . ." She began to cry.

Buzz squeezed her hand hard. "Honey, I love you and so did your mom. We understood what you needed to do. You don't have to apologize for wanting to live your life."

She reached up with her other hand and touched his face. "Dad, promise me you'll finish your journey." Buzz leaned close to ask her what she meant, she was gone.

The nursing staff gave Buzz an hour alone with her before calling Ken and Jessie. Buzz told them that her last words were that she loved them.

During the arrangements for her funeral, Buzz set up a trust fund for her stepson and offered Jessie and Ken money to help with his upbringing. They waved him off with the promise that they would ask if they it.

Before the funeral, Buzz spent an hour in the chapel with Andrea. The loneliness was unbearable. His entire family was taken from him and without closure. Even Andrea's last words were no comfort. If anything, they added to the hurt, because he had no way of knowing what she meant or how to honor her wish.

It rained the day of the funeral. No one spoke in the car as it followed the hearse to the cemetery. Jessie had been to funerals before, had seen how people behaved, and it was always the same. The women were in tears and the men were cold and stolid. This time it was different.

It was the look on Buzz's face or the lack of it. It was like he wasn't really there. Was it shock? Jessie didn't think so. It was almost as if he had stepped out of his body and walked off, like leaving a car double parked on a street. "Where could he be?" she wondered. Then it hit her, not where, but when. He had gone back in time. For a brief moment, she saw him as he was thirty years ago, a young man with his whole life ahead of him. She felt Ken's hand on her shoulder.

She looked at Buzz. "Give him some time, Jessie."

It was almost an hour before Buzz felt Ken beside him. "I know Ken. I know."

Buzz stayed for three days after the funeral so he could spend some time with his grandson. As Jessie watched them play together, she got the impression he was trying to cram a lifetime of memories into a few, short days. It wasn't any one thing he was doing. It was more like he was trying to memorize every moment.

It was approaching dusk on Buzz's last day. Jessie's attempts to help him pack were reduced to watching him empty the dresser drawers and pack his bags.

Buzz hoisted his luggage off the bed stopped at the door and looked back at the room that had been his home for the last six months. Out in the hallway, he paused briefly at Andy's door. He had been asleep for over an hour. He decided not to wake him, all of the good-byes had been said. "He's going to miss you, Buzz."

"I'll miss him too, Jessie. You'll tell him I love him?"

She touched his arm. "Of course I will."

Ken was waiting for them as Buzz stepped out of the trailer. "Are you ready?"

As they started the walk to the park gate, Jessie looked back in confusion, at Buzz's rental car, as he continued past it on foot. No one said a word until they got to the gate.

Buzz slowly placed his bag on the bench and carefully took in the surroundings, etching it in his mind for the last time. The bench, the worn brick and faded lettering on the gate entrance still proudly announcing the Westland Trailer Park. The phone booth. How many times had he walked here to make calls? It all suddenly felt like a hundred years ago. He reached out and gave Jessie a strong hug. He could feel tears on his shirt.

Releasing Jessie, he offered a hand to Ken. Ken's response was slow and measured, and with a message.

"We both know you're not coming back. I do not approve, but I understand. Where ever you go, whatever you do, don't forget us or your grandson, because we sure as hell won't forget you." As they shook hands, Ken raised his other hand and placed it on top of both their hands. The gesture was equal to Jessie's hug.

Without a word, Buzz picked up his bag and started to walk up the road, He stopped briefly and turned. He took one last look at Ken and Jessie. They watched him until he disappeared into the rapidly approaching twilight. Ken struggled for the word to describe that color, Indigo?

Jessie rubbed the red and water out of her eyes. "What the hell is going on? Why didn't he take his car? Its thirty miles just to the gas station Ken. On foot, it will take a day just to get that far."

Putting an arm around her shoulder, without taking his eyes off the road, Ken replied slowly. "He knows what he's doing, and where he is going."

CHAPTER 3
BUFFALO

"I don't know why you need to see this guy after three decades. He may not be prepared to find his past standing at his door. Are you sure this is a road you should be taking him down?"

—Jean McAlindin

A roach, a really big roach. It was the *Bradley Tank* of roaches; at least that was the opinion of the man, diner #1, at the lunch counter. The other man, diner #2, watching the fuzzy 4X4 out of the corner of his eye, as it appeared from under the napkin dispenser, was yet to form an opinion, either mental or verbal.

The roach, as far as it was capable, had definitely formed an opinion. Brother! I have wondered into a seriously bad-ass neighborhood, and if I don't get my freaking feelers out of here in a hurry, I am going to get stomped on big time."

The two men watched the insect as it crossed the counter in front of them. It stopped in front of the uneaten burger and fries, raised a feeler and decided that there are some things, and this was one of them, that even a roach wouldn't touch. The owner of the burger and fries, diner #1, thought that was one smart bug. The roach continued down the counter until it encountered diner #2. It stopped in its tracks and stared at the man.
Diner # 2 stared back.

Diner #1, watched the staring contest with interest. It appeared that these two had crossed paths before and that some form of non-verbal communication was taking place between them.

Diner #2 slowly tapped the fingers of his right hand. The roach slowly backed up without taking its eyes and feelers off him. The fingers moved faster and so did the roach. The fingers suddenly stopped and so did the bug. You could cut the tension at the counter with a knife.

Diner #2 slowly smiled. The roach tensed up like a watch spring, turned 180 degrees, and headed for the napkin dispenser as fast as its eight legs could carry it. The bug was gone. "Are you going to eat that?"

Todd pushed his lunch over to Number 2's outstretched hand. He couldn't help noticing that the man was still looking intently at the last known position of the roach. As he munched quietly on Todd's burger, a heated argument was developing in the parking lot.

Someone's wife, her character, and her fidelity were in serious question. From the sound of things, judging from the description of the offspring, the evidence was compelling. As the discussion got louder, Todd turned to watch.

Apparently, there was only one disputant in the parking lot. The rest of the crowd was trying to prevent him from entering the diner and confronting the man who had besmirched his wife's honor. In fact, the wife-besmircher was the man munching on Todd's lunch. The besmircher continued to eat, unaware of the chaos growing around him.

The owner of the diner appeared from the kitchen and looked at the small riot taking place in his parking lot. "For Christ's sake, 12, does it ever end with you?"

12 slowly finished his meal and stood up. The owner slowly backed away from the counter. Todd didn't think the guy was all that scary until he smiled. It was a warm, nice kind of smile that made you feel good about the world, just before the smiling guy pushes down a plunger, and blows up the bridge that doesn't belong to him. It was the smile of a man who really enjoys bringing his work home with him. A chain saw operator, for example. 12 took ten dollars out of his wallet and held it out. The owner

reached out and took the money. His hand was shaking badly.

He turned and smiled nicely at the people in the parking lot. The disputant and his entourage suddenly stopped struggling and backed up several feet, in unison. He put his wallet back in his pocket and went into the washroom.

The owner exhaled loudly. "Jesus!" He looked like a man who had just missed stepping into an open grave

Todd looked at the heavy steel washroom door. "Is he coming out?"

"God, I hope not! I'd nail the door shut if I didn't need the washroom."

Todd reached into his pocket to pay for his lunch. He pulled out a coin, a silver dollar. The mechanic working on his car found it jammed in the outboard seat rail on the passenger side. "Damnedest thing. I wouldn't have found it if the car wasn't on the hoist, had to be looking up under the seat to find it."

Todd turned it over in his hand slowly. It had been stuck under there for all those years. It meant a great deal to Buzz. He wondered if he ever tried to recover it.

The owner returned from cleaning up. "You mind if I have a look at that?"

He handed it to him slowly. He had a brief feeling of loss as he let it go. He reminded himself that it was only a coin.

"The name's Bill." He slowly hefted the coin in his hand and carefully looked at both sides of the coin and the edges. The man knew money. "That's odd, two heads, no tails. That's rare. You're going to want to hang on to that."

He handed it back. "A lot of sentimental value?"

"Very!" Todd handed him money for the bill.

Bill shook his head." It's on the house. Anyone who can sit next to that nut case deserves a free meal."

Todd thanked him and stepped outside. It was incredibly quiet. The angry mob had moved on. He took a deep breath of fresh air. The blown water pump that landed him here would be done by now, and he could be on his way. But to where?

The door opened behind him and he felt a hand on his shoulder. "Mister it's the damnedest thing. I remember seeing a coin like that before. Hell, it would have had to be back in the sixties when I worked the midnight shift here for the guy that I bought the place from. The guy who had the coin was a cab driver. Forgotten the name, although I remember he used to say that every coin has three sides."

Todd smiled. "Murdoch."

"Yeah, that sounds right. I think he got into construction, did all right, too, come to think of it. Hell of a thing to remember all of that from a coin. He looked down at the coin in Todd's hand. "Hell of a thing."

The walk back to the garage Todd thought about the time he and Buzz Murdoch had spent on the road, the places they went, the things they did--a lot of it good. There was also the fight that ended the journey. He winced at the things that were said. He stopped and took a deep breath. It was time to get the job done. He had a long way to go and he needed Buzz to make the journey with him. For a brief moment, he worried that he wouldn't go, that he'd put it all behind him. Maybe Buzz had passed on. No, Buzz was still out there and he needed or wanted to finish the trip as badly as Todd did.

Todd was back at the garage. The Corvette was parked outside. The mechanic looked up from a fender and walked out into the sun. He looked thoughtful as he wiped his hands on a rag. "This looks like a ride that works for a living."

"It definitely has long way to go." Todd replied.

The mechanic motioned him inside. "Let's get you settled up and on your way."

The credit card cleared and the mechanic handed it back to Todd. "I wish the hell I was going with you."

Todd reached out and shook his hand to convey understanding. "I hear the view from the horizon is really great this time of year."

As he walked out to the car he began thinking. Thinking, however, did not solve the problem of where to find Murdoch and why the hell was he in Buffalo.

He reached into his pocket and took out his cell phone. There was only one person who could answer the first question. He was on his own for the second. The phone was turned off. If he turned it on, it would melt down before he could make a call, because of all the messages in the cue, definitely, not the way to go.

Across the street was a phone booth. He smiled. If you want to take a trip back in time, just step into the first booth you find. Once inside he suddenly got the feeling he was on his way. For the first time, he knew he was headed in the right direction.

Okay, how does the damn thing work? The last time he was in a phone booth, it had a rotary dial and doors. He picked up the receiver, thought for a moment, and then put it back. Maybe he should read the instructions first. Apparently, phones now take credit cards. On the other hand, it would be kind of cool to make a collect call to his company. He lifted the receiver waited for a dial tone and pushed zero. He didn't remember it taking this long to get an operator.

A very pleasant and very young woman responded to his question. "Well, there are more of you and less of us than there were thirty years ago."

Todd thought she was pretty smart for her age and would probably end up running the company someday. "I would to make a collect call to the CTI Corporation in Los Angeles, extension 5384."

Can I have your name and the person accepting the call, Sir?

"Todd Stiles and the person accepting is Jean McAlindin. Ten seconds later, the CTI switchboard answered.

Several years ago, there was a big debate about communications. The system people wanted to eliminate the "Biosector", which was the human being in the real world, and replace it with a digital interactive, an electronic box with blinking lights that told the human to push a button. David's secretary heard about the planning group which was trying to decide what type of system to purchase. She got herself on the group and by the time she was finished, the company ended up hiring more operators. The end result was a switchboard operator who Todd, and almost no one at the plant, had ever seen, because she worked in a room at the end of an unused hallway. Even if someone did find their way to her space, they would be hard pressed to find anyone among the racks of monitors, wire-ways, servers and a monkey tree, a nasty piece of vegetation with spikes. The operator had purchased it to keep her company.

The human resources people hired her because she had an aptitude for systems, zero experience, and the ability to handle long periods of isolation. In the interview, she answered one question by saying that what they really needed was a freaking astronaut. She got the job.

I have a collect call from a Mr. Todd Stiles for a Jean McAlindin."

The operator knew that it was company policy not to accept collect calls, but something about this one set off an alarm in the back of her mind. She asked the operator to hold. She had heard something about the owner being out of town and nobody could find him. It was causing a big stink upstairs. McAlindin was the name of his secretary, so maybe this guy was legit. Operator, ask the caller if he can verify the correct extension number for J. McAlindin."

The Bell system operator was also aware of procedures and this was not one of them. On the other hand, CTI had not exactly declined the call. "Sir, what is the extension number for J. McAlindin?"

Todd actually had to think for a second. 5384."

She suddenly figured out a way to solve a problem. I have a collect call from a Mr. Todd Stiles for extension 5384.

The CTI operator smiled. This was indeed the owner. It also meant that for a brief moment, she called the shots at a company worth over 2 billion dollars. Tell the caller I will accept the call, provided he pays for a new valve job on my car and puts a window in my office. She was sure that the entire Bell system had ground to a halt.

The Bell operator would have agreed with her. "I'm sorry. Could you repeat that?"

The CTI operator repeated what she had said.

She burst out laughing. "You're kidding me. You want me to tell him that?"

"Sure, go for it! Todd was not in the loop while this was going on. When she came back, she cracked up. "Sir, I'm sorry to keep you waiting." The operator at CTI will accept the call provided you agree to pay for a valve job on her car and put a new window in her office."

Todd was struggling very hard to remember if he had ever met the switch board operator. "Sir, would you like to me to repeat that?"

This was a phone call for the books. "Yes, I'll pay for a valve job and arrange for a window."

The Bell operator gave her computer and the CTI operator a thumbs up.

"Sir, I will put you through." Her supervisor, who'd been monitoring her call, tapped her on the shoulder, smiled, and handed her a cup of coffee. Sometimes, it's okay to bend a few rules. The CTI operator forwarded the call. She leaned back in her chair, thinking that just when you were ready to give up on the world, a little magic comes along and makes things better.

Jean McAlindin glared at her phone. Every time it rang, stupid stuff came out of it. If there was one thing for which she had no tolerance, it was stupid. The call display said it was an outside line and no number. The switchboard operator was really sharp. A call like that normally wouldn't have gotten this far. She picked up the receiver and waited for a second before punching the button. She didn't say anything, waiting for the caller to speak first.

I have a collect call for a Jean McAlindin from a Mr. Todd Stiles. "Will you accept the charges?"

She desperately wanted to say that the man was a despicable reprobate and bang down the phone. "Yes. I will accept the charges."

"Hello, Jean, **how** are things going?"

The man was almost immediately annoying.

"How is it going? You up and disappear leaving a 2 billion dollar company heading for the harbor in a handcart. Well, we're all just fine here, Sir. How are you?"

Todd now knew what it felt like to be gunned down in a phone booth. "Are there any messages?"

"You're kidding me? The only one around here that does not want to talk to you is the janitor and that's because he doesn't like you. By the way, where are you?"

Todd told her he was in Buffalo.

"It serves you right!"

Todd had to admit she had a point. "Jean, I need a profile on a construction company run or owned by someone named Murdoch, first name Buzz." For a minute he thought he could hear her blood pressure going up.

"That's it sir? Just find a construction company in the U.S. run by someone named Murdoch. That shouldn't be too hard."

"I think the company is in the Buffalo area."

"Oh, well, that narrows it down to 30,000 in Upstate New York. Much better! Is there anything else I can do for you today, Sir?"

"Nope, that should just about do it. I think I will stay in Buffalo tonight. There is a Motel 8 out by Stony Brook University. You can fax the stuff there."

"What makes you think you're going to get it tonight?"

"I have the best secretary in the country."

"That's the most gratuitous load of crap I have heard in months, Sir! By the way, when can we expect to see you back in the office? The janitor needs to be kept in the loop."

'As soon as I find Murdoch and drive out to California."

"Let's see if I've got this straight. You cannot come into the work until you find a contractor who lives in Buffalo and then drive him to California."

Todd wasn't going to admit it sounded pretty bizarre. "Cool, huh?"

"I'm going to stop telling people I work for you."

"By the way, why does the janitor hate me?"

"You keep throwing your used Wrigley's in the shred documents bin. Have you got any idea how tough it is to clean gum out of a paper shredder?"

"I see your point. I better get going. I'll give you a call when I get the information."

"Jean cut him off. I'll call you. If anyone around here finds out I've been talking to you, they'll start coming in here with questions which will piss me off. Then I'll have to kill someone to make an example of them."

Todd had a very vivid image of Jean standing behind her desk with a loaded shotgun, casually challenging anyone to leave a message.

"Okay, that sounds fine."

Jean listened as Todd passed on some additional requests and then hung up. She was going have a chat with the switchboard operator as soon as she figured where she was.

Todd walked back to the car and got behind the wheel. It felt good to have a goal and a sense of direction. Thinking back over the years that he and Buzz had spent in this car, he wondered if they knew then that they were headed in any particular direction, they were. But when you're young, you miss the big picture.

He pulled into the Super Eight around seven. It was later than he planned, but it was too nice a night to be wasted sitting in a hotel room. Jean's faxes were waiting for him at the counter. They consisted of eight pages of information and photographs on Whithers-Murdoch, including a list of past and current directors. Murdoch's name was identified as President and CEO.

Todd got a drink from the mini bar sat down and started to read. The list of projects filled two pages. The company was a monster. One project caught his attention. It was an integrated circuit company in Texas. CTI owned the company for eight years and sold it three years ago. David had overseen its upgrade and operation. The company that had built the expansion was Whithers-Murdoch. He shook his head in disbelief. "I never knew."

Jean had placed a note on the last page. "Call me when you get this."

He looked at his watch. It would be past six in L.A. She would be home by now. He decided to call the office and leave her a message that he'd received the faxes she had sent. She answered on the second ring.

"I got the information, Jean. Thanks."

She chose her words carefully. "How long has it been since you talked to him?"

"About thirty years. Why?"

"There's background on this guy that you should hear verbally before you follow through on your plans."

"Go ahead, Jean. I am going to need to hear this."

"His family has been wiped out, boy and two girls. The son died in a plane crash, and the wife and daughter in a car accident six years ago."

"What about his surviving daughter?"

"She died of cancer two months ago. I will fax the complete history to you now. I thought you should hear it from me first."

"Thanks Jean, it was the right thing to do."

"I don't know why you need to see this guy after decades, but I know you have a good reason. He may not want his past showing at his door. Are you sure this is a road you should be taking him down?"

"Good advice. I'll be careful. It's after six. Call it a day."

"I'm on my way. By the way, it took a long time to turn you into a great boss, don't screw up." She hung up.

Todd looked at the receiver and smiled. A compliment from Jean McAlindin, she'd deny it until hell froze over.

There was a knock on the door. The manager was there with Jean's faxes. It was nearly twenty pages and it did not make for very good reading. The last eight years of Buzz's life read like a horror novel. He'd done everything right and his life still ended up a train wreck.

Todd was beginning to have serious doubts about going through with the trip. He skimmed through the rest of the report. There was only photo of Buzz taken in 1973 at an ANSI conference. It was a group photo taken at a distance. It took a minute to pick him out of a crowd. Todd barely recognized him in a suit. His conference biography was pretty thin. There was no indication that he had gone back to school or earned any professional accreditations. It did not make any sense. He was on top of a company that was half again the size of his. There wasn't even an honorable mention in the trade journals. He did not sit on any boards and certainly his company hadn't made the Fortune 500.

Todd closed the file folder and poured another drink. He was going to have to make a decision, but not now. It was going to be a long night, and from the feel of things, a sleepless one. He decided to go for a walk.

It was dark. The rain had come and gone, leaving the pavement covered in diamonds lit by moonlight. He didn't know which way to go and maybe it didn't matter. The wind had come up a bit, but it wasn't cold. In the distance, he could see a neon light. He decided to head in that direction. It looked like the only thing out there. He stopped at the parking lot exit, looked for traffic, and crossed the road.

Ten minutes later, he was beginning to wonder how far that sign really was. It did not seem to be getting any closer. He stopped and looked up at the sound of metal rattling. The sign said Interstate 75 ten miles. The wind gave it another gentle tap and moved on. He looked back at the hotel, considered calling it a night, zipped up his jacket, and decided to press on. Eventually, the sign relented and began to get larger. Still, he could not say for sure how long he had had been walking. His watch said sixteen minutes, but it felt closer to an hour.

The place looked old and out of place for Upstate New York. It looked like the kind of bar you'd expect to find in Arizona. He looked in the window. The lights were on but the place looked deserted. Having come this far he might as well go in. As he pushed open the door, he looked up at the light. That type of bulb hadn't been made in years.

The place was amazing. It was an exact replica of an 1890's bar. In a corner, a railroad regulator clock chimed softly. Todd whistled quietly.

"This is incredible!"

"Thank you."

Todd turned to find a man behind him, smiling. It was hard to tell his age. He could have been fifty or eighty, not tall, but solid. He was wearing those arm bands on the sleeves men used to wear, although he couldn't remember why.

"May I help you?"

"Well, I think I'd like a drink."

He laughed. "You've come to the right place. Step over to the bar and let's see if your poison is up there."

Todd followed him over to the bar and sat down. The stool was really comfortable. The man walked behind the counter and sized Todd up.

"I'm thinking you're a scotch drinker?"

Todd agreed that he was.

"So am I. He thought for a moment before speaking. You know, Scotch is a fine animal. But if you ride it too often, it starts to get a bit lame.

Tonight, we need something that will oil a conversation." He walked to the end of the bar. Todd could barely see him in the shadows.

"Let's see, Ouzo? No, not unless you plan on burning down someone's house. Sherry isn't going to do it either. Hello? There's the answer, Metaxa!"

He reached up and pulled down a bottle that had not seen the light of day in years. He pulled out the cork and waved it slowly under Todd's nose. "What do you think?"

"It reminds me of--I'm not sure, but I hope it drinks as well as it smells."

"That's the great thing about this stuff. It can be anything you want. Hell, I might as well have one with you. He pulled down a couple of brandy glasses and poured.

Todd had just lifted his glass when the bartender stopped him.   "Care for a cigar?"

"You're kidding!"

"You don't smoke? He looked surprised.

"No, the cigar sounds great, but isn't smoking in public places an issue these days?"

The bartender reached under the bar and produced a box of cigars and two ash trays. Taking two out of the box, he cut the tips and handed one to Todd. "Not in 1891 it isn't."

He lit Todd's cigar, telling him to draw slowly and let it burn at its own rate. He had to admit he couldn't remember a cigar tasting that good.

"It's been a long time since you had a good smoke, huh?"

"It's been a long time since I've had a chance to enjoy one that's for sure."

The bartender nodded but remained silent.

Todd looked over his shoulder. "Where did you get all the antiques?"

"I didn't buy anything. It was all here, just as you see it, when I took over the place."

The stuff must have been old when you bought it."

The bartender scratched his head and thought carefully. "Let's see. I'm the third owner and I've been here for forty-six years. The woman I bought the place from was as old as I am now.

"What about the first owner?"

"Well, if I remember right, she said the first owner was a colored fell who came north from New Mexico after the Klan burned him and his family out. He owned this bar and was doing a right smart job of running it until they came after him. With his home gone, all he had was what was in the business, so he stripped it right down to the studs and came north. Everything you see in here is what was in that bar. For the first few years, he lived here until he could afford a home. He must have done alright because the place is still here."

Todd tried to imagine what the place looked like in 1890, when the man showed up with everything he owned in the back of a covered wagon.

The bartender's voice brought him back to the present. "How about you, got a story to tell? That's why I am here. People will tell their bartender things they'll never tell their doctor."

Todd nodded, but he didn't know where to start or if his problem was worth telling. The man had probably heard it all before.

"Look, nobody walks into a place like this, at this hour, looking for entertainment. Besides, we got to talk about something."

"You've probably heard the story a hundred times."

The bartender laughed. "You can always prove me wrong. Besides, don't do it for me. Do it for the bar."

Todd frowned. "The bar?"

"Sure. You are sitting here surrounded by the past. Thousands of people have come through those doors, each with one with a story to tell. Each one of them has become a part of the place. So here you are, on a cold rainy night, with your own story to tell. Make some history!"

Todd couldn't argue with that, he raised his hands and clapped. "That was a fine and eloquent speech, Sir.

The bartender took a bow. "I do my part, worthy patron."

So, Todd told him the story, his time on the road with Buzz, the fight that drove them apart, his family, and the loss of Marcie. He tried to explain why he was making the trip, but failed on that one. His indecision was whether it was worth it to drag Buzz into something he was not even sure about himself.

The bartender listened intently, stopping Todd to ask a question or for clarification, letting him tell the story at his own pace.

It was surprisingly late when Todd finished. The bartender looked at the clock and the bottle which was nearly empty. "I ought to be getting home and you have a long day ahead of you."

As Todd reached for his wallet, the bartender put hand on his sleeve. "It's on the house."

Todd shook his head. "That was a lot of booze."

He just smiled. "That bottle was bought and paid for twenty years ago; it's earned its keep."

Reaching over the counter, he shook Todd's hand. "Whatever happens out there; take care of your self and take care of Buzz.

His words were sincere and Todd promised he would. "I never did get your name."

The man smiled. "Does it matter?"

Todd shook his head. "No, I guess it doesn't"

When he got to the door, the Bartender called out to him. "You said you weren't sure about going through with it. What do you think Buzz would tell you?"

"I wish I knew, but he's not here."

The bartender pointed at his pocket. "No he isn't, but his coin is. Let it decide on his behalf. If my read of the man and you is worth anything, he'd trust it to decide right.

The next morning, Todd could remember very little of the walk back to the hotel, except that he'd turned briefly to look back at the bar as the bartender turned off the neon light for the night. When he closed his eyes, he could still see the image on the back of his eyes, like a TV holds a picture for a few seconds after it's turned off. It was 9:30 in the morning and time to go. Bags packed, he went around the room to make sure he had not forgotten anything. This was a room that he would never return to.

He pulled on his coat and checked the contents of his pockets. Keys, and a coin. He reached in and pulled it out, Buzz's coin. He sat on the edge of the bed and turned it over in his hands. It was time to make a decision. It was definitely a heart and head choice. He knew, deep down in that spot where people rarely go, that this trip was something that needed to be done. On the other hand, Jean was right. Buzz Murdoch didn't need his past showing up at his door thirty-plus-years later.

"Hi there, your life has gone to hell. Let's go for a ride!

He turned the coin over slowly. It shone like a diamond in the sunlight. In the hall, he could hear the housekeeping staff. They would soon be at the door wanting to groom the room. "What did the bartender say?" Todd struggled to remember what he said through a night of Metaxa.

"Why don't you let the coin decide, on Buzz's behalf? After all, it was his coin."

He tossed the coin. It dazzled as it spun in the sunlight. Todd reached out to catch it and missed. It hit the floor, bounced once, and then disappeared under the dresser. "Damn!"

He got down on his hands and knees, but couldn't see it. Well, he wasn't going to leave without it.

"Sir, is there a problem?

He looked up at a stout woman carrying an armful of towels. She looked down at him without the least bit of surprise on her face. "She had seen it all."

He smiled carefully. "I seem to have lost something of value behind the dresser and I'm trying to find it before I leave."

Without a word, she stepped over him and pulled the dresser away from the wall. "Can you see it now?"

Todd replied that he couldn't see it.

She walked to the other end and pulled it away from the wall. "What is it?"

"A coin."

She motioned him over. It was sitting upright on its edge between the wall and the dresser leg. She reached down, picked it up, and hefted it in her hand without looking at it. Her face broke into a smile as she handed it to him.

Todd thanked her as he put the coin in his pocket. He helped her move the furniture back and reached for his wallet to give her a tip. She declined it.

As he reached the door she stopped him. "A silver dollar with two heads is a pretty valuable coin to go tossing around. I suspect the owner will be pretty happy to get it back."

Todd turned to reply, but she had already forgotten him and was concentrating on preparing the room for the next occupant.

Ten minutes later, the bill was paid and he was loading the car. He looked up. It was going to be a nice day. Another ten minutes, the top was down, and he was easing out of the parking space. He pulled over, reached into his pocket, and took out the coin. The housekeeper had a point, and he needed a safe place to put it. How many times had Buzz lost it? Well, now that he thought about it, it had always ended up in a frantic search, with one of them finding it under the passenger seat. He got out, walked around the car, and opened the door. He dropped the coin and it immediately rolled out of sight between the seat and door sill. The coin had made its decision.

As he pulled out of the parking lot, he looked up the road towards the bar. The sun was well up in the sky and in his eyes. He couldn't make it out in the morning heat. It didn't really matter. He was headed in a different direction, and he knew he'd never be back.

Up until now, he had been drifting, or at least it felt that way. Now, he wasn't sure. He didn't believe in fate or cosmic tumblers, but it sure wasn't a coincidence that he ended up finding his answers in a seriously run down diner in Buffalo.

Well, he was definitely going somewhere now. He was tired from the night before and it would take the entire day to get from Buffalo down to New York and the offices of Whithers-Murdoch. Apart from steering the car, he didn't have to do a lot of thinking. "Damn. It felt good to be back out here again!"

He got to New York just as the sun was setting below the skyline. It had been a long day and to tell the truth, a little melancholy was starting to set in. He knew tomorrow was going to be a tough day and he really didn't have a game plan. This was a bad time to be flying by the seat of his pants. But right now, he needed a place to spend the night. He found a room, in a three-story walk-up, fifteen minutes from the Empire State Building. The place turned out to be pretty clean, complete with a neon sign right outside the window. No doubt about it, the building was a classic.

Tossing his bag on the bed, he walked over to the window. Buzz would have loved this place. The place has a lot of class, *all low*. He smiled at the thought and wondered if Buzz still had a dry sense of humor. A last sliver of sunlight shot between two buildings and hovered briefly on the far wall before giving way to twilight. It was almost eight o'clock and he couldn't figure out what to do. He was definitely tired, but sleep was out of the question, at least for a while. Booze was definitely not an option, especially after last night.

There was a diner a block east of the hotel. He'd passed it on the way in. He wasn't hungry, but the food wouldn't kill him. Lunch felt like ten years ago.

The walk to the diner was a lot shorter than the one he took yesterday, which was a good thing, because he sure felt a day older. The place was tidy, quiet, and modern. He picked a booth and sat down. After a minute, he looked around for a waitress, but the place looked deserted. He picked up a menu and thumbed through it. Nothing turned his crank.

"Don't waste your time. The only thing edible on the menu is the plastic." The waitress had arrived.

He closed the menu and put it back in the rack. "What do you recommend?"

"Try the restaurant across the street."

Todd laughed. "Are you the waitress or the entertainment?"

"They don't pay me enough to wait on tables. Go with the chicken salad and coffee. It is only two-hours-old and the cook hasn't had a chance to ruin it yet."

"That sounds great. Thank you."

She didn't move, staring at him over her glasses. "A polite, all-American boy, where were you thirty years ago?"

"Eating at that dump of a diner across the across the street."

"And funny too." She left to fill his order.

A man in a plaid work jacket came in and called for her at the counter. She appeared in a couple of minutes with a paper lunch bag. Handing her a couple of bills, they chatted for a few minutes. He declined the change, said good night, and left for work. Ten minutes later, she returned with his chicken salad and coffee.

She wrote the total on the bill and put it on the table. "If you're still here when we close, you can walk me home."

"You're serious?"

"Hey, do you see any ha, ha, coming out of my mouth? Eleven o'clock." She returned to the kitchen.

Todd watched her walking away. He had to admit she looked pretty good. She had the kind of walk that said, "I know exactly where I am in the world." This was the kind of walk that comes from absolute confidence, solid and strong, the shoulders straight, and the head up.

He felt a sharp hurt. That was Marcie's walk and that's how it would have looked. God, he missed her. Todd put some money on the table, cleared his eyes, and got up. Outside, it was a good night for a walk. He checked his watch. He had some time to kill. He decided to check out an antique shop across the street. At 10:30, he returned to the diner. She was waiting with a sweater over her shoulders. He hadn't seen a woman do that in years.

She took his arm as they stepped out on to the street. "I'm three blocks up in the battery. It takes about fifteen minutes. It's a nice evening. Let's try dragging it out to an hour."

He nodded silently. They did not complicate the time with discussions about where they were from, or where they were going. By agreement, the conversation was limited to the present.

Ninety minutes later, they were at her front door. There were a few minutes of awkward silence. Todd looked back the way they had come. "I have a long day ahead of me, so I had better be going."

She nodded. "Thanks for the walk. It has been a long time since I've done that. Look, I'll try to put it into words. Good people are hard to find these days. I asked for the some of your time because the world could do with a little magic every once and a while, don't you think?"

Todd reached out and gently touched her shoulder. "Magic is exactly what this all about, now, or thirty years ago. Thank you for lending me some of yours. Good night."

As she walked to the door, she turned back and watched him walk away. She would never see him again, she did not have to. Magic moments lasted forever.

As Todd climbed the stairs to his room, he could hear music start up, Mexican music-- really bad Mexican music. Brother was that stuff awful, right up there with fingernails on a blackboard! Four bars into the tune, someone screamed in agony. "Oh God no, not the damn maracas, anything but the maracas!"

As he continued to climb the stairs, the screaming got louder. Apparently, a lot of people in the building didn't appreciate really bad Mexican music. By the time he got to the third floor, he had discovered that the artist, perpetrator, or criminal's name, depending on who you asked in the building, was El Grande, King of the Maracas. He could hear someone in an apartment on the floor below threatening to come up there and personally remove El Grande's maracas with a dull implement. She sounded serious.

As he approached the door to his room, it was obvious that El Grande was, in fact, staying in the room next to his. He unlocked the door. It would only take a couple of minutes to pack and be on the street, looking for a building that played jazz or country and western. He pushed open the door and, for at least a minute, his brain could not process what it was seeing.

The bed was half way across the room and headed for what looked like the bathroom. It seemed to be powered by a force coming from the wall where it had started. It stopped briefly to acknowledge his presence before continuing on its way. The photo on the wall where the bed used to sit flung itself from the wall, in a vain attempt to follow the bed to safety. Then, suddenly it stopped--the bed, the music, the picture, everything. The only sound was a soft buzz from the neon sign outside the window. It seemed like the entire building had exhaled.

Then, just as quickly as it stopped, someone screamed, "Oh my God Almighty, not again!" On cue, the whole thing started up again. When the bed discovered that it couldn't fit through the bathroom door, it reversed direction and headed back to the wall. It became obvious, after about ten minutes, that the couple in the next room were having sex to the rhythm of El Grande. It was a little hard to understand--four minutes on and three minutes off. Neither could anyone else in the building. Todd walked in, closed the door, threw his jacket on the bed, and shrugged. When he tried to climb into bed, he had to chase it around for a minute before jumping on it. He figured he'd slept in bigger dumps than this one. He was asleep in minutes.

Around one in the morning, someone in the building, driven to the brink of insanity, stormed out into the hall and screamed, "For the love of Christ, finish her off!"

El Grande, his chorus of maracas and the tempo began to ascend to a climax. The bed, having made at least four trips to the bathroom and back, two of them with Todd on it asleep, had decided to wait out the climax in the middle of the room. It was safer there. In the next room over the sound of the maracas, Todd had awakened to hear someone very heavy climbing onto furniture, which was not designed to carry overweight Mexicans. He could hear the sound wood makes when it does not like being abused.

El Grande's voice, now much closer to the ceiling than the floor, roared. The arrival of the great flying squirrel is upon us!"

The woman who was clearly close to being finished off screamed. "Holy Christ, look at the size of that furry bugger!"

El Grande screamed over the sound of the furniture that wanted to him get back on the floor where he belonged. "Yeah, and look at these maracas. Bet you haven't seen a pair of grenades like these before!"

"Baby, come on over here, so I can yank your pins!"

El Grande screamed "Incoming!

The finale, at long last, had arrived.

A lifetime's worth of burritos, about 300 pounds, launched itself into the air and landed on the bed and its now waiting, to be finished off, occupant. Walt Disney tried making a ride like that once, but gave up when every religion in the world sued them.

First, there was a thunder clap of wood and metal, and then, everything in the room, including Todd, moved simultaneously and violently back towards the bathroom. Then, just as quickly, everything rebounded towards the center of the room. The picture on the wall finally succeeded in joining the bed in the center of the room. A huge crack appeared in the wall in the shape of a headboard followed by the sound of springs hitting the floor.

Todd could hear the sound of a woman, on the floor below, screaming that everyone was going to die. Then, a man's voice overrode hers. "The ceiling, there are fucking legs sticking out of our ceiling! I just painted that fucking thing!"

Todd got up, opened the window, and took a deep breath of fresh air. It was a nice evening and he decided that he was glad that he'd checked in here. With all hell breaking loose around him, he thought to himself that everything was going to be just fine. He climbed back into bed and was asleep in less than a minute.

Although it promised to be a nice day, the sun rose reluctantly over the Griesmont Hotel. A few rays wandered in through the window, didn't like the look of the place, and left.

Todd was up at 8:00. He glanced out the window at the now dark neon sign. Life was beginning to appear on the streets. A couple of men with lunch pails met on the street and walked off together, it was a practiced ritual. In the distance, he could hear a woman admonish someone for being late for school, and the unmistakable sound of a garbage truck.

These were sounds of peace and continuity. The people who lived here had traded excitement and uncertainty for a guarantee that there would be a tomorrow, exactly like today. About the only excitement these people had to deal with was The Griesmont. He took a couple of deep breaths. He was going to miss this place. It was time to go.

It took him a little longer than usual to pack because of the redecoration the room had received the night before. Because the bed had covered a lot of ground, he had a lot of ground to cover. Eventually, he rounded up everything, got packed, and went out to the door. He closed it quietly because the neighbors didn't need any more noise. Actually, Todd could have slammed the door twenty-five times and it would not have made any difference.

As he passed his neighbor's door, home of El Grande King of the Maracas, he could see that the peep hole in the door had been replaced by a fist-sized hole. There was a slipper jammed in the door, about two feet from the floor. On the way out, he slipped the key under the care-takers door. Ten minutes later, as he slipped the wheel, he realized that he had never been to the Empire State Building.

The drive up to 33rd Street and Broadway brought back a flood of memories, his dad taking him on business trips to the city, or the time his mom woke him up in the middle of the night, telling him to get dressed. She was dressed in her best clothes and had a smile on her face. When the confusion got the better of him, she said to him quietly, "We're going on your first adventure."

He remembered the smell of her perfume, the light from the locomotive in the distance, like a star on the horizon, and the sun rising over New York City. They went to the museum, the library, took a ride on the Staten Island Ferry, and had lunch on Coney Island. When the day was over and finally on their way home, she asked him what he learned that day.

Todd told her that you really had to keep your eyes open when you were on an adventure.

Boy was she was proud of him that day!

The memories started as a trickle and then, began to flood in. It was all coming back, the good and the bad. He remembered his first trip into the city with the Corvette, a gift from his dad, how concerned he was about totaling the car and that it was damn near all he had left to remember his Dad, after his suicide.

33rd Street. He turned right, two blocks up, and there it was, The Empire State Building. It was not like you could miss it. It had a hell of a foot print that cast a shadow four blocks long. He found a parking lot on the south side of the building.

As he walked behind the car and out on to the sidewalk, he looked up. The thing just kept getting bigger. He shook his head, the Empire State was hardly a giant anymore, and maybe it was because he didn't spend a lot of time inside tall buildings.

He stepped through the lobby doors and waited briefly for his eyes to adjust. This was still an impressive building. In eighty years, she had not surrendered an inch of class. There was history here, and power, a lot of power. The people who worked here did not make integrated circuits. They decided what kind of circuits were to be used, who used them, and where.

As he approached the security desk, the officer looked up at him, smiled, and asked politely where he wished to go and whom he wished to see. The man's eyes were calm, focused, and experienced.

"I understand that Whithers-Murdoch has its head offices here."

"Yes, Sir, they are here. Whom do you wish to see?"

"Buzz Murdoch." Todd answered, reflectively.

The smile slowly receded. "I'm sorry, Sir, there is no one by that name at Whithers-Murdoch."

Todd briefly panicked. Buzz wouldn't use a nickname in a business like this. What was his given name? Hell! He couldn't remember!

"Sir?" The guard wanted his attention.

"Sorry. Wait. Robert Murdoch."

The guard relaxed slightly. "Do you have an appointment?"

He reached behind the desk and retrieved a metal detector and log book.

"No, but I am a friend of his."

He was asked to raise his arms as the man passed the detector over him. He found nothing suspicious and made an entry in the log. "How long have you known Mister Murdoch?"

"We met in a place called Toots Shore's. He worked for my father's company."

The smile returned knowingly. "I'll bet you've got a few stories to tell about that place."

Todd chuckled. "A few, we knocked around the country for a couple of years."

He finished making his entries. "20th floor, turn right off the elevator. "

Todd wished him a good day and left.

When he got to the elevator, the guard called out. "Mr. Stiles. Take the last one on the left. It's faster."

Todd waved as he pushed the button and waited. It only took a minute. It didn't register with him that the guard had called him by name.

As he walked off the elevator, someone stepped out of the shadows. "Mr. Stiles?"

He was directed to an outer office that made his own in L.A. look like the lobby of a cheap hotel. The security guard crossed to the far side, opened a door, and ushered him into another office. "Sir, if you'll make yourself comfortable, someone will be along in about five minutes to see you."

Todd nodded silently as the man left, slowly closing the door behind him.

He walked slowly around the office, taking in the look and feel of the room. This was definitely Buzz's office. But there was nothing here of the man he knew thirty-five years ago, everything in the room belonged to someone who was years away from 1962. To be fair, he had changed as well, but he thought he had hung on to some of the things he used to be.

He stopped at a wall covered in documents and photographs. There were awards and commendations next to photographs of presidents, industrialists, some of whom he knew personally, and astronauts. It was impressive.

"That's Gene Kranz. Todd turned to see a woman in her fifties standing at the door. She was shorter and smaller than his secretary Jean, but she was every bit her equal: tough and smart, and when she talked to you, she looked you right in the eyes. She walked over and extended a hand.

"Mr. Stiles?"

He nodded. "Todd."

She smiled. "Bonnie Davids. I'm Mr. Murdoch's executive secretary."

"It's quite a history", turning and looking at the wall.

"Gene Kranz. Wasn't he the flight director on Apollo Eleven?"

"Yes, one of them. That's Chris Kraft and Thomas Paine pointing to a photograph of two men standing next to a capsule.

Bonnie reached out and gently touched the photo of Gene Kranz. "It was the only photo up here that he really liked; he didn't want to put up any photographs."

"I can see that. He was never big on advertising." Todd was glad that this was one part of Buzz that hadn't changed.

"Buzz's wife insisted on it. When he objected that no one was interested in that sort of thing, she told him it was for her, that she wanted to see them because she was so damned proud of him."

He tried to visualize her. There were no photographs of her in Buzz's bio. "It would have been an honor to meet her."

Bonnie turned to him slowly. Molly passed away a number of years ago. "He took it hard. She would have liked you."

Todd thanked her.

"In the last year, things have gotten worse."

"I know. His daughter passed away a couple of months ago. He stopped. "I'm sorry. I did some research before I came. Invasion of privacy, research, it's all the same. But I couldn't go into this blind.

She put a hand on his sleeve. "Who do you think gave Jean the information?"

Todd laughed to himself. "We are not really in control, are we?"

"No. You never have been. I'll be back in a moment."

She returned with a small suit case. "I packed this for him shortly after I spoke to Jean. This should be enough to get him started. There are a couple of changes of clothes and his shaving kit. He'll find an overcoat and windbreaker behind the seat of your car."

She directed him to a couple of chairs, sat down, and asked him to join her. In all the years I have known him, Buzz only talked once about the time you two were out there. It was the damnedest thing I've ever seen. Even Molly couldn't believe it, and she knew him better than anyone. It was almost like he wasn't even there. There was nothing there but road.   You could almost reach down and touch. It felt that real, flat and straight right out to the horizon and beyond. You could actually feel the heat coming off the asphalt, and the passion. You could sense his need to go back. I remember Molly telling me later that it was the first time since she'd met him that she'd have to share him with something else."

"Was she hurt by that?"

"No, she knew that it meant something really important to him.

Todd took sometime before he spoke." I can't speak to what you and Molly have felt. I do know that we never thought of it that way. Of course, we had fun and didn't take ourselves seriously. In the end, it was just about another town and another job. It was about putting enough money in our pockets, and then, moving on. We probably did have a sense of direction and purpose, but if you asked us at the time, we would just say we were passing through. We were young and complicated answers didn't come easy."

Bonnie took a deep breath and looked slowly around Buzz's office. She stood up, reached down, and handed the bag to him slowly. "He's not here. He spends every Tuesday at the New York Port Authority docks having lunch with a man named Bertie."

She stopped him at the door. "Molly made me promise to look after him. Make sure he gets home safe."

"I will."

Back at the car, he looked up at the building. For the first time in decades, he heard something familiar, a voice. "You are free to do anything you want with your life. It's an open book with blank pages. Feel free to write whatever you want." He opened the trunk and tossed in Buzz's bag.

It took longer than he planned to find his way to the dock. It'd been a long time since he'd been there. It was hard to believe that his father's main office and warehouse were still standing. The company name, of course, was long gone from the side of the building. There had been many owners over the years.

He couldn't see anything through the windows because of decades of dirt and grime, and it was locked. He went back to the car. He still had the key his dad gave him. He could still see him handing it to him, saying that the first key you get to a business is a lot more important than the first dollar.

The key went in like it was 1959, but the lock would not turn. He tried both ways but it refused to budge. Of course, he could keep increasing the pressure, but he would probably end up breaking the key off in the lock.

"Pull the door toward you, it'll move. The voice had a lot of power, enough to turn Todd around quickly. Bertie Becker.

He was a retired longshoreman and stevedore. He looked old, wide and tough, really tough, just like he did in 1961. Still was. Becker shouldered Todd aside, simultaneously pulling on the door and the key. It opened in seconds. He stepped aside and Todd followed him in. Becker reached for a light switch just inside the door.

When the lights came on, there was a rush of memories so strong Todd could actually feel them. Of course, the people and the furniture were gone, but that did not lesson anything. He could walk around the room and know precisely who sat where, thirty years later. Becker pointed to the far wall "upstairs."

It was a long climb. He hadn't been on these stairs in decades, since his father's funeral.

At the end of the hall on the right was his office. Becker had followed him stopping in the hall, and watched him go into the office. He turned and went back down the stairs. Becker had never met Jean or Bonnie, didn't even know their names, but he had an intuitive sense of who they were and their objectives. It is an art a good man learns, just by looking at what's around him, when he walks into a room. He was an equal partner in their plans. Just like working on the docks, everyone had a role to play. It was good to have a purpose again.

Buzz was right where he always was, standing on Pier 4, looking out to sea. Bertie put a hand on his shoulder. Buzz immediately knew that today, there weren't going to be slow walks on the docks any more, no quiet conversation about health and family, or lunch at Softies Deli. When they got back to the warehouse door Bertie stopped, took a hard look at Buzz, and held out his hand. Buzz, for a full minute, refused to take it because this handshake was a good-bye. Bertie Becker was a constant. A connection to the past and all that was good and decent in the world. The hand stayed out until Buzz finally reached out and answered it. Bertie's work was done.

Buzz pushed open the door, stepped inside and closed it behind him. From a long forgotten memory, he gave it a gentle push, and the lock seated with a click. He stood motionless, his hands in his overcoat, listening for sounds. Utter silence. Looking down there were footprints in the dust. Two sets leading across the floor to the stairs and one set returning. Bertie's.

Buzz turned and looked back at the door. He didn't have to do this; he could go back the way he had come. Back to his office and spend the rest of his life behind a desk, running a company that no longer needed him. Watching the money, his personal wealth, pile up until he eventually drowned in it.

His memory of the building was about equal to Todd's. It didn't take him long to find the office. Hesitating briefly, he pushed open the door and stepped inside. Cloudy sunlight was coming through a skylight, making it difficult to see clearly. It took a few minutes for his eyes to adjust enough to see the figure standing at the window.

Meeting someone after more than thirty years is not like in the movies. No profound words, grand gestures, just awkward silence and staring. In Todd and Buzz's reunion, confusion reigned, because they were not sure why they were in this room after so many years. "You're well?"

Todd shrugged. "Can't complain, you?"

"Fine, never better."

Todd felt a flash of anger. Three decades and the first thing he does is to lie to me. He caught himself and realized that he would have reacted the same way.

The conversation stalled. Buzz walked over to the window and stared out. He was relieved that the skyline had barely changed. He tried to draw it in, to smell it, to touch it. He reached up and turned the latch and pushed open the window. Sound rushed in driving out the silence and giving them a chance to reign in their emotions. They stayed at the window for fifteen minutes. Neither of them noticed Bertie standing on the dock, looking up at them briefly before turning away.

Buzz finally broke the silence. "Whatever happened to the Corvette?"

"It's parked over at the Crane House."

Buzz smiled to himself and shook his head in amazement. "Where the hell are we going to go in a thirty-five-year-old car?"

Todd looked up at the skyline, as though he was searching for something in the distance, and then, answered quietly. "Back the way we came."

"Why? What's out there that's so damned important that we have to go back and do it all over again? We're not kids anymore."

"Because when you're alone, you can feel it, the heat from the road, the wind. When you put your hand down on a table, you can feel the vibration in the steering in your finger tips."

Buzz knew Todd was right. He knew now that this moment had been coming for a long time. He turned, walked to the door, and waited for Todd. "Give me a few minutes; I'll meet you out side. Buzz nodded silently and left.

He closed the window carefully and locked it. He spent a full ten minutes in the room recalling how it was, saying a silent, and long overdue good-bye to his father.

Back outside, he was surprised to find Buzz waiting for him. Neither of them said a word as they walked to the car. Todd opened the drivers door and handed Buzz the keys while he shrugged off his overcoat, stopped and stared into the trunk. Concerned, Todd joined him at the back of the car.

Buzz pointed at the bag. "You were pretty damned sure of yourself.

Todd pulled off his coat and tossed it in. "Nope, but your secretary was. You want to take the first leg?"

Buzz hefted the keys in his hand. It felt good, like finding an old friend you hadn't seen in years.

Murdoch turned and looked out into the harbor. "You mind?"

"Sure, I'll go with you."

They stood at the edge of the dock. Buzz took a deep breath of harbor air. "It's been a long time for you, hasn't it?"

"Yeah, it has. Does the construction business pay well?"

"The last time I checked, about 4 and half billion in assets."

"Not bad!"

Buzz scratched his chin and drew in a deep breath.

Todd smiled. That was the Murdoch he remembered, reflective before he spoke.

"You?"

"I did alright, didn't get anywhere near 4 billion. I went into electrical engineering in 1965. If I sold everything, it might be worth 2 and half billion. Anyway, it's not about the money. It's the work and people that matter."

Todd reached into his pocket, took out his cell phone and thought for a second. "7 billion dollars in thirty-five years, I would say that we're owed some time off. Have you got one of these on you?"

"Sure. My secretary won't let me out the door unless she knows I've got it."

He reached out and took Buzz's phone out of his hand.

Buzz took a long breath before speaking. "I can't see what this is going to accomplish. Our mistakes are three decades in the past."

Todd looked back towards to the city. "I agree, but consider the alternative."

Buzz stuck his hands in his pockets. "We go back to our jobs and look after our people."

Todd took a step forward, took one last look at the phones in his hand, and threw them as far as he could out into the harbor. "We're done, Buzz. They don't need us anymore."

He looked at Todd. "Back the way we came is pretty open ended."

Todd smiled. "I know."

Buzz drew a deep breath before speaking. "35 years, 7 billion dollars,... we are done.

They waited another five minutes before Todd answered him. "It's time."

As they passed the Empire State Building, Buzz saw it as part of the past, another life. It already felt like a long time ago. "Seriously, what are we going to do if we need to talk to someone?

Todd reached down between the seats and pulled out a baseball cap. "You should see the pay phones they've got these days."

Two hours and sixty miles away, Herman T. Spud was waiting for them.

CHAPTER 4
HERMAN
T. SPUD

The average person puts only twenty-five percent of his energy and ability into his work. The world takes off its hat to those who put in more than fifty percent of their capacity, and stands on its head for those few and far between souls who devote 100 percent.

—Andrew Carnegie

     At a distance, you would guess that Herman T. Spud was a garbage collector. Up close, you would be right. Herman T. Spud was a sanitation worker for the State of New Jersey. This was a perfectly respectable profession employing hundreds, if not thousands, of dedicated women and men, including Spud, who provide a valuable service to the good citizens of New Jersey. The honor of employment is also extended to the state's less worthy one's as well, but that's how democracy works. You would have said that. If you were Warren Oates, the supervisor of District 6, you would agree with everything except the part that had Spud's name in it, and the part about those dedicated sanitation workers, because they were always coming into his to complain about stuff. People who spent eight hours a day standing in other people's trash did not smell nice. His repeated requests that employees wipe their feet before coming into his office went ignored, although a great many of those dedicated sanitation workers have no problem remembering to wipe their feet when they are in his office, five carpet replacements in three years.

   Herman T. Spud was a small man, barely five-feet tall, with glasses and a receding hairline. He had a gap between his front teeth that he used to make an annoying whistle, which reminded people of that guy on the front of that magazine. Of course, you wouldn't see any of this when Spud was behind the wheel of his garbage truck. All you saw was a baseball cap, a set of eyes peering through the gap between the spokes in the steering wheel, and a pair of hands at the top of the wheel. Herman T. Spud was the ultimate low rider.

   Spud was one of those people who didn't fit in. He was the proverbial square peg in the round hole of life. He drove a garbage truck because he just wasn't going to work out in any other position. His sister, who was very successful, wealthy, and did fit in, got him the job. A lot of people would be pretty unhappy with being relegated to the clearance bin of life. Herman had no such problems or illusions about this. He was comfortable with his life. He really liked his job, which provided a valuable service to the community and he was meeting nice people. But mostly, he just liked driving his truck. Behind the wheel, he was king of the road, and the ultimate road warrior.

   The only flies in Herman's ointment were the women in his life. There was a cashier at the *Piggy Wiggly* that he still hadn't gotten to first base with, after two years; Sally, a stripper at "*Dirty Pete's Bango Rama*," who would literally give Herman the shirt off her back, when he stopped by for a drink on Friday nights. And Herman's sister, Victoria, who made piles of money, and a career out of preventing Herman from having any kind of meaningful relationship. Women, as far as she was concerned, were not to be trusted. So far, she had successfully sabotaged every attempt Herman had made to get a date. The owner of Dirty Pete's, who had a thing for Herman's sister, was one of the few people in the world, or at least New Jersey, who truly enjoyed Herman's company.

On the road of life, many lives had converged for any number of reasons. On this particular day, life brought together a group of relatively decent people: two men in a sports car, a garbage truck driver, an assortment of oddballs, and a stripper, in the hope of sorting a few things out. Shaken, not stirred. It was just about dusk as Murdoch and Stiles left New York and drove into New Jersey. It would have been easy for them to head to Todd's place and to have spent the night, but that's not what the journey was all about.

The place was not exactly a dump, but it was definitely not five stars, but the view was. It was one of those "no tell motels" that backed onto a ridge overlooking the Hudson. In the distance, the New York skyline glowed in the evening sun. In the sky, the moon was already bright and full. There was a small playground with a picnic table at the back of the hotel. Buzz and Todd decided to take the bottle of scotch outside, and talk.

Todd got up from the table and walked out to the edge of the bluff. "I've lived in New Jersey damn near twenty years, and I could have gone anywhere, done anything I wanted, and yet, I never bothered to look out my back door. This has been here every night, for twenty years. What the hell was so important that I couldn't take the time to look at this?"

Buzz held his glass up in front of the moon's light and let it shine through. "Money does that to you. You live in a world of answered calls, waiting limos, and attending another meeting. The more you make, the less control of your own life you have. By the way, did you put in a wake-up call for seven with the front desk?"

Todd was raising his glass for a drink when he stopped. "You know, she said we wouldn't need one."

Friday morning arrived right on time at the Ocean Grove motel, 6:57 a.m. to be exact. It brought sunshine, birds singing, a nice breeze, and a garbage truck, Herman T. Spud's garbage truck, to be exact. The owner of the motel was aware of all this because she checked the weather and the calendar every morning. She kept a big one in her office. She would mark off all her appointments, special events, birthdays, and anniversaries--all marked in green or blue, depending on either the importance or which relatives were in and which relatives had fallen out of favor. A more careful examination would reveal that every second Friday was marked with a large red X. You would assume that these were truly important days. You would have assumed, also, that someone else was marking these X's, because they appeared harried and angry next to the graceful handwriting identifying a niece's birthday. You would also assume wrong. They were all from the same hand. The X's that were harried, angry, and filled with anxiety identified garbage pick-up day.

"Rumbling?" Murdoch cracked open an eye and stared malevolently at the glass of orange liquid on the night stand. For a moment, he did not recognize the room and he wondered why he was not in his bedroom in his apartment in Central Park, then, he remembered,...road trip. The orange liquid had apparently developed some mysterious power source during the night and had taken up humming as a hobby. He looked at the alarm clock. The numbers hesitated briefly before flipping from 6:57 to 6:58 a.m. The mysterious energy living in his orange juice had grown in magnitude and decided to move up to the picture over the bed.

In the room next door, Todd Stiles was having a Griesmont flashback. Every piece of furniture in the room had suddenly come alive. At any moment, the great flying squirrel dressed up as El Grande was going to come crashing through the bathroom door.

Emerging from the motel, Todd and Buzz were presented with a uniquely American scene, a garbage truck delivering trash! The owner of the hotel, one Greta Gebauer, did not do unique well. In fact, she detested unique, had no use for it, and did not want it hanging around her parking lot. Gebauer, from where Murdoch and Stiles where standing, looked like an enraged bridge troll in a pink floral house coat and slippers carrying what appeared to be a fully functional broadsword. Her dead husband had borrowed it from a castle, in Wunsdorf, Germany. The Castle had been converted into a cheap hotel during the Korean War. George Gebauer had never set foot in Korea and probably couldn't have found it on a map if he tried. George was a duty driver in Berlin who managed to get himself drunk and lost returning from a cheap bordello. George wasn't just cheap; he didn't have a lot of class either.

Todd had read the *Hobbit, or There and Back again*, which had contained a number of trolls as characters. He couldn't remember any of them wearing pink floral house coats and bear claw slippers.

Buzz thought out loud. "Maybe she's a bridge troll. That might explain the way she was dressed."

"Clang!"

From the window sill, Spud's voice came from under the ball cap. "Hey, you old buzzard! Stop that! This is government property."

"Clang!

"Come down here, you rotten little turd, so I can chop you up and feed you to my Rottweiler, Cromwell! Yelled Greta.

The baseball cap bounced up and down in the window.
"Rottweiler! Hell, that ain't even a dog. That's an ass-hole with a Chihuahua sticking out of it!" Challenged Spud.

Again, the noise of sword on garbage truck, "Clang, clang, hiss. CLANG,... hiss."

"You rotten old bag, those are $500 dollar tires! You are going to answer to the New Jersey Department of Sanitation for that!" Spud yelled angrily.

Todd and Buzz watched as Cromwell chewed her way through a tire thick enough to hold up a 35,000-pound truck.

"Good doggie," Chuckled Greta.

The bridge troll was doing a happy dance, having finally slayed the foul smelling green outhouse disguised as a garbage truck.

She yelled, "You dumb ass! Every week you do the same thing and every week I have to come out here and explain to you how it works."

The baseball cap bounced up and down in the window. "How does it work, Fatso?"

She looked at Todd suddenly. "What did he call me?"

"Fatso."

"Really?"

"I'm afraid so."

Buzz tapped Todd on the shoulder. "You know, that wasn't very nice calling her fatso."

"I didn't call her that, the guy in the truck did."

"Well, you could have worded it a little nicer."

"What's a nice word for Fatso?"

Buzz just stood there and grinned at Todd.

"You know, Buzz, you weren't as nasty in the 1960's."

Buzz continued to grin, "Was so."

The bridge troll took another swing at the truck, just to make sure it was dead. "You pick up garbage and take it away. You do not deliver garbage. That's why it is called garbage. The stuff goes away and it doesn't come back."

The smile under the baseball cap got bigger. "It's really nice trash, not like that crap you are producing. This is really high grade waste from the best hotel in New Jersey. When people drive past this place, they see a flea bag motel. I'm doing you a favor. Now, when people pull in here and look in the old Dempsey dumpster, they see class!"

Greta Gebauer clearly had had enough of the chit-chat, and raised her sword to dispatch either Spud, the truck, or both, it didn't matter. Suddenly, she discovered Todd and Buzz, who had seemed to have appeared out of nowhere.

"Who are you guys, anyway?"

"We're guests in the hotel. You checked us in yesterday."

"I did?"

They nodded together.

Spud, who had climbed down out of his truck because he was feeling left out of the conversation, looked Todd up and down, slowly.

"Hey, pal, you think maybe it's time to spring for a new pair of jammies?"

Greta, being a people person, suddenly lost interest in the nasty old garbage truck. "My husband was about your size, except he's dead. I still got a pair of his night shiners you can have. Had one arm longer than the other, looked like a damned monkey, but it shouldn't matter none. Ain't anyone going to see you with the light off anyway. Come to think of it, that was the only time when he didn't look like a gorilla."

Todd began to pick defensively at the afore-mentioned shirt, and looked at Buzz for moral support. Murdoch was suddenly working very hard at watching Cromwell gnaw on his 35,000 pound doggie chew and was suddenly unavailable to speak up on his behalf.

Spud and Gebauer had gotten back to the business at hand as a car pulled into the parking lot. District 3 supervisor Warren Oates was not having a good day. It was only 7:30 in the morning and Herman T. Spud was already getting on his nerves. If pressed, he would respond by asking, "How was this different from any other day?

"Spud! What the hell are you doing? I haven't even had a cup of coffee and I've got some old bag screaming at me on the phone about you."

Spud pointed at Oates tie. "Yes, you did. You had coffee. I can see it right there."

"That's right, you pecker wood. It is coffee. But as you can clearly see, I am wearing it because some harpy started screaming at me about you before I could start drinking it. You know how much I hate it when people start talking to me about you, don't you, Spud?"

"Clang, sqwack, hzzt."

Oates turned to find that the bridge troll was chopping up his car. First impressions are important. Oates took a long step back as she raised the sword overhead and hacked off the roof light in one slice. She looked experienced at hacking things off.

Buzz politely tapped Oates on the shoulder. "That would be the old bag."

Spud corrected him. "No, I distinctly heard him call her a harpy."

Greta took a break from car chopping, stepped up to Oates, real close, and whispered, nicely. *First impressions are important.* "How about I cut some new pockets in that cheap suit of yours?"

Oates was suddenly having trouble with his mouth. "So what is the problem here, Ma'am?

When someone is waving a six-foot broadsword in your face, it is important to be polite. *First impressions matter.*

She pointed at Spud. This time everyone took a step back. "That stupid sack of crap is delivering garbage."

Oates had to admit that was a problem. "Well, that's not our policy. We're only supposed to pick trash up."

He looked out over the parking lot looking for divine inspiration, something that would sweep all these awful people away. In the distance, he could see New York shimmering in the morning light, nope, not a shred of inspiration over there. After all, there is only so much you can expect from a parking lot and New York was busy.

"Spud, I want to see you in my office in an hour!"

Greta was not going to be left out. "Well, you can count me in."

Oates had a sudden vivid image of being trapped in a small room with a large woman in a paisley housecoat; bear claw slippers, and carrying a large sword. "You are not bringing that letter opener with you."

She smiled sweetly, "Of course not."

He turned to Todd and Buzz. "What about you guys?"

"Sure, we'll be there."

Oates took a hard look at Todd. "What's your problem fella,... can't afford a decent pair of jammies?"

He took a second look at Todd, and shook his head as he walked back to his car.

When they were alone in the parking lot, Buzz looked Todd up and down. "How long have you had those things, anyway?

Todd was getting way past defensive. "What?"

Buzz pulled on a sleeve, "Webb City? You got these in 1961. You were putting the moves on a car hop at an A&W."

"Well, they worked! I got way past first base."

A really evil grin appeared on Buzz's face. "No, you didn't, because her husband said she couldn't play with you anymore."

Todd picked furiously at the shirt. "She was not married, just seriously engaged."

The evil grin liked being where it was and it refused to leave. "If you're short of cash, I can lend you a couple of bucks for a new pair, with interest, of course.

Todd burst out laughing. "Fuck off!"

An hour and twenty minutes later, the first meeting of the New Jersey Sanitation Department Glee Club got under way. District 3 supervisor Oates was presiding. "Hey, you old bag, what do you think you are doing?"

"You can't talk to me like that. Do you say things like that to your wife?"

"I do when she is sitting in my chair. Out!"

"Bite me, asshole!"

"You ain't so tough when you don't have that freakin NAZI swizzle stick." Oates grabbed the back of the chair and dumped her on the floor.

She got up and promptly took a swing at Oates. She missed and put her fist through the shade on the floor lamp next to the window.

Oates laughed and blew a big fat raspberry at her. She responded with a nice left jab that connected. The shiner she gave him was going to put his eye out of action for at least a week.

Todd and Buzz had taken up positions next to a bookshelf.
"Buzz, did you ever have meetings like this?"

"Sure, lots, but they weren't this civilized. What's that?" He pointed to the object that Todd had picked up off the bookshelf.

Spud, who was an authority on all things trashed, directed their attention to the plaque on the side of the solid silver garbage truck. "That is the Front End Loader Award. They give it to the driver with the highest tonnage collected in a single day".

Buzz turned the trophy around to read the inscription and let out a low whistle, "80 tons."

Spud reverently took the trophy. "They've only given out two of them and no one has broken the record in eighteen years."

"I could use a little help here!" Greta had Oates by the throat and was trying to wipe a note off of his desk blotter with his forehead. It took the three of them to remove her hold on him. It's like that with people who are having too much fun.

Oates collapsed in his chair, picked up a piece of paper, and tried to read it with his remaining eye. Nope. He threw it back on the desk.

The problem here is a fairly simple one that can be corrected quite easily. He was speaking in a calm professional voice until this moment.

"Spud, you shit-for-brains, peckerhead! We pick up garbage. We take it to a place where people do not live, it's called a dump. It's called a dump because that is where we dump the garbage. What we do not do is drive around town and leaves the garbage it at someone else's address. Why don't we do this, Spud? I'll tell you why. Because people already have their own garbage and do not pay taxes to get someone else's."

Spud responded that the world would be a lot better place if everyone tried to get along and learn to love each other's waste. He stopped mid-sentence.

Oates, who was still standing behind his desk, began turning a sort of crimson color. Spud pleaded. "Sir, you're not going to fire me, are you? I really love my job."

Oates responded speaking in a low, menacing voice, which contrasted with the weird smile stuck to his face. "Fire you! I wouldn't dream of it. That would be just wrong. No, I am going to *kill* you. I am going to rid the world of that stupid spud face. They will call it justifiable homicide. They will give me a medal!"

Oates lunged for the lamp, yanked the cord out of the wall, and went after Spud with it.

Spud was fast and just managed to make it to the door and yank it shut after him before Oates got there. Oates had no intention of stopping. The lamp, all six feet of it, went through the door like it was cardboard, shearing off the lampshade and pushing it up the shaft until it jammed on the base with a loud crunch. Oates took a deep breath, yanked open the door, and broking the lamp in half. He could be heard somewhere in the building screaming. "Spud, you filthy tater tot, when I get my hands on you! The rest was cut off by a corner.

Todd had wandered over to the door and was inspecting the lamp shade when Herman suddenly reappeared. Buzz looked passed him down the hall. "Where's your boss?"

He shrugged. "I'm not sure. The parking lot, I think."

"You don't seem too worried about this. You could get fired."

"No, I should be Okay. Mr. Oates just gets a little cranky in the morning when he doesn't get his coffee. He'll calm down in a while. Besides, he has a thing for my sister.

Buzz had to admit that would provide a measure of security. Spud thoughtfully adding that she was also sleeping with the Mayor.

"Bulletproof!" Todd nodded in agreement.

Greta had made herself comfortable again behind Oates desk. "When I first saw old feed-bag-boy, it didn't look like he had a lot of lead in his pencil. But he sure impressed me with the way he handled that lamp. He has the potential to be a real sword's man. I am going to have to arrange for him to check into my motel for a couple of days."

The room suddenly went quiet for a few minutes. Spud calmly asked if anyone wanted to go for a burger. "We can take my car."

His car, like everything else that came into contact with Herman T. Spud, was a lesson in contrast. It was spotless. Every last bit of dust, dirt, and lint was hunted down and disposed of. Not a scrap of paper was to be found. The motor, perfectly tuned, started in half a crank and settled down to a soft rumble. Nice hearse."

Murdoch, Stiles, and Spud were in the front seat, which was actually the only seat. Frau Gebauer was comfortably laid out in the back, but there weren't any cushions. It didn't matter. She came equipped with her own padding, factory installed.

"Herman, *this-is-a-hearse.*"

Spud nodded in agreement and proceeded to provide the explanation that was inevitable. "I needed a car. The dating service said I should get a set of wheels. Now, it is important to remember when buying a car, that it's in good running order, clean, and low mileage. The division was okay with me taking the top loader home, but you can imagine trying to get it through the drive-through when you are on a date. Anyway, the suspension is a bit stiff and I guess women prefer a softer ride."

In the back, Greta was humming a tune by the Grateful Dead. Buzz and Todd looked at each other without saying a word, but the same thing was going through both of their minds. "Four hours ago, we were Captains of industry, men of influence, power and control. When we spoke, people listened. Now, we are sitting in a hearse driven by a garbage truck driver who has phone books strapped to the pedals with an over sized *fraumeister* in the back."

Buzz leaned forward and looked across at Spud and then at Todd. "Good to be back, huh?"

Todd reached into his shirt pocket and took out a pair of sunglasses. He put them on, looking straight ahead. "We are living the dream."

Murdoch rolled down the window, put his arm out, and took a deep breath. It felt good. He did not know how this was all going to turn out, but for the first time in years, life felt good. He could finally go on with living.

At 11:29:29, Herman T. Spud was a man who also thrived on precision, The Mighty Rider as Greta had taken to calling it, swung into the drive-through at what could be generously called the worst looking fast food joint on the planet. The place made *Weird Walt's* look like a five star. *Bert's Dine and Dash* did not put a premium on presentation, it was a dump.

Buzz looked out his window and down at the gap between the car and the curb, wanting to know if the car was going to fit inside the curb. Spud assured him it would and that it would be a walk in the park.

The voice out of the speaker order box was a perfect fit for the outside of the place. "Whadda ya want, Spud?"

"I'll have the usual, Charlie. The same thing I order every time I come here."

"You're a loser, Spud, and look you brought more losers with you. What do they want, food or bananas?"

"Hey--that's not a nice thing to say about my friends."

The speaker went silent for a moment. "Bite me, loser!"

There was a brief pause. "Hey, what've you got in the back, a dead beaver? It's a big hairy sucker, ain't it? I'll go see if I got a log you can feed it."

Greta sat up like she had been shot. "Who said that?"

The speaker erupted in a nasty cackle. "Hey, whadda you know? It talks. C'mon, let me see that big fat tail of yours. C'mon show me a nice hairy wrinkle."

She was way past annoyed. It took a couple of seconds to figure out the latch on the back door of the hearse. As a rule, people don't usually let themselves out of the back of a hearse because they are lying down quietly being dead. She eventually figured it out, which saved her the trouble of kicking out the window. Blind with anger, she could not decide to go left or right. She stopped for a second and looked at the rear door of the hearse. "Nice curtains."

Another cackle erupted from the speaker. She grabbed the menu board and tried to pull it out of the curb, unsuccessfully. She stepped back, out of breath.

The menu board did not like being abused, "Saggy tits!

She delivered a right cross that ripped the Mr. Snacky statue off the top of the menu board. Greta leaned into the menu board and spoke slowly and quietly. "I'm coming for you, pecker wood, and I know where you live."

She disappeared around the corner of the diner.

The cackling and insults continued for a few more minutes and then suddenly stopped. Voices could be heard in the background. "Hey, you can't come in here!"

Todd and Buzz could hear the sound of something heavy being dragged across the floor, followed by screaming, "You can't touch that, that's the shake machine,...put that down!

"So, what are you going to have, Buzz?"

Normally, it takes about four minutes for the average customer to get their food at a drive through. The Spud party took somewhat longer because Greta had to walk to the car carrying five large salads.

"What? I'm trying to watch my waist line."

The three men in the front seat nodded silently in agreement

They arrived back at the sanitation department around 2:00 pm. It could have ended there, with everyone shaking hands and going their separate ways.

"So, what are you pecker woods doing tonight?"

Herman was not too sure about unloading his lack of a love life on strangers. I'm going to the supermarket to pick up a few things. Actually, I am interested in one of the cashiers who works there, but to be honest, I don't think she has the same level of interest. His face suddenly brightened.

"Maybe she really does like me and is just playing hard to get. Yes, I think that's it!"

Greta put an ample arm around his shoulder and gave him a reassuring squeeze, gentle like. You could hear his collar bones groan. "I'm going to give you the benefit of my vast experience. Your situation obviously requires a woman's touch. By the time I'm done, she will be eating out of your left pocket."

Todd looked at Spud, whose head was sticking out from one of her armpits. "You're a lucky man, Herman."

Todd and Buzz had planned on being on the road by then. They had a lot of ground to cover. On the other hand, the understanding between them was that it wasn't just about retracing their steps. That wouldn't accomplish anything. It was about making the world a little better, fixing stuff, one step at a time. The journey was the destination.

"Live the dream."

"Todd, you said that already."

"No, I didn't"

New Jersey was a place that could get hot when it wanted to, and on this particular day, the place decided to take a match to itself.

Todd and Buzz stopped on the way back to the hotel and bought water and booze. Spud dropped Greta off at a store to purchase a new dress. The plan was to meet at 5:00 pm at the hotel. First stop, the *Piggly Wiggly,* to assess Herman's romantic situation.

The cashier hit Herman with two sixteen ounce steaks--one on each side of the head, kind of like large meat cymbals. At half pound each, it was not exactly five-star dining. When swung by a severely annoyed and underpaid cashier, a blade steak can really punch above its weight.

"Maybe we should give him hand?"

Greta held up a hand. "Let's see what kind of mood she's in. She might be testing to see if he can make a commitment, by playing hard to get."

Hard to get had her hands around Herman's neck and was trying to jam his head into a five-gallon pail of lard.

It took the three of them to finally get Susan Panzarella off Spud. Threats followed, all physical, detailed, and very vivid. Buzz thought out loud that she certainly talked a good killing.

"I'm sending my brother after you, Spud. By the time he is done with you, you are going to be riding in the back of your own truck. He's tough and doesn't take crap from anyone."

"He drives a milk truck."

Everyone looked at him. "What? That's what he does. I mean--someone has to do it."

"That's right, Spud. You have to be one tough bastard to drive a milk truck and he is tough as the day is long! Nobody screws with the lead driver of Milkmeister Dairy. He's coming for you and that dirt bag-mobile of yours."

You can insult Herman T. Spud till hell freezes over and all you get is a smile and a shrug. Besmirch his truck, and you had a fight on your hands.

"You take that back! I've got the best front end compactor on the road. Someday, I am going to win the Front Loader Award. I am going to be somebody someday, not like your brother, who spends all day driving an udder with wheels."

She took a sudden leap at him and the both of them ended up in the cheese cooler. This time it took ten minutes to get them out and separated. Spud had bruises on his head where Panzarella had tried to beat him to death with a ten pound block of mozzarella.

"Tonight, Spud. The Drag Line Road, midnight, you and that crud-mobile of yours. Don't keep us waiting!"

Herman tried to straighten what was left of his shirt and hair. "You know, she really does like me. She's just having trouble trying to make a commitment. So, who's hungry?"

"Clean up in the dairy aisle!"

Back in the parking lot, Todd and Buzz had to answer two really important questions. Why was a man who had just been roughed up in a cheese cooler so calm? What kind of bug crap had they stepped into, anyway?

Herman's ability to get a thirty-foot vehicle into a drive through with a forty-five degree bend in it was impressive. As the Dine and Dash was only taking walk-in customers, they decided on the local McDonald's. It went well, the order was correct. Greta stayed in the car and the menu board was spared a mugging.

"Herman, have you ever considered eating inside. These places have furniture you can actually sit on."

He shook his head and pointed between mouthfuls. "That's what the dashboard is for."

Buzz looked down at the hand, not one of his own, that was fondling his burger. Greta wanted to know if he was going to eat that.

Todd thought that was pretty funny until the hand reappeared on his shoulder. He wisely gave it his burger and it went away. Buzz reached into his pocket, pulled out a Mickey of Rye, and poured a shot into Todd's coke, one into his own, and put the bottle back in his pocket. Looking into his cup, Todd said he didn't remember it tasting like this.

Buzz looked out the window for a moment before replying. "It did. We just let thirty-five years of letting other people live our lives for us get in the way. We're getting a second chance in a world which has changed right out from under us."

Todd nodded in agreement and looked at Herman. "So, what is next, Mr. Spud? You are most definitely in the driver's seat."

Herman, who was busy chasing a crumb out of the car, looked up in surprise. It was not very often that he was referred to as mister. "It's Friday, so I have a drink with Sally when she gets off work. But we have a couple of hours to kill before I get there.

The sun was beginning to set as they left the local Kart Track and Mini Putt. Sunsets can be a special time--magic under the right circumstances. The transition from the work of the day to the life of the night is when dreams are made and come to life.

Dirty Pete's place was a dump and the name was none too tidy, either. As they pulled into the parking lot, Spud's hearse was starting to look pretty good. Todd wanted to know if they were in the right place.

Doesn't it just figure that I left my brass knuckles in my other purse? Silence as the men turned to and stared at Greta.

Todd and Buzz stopped at the front door, steel with handles and dead bolts." I'm thinking we are going to be seeing a lot of places like this."

Buzz agreed. "Wait here for a second."

He walked over to a shrub, reached in, and retrieved a much scarred length of 2X4. Returning to the door, he swung and sheared the light over the door cleanly off the wall. The lamp bounced once and skidded across the pavement, coming to rest under a car. Buzz had everyone wait a minute for their eyes to adjust to the reduced light, before opening the door, "Ladies first."

We all have our moments when we walk into a room we've never been in before and know we have come home. Buzz had that feeling as soon as he stepped inside, the bartender's baseball bat behind the counter, the fare from hell. The place was quiet but said "Watch your step."

A man yelled and detached himself from the crowd, "Spud! A big man, beard and a weathered face, that had spent many years in the wind, a biker.

"   "Jonathon, it's good to see you." Spud could have stood on a chair and still not reach his shoulders.

Hammer, as he was more commonly called, glowered at Spud's companions. "Hey, these are my friends, Todd, Buzz and Greta."

Hammer extended a hand full of rings and calluses. He wriggled his fingers speculatively, after shaking hands with Greta, a couple of his them were pretty numb.

They headed for a table while Herman elected for trip to the washroom. Todd ordered beers all around and a coke for Herman. Greta ordered something decidedly upscale, which to the bartender, sounded suspiciously like a Zombie.

Hammer added a few more pieces to the puzzle that was Herman T. Spud. "He came in here about three years ago. He used to hang out at an upscale place, said it was tough to enjoy your self when people were laughing at you. We were shooting pool, four of the brothers. Herman just walked up and asked to play a game. I played a round with him, you know, just for laughs. He played well, nothing spectacular, but a solid game. I was severely pissed, when he won, and was going to drive him into the floor like a post. I was really going to do it, until I realized that he wasn't afraid of me. Five feet and 100 pounds, wet. Spud never even blinked. He just asked real polite for his twenty bucks. I gave him the money, and he used it to buy all of us a round. Herman's got his respect around here the old fashioned way,... he worked for it."

The waitress arrived with the drinks and looked around the table. "Sitting with people who take baths, are you are going upscale on me Hammer,... how much are you paying them?"

Hammer just growled back. "Some talk! Gave you ten bucks, and all I got was a wrinkle."

She stuck out her hand. "Hi, nice to meet you. We left the kitchen door open and we've never been able to get rid of him. Now we just keep him around as a pet, he bit someone from the humane society, now they won't come and get him."

"He pointed to the table these are friends of Herman's"

Her face brightened up. "You have good taste in people. Herman comes in to see Sally on her break. They usually manage to get in a couple of hands of crib or just shoot the breeze on her break."

Todd looked around at the women serving tables, wondering which one was Sally. She tapped him on the shoulder. "Sally is one of the dancers. Her stage name is Blaze."

She looked over her glasses at Hammer. "They don't know?"

Hammer smiled, "They don't know!"

She looked around the table. "Wait till you see Sally."

Spud returned to the table and settled in with his Coke, a lemon on the side. The conversation began with Hammer and the waitress impugning Herman's character and questioning his sexual prowess. The fact that his character was beyond reproach and that he couldn't get a date with a hundred dollar bill didn't prevent him from simultaneously denying and encouraging the doubts about his character.

Greta graciously offered the services of her vast sexual experience, for a reasonable fee, of course. Herman politely declined the offer, although Todd and Buzz were more than willing to lend him the money. Herman replied that it would cheapen the experience to borrow the money for the privilege of spending time in the august company of a woman of Greta's stature.

She leaned across the table and purred. "I'll do it for free."

Spud smiled back. "Good luck getting past my whip and chair."

Greta put her hand on top of his and whispered. "I like whips and chairs, they make me frisky. Bring Hammer. That way, I can have a snack afterwards."

"Spud! The voice sounded like freight train going off the rails, big, loud, heavy and seriously out of control. The room went silent as everyone looked around for the source.

Gary Panzarella was a walking, talking comic book character, complete with ten gallon hat, boots and string tie hung on a five-foot one inch body. When he reached the table, Hammer started to get out of his chair. Herman put a hand on his shoulder to stop him as he stepped around the table and stood in front of Panzarella.

"Spud, I'm calling you out tonight, you and that bug mobile of yours. Nobody screws with my sister and walks away. You have been dirtying up the streets for years and I'm going to put a stop to it. He looked at Hammer with disgust. Your muscle isn't going to help you tonight."

Todd stood up from the table and directed his attention away from Hammer. He had to admit that Panzarella was tough. He never flinched, despite the difference in height between the two of them. "This isn't the man you should be worried about. It's me and the gentleman who is sitting behind me. Mr. Murdoch and I are worth about seven billion dollars. It only takes a phone call and Milkmeister Dairies is under new management. Do you happen to have that much money, Sir? Mr. Spud is a friend of ours and we have taken an interest in his affairs. You do not want to make him, or us, angry."

Buzz, who had remained seated, added in a low menacing voice. "The Old Mill Road, Midnight, do not keep us waiting."

It was 10:00 p.m. and Sally K. Large, aka Blaze, took a final look in the mirror. There were ten dancers at Dirty Pete's, and they all took turns as the lead, but it was agreed by all of them that starting

Thursday night, the stage belonged to Sally. The stage belonged to her, no doubt about it. But she never took advantage of it, or took her looks or status for granted. Looks would only take you so far in life. She worked hard on stage and at everything she did. But she still caught herself doing double takes and asking how the hell anyone could actually look like that. From her side of the eyeballs, the world looked exactly the same way everyone else saw it, until she stepped in front of the mirror. She took a step back to make sure everything moved correctly. "Show time!"

It took her exactly twenty-nine steps from the mirror to the stage; the last five were the best because she was always smoking. The lights would come up and the place would go nuts. Halfway to the pole she ran into the waitress standing there with a drink in her hand. "What are you doing up here I am starting my show?"

The waitress handed Sally a glass. "Here have a drink. As a matter of fact, I'll even have one with you."

Sally was totally off her game by this point. "Look, I have to get to work."

She stepped around the waitress and continued on to the pole with the drink in her hand, but was a bit confused as to where to put it. She looked out in the bar, turning left and then right, deciding to hand it to a customer, but the place was empty, not a single body. Even the bartender was missing in action. The waitress reappeared with her trench coat and put it over her shoulders.

"You play a pretty good hand of crib. I'd ask the barkeep, to join us but he is in the back working on a crossword that will take him three years to finish.

When they got to the bar, she told Sally the saga of the empty bar. Panzarella and Herman were going to the Old Mill Road to have it out, once and for all over his sister, Mano-a-Mano. The whole place got in on it and off they went. After all, Dirty Pete's reputation is on the line."

"What's the contest going to involve, a fight, arm wrestling, or broom ball?"

"I'm thinking they are going out to drag race."

For a moment, Sally thought that sounded pretty safe, until the numbers started to add up. Herman didn't have a car, and she didn't know about the hearse, making the garbage truck the only vehicle that Herman had access to. Second, and this was a big one, he was going out to the Old Mill Road to race someone in a 35,000 pound truck.

The waitress burst out laughing at the image.

"It's not funny."

She laughed again. "Sure it is. It will take them all night just to get to fifty miles per hour."

Sally was suddenly deadly serious. "They don't have all night."

She looked over her glass of rye. "What are you talking about? The Old Mill Road runs, concession to concession, for thirty-five miles."

"Not anymore. The mill extended the tailing lagoon. The Old Mill ends about 100-yards past the gate. If they overshoot and go through the barricade, they will be into water a quarter mile wide and 100-feet deep."

She put the glass down slowly. "They don't know that! It's dark as hell out there and less than a quarter mile from the road to the gate."

"We'll take your car. Let's hope the hell we get there in time."

The waitress insisted on a costume change for Sally.

She shook her head and got up to leave. "We may already be out of time. Let's hope we don't get stopped."

The waitress threw her the coat. "You'll need it!"

When Herman and his pit crew left the bar, he was definitely on a mission. Honor was at stake.

"Spud I can't let you do this! Breaking and entering is one thing but stealing a city garbage truck is something else."

"It's okay, Jonathon."Herman produced a key from his pocket and unlocked the gate.

"You've got your own key?"

Sure. Sometimes we get a call to pick up stuff after hours, so we need to get in for the truck. Open the gate for me and I will be back in a minute."

Todd stopped him. "Herman, you are not picking up garbage. You're taking state property out illegally and drag racing with it. You could get into serious trouble."

Herman Spud could be surprisingly insightful when he needed to be. "I know,... I know but I have spent my entire life driving on the right side of the road. I could coast through the rest of my life without a worry. But what do I do when I'm done, and I've never once stepped up to plate or walked out to the edge?"

No one could argue with that. "Well, Mr. Spud, you won't step up to the plate alone tonight."

Greta spoke for all of them as she watched him walk away. "He's his own man. I'll grant you that."

"He stands some taller that," Hammer added softly.

Herman was back with his truck in five minutes. "Could you guys close the gate?"

Buzz asked Hammer if he wouldn't mind bringing Greta in the hearse and then looked up at Herman.

"Shotgun!"

They climbed up and Buzz pulled the door shut behind them.   Sitting three across, Buzz turned to Herman, whose face was illuminated by the dash lights. 'Show us the magic, Herman. Show us the magic."

The Old Mill Road was poorly lit, but it was possible to see that it was well looked after. Panzarella and his group were already there.

They gathered in front of the headlights to work out the details. To make it fair, both trucks were empty. The first truck to pass the gate was the winner. There would be one person on each side of the road to see who got there first. They would use the turn out a mile past the gate to turn around and come back. One race, winner takes all. It was agreed that Greta would sound the horn on Herman's hearse to start the race.

Spud and Bannister climbed in, buckled up, and started their engines. In the quiet of the night, the sound was deafening. There was some serious pushing and shoving with pistons as they revved up their engines.

Hammer and Greta were getting acquainted and deeply engrossed in the relative merits of brass knuckles vs. blackjacks in a brawl, when they were interrupted by a face that suggested that they could blow the horn anytime they had a moment.

Three miles away on the concession road, Sally came to the conclusion that they weren't going to make it. She gave directions. "A quarter a mile up the road on the left, turn off and stop at the visitor's gate."

When the car came to a stop, she got out. "Where the hell are you going dressed like that?"

Sally leaned in the window. "In about fifteen minutes, seventy tons of truck are going to run out of asphalt. "There's a safety station across the road. There's a boat there for inspecting the lagoon. You go out to the race. Maybe you can stop it before it gets started. I'll take the boat to the other end of the road. Either way, we'll have someone at both ends."

"How do you know all this?"

Sally laughed. "I'm not just a pretty face."

She put the car in gear. "When was the last time you looked in a mirror?"

It was close, but she didn't make it in time. The group stepped aside as she pulled up. As she got out, someone laughed that she just missed the first race. She could hear the diesels receding rapidly in the darkness.

"There won't be another race, because there won't be anything to race with."

Panzarella's sister yelled at her. "What the hell are you talking about? There is nothing out there to run into."

The waitress looked at her carefully. "You're right. There is nothing out there, including the road. It ends 1000 feet past the gate."

In the two cabs, it was a struggle. Panzarella's truck was lighter than Herman's, but he had more power. However, both trucks had the same transmission, which made the odds even. It was about who got through the gears faster.

Panzarella smoked through the first six gears and gained ground. But Herman pulled a seriously sweet axle shift between seven and eight and gained it back. The ground shook under a twenty-wheel footprint.

The guy at the gate with the flag, and his girlfriend, watched as the two trucks appeared out of the darkness. They looked and sounded like freight trains coming out of a tunnel. Running flat out, the sound was deafening as they passed the gate. There was a rush of wind and then sudden silence as both drivers took their feet off the accelerators followed by the sound of high pressure air escaping as the brakes came on.

The guy at the gate was tapped on the shoulder by his girlfriend. "Hey, look. Everyone's coming."

He turned and saw headlights approaching, *fast*. Almost simultaneously came the sound of gears whining and tires howling on the pavement.

Spud and Panzarella were coming to the end of the Old Mill Road.

Both trucks were moving at more than fifty-miles-per-hour, when they saw water reflecting back where the road should have been, giving them only seconds to react. In desperation, Panzarella jammed the brake down with both feet. Herman used both the brakes and the gears. When Spud saw Panzarella wheels starting to smoke, he knew they weren't going to make it. He tightened his seat belt and rolled down his window. He took one last look to the right and saw Panzarella in the dash lights, both hands on the wheel, and terror on his face.

The trucks went into the water at forty-miles-per-hour. Herman's truck hit the water slightly nose up, blowing out the right-hand window. Panzarella's, with a conventional cab, went in nose down, ripping off the hood on impact and knocking him out.

With the cab filling with water, Spud released his seat belt and went out the missing window, coming to the surface immediately. Half of the garbage truck was already under water. In the darkness, Herman could just make out the milk truck with the cab just under the surface, but there was no sign of Panzarella. He swam over to the truck, ducked down, and looked in the window. He could see him still in the seat, clutching the wheel.

It took everything Spud had to get down to the door handle and force open the door, fortunately, the cab was completely flooded. He came to the surface, took another breath and went back, this time returning with Panzarella. Almost on cue, he started to choke and cough as soon as he reached the open air.

At the edge of the road, all they could hear was a hissing sound of air venting from the trucks as they slowly sank.

"Buzz, we could have stopped this."

He nodded grimly and started to pull off his shirt. "I'm still a good swimmer.

Someone yelled. "Hey, I think someone's out there with a boat!"

From a distance, they could hear the sound of an outboard and voices in the darkness. Someone waved a flashlight. "Over here."

In a couple of minutes, the boat appeared and Panzarella yelled that they were all right. When the boat approached the shore, someone tossed out a rope so it could be secured. Hammer looked in the dark, wondering who was driving it. A few minutes later, everyone climbed out onto the road. Greta was carefully poking Spud to make sure nothing was broken. Panzarella suddenly grabbed Herman by the shoulder and spun him around. For a moment, it looked ugly. He slowly extended a hand. Herman took it and for a minute they stood there, silently knowing that this was a moment that only belonged to them. Panzarella turned, looked back up the road, and asked if someone could give him a ride into town.

Herman, ever the optimist, smiled. "I guess I won, didn't I?"

He turned around. Sally was standing silently behind him. "Todd and Buzz, I'd like to you to meet Sally, my crib partner."

Sally stepped out of the shadows and extended a hand. Greta croaked, "Oh, my God!"

Someone in the crowd pleaded for someone to teach him how to play cards. Todd smiled as he shook her hand and Buzz managed a pleasure to meet you. She turned to Herman. "We'll give you a lift home."

Herman asked her to give him a moment to talk to Todd and Buzz.

"Sure, I'll meet you at the car."

They watched as Sally walked to the car. Todd shook his head as if to clear it."She can't be real?"

Herman laughed. "Believe me, she is most definitely real."

They walked to the end of the road and looked out. The trucks were gone in a hundred feet of water. Herman looked down at his feet briefly." I'm a lot of trouble, aren't I Buzz?"

Buzz put a hand on Herman's shoulder. "You both are. We'd better go. We can start dealing with this in the morning."

Greta was in the Ocean Grove parking lot the next morning waiting for Herman and Todd. They had called to say that they were on their back from their meeting with Oates. It had been a very long morning. Greta told them that Buzz had just returned from Milkmeister Dairies. He'd managed to prevent the company from charging Panzarella with theft, but he lost his job. However, the owner agreed to give him a good reference and Buzz arranged to replace the truck that was destroyed. The hearse pulled up with Todd driving and Herman looking pretty worn out.

Oates's office had been very crowded. In attendance was the district supervisor, the heavy maintenance supervisor, the security supervisor, a representative from the union, the police, Herman's sister, Supervisor Oates, and of course, his now totally trashed carpet. They all took turns taking out their wrath on Herman, except the carpet which just got dirtier.

When everyone had their turn, Oates started by stating that he was truly confused, not knowing whether to be insane with anger or drunk with joy. He was finally going to be rid of Spud, *not his exact words*. Finally, totally, the evil troll was going to be hauled off to jail. He worked himself into such a frenzy, that in front of the terrified group, he climbed up on his desk and screamed, slap the cuffs on the Spudmeister and haul his rotten French fried ass off to jail!"

Oates phone rang and he sat down cross legged on the desk to answer it, yelling Cheerio into the receiver. His happy face slowly began to vanish following a series of Yes, Sir' sand No, Sir's. He handed the phone to the police officer, who listened for a few minutes, and then handed the phone back to Oates. Oates bid everyone good-day, and left the office, slamming the door three times to make sure it was shut.

In the end, Herman lost his job driving a garbage truck, would never be allowed to operate a government vehicle again, and was ordered to pay for the repairs to the truck. However, the good news was that he would still have job. He was going to be reassigned to a supply depot as a stock clerk.

Herman took a deep breath before speaking. "It's going to take a long time to pay for the damage to my truck. I'd give anything to take it back."

Buzz put a hand on his shoulder. "We can't change the past but we can pay for it. We've arranged to replace the truck."

Greta looked at the both of them like they were nuts. "One of those things is worth a couple hundred thousand bucks. You got that kind of cash?"

Todd smiled at Greta and wiggled his eyebrows. "We've managed to save a few bucks."

Buzz reached out and shook Herman's hand. Todd followed suit and they both gave Greta a hug.

Spud was extremely grateful. "You guys have been great. I really appreciate everything you've done. I have learned a few things, as well."

"What did you learn, Spud?" Greta wanted to know.

"It can get pretty windy out there on the edge."

"Unfortunately, we didn't do a very good job, Herman. If we had, things might have worked out better for you."

Herman understood, waved goodbye, and returned to the hearse.

As they watched him pull out of the parking lot, Buzz added. "But I think we're starting to get the hang of it, again."

Before they said goodbye, Todd asked Greta to look after Herman for them. She promised she would.

It was 1:30 in the afternoon when Todd and Buzz pulled out of the parking lot of the Ocean Grove Motel. It was as deserted as it was the two very long days ago when they arrived. They turned west on Delmar Boulevard. In a few short minutes, they'd disappeared into traffic.

CHAPTER 5
PECHERSNOOT

"You know things are not going well when you're at the nursing station, at that nice quiet place you put Aunt Zorma, after she showed

up at the church bake sale claiming she was a nudist, and you discover that all of her nice new friends are on the wrong side of the barn.

— anonymous

What was the distance from Frenchman's Knob to Jetson, Kentucky? Close to a hundred miles, if you are coming from Lebanon. Nice drive, plenty of forest and old bridges, that's the great thing about Kentucky. It's a really pretty state. People are nice, too.

Todd and Buzz had been on the road almost a week, good days getting reacquainted. They were adjusting to the rhythm of the road, rediscovering the car's idiosyncrasies, and most importantly, relearning the routine of the drive. Deciding who drove had, once again, become subtle and unspoken. That's the way it is when you are out there. You just know. That's the way it was 62. They just knew.

That's how it was on a nearly perfect day in a nearly perfect state, when they found themselves on the road between Frenchman's Knob and Jetson, Kentucky, about a hundred miles, if they were coming from Lebanon. It was a coin toss, call it a day in Cub Run, or keep going to Jetson.

Cub Run had been in the rear-view mirror for about thirty minutes, when they agreed to stop for dinner and gas in the next town. If it looked half decent, they'd stay. The road sign declared Jetson 80 miles, Hybach 45 miles. The sign also said

Pechersnoot 28 miles, or at least it used to, until someone painted over it. A group of local malcontents with a unique command of the English language kept painting out one of the *O's,* and messing with the H which resulted resulting in a town called Peckersnot.   Every couple of days, someone from the town, at considerable expense, would correct the name and within a day, someone else, at considerably less expense, would show up and screw with it again.   Eventually, the citizens of Peckersnot gave up and got rid of the name altogether, which was unfortunate for everyone concerned. This was particularly true for the people who repaired the sign, as they were making a killing in overtime hours. Unfortunately, this was also true for the people who defaced the signs, as now they had a lot of free time to spend with their wives. In any case, if you still wanted to get to Jetson, you still had to go through Peckersnot. Todd looked over his shoulder as they passed the sign. I wonder what the 28 means?"

Larry Wallace stood on the street in front of Bert's Grill, which he owned, and he knew exactly what the 28 on the sign meant. He looked up the road. He wouldn't see the red and white sports car for another fifteen minutes. What he could see was across the street, and Bert Wallace, the owner of Larry's Bar. He waved at Bert who waved back and went inside. They had known each other since grade four, and they went to high school together. They even served two tours in Vietnam, eventually ending up back in Peckersnot, staring at each other from opposite sides of the street.

Larry went back inside the restaurant. From the kitchen, he did not see the red and white sports car as it passed. He was busy transferring thirty gallons of spoiled baked beans into a canvas sack. As he worked, he thought about how much he really hated Bert Wallace and how much he was going to enjoy getting rid of those beans.

Buzz looked down at the gas gauge. "We'd better fill up."

Todd pointed to the left. "Two blocks up from the look of it."

It was one of those old gas stations, the stations with the bell hose in the driveway which rang when someone drove over it. The bell clanked indifferently under the front wheels, not bothering to ring at all with the rear wheels. From the passenger seat, Todd looked at the station.

"Are we seeing full serve or self?"

Buzz followed his gaze. "I'm thinking no serve."

They got out of the car and inspected the pumps. Todd couldn't see anyone moving inside. "It doesn't look like the power is on."

"Hi there!" A woman in her late fifties appeared at the door. She glanced up at the sky, expecting to see clouds, as she stepped out into the driveway. An oily rag was clutched in her hands.

"You fellas will be looking to stay for a couple of days."

Buzz extended a hand. She finished cleaning off the grease and returned the handshake." No, we're just getting some gas and passing through."

She smiled knowingly. "No, I think you two will be making yourselves comfortable for a couple of days. "

Walking around the Corvette, she ran a hand across a fender and nodded with approval. "I can't sell you any gas until Tuesday, and my guess is you got less than a quarter of a tank on the gauge. That won't be enough to get you to anywhere from here."

Todd joined them in the driveway. "You can't sell gas until Tuesday?"

She nodded. "Three days a week."

"What kind of a deal is that?"

She rubbed her nose with the rag. "By law says so."

They responded. "A gas by law?"

"Yep, council passed it about a year ago now. Says each gas station in town can only sell three days a week. That way everyone gets a chance to make a little money."

"Okay, we'll just go to the other station. No law against that, is there?"

"Nope, no law at all."

"Well, I guess we'll be getting gas at the other location."

"Can't."

Todd rubbed his eyes in frustration. "Can't?"

"Other station burned down."

Buzz looked up the road and then at Buzz. "There should be a gas station between here and Jetson."

"Nope, burned down."

"Don't you find that a little odd? They found this an incredible coincidence.

"You know, now that you mention it, seems a little queer that they both went up in flames within a month. Said it was smoking in bed that caused the fires, except, old Smitty didn't smoke. He liked to fool around with dynamite a bit, but didn't care much for tobacco. Old man Lammerstein enjoyed a toke in the evenings, but then he'd go and bother the critters in the bush behind his place. Can't see how that would cause a fire. But it has been good for business now that people are staying longer. Sell a lot more gasoline, too, especially on Tuesday. that's the next day. Best you come early to avoid the line up."

She looked at them. "There's a motel a mile past the road sign on the left side of the road. You can get eats and a drink back in town. Look for Larry's Bar on the left and Bert's Grill on the right. You guys like beans?"

As Buzz and Todd pulled out of the gas station, the woman yelled "Welcome to Peckersnot! "

Driving back into town, Todd looked at the gas gauge. She had it exactly right. "What was the name of that place?"

The woman at the gas station had that exactly right too. Bert's Grill was on the right across the street from Larry's Bar. The inside of Bert's Grill did not look half bad. It was clean, beige, and with the prerequisite red vinyl seats. The decor looked like it started out in the fifties, got as far as the seventies, got stuck, made one shot at the eighties, and finally gave up altogether. A voice from the kitchen said it would be out in a minute.

Buzz perused a menu while he tapped his fingers on the table. He looked out the window. Across the street, a man in an apron, presumably the proprietor was tying what looked like tape between two poles in front of the door.

The voice from the kitchen had appeared from the kitchen. "What would you like, fellas?"

Buzz looked up from the menu. "You know, that ham and cheese sounds good, and I'll have a coffee with that."

Todd took the menu and glanced at it. "That sounds good. I'll have the same."

"You like beans?" The voice wanted to know.

Todd looked at the menu again. Beans weren't listed. "Sure, I like beans fine, but if it's all the same, I'll go with the sandwich and coffee."

"Sure you wouldn't like beans? We just made a fresh batch, homemade."

"No, I'm pretty sure we'll go with the sandwiches."

The voice, cook or waiter, depending on where he happened to be in the building, was apologetic. "Sorry, all we got is beans. Fresh, though."

They both looked up in amazement. "That's it, just beans!"

He shook his head. "Oh, we got all sorts of stuff, but we can only sell beans three days a week."

Buzz rubbed the back of his neck. Let me get this straight. "You have to serve beans three days a week even though you have a full menu?"

"Yep, that's about right."

"Why? That doesn't make any sense!"

"It's the By law."

"You mean like the one that says you can only sell fuel three days a week?"

The cook brightened up. "No, no! That's a different one. You can only sell fuel three days a week. This one says you can only sell beans three days a week."

He looked speculatively at them, hoping to see understanding. See the difference?"

Todd said, thoughtfully, "This is so that the other restaurant in town can take turns selling food?"

"No, that only applies to fuel. There's only one restaurant in town. The council just likes beans, that and the only other place burned down."

Buzz wanted to know if the cook-waiter was related to the woman who worked at the gas station.

"Gus? No, we're not related been stuffing her regular for the last fifteen years, though. She's got an old DeSoto out back we use; had to break the rear window so she could get her legs out. Best part is the wife hasn't said a word about it."

"How's that, she must know by now?

"Oh sure she knows, but she won't make a fuss because she knows I know she's doing Gus's other half!"

"Well, that should make the guy feel a little better about you doing his wife."

"No, the husband has been dead for years. She's been porking Gus's mother. You fellas want your coffee now or with your beans?" He looked up at the sound of someone walking on the roof.

Above them, the footsteps were becoming more intense along with something heavy being dragged. Ten minutes later, the waiter returned with their orders. As he was about to set the orders down on the table, a voice could be heard through several inches of ceiling, roofing tar, wood, and tin, the type of voice God would make, if he had been drinking and swearing.

"I hate your guts, always have, you no-good-for-nothing, dirt bag full of scratchy ass-holes, and I have got just the thing for someone like you. A forty pound sack of crap! Are you ready dirt bag? Here it comes!"

The three of them continued to stare at the ceiling, as the lights moved menacingly as the voice continued dragging the sack across the roof. "Why don't you fellas come out to the kitchen? It's cooler there and safer."

Looking out the window, they could see the front door of the bar across the street and the owner, Bert who suddenly went inside and was attempting to secure the door. Buzz looked at his watch, thinking Bert was closing a little early.

Todd looked at his beans, and then at the kitchen door. "You may be right."

Halfway to the kitchen, the footsteps on the roof stopped. The waiter's pace quickened and by the time he reached the door, it was close to a run. Something on the roof made a large thump, followed by a *thwang*. The ceiling lights reacted by swinging violently.

Two seconds later, the front door of *Larry's Bar* imploded, when it was struck by a forty-pound sack of rancid baked beans, which had been cooking all morning in the hot sun. It was a door Bert Wallace had spent four months making, a door that Bert had hand-made out of real oak with a stained glass window of the Virgin Mary standing in a field of corn. It had been personally blessed by the Pope, complete with documentation. It imploded when it was struck by a forty-pound sack of rancid baked beans which had been cooking all morning in the hot sun.

Bert watched through the peephole in the door, as the bean bomb sailed across the street. "No doubt about it, this was going to be a strike, right down the middle of the alley." He said a quick prayer, but he had a feeling God was out of town on a business trip. At the last second, he threw himself under a table. The door exploded inward in a shower of splinters. The sack of beans, behaving like a mushy cluster bomb, exploded, covering every square inch of the room. It also deposited a considerable amount on the furniture and lighting, and then it made a huge pile against the back wall.

Bertram K. Wallace staggered out from what was left of the table he'd been hiding under. A piece of stained glass with the Virgin Mary's left arm pit was embedded in the table top. The damage was impressive. It was like being inside a giant fart.

Across the street on the roof of *Bert's Grill* Lawrence K. Wallace, no relation, was doing the "I just bombed my neighbor with a bag of beans" happy dance. For a brief moment, he stopped and wondered what had driven him to such carnage. Was it a slight, insult, a business deal gone badly? He shrugged and resumed the dance because he couldn't remember. And like a man using an illegal narcotic for recreational purposes, he didn't care. Down on the street, the object of his affection appeared at the remnants of the front door of Larry's Bar, bruised, battered, and with a disgusting smell, was Bert Wallace. He raised an arm and pointed at the evil specter on the roof of Bert's Grill. An image, embellished by the sun directly behind it. grade school, high school, college,... Nam. "Well, we are there, bucko! This will not stand!"

The evil specter suddenly stopped basking in glory. "This is not good!"

The waiter, Doug to his friends, appeared at the front door of Bert's Grill and yelled across the street at Bert, who was pulling on the massive rubber band strung between two poles. "Bert! For Christ's sake, don't do this!

"Don't care!"

"What is this going to prove? Doug yelled back.

"Don't care!"

"That's right, Doug, you tell him."

He looked up at the owner of *Bert's Grill* peering over the roof like a demented vulture. "Larry, will you shut the hell up!"

Across the street, Bert Wallace had appeared, dragging a sack of his own.

Doug felt a tap on his shoulder. His customers had finished their beans. He asked them to wait until he could write a bill. "C'mon, can we just calm down here? Maybe we can just talk this over."

Bert was busy hooking up his sack to the rubber band. "He messed with the Virgin Mary. He has to say he's sorry!"

Doug looked up at Larry, who was still perched on the edge of the roof. "All you have to do is apologize. Let's end this. We're not enemies here, you know that. We know who the bad guys are around here. Larry, are you listening to me?"

Larry K Wallace, the owner of Bert's Grill, stood up, looked at the sky and then down Main Street. From where he stood, he had command of an entire town that was holding its breath, waiting for him to make the big decision, the momentous one that counted. It was the moment that would be remembered for years, the one that would bring everyone together to vanquish a common enemy. All he had to do was to say I am sorry for besmirching the Virgin Mary;..."She had it coming!"

Doug turned to Todd and Buzz. "The meal is on the house. Enjoy your stay in Peckersnot."

Todd grabbed Buzz and yanked him into the street and out of the line of fire. "We don't need to be here. Let's find the hotel."

Buzz didn't move. "This is like watching a train wreck. You can't take your eyes off it."

Bert Wallace grabbed the rubber band and dragged it through what was left of the front door. The poles quivered as the tension increased. Grunting and cursing could be heard in the darkness of the bar.

Todd walked over to the now desperate waiter. "Where's the hotel?"

The waiter turned with a "the world is going to end look", and asked, "What?"

"Hotel, where's the hotel?"

"You two are actually going to stay here?"

"We haven't got any choice. There is no gas until Tuesday. Besides, you did say Welcome to Peckersnot."

"Look, I was just kidding. Okay, go west past the gas station about a half mile on the left. It's called the Happy Tumbleweed. I'll stop by this evening with a couple of Jerry cans of gas that I keep around for emergencies. That should get your on your way."

Outside Larry's Bar, it was possible to hear the sound of a heavy sack being dragged across broken furniture, a sack, not unlike the one that had obliterated the inside of Bert's beloved bar. Except for the contents, it would be difficult to tell them apart.

The sack that came *in* was forty pounds of badly overcooked baked beans, well past their due date. The sack going *out* was forty pounds of badly baked vanilla custard soaked in cheap rum that had gone bad well before its due date. It was forty pounds of Bert Wallace's one and only attempt at cooking. It was a desert designed to class up the place, consisting of off-the-shelf pudding mix, condensed goat's milk, vanilla extract, and two-dollar rum. He covered it with off-the-shelf dollar brandy. Light it and you got *Bert's Flambé.* The concoction torched four ties and seven table clothes before anyone could get close enough to eat it.

Bert heaved the sack onto the table and dragged it over to the slingshot, which was anchored to a post. It took a couple of minutes to load it into the slingshot and to perform a little tweaking, to ensure that it would go through the door and hit its intended target. Out on street, Bert could hear voices. He started for the door, and then decided that it might be safer standing at the window. It took a while to open the window, because it was welded shut with a hardened seam of baked beans. Across the street, he could see his counterpart, peering through his own window. "Can you hear me, dicknose?"

Larry cackled. "Yeah, I can hear you and smell you, too, Fart face!"

"Forty years I have to look at your crummy face. Forty years of you eating my lunch, stealing my parking spot, and sleeping with my wife!

"You don't have a wife. You've never been married."

"Well, you would have slept with her if I had a wife. So, you slept with my girlfriend!"

"Myrtle was not your girlfriend and everyone slept with her, including your mother."

"Who told you an awful thing like that? Bert yelled through the window.

"Your mother!" Larry cackled.

"My mother was a saint. She wouldn't have done a thing like that for all the money on earth!"

"You're right! She only paid me a hundred bucks and I didn't have to make her breakfast in the morning."

Bert had begun to look and sound like one of those raving imprisoned souls you see in the windows of insane asylums. "No more Mr. Mister Nice Guy!"

Larry was now looking at an empty window. "Maybe I shouldn't have said that stuff about his mother?"

Thirty seconds later, a flaming sack of rancid custard retraced the path of Larry's bean bag. The concussion was tremendous, blowing the kitchen door off the back of the building. The freezer door and most of its contents were embedded in the side of Betty Davenport's Oldsmobile. Every inch of the inside of *Bert's Grill*, including Larry, was covered with rancid and rapidly hardening, caramelized vanilla custard.

"Buzz, you feel like dessert?"

Buzz shook his head as they turned to walk back to the car. "Pass. I'm trying to watch my waistline."

Todd looked down at his belt. "Yeah, so am I."

On the windshield was a bright yellow ticket. Buzz pulled it off the windshield, read it, and handed it to Todd.

"It's a ticket for overtime parking, $200?" He looked around but there wasn't a single sign anywhere. He handed it back to Buzz.

Buzz turned it over and read the payment instructions. All it said was "Welcome to Pechersnoot."

"The ticket, or the hotel first?"

Todd walked around the car and stared up the street. The road seemed to go forever, and then, it disappeared in the afternoon sun. He could barely see it but there was a single dark cloud right at the horizon.   "Let the coin decide."

Buzz got the coin out of the car gave it a toss over the hood. It shone like a star in the sunlight. It bounced twice on the hood, threatening to fall to the left and then to the right, before stopping in the middle of the hood.

Todd bent over and looked at the coin sitting on it's its edge. "How does it do that?"

The coin had spoken. Todd carefully picked it up leaned over and handed it to Buzz, who put it back in the car.

"I'm guessing they pay tickets at City Hall."

Buzz looked up at the sky. "Nice day for a walk."

Pechersnoot City Hall was like the city halls of every town in the country. It was the heart and soul of the town. Humming with purpose, decisions large and small directed to the benefit of the lives its citizens, twenty-four-hours per day, seven days a week, fifty-two weeks a year, it was constantly vigilant, standing guard, an example of democracy in action.

As they walked up the steps to the front door, two pairs of eyes watched them through the slats in a window blind.

"What was that in the window?"

"I think they were gophers."

"Are you sure? I don't remember them being that big," Buzz mused.

"Yeah, you're probably right. I've never seen them that large, either. Come to think of it, I didn't think they could smile like that, either."

The place inside was a typical town hall. As Buzz looked around for directions, Todd wandered across the hall to look at a wall plaque, which stated, "The Hammerflap Award for outstanding community achievement."

Although the recipient had experienced a great deal of personal distress, it was unclear as to what he'd done to be so honored. At the bottom of the plaque was a photo of a large, unkempt man in his forties. His pant legs were missing below the knees, and the left sleeve of his shit was also gone. He was holding what appeared to be a badly damaged microwave. The recipient was Bert Johnson.

Buzz looked up the stairwell to the second floor. "It looks like we pay the ticket on the second floor."

"Are you sure you want to go up there? Who the hell knows what's waiting at the top of the stairs?"

Buzz chuckled and pointed to the sign directing them to the second floor. "Some guy with a sharp crayon."

Two doors on the left, the Parking Ticket Office was a large room with a heavy oak door. The door knob was on the opposite side because the door had been installed upside down. It was also installed backwards, causing it to open into the hallway. The two of them stood there looking at the door that was now jammed against the opposite wall.

Todd stuck his hands in his pockets. "You know, we could just sleep in the car until Tuesday."

Buzz pushed the door away from the wall and stepped around it. "No, we'll just end up getting a ticket for sleeping in a loading zone."

Todd followed him and pulled the door shut behind him. The doorknob came off in his hand.   They were definitely in a court room. On the wall, a clock ticked quietly. The benches were polished and clean. There were two tables for the prosecution and the defense, a small chair and table for the court reporter, and of course, the judge's bench and the witness stand. Everything seemed to be in order. They were definitely in the right place. The only thing that seemed to be out of place was a large red button under a photo of Grover Cleveland. The button said "Push button if you wish to plead guilty." Next to it was a small door that said "Pay fine here."

"What do you think?"

Buzz shrugged, "Beats taking a number."

He reached out and pushed the button as Todd looked around the room. "I didn't hear anything and it doesn't sound like anyone's coming."

Todd looked at his watch. It's nearly five. "Maybe everyone's gone home or we're not hearing anything because the alarm is someplace in the building."

Buzz acknowledged Todd's reasoning. "You're probably right, although if there was someone in the building, it would be locked. Let's give it one more shot." He held the button for a full minute.

"Hey! What are you trying to do to my ears, you stupid dumb ass."

Todd grinned and pointed at the portrait of Cleveland. The speaker was behind the picture. "Yep, there's someone here alright, but I always thought his voice was taller."

Grover told them to pay the fine by depositing the money in the payment box in the wall next to the button. Buzz pulled open the door and peered in. There was a trapdoor in the bottom allowing the money to fall through to who knew where. "You gonna pay the fine? I ain't got all day!"

Todd stepped up to the picture and spoke really quietly. "Can you hear me?"

"Sure, I can hear you."

He got as close to the speaker as possible and screamed, "I'm not paying!"

Cleveland clearly preferred a quiet court. "You freaking chicken whacker. What's the matter with you? You are guilty as hell! You admitted it in front of the entire court."

They turned around to make sure the court was still empty. It was. "What are you talking about? The place is empty. You can't plead guilty to an empty room."

"Can so, if you push the button, which is what you did, and now you got to pay."

Buzz got a real wicked look in his face. "So, if you push the button, you're automatically guilty. Have I got that right?"

"That's right, feller!"

"You mean like this!" Todd yelled and jammed the button in and held it down. For dramatic effect, he checked his watch to make sure it was a full minute.

A string of profanities erupted from Grover Cleveland's picture as he released the button. "You filthy, rotten dirt-bag, my ears are ringing so badly, I can't hear my own farts! Damn, I shouldn't have said that. You're going to pay big time for that. The fine is doubled because you assaulted a judge."

"Got any witnesses?"

"I don't need any witnesses, I'm a judge. I could throw your sorry asses in jail, but I'd rather clean out your cash instead. Shit, I shouldn't have said that either!"

"We're not paying. We're going to appeal."

Todd tapped Buzz on the shoulder. "Who exactly are we going to appeal to?"

President Cleveland piped up with an answer. "You can appeal to the Mayor. He's the only one besides the judge who can overturn a conviction."

"Where can we find the Mayor?"

"He's on the third floor, the first door on the right. Crap, I got to stop saying that stuff."

The journey to the third floor was pretty much the same as the trip to the second. The door to the Mayor's office, however, had been installed correctly and opened inward, but only for about two feet, just enough for someone to barely squeeze between the wall and the door. The doorstop had been installed incorrectly.

Todd stopped at small fridge with a sign over it which humbly stated, for your convenience. Inside were two opened large bottles of Shasta orange soda and Styrofoam cups. The secretary's desk was unoccupied and the lights in the Mayor's office were off.

On the opposite wall was a button and box identical to those in the court downstairs, complete with the portrait of a greasy looking man in a suit.

"I know it sounds crazy but I've actually seen this guy somewhere."

Buzz nodded, looking at the plaque on the frame. "To the boys from Otto Meyer, never leave a sucker with a buck in his pocket."

Todd opened the box and looked inside. It didn't take a rocket scientist to realize it was connected to the one downstairs. This button said appeals to the Mayor. He pushed in the button and held it down for a good thirty seconds.

Otto responded with a string of profanity. "You know, this guy's language is even worse than the president and wait a minute! This guy sounds just like Grover Cleveland. You're the same guy we were talking to in the court!"

The voice suddenly doubled in a really lousy attempt to disguise itself. "No, it's not. That was the judge. I'm the Mayor."

"If you're the Mayor, why aren't you up here?"

"Because I'm down here, that's why. State your case."

"We're not paying the fine because there were no posted signs saying no parking, and we didn't get a fair hearing in court."

"You pushed the button, didn't you?"

"Yes we did, and now we're appealing because there weren't any signs posted."

"Ignorance is no excuse for breaking the law, feller. Guilty as *Hell*,...charged. Pay the fine."

Todd appeared with the two bottles of Shasta. He opened one, dropped in an Alka Seltzer tablet, and recapped it. The bottle bulged ominously as the pressure built up. Just for fun, he gave the bottle a good shake. He handed it to Buzz, who knew a bomb when he saw one, and repeated the process with the second bottle. "Where did you get the Seltzer tablets, anyway?"

"They were in the First Aid cupboard."

Buzz looked at him in disbelief." Who'd put Alka Seltzer in a first aid box?"

"Ever seen a sack of beans used as artillery before?" Buzz had to admit that he had a point and handed back the other bottle.

Todd was now holding the explosive equivalent of a small land mine. He jammed both bottles into the box so that they would fall into the tube, one at a time.

"I'll need a piece of cardboard."

"What the hell for?"

Todd smiled. "All will be revealed, Grasshopper."

He opened the fine box as Buzz went looking for the cardboard. The bottles had expanded again and were well past a small land mine. Todd slowly closed the door and backed away without taking his eyes off the box. Buzz returned with the cardboard and handed it to Todd.

Todd carefully folded it to what he thought were the right dimensions. "Let's see, three floors to the basement. If they don't hit anything, it should take ten seconds to get to the basement.

"Okay, push the button and hold it down."

Buzz held the button down and Todd jammed the cardboard in so that it would not release. Somewhere, an alarm was rubbing someone the wrong way.

"Enough with the button already, what the hell are you two doing up there?"

"Hey, Otto, we're pleading guilty. Wanna hear it again?"

They timed it exactly right. The explosion blew the basement windows out of the courthouse and halfway across the lawn.

As they walked out of the courthouse, Buzz wanted to know where Todd had learned to do that.

"Fraternity, Cal Tech"

"What the hell kind of a fraternity teaches you how to blow up a courthouse?"

"Lambda-Chi, watch where you step, there's glass everywhere."

The Happy Tumbleweed Motel was right where Doug the waiter said it was.

Unfortunately, the sign was not where he said it was which was why they had such a hard time finding it. The sign had been knocked down and dragged by a car several hundred yards before being dumped in the ditch.

Buzz followed line the tires made in the dirt shoulder leading to the sign. "Looks kind of deliberate, doesn't it?

It didn't help that the Happy Tumbleweed looked less like a motel and more like a bunch of RV's, campers, and construction trailers lying in an open field. In fact, up close or even at a distance, say from across the road, it looked a lot like Gary Lamplighters RV Salvage Yard. Grizelda Lamplighter, Griz to her friends, who, at 280 pounds, was half of her brother's size, but twice as smart, took over the business after he went upstate for an extended vacation in a straight jacket because he wouldn't leave squirrels alone. He now spends most of his time making wallets out of fur and feeding the squirrels, as he as long as he did not stick them down his pants, which got him into trouble in the first place.

The first thing Griz did when her brother was safely locked and the state wasn't in any danger of running out of squirrels, was to hook up power and water to the first ten habitable trailers and RV's. The second thing she did was to knock down Gary's sign, put up her own, and the Happy Tumbleweed Motel was born. She still sent a five-pound bag of nuts to Gary up at the farm. His back teeth had to be bridged after he broke them eating the nuts that were supposed to be for the squirrels.

Parked on the shoulder of the road, they were having trouble making a connection between the sign and what they were seeing.

Todd got out of the car and walked around to the driver's door. "This can't be the right place, can it?"

"How long have we been here, Todd?"

Todd replied without taking his eyes off the entrance to the motel. "A food fight covering a half a city block, a $200 parking ticket, a town that only sells gas on Tuesdays and Thursdays, and beans three days a week. Add a Mayor and Judge in a Jack-in-a- Box. Total time: Five hours and twenty-seven minutes."

Buzz laughed. "You forgot about the part where you blew up the City Hall."

"That doesn't count."

"How do you figure that?"

Todd imitated a righteous voice. "That, sir, was a classic case of justifiable civil disobedience!"

Buzz pointed across the road. "And that is the Happy Tumbleweed Motel."

"I guess it's time to start paying for our sins."

The place didn't look any better close up. When you are talking about the Happy Tumbleweed, distance is your friend.

"Howdy!"

Griz Lamplighter appeared from behind one of the many piles of broken machinery that littered the driveway. "You boys staying till Tuesday, is that right?"

They got out of the car slowly and carefully. Buzz put both hands in his pockets and told Todd not to make any sudden moves.

"Dave! We got guests. C'mon out here and say hello. Try showing some class for a change. Haven't I taught you anything, you dumb ass?"

A voice could be heard from a window. "No God Damn way I'm coming out there while you're carrying Fluffy around."

"That's a load! Fluffy ain't here!"

"It just ain't happening, you fat bag of crap, no way!"

Griz shook her head. "Man ain't got no manners at all. Don't know why I married him."

She suddenly got a real evil look on her face. "Oh, right. Still not right to at least to step out and say hello, don't you think?"

They nodded silently in unison.

"Excellent! Come on in and we'll get you set up. You're really going to enjoy your stay."

The office looked just like the driveway except that it was inside as opposed to outside. They stepped aside as Griz walked to the end of the counter. She flipped up the counter end and tried to walk through. She got stuck.

"Dave! How many times I gotta tell you to fix this counter?"

His voice was now coming from even farther back in the office. "There's nothing wrong with that counter. You just can't drive a bus through a toaster hole."

Griz stopped struggling as a bright red line crawled up her face. "That's low!"

They had to admit it was but nodded silently. Fluffy could be anywhere, or anything.

She gave one final heave, popped through the opening, and handed each of them a key. Then she took down some information in the guest book."Just a formality, you understand."

"Now, Buzz. I've got that right? You take trailer #4. That's the Moose Room. Todd, you're in the Caribou Room. You can't miss either of them because they are side-by- side. But if you do get lost out there, just look for the trailers with the heads on the sides of them. Shot them myself, me and Fluffy."

The drive to the trailers was a slow, dusty five minutes on a dirt road that wound its way around broken trailers, RV's, and the occasional chunk of mining equipment. Questioning eyes watched them from the shadows under machinery and through dirty, sand blasted windows.

The Moose and Caribou Rooms were right where Griz said they would be. "Did she say you had the Moose Room?

Bolted, screwed, and nailed to the side of trailer #4 was the head of a moose. "What did she say? She shot the thing herself."

"What, did she use, a bazooka?"

It was an incredible display of marksmanship. The right ear and antler of what had been an impressive 12-point animal had been shot clean off. Worse, what was clearly the work of an insane taxidermist was the setting of the eyes, deliberately installed cross-eyed. The end result was

Bullwinkle the Moose, who had stepped off a curb to get on a bus, that hadn't come to a full stop.

Buzz looked at Todd. "What's so funny?"

He choked back a laugh and then totally lost it. "Okay, it's a little tragic, but c'mon, you have to admit that's pretty damned funny!"

Murdoch slowly pointed to the next trailer. "Funny? You are staying in the Caribou Room trailer."

Stiles suddenly stopped laughing. Mounted, screwed, bolted, and nailed to the side of the Caribou Room was the head of a bison, a spectacular animal, a king among its kind, a Cadillac among tarandus fennicus. It was beautifully and lovingly stuffed to preserve the essence of the animal's magnificence. It's upside down."

"You want to know something, Buzz?"

"What's that?"

"America has gotten one whole lot stranger in the thirty-some odd years we have been away."

Buzz shook his head. "I think its right where we left it."

"How do you explain that, Buzz?"

He walked up to the head and gave it a close look. It was a good job. "Thirty years ago, we wouldn't have given this a second look. It's amazing what you miss when you're young. Back in 1962, we were more concerned with where we were going than where we were. It was about putting as much wind between us and what was behind us."

In the distance, they could hear Griz looking for her guests. In her hand were three bottles. "Boys, you two are right popular! Only been here an hour and already you got visitors. Here you go, home brew on the house, real smooth. Just don't drink any of it if you're planning on operating any kind of machinery, or having a smoke. Come to think of it, I wouldn't be brushing my teeth, friction could set it off. Anyway, that feller from the restaurant is here and he wants to see you real bad."

Griz gave her back side a good scratch and leered. "Now which one of you am I going to tuck in tonight?"

"We'd better go talk to him!" Buzz quickly agreed with Todd.

As they walked back to the office, they could hear Griz screaming at Dave, who could have been in a parallel dimension for all the difference it made. "You dumb ass, you nailed the Caribou on upside down."

Doug was waiting for them out front with two Jerry cans of gas and a story to tell. "Is that Griz's hooch you got there?"

They looked down at the bottles and nodded silently.

"You mind?" Todd handed him his bottle.

"She makes the best shine in the county, best not to get any on your clothes though." He took a long stiff pull on the battle and handed it back.

Todd held the bottle up to the light and decided after looking at Doug that the stuff might actually be safe to drink. He tipped the bottle back and took a drink. With less than a mouthful down, he was pretty sure he was losing his eyesight.

"How's it taste?"

"I'm over the legal limit."

"On one mouthful, what's in this stuff, anyway?" He looked at his bottle and decided to try it. The stuff definitely went down smooth, like being run over by a Cadillac.

Doug pointed to the red containers. "Well, here's your gas, should be more than enough there to get you to Jetson. I'm thinking you'll be on your way in the morning."

Todd agreed. That's pretty much the plan."

He was having trouble organizing his thoughts and he was pretty sure that the picnic table had moved on its own. "So, what's going on with this lame ass, low down, good for nothing, dumb fart, waste lagoon, dump of a town anyway?"

Buzz stopped Todd in the middle of the next sentence and looked at him in confusion. What's wrong with you, anyway?"

"You know, I'm not sure where that came from."

Doug had the answer. "It's Griz's rocket fuel, the final answer in behavior modification. I got bent on the stuff a couple of summers back and went after her Doberman. Damn dog still won't let me get near it."

Okay, let's go sit down at the picnic table because it's a nice evening and standing up is getting seriously difficult." Everyone sat down except Todd, who was staring suspiciously at the table.

"Something wrong, Todd?"

" Okay, let's bring you up to speed on the Pechersnoot, snot's story. Griz's Doberman made an appearance from behind the office.

"Here boy, nice doggy, got a treat for you."

The dog backed around the corner with a look that said. "Not in a month of Sunday's, you dirty old man!"

Doug gave up on enticing the dog and got down to the story. "Beckercrotch was named after, well, some guy. How am I doing so far? Okay, it doesn't much matter, dumb name, anyway. Fact is nobody in the town has a clue how the place got its name or got started. Town went through its growing stage, which lasted about a week. Then came the rail phase, which was another week. Fact is, you got to have a reason for a train to show up and the place was hard pressed to come up with one. Everyone in town pretty much adjusted to the fact that its only claim to fame was that it was half way between Cub Run and Jetson."

"For the first 175 years or so, folks were happy to pump gas and feed anyone who passed through. With just enough agriculture and a doorknob factory just outside of town, Peckersmut sailed through the 20th century without a scratch. Of course, there were scratchy patches. The widow Smith got hammered out of her skull on corn squeezings, and drove her recently deceased husband up to the cemetery with him tied to the roof of his Nodwell. It took two days for the damn thing to run out of gas. It was the longest police pursuit in the county's history. Judge Hardpecker insisted on presiding from the bench in the nude because the town refused to spring for an air conditioner in the court."

Todd wanted to know if the widow's husband ever made it to the cemetery.

"Sure, they just took a cab."

"How did they get a casket into the back of a cab?"

"Casket?"

Doug took a long drink from *Griz's* bottle of 24-carat shine. "I digress. Fact is things weren't going half bad around here until the prodigal sons came home--Bert and Larry. You met them. They own the Bar and Grill. It's bad enough with those two, they never liked each other. The real problem is Horace and that damn brother of his, Freddy.

Doug was having a trouble getting his thoughts to line up in single file. Griz's shine had that effect. Where was I going with this?"

"It was about Horace and some other guy. Buzz was a little fuzzy on that other name.

Doug suddenly found an undamaged brain cell."Oh, right the money. You see, these guys from the Federal government showed up one day with a pile of money. They wanted to see the Mayor and the Council."

"That doesn't sound like a big deal. What happened?"

"Nothing, we didn't have any, never needed one. Those fellas were really upset. They said we qualified for federal funding and that we had to have a municipal government to manage it. Of course, it didn't make a lick of difference to them that we didn't want any money or a council to manage it. They just said that they were going to be back with the money in a month and there had better be a government here to sign for it. So, we got a book out of the library on government--the French Republic. It took a while to figure it out and we had to skip the parts about royalty, kings and vengeance, which seemed to happen a lot. But, we managed to get something figured out."

"Then, what happened? Buzz wanted to know.

'That's where we ran into trouble, because you actually have to elect somebody who can do the job."

"Well so far, so good!" Buzz was enthusiastic.

"We looked for someone who had the training and skill to do it properly."

"Also good," Buzz agreed.

"Problem is that most of the citizens of Peckersnot spend most of their free time swimming in the shallow end of the gene pool."

"Understandable," Buzz commented.

"There are only two people in the town who have college training, right smart, too. So we all got together and elected them."

Todd, who was having an Eddie Gluck flashback, suddenly broke out of the cloud his brain was flying in. "So, what went wrong?"

"The two people we elected didn't cast ballots."

"That's not a problem. You don't have to vote, even if you are a candidate."

Doug shook his head slowly, because he wasn't sure if his head would come off his shoulders. "No one told them we had elected them."

"You forgot to tell them they had won!"

"No, we forgot to tell them we had an election."

Todd suggested that they should work on their communication skills. "You'd think they'd be honored to be elected. That is quite a privilege."

Doug nodded. "You'd be right. Any normal person would be pleased as punch to be elected to office."

"So, who did the people of Peckersnot elect?"

"We got Bert and Larry Wallace."

"Well, I guess normal isn't everything, Buzz observed, sort of.

Democracy is a messy business."

"That's a Bummer."

"They tried everything to get out of it. They even showed up at the council meeting in chicken suits."

"Wait a minute." Buzz wanted to know why they didn't consider Judge Hardpecker, because he must have gone to college.

Doug nodded. "Yeah, he did, back East, real good one, too. But he doesn't count because he's a nudist. Got him self disqualified by the State Bar Association because he insisted on using a gavel that wasn't approved for use in court. Women didn't mind so much, but the men folk weren't going to put up with all that bragging. Anyway, the Feds just sat there as the Wallace boys gave them a bird's eye view of how a chicken would run the county. They didn't even bat an eye, just called us amateurs. As God is my witness, they were reaching for the check book when Bert and Larry did the nasty!"

"Not in the Courthouse?"

"Verily, they did, right, in front of representatives of the government of the United States."

"That's low!"

"You bet and then torched their car in the Court House parking lot. And you can imagine, they were none too pleased, and without a car, it was going to be mighty tough getting back to, what's the name of that place that they come from?"

"Washington."

Todd, who was listening intently, head in hands, and who was having another Amanda flashback, suddenly found a brain cell that had not been run down by home brew. "So, what happened?"

"Horace and Freddy, that's what, happened."

Griz returned with another bottle of firewater and handed a bottle to Doug. "They're two of the lowest, greasiest, greediest weasels on the face of the planet. They'd sell the wheels off their grandmother's Zimmer for a buck! "

"They did?"

"I was just joking. I mean, nobody would sell someone's wheel chair while they are sitting in it, would they?"

Doug's head nodded back and forth like the hinge on a screen door. "Yep,... you bet!"

Griz topped up Buzz's glass. "I'm going to die in this RV hell. They are going to have me stuffed, and mounted upside down, right next to the moose.

Todd looked up as she refilled his glass, unconsciously thinking aloud. "How much of this stuff has she got anyway, and when was the last time I had sex? Maybe I should give Amanda a call. I wonder if she ever made bail."

Everyone had stopped talking and was staring at him. "What?"

"Who's Amanda? Sounds like my kind of people." Griz was interested.

There was awkward silence. "My gardener."

"Anyway, where was I going with this? Oh yeah, the Bender boys, been swimming in the shallow end of the gene pool, pretty much since day one. In fact, between the two of them, they couldn't outsmart a fence post, except when it comes to money. They can smell a dollar at the bottom of a septic tank. Anyway, those federal fellows hadn't been in town long enough to change their underwear when Horace and Freddy popped up like a couple of demented jack-in-the- boxes. Of course, the feds didn't exactly fall off the turnip truck and land on their heads. They could see right off that the Benders were a couple of dyed-in- the-wool bridge trolls. I mean, they weren't really going to give 28 million dollars to those two shysters."

Todd and Buzz said it was nice to see the government make a smart decision, for a change.

"Oh, they gave them the money all right."

Buzz had given up trying to identify specific colors and decided to switch to black and white while he could still experience some physical sensation. "Why?"

"Well, those government fellas needed to get back to Washington really bad, except they didn't have a car. So, the Bender boys stepped right up to the plate and sold them one, a real beauty, 61 Plymouth Valiant. Nice."

"The federal government paid someone 28 million dollars for a used car?"

"Yes sir, that and the deed for the town! Lock, stock, and barrel. Well, not exactly the town itself, just the signing authority for the civic accounts, which is pretty much the town, when you think about."

Todd wanted to know how many miles the car had on it.

"I'm thinking, 28 thousand original miles,...

Nice!"

Everybody thought that was as close to winning the lottery as you could get. "Nobody had to get elected to anything and the place pretty much ran itself anyway, or at least, Perky McClusky the county clerk did, and Horace and Freddy were just too stupid to do any real harm. Problem was, no one bothered to consider that the Benders could figure out that they could actually make money out of the deal. At first, it was small stuff, like parking tickets and fines for vagrancy, you know, tiny stuff. Then it started to really get out of hand."

:"You mean like only selling gas three days a week."

Doug brightened up. "Yeah you bet! The plan was to build their own station and sell gas the rest of the week at seriously marked up prices. Then they discovered that it was just easier to keep people in town, overcharge them for everything that wasn't nailed down, and then hit them with parking tickets. They even tried to get Griz to go along with it. Even threatened to set up a hotel and put her out of business, but she disabused them of that idea right quick."

Everyone turned to look at her in silence. "I had the boys over for a sleepover."

"They had better luck with Bert and Larry Wallace. Of course, they didn't like each other much to start with, but by the time the Benders were done, they were at it big time."

You mean the story about his mother sleeping with his girlfriend."

Doug nodded. "Now, that part is all true. Everyone slept with her. No, wait. Bert was the only one who didn't do her."

"So, Bert was angry because he was the only one who didn't get to climb Mount Myrtle?"

Doug took a couple of seconds trying to get both eyes open at the same time. "Nope, Bert didn't give a rat's ass and now that I think about it, Larry wasn't exactly wrapped around the axle, either. What got them going was the sign."

"What sign?"

"The sign just outside of town, it offered a free drink and a meal to anyone who got the guy who did Bert's mother to show them the pictures,...
just ask for Larry."

"Who the hell would put up a sign like that?"

"Horace and Freddy Bender, that's who!"

"Nice job, too, only charged Larry three grand for it. I digress. Oh, yeah. So, they really got into it after that and the Benders just sat back and raked in the dough. Every time Larry and Bert took a shot at each other, Freddy or Horace would up their taxes or fine them for littering. As long as those two kept it up, they would just keep raking in the dough!"

As the evening wore on and night settled in, Griz got the idea to go duck hunting for Sunday dinner. She made it clear it was to be a black tie affair, nothing else--just black ties.

Armed with a flashlight with its batteries on their last legs and a fresh jug, the group and Fluffy marched to the back of the junkyard and set up shop. Partly because it was a pitch black moonless night, Griz being blind drunk, and the fact that no self-respecting duck had set foot in the place in twenty-three years, the odds of a duck dinner that wasn't store bought were slim to none. With everyone cheering her on, Griz made short work of Homer

Haverstock's windmill, which made a reasonably good imitation of a flock of ducks. Suddenly, someone who was hammered out of their tree in the dark came to a conclusion.

"You know something Todd; I think we should hang around for a couple of days."

"Sounds like a plan, Stanley. Besides, it's going to take that long before we can legally drive anyway. Hell, it's going to take at least a day before I'm sober enough to operate a can opener."

Around three in the morning, Griz had succeeded in shooting all the vanes off Homer's windmill and then moved on to gophers. Todd and Buzz decided that it was a good time to move on as well. The last thing they saw was Doug holding the flashlight as Griz fended off an enraged ten-pound rodent with the butt end of Fluffy, as it chased her around a darkened field filled with scrap metal.

As they approached their trailers, Buzz stopped and looked hard at the moose on the side of his trailer. Griz's shine, combined with the dark, made it hard to focus. Tomorrow was going to be a long day.

Dawn rose over the Happy Tumbleweed Trailer Park right on schedule, but it made it clear, that it wasn't happy about it. The sky clouded over almost immediately. Good thing, too. Anyone who had spent a night in the clutches of Griz Lamplighter and her home brew was going to wake up in the morning feeling like they had been mugged by a bunch of criminally insane Girl Guides packing Brownie cameras.

It was close to 11:30 am. by the time Buzz and Todd were getting into the car. "Where did you put the gas that Doug gave us?"

"'s behind your trailer next to Griz's booze."

"How are you going to tell the difference?"

"She keeps the booze in the gas cans."

The plan was to drive over to Larry's place for breakfast. Buzz and Todd looked like crap, to put it mildly. Buzz, who wasn't driving, was sitting so low in his seat; he had to look up see out the window. "What time is it?"

"Monday"

"Are you sure you can drive?"

Todd shook his head. "I'm not sure I am ever going to be sober again."

Doug was coming out of the kitchen as they walked in.

"How did you get home? The last time we saw you, you had a dog bone in your mouth heading for Griz's trailer screaming here, "kitty, kitty!"

"I haven't got a clue. By the way, I'm glad you guys are here. I wasn't sure if I worked here or across the street, and I can't seem to remember my name."

The name tag on the shirt he was wearing said, "I am happy to serve you. My name is Ethel."

Buzz pointed at his shirt. "The name tag says Ethel, Doug."

He looked down at the shirt tag. "It's a bit wordy. By the way, what day is it?"

Todd told him it was March.

Buzz ordered the breakfast special with no beans. Todd went with coffee and toast, and no beans.

Ethel told them they did not have any. "There'd been another shootout yesterday and the entire week's worth of beans was over at Larry's Bar.

Breakfast was surprisingly good. They ate in silence, both lost in their own thoughts and thinking about the road ahead.

Doug refilled their coffees. "I got another Jerry can of gas for you fellows, just in case you need it. As soon as you are ready to go, we'll get you gassed up and on your way."

"Thanks, Doug, we'll come back and pick it up as soon as we pay the bill."

"No worries. I'll bring it out. It's in the kitchen. Breakfast is on the house."

They thanked him for everything and headed out to the car, which was parked across the street. Buzz suddenly came to a stop. Todd turned and looked back at him. "What?"

We weren't serious about actually staying here, were we?"

"We were drunk, Buzz. Seriously up a river without a canoe. Besides, what can we do? Everyone here has learned to live with the fact that the crazy people are on the wrong side of the bars."

Fifteen minutes later, the gas was emptied into the tank. The gauge read half of a tank, more than enough to get back to Cub Run. With what they had at the trailer, there was enough to get the Corvette to Jetson. Buzz took another look at the gauges and reached for the key. Todd tapped him on the shoulder and pointed out the window. They slowly got out of the car and looked at the two pieces of yellow paper neatly folded under the right-hand wiper. Todd pulled them out, looked at one and the other, before handing them across to Buzz without saying a word.

"Swell, $400 dollars for the unpaid ticket from yesterday plus court costs plus another $200 for illegal parking."

"What's that?" Buzz was pointing to a white piece of paper.

Buzz turned it over, opened it and burst out laughing. "It's a bill for the basement window and blinds in the Court House, $650.00."

Todd walked around the car and joined Buzz. They both looked up the street to City Hall. "They're really starting to make this personal."

Todd took the papers out of Buzz's hand. "Uh, huh, but they say you can't fight City Hall."

"But you know what they didn't say Todd?"

"What's that?"

"My friend, no one said anything about buying City Hall."

Todd looked at Buzz, and for a moment and thought he was having a Griz-induced flashback from last night.

Buzz shook his head to clear it. "No, let's move on. That's just last night talking."

He looked back up the street at City Hall and the third floor right window and then second floor center window. "That was the court room, wasn't it?

Peering out of each was a large, round, chubby face, complete with beady little eyes, pushed in nose and big ears. The faces had smiles on them as they looked across the street at the two men standing next to their car. The face in the 3rd floor window made eye contact with Buzz. There was a second of recognition, and then, the smile disappeared. The smile on the face in the 3rd floor window returned, and then it blew Buzz a big fat raspberry.

"We're staying!"

It was Todd's turn to take a look at Buzz. "Doesn't take much to set you off, does it?"

Without taking his eyes off the face in the window, he reminisced. "You remember the class big mouth who always found a way to get under your skin, the guy who always knew how to push your buttons?"

"Yeah sure, Arnie Collinger. He wound me up like a cheap watch. I took a swing at him in history class and ended up with two weeks of detention. He walked"

Buzz nodded. "Gus Tinker, royal pain in the ass. Everyone wanted a piece of him but he was bullet proof. He was dating the principle's daughter."

Todd looked over at City Hall, at the faces in the windows. He got a really big smile on his face. "Yeah, this time it's personal."

Almost simultaneously, the smiles on the two faces slowly disappeared. The message was clear. There was, most definitely, a new guy in town. "Let's go back to the trailer park office and make a phone call."

"Can't make any phone calls, no phone." Griz was emphatic.

Todd pointed to the desk behind her. "What's that? It looks like a phone to me."

Griz smiled, nice like. "That's right. It's a phone, sure enough, ordered it myself out of one of those catalogs."

Buzz looked over Griz's other shoulder, no small feat, at the black rotary dial. "You ordered that out of a catalog?"

"Sure did! It's a beauty, too. Works like a charm."

Todd was beginning to feel his hangover coming back. "I thought you said the phone didn't work."

"I didn't say the phone wasn't working. It works fine. It's the wires. They only work three days a week."

"You mean like the gas station and the restaurant?"

"Oh no, no sir, not like that all. They work on opposite days. Gas, booze, beans. See?"

Buzz wanted to know about the phones. "Which day do they work on?"

Griz started to think real hard, not a pretty sight, like watching a wheel bearing burn out on a really slow moving train. "Well, you know we're not too sure which days the phones are working and which days they ain't." She yelled to Dave. "Which days are the phones working?"

They'd been at Happy Tumbleweed for forty-eight hours, and Dave , who still hadn't put in an appearance, yelled from someplace in the back. "It isn't working any day of the week."

Griz thought now would be a good time to blow a gasket. "What the hell are you talking about? It's supposed to be working three days a week!"

"Of course, it works three days a week or it would, if you paid the bill, you fat sack of crap!"

She turned and looked into the back of the office. "Honestly, I don't know where that man gets his manners, that's no way to talk to a lady, I am not,... FAT!"

Buzz suggested that they had plenty of time and would come back later.

Griz was having none of that and put up her hand. "You just wait here, gentlemen, while I get this straightened out."

As much as they would have preferred to wait outside, possibly in another town, morbid curiosity kept them waiting at the counter, as Griz pushed her way past a large number of obstacles strategically placed, presumably by Dave, to drive her crazy.

From the counter they could hear Dave and Griz having a conversation. Buzz commented about the mood of the conversation. "Well, I got to admit, they sound pretty civilized back there."

Todd agreed. "Maybe the rest of that stuff is for show, like when you use steel wool on furniture to make it look rustic."

Buzz looked at him with real concern. "You're sure you're all right, not brain damaged or anything like that?"

Todd frowned. "Sure, fine, never better. I mean, if someone was really brain damaged, how would they know?"

The conversation in the back came to an end. There was a brief moment of silence, followed by an enormous crash that sounded exactly like a bowling ball being dropped on the keyboard of a piano. Griz returned shortly with an old linesman phone and an impressive black eye.

Todd and Buzz were not impressed. Hitting a woman was simply not on! They made it clear they were ready to explain that fact to Dave. Griz was surprised and grateful, but raised her hand. "Relax, boys. I threw the first punch and he gave as good as he got."

"He had no right to talk to you like that."

Something odd happened with Griz's face and voice. For a moment, the space she occupied seemed to be owned by someone else. *"You boys have been away from the road way too long. We are going to have to get you two tuned up for the journey. Tick, Tock, boys, time is a flying. Tick, Tock,..* Sorry, must have drifted off for a moment."

"Where was I going? Oh, right, Dave and I go way back. No harm done."

She pushed the phone across the counter. "This is one of those repair guy phones. I am not sure how they work, except that you have to climb up a pole to use one. Dave says to look for the pole with the chrome on it. It's a mile out of town toward Jetson. Better you should take my car. It's out back in the garage. That little red smoke wagon of yours will attract attention and the Bender boys will be watching to see what you are up to. Which reminds me, what are you two up to, anyway?"

Buzz grinned. Wait for it."

Griz grinned back. "Don't disappoint me!"

Her car was most definitely out back but she was being a bit generous with the term, *automobile.* The car, at best, had wheels and a steering wheel. "We could take the Corvette."

Buzz stuffed his hands in his pockets. She did say there was a car back here. Maybe we are looking in the wrong place?"

"No, I think we're in the right place and this is Griz's car."

"Well, a wise man once said that it is not just a career, it's an adventure."

They stood there and looked at what was the strangest piece of machinery on four wheels. It was five tons of confusion that could not make up its mind if it wanted to be a car, a boat, or an air plane. "How come it only has one wing?"

Buzz looked at Todd. It's your turn to drive."

They climbed in on both sides and eased into the seats. "Does it need all these seat belts? Seriously, how fast can this thing go?"

"This looks like the inside of an aircraft cockpit."

"How do you figure that?"

"Well, for one thing, these instruments are definitely out of an air plane. I did some aircraft electronics studies in college."

"What's the second thing?"

"You're sitting in an ejection seat."

As they careened from shoulder to shoulder, the drive to the telephone could generously be described as the worst example of taxiing of an aircraft in transportation history. "I think the steering is a little loose, but I'm starting to get the hang of it."

Buzz looked at him like he was crazy, and then yelled over the sound of the engine. "Yeah, I am actually starting to see the line on the road as much as the telephone poles."

In the distance, they could briefly see a pole with a lot of chrome on it.

"Brakes use the brakes!"

"Where are they?"

"What do you mean, where are they?

Buzz grabbed Todd by the shoulder and looked over at what he thought might be the speedometer. "Didn't you check to see if they were working?"

Todd looked down at the floor where a brake pedal should have been and saw two aircraft rudder pedals staring back at him. They seemed to jeer at him. "Bet you can't guess which one?" He stomped on both of them. Nothing happened.

He yelled over to Buzz, pointing down at the pedals. "You try!"

Buzz put both feet on the pedals and jammed them down hard. The machine shuddered, followed by a high pitch squeal coming from the wheels, and then smoke appeared as it began to slow down. It came to a stop four feet short of the pole.

Todd stood up, looked at the bumper wrapped around the pole, and then glanced back at the contraption they were riding in. "How fast do you think Griz was going to get a bumper that far up a pole?"

"Is that's the back bumper we're looking at?"

"Looks like it."

Buzz got out and looked up at what was left of the bumper. "That is one tough telephone pole."

Todd pointed up at the junction box. "Do you think we attracted any attention?"

"Nope."

"Neither do I."

"Who are you going to call?"

"We need someone with the financial skills to handle such an august operation."

"Who are you going to call?"

"A specialist with a wealth of financial experience."

"Who are you going to call?"

"A man who knows his way around the intricacies of complicated financial systems."

Buzz tapped Todd on the shoulder. "Who are you going to call?"

"J. Bernard Costello."

He struggled to put a name and face together. "Costello, Bernard Costello? I've heard the name. Am I supposed to know him?"

Todd was still looking up at the pole trying to figure out how to climb and dial at the same time. "Only by the reputation."

A headline from *The Washington Post* suddenly appeared on the back of Buzz's eyeballs. "You're kidding! Please tell me you're pulling my leg. Bernie the Bookie, two books Bernie, fast paper Costello. Every government in the western hemisphere is looking for his phone number. Looking is an understatement! He's on every Ten Most Wanted Poster in the country."

Todd smiled. "Thirty years in the business and not even a parking ticket."

"Not in the state of California. The man is a legend because he accidentally wiped out the state's DMV data base, fixing a ticket for parking in handicap zone. Then, he gets the computer to arrange an out-of-court settlement for the fine."

"So?"

"The state, or more precisely the state's computer, awarded him the court costs."

"So?"

"It didn't just give him his court costs. It gave him the court costs for the entire state.

"So?"

"You can't settle out of court on a parking ticket!"

Todd whistled. "He is good!"

"Are you listening to me? The man is a crook."

"So?"

Buzz threw his hands up in the air and surrendered. "Okay, how are you going to get a guy that every law enforcement agency in the free world is looking for, here, in this dump, a town that we can't even get out of? How are you are going to do that, Mr. Smarty Pants?"

"I'm going to have to make a long distance phone call."

"Of course, it's so simple, a phone call. How come I didn't think of it?"

Todd burst out of laughing. "I'm just going to climb up that pole and call rent-a-felon and all our problems will be solved."

Buzz just stood there stone-faced as Todd egged him on. "I know you want to laugh. C'mon!"

"This is so stupid, it's funny but I'm not going to admit it."

The call took twenty minutes.

The person on the other end of the line listened quietly. The connection was bad. Questions were asked for clarification, but otherwise, little was said. The hand holding the receiver was large and heavy with rings, brass. Remuneration was offered. But there was only silence. The person passed on condolences for Marcie's passing and asked how he was getting along, were the children well? After five minutes, he was climbing down the pole.

"So, how did it go?"

He grinned, followed by a frown. "The fix is in. Our friend Costello will be here within a week."

"What's the problem?"

"You know it hurts when you have way too much money and good people won't let you give some of it back."

Buzz looked up at the pole and then up the road, nodded, and put a hand on Todd's shoulder before speaking quietly. "I know."

Todd started back to the car, stopped, and looked back. Buzz hadn't moved. He walked back. "Okay, what's eating you?"

"You said it would take about a week to get that guy here, right?"

"Yeah, something like that."

"I don't think my liver is going to that last long."

Twenty-four hours later, the object of interest to Buzz, Todd, and just about every law enforcement agency in the known world, was suddenly awake. J. Bernard Costello was a man with very sensitive personal radar, and at this particular moment, in the darkness of the bedroom of his current address, 22 Lakeshore Boulevard, one-half mile from Venice Beach, his screen was lit."

Costello, a small wiry man who bore an uncanny resemblance to Don Knott's, wasn't strong enough to lift a sack of wet cotton. He made up for this short coming with a really big brain. He could've done or been anything he wanted to in life, but for a number of complex reasons, he decided on a lucrative career in financial crime. Over the three-plus decades in the business, he'd amassed an incredible fortune which he had successfully hidden in accounts all over the globe. He protected himself by adhering to a few simple rules: work alone; never own more than you can carry; live within your means; and keep your interests mobile.

He could have lived in a castle, but preferred the other side of the tracks, living in low rentals, paying cash for everything, and not owning a car. He rarely went out, except to eat. His only concession to the modern era was a very expensive lap top which he used only for work, and a black 2500 telephone that he carried with him wherever he went. Bernie hated crowds, was terrified of big people, and got air sick crossing a thick carpet. His primary mode of transportation was the train. If he was feeling extravagant, he ate in the dining car.

In less than twenty minutes, he was dressed, packed, and on the street hailing a cab. The apartment, paid monthly was yesterday's news. Costello had memorized every train and bus schedule of every rail service in the country. He preferred an empty station, which is why he always took a very late train to wherever he was going, usually a destination he'd decided on when he was actually standing at the ticket window. With his ticket in hand, he decided to check out the facilities. It was going to be a long trip and night trains, although equipped with washrooms, were often long on odor and short on servicing. As he expected, the washroom was empty and surprisingly clean. At two in the morning in an empty train station, he expected to be safe, but he checked under a few stall doors, anyway. He was alone. It was taking a little longer than usual. It had been a long evening and he couldn't remember the last time he had been to the little boys' room. He decided to relax, let his guard down, and let nature take its course.

He suddenly felt something light fall on his shoulder. For a moment, he thought dust from the ceiling had come loose and had fallen on his jacket. Turning to look, he froze. A hand, a really enormous hand, was resting comfortably on his shoulder, like it belonged there. For a moment, he couldn't believe something that big could be so light. The jewelry on the fingers smiled back at him, even the ring with the skull on it. A head appeared from behind him over his right ear and looked down over his shoulder. It nodded with approval. "Take your time, Bernie."

Costello tried to back away. The hand on his shoulder tightened perceptibly. Was that perfume he smelled?

Four days later, Todd and Buzz were standing on the road in front of the Happy Tumbleweed. A lot had happened in a short period of time and it was becoming difficult to recognize either of them. Todd had given up shaving and had developed a ratty looking stubble. Buzz had shed weight, and combined with a shirt missing the right sleeve, had begun to look like a horse thief who had ended up on the wrong side of the saddle on a real ornery animal.

"Where did you get that thing, anyway?"

"What thing?" Buzz asked.

"That shirt you're wearing, where did you get a piece of crap like that anyway?"

"Out of your closet."

"Well, the least you could have done is stolen one with a right sleeve."

Buzz pointed at the shirt he was wearing. "All of your shirts are like that."

"I'm thinking we're going to need a wardrobe upgrade when we get out of here."

Buzz agreed with him, as he looked down at the point where the right cuff was supposed to be. "After a week of drinking Griz's home brew, I am surprised that I have an arm to put in it."

Todd nodded silently as he scratched his chin. He caught Buzz looking at him. "What?"

"You need a shave."

It had been a long four days since the drive out to the phone call. They had gotten another two tickets totaling $1800 the afternoon of the phone call. The Corvette was now persona non auto on Main Street in Peckersnot.

Without transportation, they had to wait it out in the trailer park, alone with Griz, or rely on her mystery automobile, which had suddenly decided to give up making right turns. Dave, still unseen, was surrounded by enough of Griz's moonshine, if it exploded, to remove the state of Kentucky from the surface of the planet.

The widow Smith lent them her Nodwell, a tracked vehicle used in the arctic to transport supplies. Bill her husband, now deceased. decided one Christmas to go for, in his words, a wee drive to deliver presents to the needy. The state police, not equipped to pull over a forty-ton tracked vehicle, had to be content to pursue Bill through the streets of Peckersnot at a top speed of twenty-five-miles-per hour, until he ran out of fuel. The machine, equipped with long range tanks and two cases of Griz's fire water took four days to run out of gas. Except for the widow getting lost on the way to the cemetery with what was left of his mortal coil it was on the record as the longest police pursuit in U.S. history.

Todd went into town with it to pick up 800 pounds of raisin mash which Buzz could not bring back, because it wouldn't fit in the Corvette.

For reasons that he has unable to provide, he took a short cut across The City Hall lawn and parking lot. It was bad enough that the town was going to have to replace 2,400 square feet of sod and sidewalk, but running over Horace Bender's limo was a bit over the top. Horace was justifiably annoyed and made it clear that he wasn't very happy either. It would have ended there, if he hadn't yelled at Todd and called him a no good-for-nothing beach bum. *Not his exact words.*

Todd had already crossed the parking lot and was almost to the street when he heard what Horace yelled at him over the rumble of the Nodwell's engine. He stomped on the brakes with both feet and looked out the window, back at Horace. From where Horace was standing, Todd looked like Willie Nelson on a really bad acid trip.

Gears groaned and screeched as the machine began to back up. Horace was looking forward to a confrontation. He'd even taken his ticket book out with a flourish, when he realized that the driver of the Nodwell was not actually looking out a window to see where he was going. To be fair, Todd was looking in the rear view mirror, carefully examining the rapidly growing shrubbery under his chin. This had nothing to do with looking to see where he was going. Horace was now sharing the parking lot with forty tons of machinery, driven by a distracted man with a really big hangover,

Todd was back by four o'clock with Griz's raisin mash. They were waiting for him when he stepped into the office. Dave had been on the phone, which was suddenly working, at least for the time Freddie Bender needed to give Griz hell for what Todd had done to Horace's limo. Apparently, there was going to be a police car attending the Happy Tumbleweed Trailer Park, within the hour, to haul Todd's miserable ass off to jail. *Not his exact words.*

Todd grabbed a fresh bottle of Griz water, which was sitting on the counter, and headed for the door. "Police car, you say?"

"That's right!"

Todd yelled into the back of the office. "Within the hour, did I hear that right, Dave?"

"Yep, that's what the greasy little troll said."

Todd took a long slow pull from the bottle and walked out the door rock steady. "Not unless they inflate it first."

"Todd, old buddy, I do believe that you're becoming immune to Griz's medicinal!"

"You may be right."

Buzz was aghast. "What the hell-kind-of-medicine do you call that?"

"Highly flammable."

Buzz looked down at stone on the pavement and gave it a nudge with his foot before looking west, up the road. "So, why are we out here anyway? It can't be for the view."

Todd shrugged. "I don't know or I can't remember. I'm pretty sure it's one or the other."

Buzz looked down at the stone and could see a large brown bug looking at the stone with interest. When it discovered the stone was as boring as it looked, it moved over to the white line, unsure which direction to take. It suddenly made a right turn and picked up speed heading out of town. He thought that it was a pretty smart bug. He slowly turned and faced the wind. He could feel it, just a low frequency, high energy rumble. Something was out there, and heading their way.

Todd had known Buzz a long enough to know that he was a man that meant what he said. If he thought there was a something out there, you could be sure there was. On the other hand, between the two of them, they had drunk so much Griz water that they would have trouble telling the difference between the Philadelphia Philharmonic and a passing train.

"Motorcycle, a big one. A Harley with a knuckle-head."

Todd followed Buzz's gaze into the distance. As far as he could see, there was nothing out there. The road was clean and straight, and looked like it went right out to the horizon and beyond. He felt a surge of adrenalin. The hangover he had been carrying around for the last four days vanished in the afternoon sun. "You sure?"

Buzz smiled. "I'm sure. Are you starting to feel better?"

"Yeah, I am. How about you?"

"So am I." He looked down again, noticing that the bug was almost out of sight and it appeared to be picking up more speed.

"You'll be able to hear it in about a minute."

He was right. It came on the wind--a low rumble that they could feel before they could hear it. As the source of the sound got closer, it settled down to a steady deep rumble that only a Harley Davidson can make.

Buzz raised an arm. "There, can you see it?"

Stiles raised an arm to block the sun. A sharp flash of chrome exploded in the afternoon light.

He had it right. A Harley stripped for travel by someone who kept their interests mobile. As it approached, the driver slowed, but made no effort to pull to the shoulder. They were going to have to step out of the way.   The Harley slowed to a stop in the center of the road. The owner placed two hob nailed boots on the road and waited patiently for them to approach.

Todd moved first and slowly extended a hand. The rider reached out and returned the handshake. His hand disappeared in an ocean of fingers and jewelry. "It's been a long time, Ollie."

"Modesto, 78, now, that was a train wreck!"

Her smile faded. Marcie?"

"Four years. MS."

The grip on his hand tightened. "I heard and you don't need more wasted words, when we're done doing business, I want some of your time to talk about her."

He agreed that it would be good for the both of them.

She looked at Buzz, who had been standing silently next to Todd. "I don't know you."

"Buzz Murdoch. Todd and I are traveling together."

Ollie extended a hand. "You keep good company."

Buzz's fingers felt like they had been in a vice. He wiggled them to get the circulation back.

Leaning back on her bike, she unzipped her jacket. "I brought your package."

As the zipper came down, a face appeared. J. Bernard Costello coughed and gasped for air. "I want a god damned lawyer, kidnapping across state lines is a federal offense!"

Ollie laughed and gave his head a rub. "No problem, we'll just call the feds and you can tell them everything!"

Costello suddenly stopped talking as the woman finished unzipping her jacket and he fell out of the coat.

They pulled him off the bike and tried to straighten up his clothes. Todd tried to put him at ease when Costello resisted any help. "Relax; we're on your side. We've got a problem here that we need your help with. When it's done, you're on your way to wherever you want to go."

Costello's instincts immediately kicked in. "What's in it for me?"

Todd smiled nastily as he looked at Ollie and back at Costello.   "Like I said, Bernie, you get to go wherever you want."

"That's it! That's all I get out of this?"

Buzz leaned over to Costello. "You get to pass go, a get out of jail free card, get to collect your $200.00.

"Okay, you've got my attention, but what about Girlzilla here?"

"Oh, you can take her with you if you want."

Costello said No! *Not his exact words.*

Ollie smiled and asked where a lady could go to freshen up.

Buzz pointed across the road to the entrance to the Happy Tumbleweed, just as a gust of wind tore the sign off the pole and flung it into the ditch.

She nodded. "Nice. I think I'll lay up for a couple of days. You may need an extra pair of hands."

"Ask for Griz, she'll get you squared away."

"You want a ride Bernie?"

He told her to have sex with herself and that he preferred to walk. *Not his exact words.*

She chuckled. "I love it when a man plays hard to get."

The Happy Tumbleweed hadn't been this busy in as long as Griz could remember, about three weeks. Traffic depended, in large measure, on the quality of her current brew.

Costello immediately started to make demands about the quality of the room and his requirements.

"Hey, you're getting the Emu room, that's high class. If you want electricity, that's extra."

Buzz tapped him on the shoulder. "That's a good deal. You're between an RV and a semi and the place backs onto a tailing pond. It's real quiet back there."

Griz handed him a bottle of fire water and a lifesaver along with his key. "By the way, we're non-smoking here at The Happy Tumbleweed. "

Ollie stepped up to the counter and asked for a room. Griz, who didn't scare easily, stepped back in fear. "How the hell did you get so big?"

Ollie grinned wickedly. "I ate all the boys in my grade 4 class."

Griz pushed a key across the counter without getting any closer. "Grizzly room, it's to your left down the road, the third trailer on the right. There's a raccoon under the stairs that you don't want to be bothering. By the way, you're not gay, bi-national, or whatever they call it?"

Ollie laughed. "No, sorry can't help you."

Griz let a deep sigh of relief. "Thank God for that."

So, it was in the twilight of that August evening that a plan was devised to rid Peckersnot of the less than beloved Bender brothers, and return it to its rightful owners--its seriously indifferent citizens--for the bargain basement price of 28 million dollars.

"We are boned! How are we going to buy back the town?"

Doug suggested robbing the bank, but the idea was discounted because the jail wasn't big enough to accommodate six people.

Bernard had finally succeeded in prying Griz's dog off his leg with an axe handle. "You have to find out whether the money was a grant or a contribution and which department it came from, because they all have different terms and mandates. The information will be on the document next to the file number."

Buzz shook his head. There's no way the Benders are going to let us near that kind of paperwork."

The dog was after his leg again with a vengeance. "You can get the information from the government accounting office in Washington."

"And then what?" Everyone wanted to know.

Before he answered, Costello looked down and discovered that Griz's dog had switched direction, established a firm grip on his other leg, and had made it clear that it was going to take more than a stick to get him off this time. Someone was going to get a hell of a dry cleaning bill. "Find out what the conditions of the disbursement were. Was it a grant, a contribution, or a loan? Are there time limits in the conditions? How is the money to be spent, etc.? What happens if the conditions are not met? Does all or part of the money have to be returned? Every government funding agreement comes with attachments of some sort."

"So, what could happen if the Benders screw it up?"

"The money would have to be returned and the government assumes control. The government appoints someone to run the place until it is satisfied that a proper municipal government has been set up."

"The problem is those Bender boys will be on to us right quick if we try phoning Washington. How are we going to get a letter back here without them getting their hands on it?"

Buzz nodded to Todd and they silently got up and walked back to the trailers. Todd walked over to the Corvette and retrieved the coin. "Heads your secretary, tails, it's mine."

"Sounds good to me."

The coin shone in the afternoon sun as it tumbled end over end before bouncing twice on the hood. It came to rest near the windshield, upright on the edge, sitting rock-steady in the setting sun. Ollie's hand reached out and carefully lifted it off the hood. She held it up to the sun turning it one way and then the other, carefully examining the faces. "That's a beautiful coin."

She handed it back to Buzz. "Gentlemen, leave your problem with me. I should be back inside of a week with the information you need."

"Ollie we appreciate it, but . . . ."

She raised a hand and stopped him. "This is important and I want to be a part of it. Besides, you two are going west and Washington would be heading in the wrong direction."

She left that afternoon with instructions to drop the information at Whithers-Murdoch in New York. They would deliver it as Buzz instructed, just in case she was intercepted on the road by minions of the Benders.

When she left, they went looking for Costello. "Okay, Bernie, we're going into town, to the records office to see if we can find anything."

"What do you need me for?"

"Look, you know this stuff better than anyone. Besides, the clerk is a forty-eight-year-old spinster who is really going to take a shine to you." Buzz smirked.

"Pass, I've been shined enough, thank you very much, and there is no way you can make me do anything!"

Todd put a friendly arm around Costello's shoulder and looked up at the sky. "You know, Bernie, you are totally correct. We can't make you go. But, on the other hand, life is not always that simple. Life is about choices. Yes, indeed, it is most definitely about choices."

"Get to the point, Stiles, you're making my teeth hurt."

"It's really about deciding between the forty-eight-year old records clerk and Ollie."

"Okay, okay. But we have an agreement. As soon as this is done, I am out of here, free and clear!"

They agreed enthusiastically. "Sure, right, you bet, Bernie."

"It's Bernard!"

The Peckersnot records office, overseen by Ms. Perky McClusky, was exactly the sort of place where records like to hang out, in dark, dingy basements of old small town city halls. McClusky, on the other hand, was neither dark nor dingy. She was widowed. Her husband died of a heart attack ten years ago. She was stacked like pancakes, as they used to say and it didn't take a lot imagination to figure out that old McClusky died horizontally with more than his boots on.

Perky McClusky was justifiably pleased to see Costello. She hadn't seen an eligible male in four years. 'How can I help you, sir?"

"Yes, well. I'd like to see the records and financial statements for the town of Peckersnot."

"It's pronounced Pechersnoot, Sir, and I'm afraid they are located in the basement and unavailable to the public. However, if you would like to see the public accounts for New York, I would be happy to arrange it."

"Kentucky has a town called New York?"

"No, it doesn't. They are the New York accounts.

Costello was briefly stunned. "You're talking about the one that sits on the river, right?"

"Yes, that's the one."

"Why would the City of New York send you their public accounts? That doesn't make any sense."

McClusky shrugged. "I have no idea, but they show up every year on April 15th by courier. Would you like to see them?"

Buzz tapped Costello on the shoulder to remind him exactly which town he was supposed to be looking at. "Actually, I am willing to go to the basement if I could see Peckersnot's as well."

"You are?"

"Yes, of course."

Perky undid the top button of the collar of her shirt, which had suddenly become uncomfortably tight." If you're willing to go to the basement, with me, I guess we can work something out."

The basement looked exactly like the records office except it was in the basement. It took a about few minutes for her to find the New York documents Costello really wanted to see.

"If you like, I can help you find what you are looking for?" Costello thought she was standing far too close and wondered why she was whispering.

The image of Ollie appeared in the back of his mind and he suddenly remembered what he was supposed to be looking for. "If you don't mind, what I am really interested in is the town records and correspondence."

Perky reached over his shoulders with both arms, grabbed the cabinet behind him, and backed him into it. "Well, I am sorry, Sir, but they are confidential and I couldn't possibly allow you to access them."

Costello's understanding of women had ended somewhere around grade six, but he suddenly remembered a scene from an old black and white movie. He leaned forward and blew in her right ear. "Just between the two of us, I promise not to tell."

"You just stay right here. I'll got get the keys."

Four hours later, he had all the information he needed and was back out in the street waiting for Todd and Buzz to pick him up. Griz showed up instead. She looked him up and down as he got into the car. "Where the hell are your strides? You can't go walking around in your undie things like that, it ain't decent."

Perky appeared at a window waving his pants and screamed. "Call me!"

Griz looked up at the window and then at Costello. "You must be good. Perky hasn't been that excited since she won a C-note at Bingo."

"Are all women like that?"

Griz laughed. "Hell, boy, we're worse. You're lucky you still got hair on your Weed Whacker! In fact, I'm thinking I might as well finish the job tonight."

Costello grabbed what was left of his shirt and pulled it together. "Don't touch me!"

Todd looked at the back of Costello's shredded shirt. "What the hell happened to you, anyway? You were only going to the basement to get the arrangements the Benders made with the Feds."

Griz appeared at the door with hot dogs for dinner. "Ole Bernie here took one for the team. He went to heel to toe with Perky McClusky, who hasn't hauled anyone's ashes in four years and has nails sharp enough to cut glass."

"It's Bernard!"

"Okay, what did you find out?"

It was a quite a story. The Benders had, indeed, received a check for the sum of 28 million dollars. It was duly deposited in the town accounts, and promptly went out again. According to the records, every last dollar belonging to the town was transferred to the Danby Corporation. In the remarks column, the decision was made because public funds were safer in the custody of private companies, because governments could not be trusted with the publics' money.

According to Costello, it was perfectly legitimate for governments to transfer money to private companies. It happens all the time for the purpose of investment or management.

However, he had to admit that the explanation was a bit unique. It was not every day that a government admitted that it was as crooked as a dog's hind leg. All that was required was a warrant drawn up by the council, which requires a vote to make it legal. With the Benders being the only duly elected members of council, it wasn't difficult to arrange the paperwork and vote on it.

Buzz looked at Todd. "Ever heard of the Danby Corporation?"

Todd shook his head and shrugged. "So, what have they spent the money on?"

Costello brightened up. "Oh lots of things. You name it, streets, sewers, etc. There were at least ten projects for municipal work, you know, infrastructure."

Griz looked up from a hot dog that she was happily turning into a chunk of fire hose. "What's infrastructure, some kind of sex toy?"

Buzz said to no one in particular that it meant manhole covers.

"Oh, right, I know what those are, and, now that I think of it, that pothole over on Hammerflap circle still ain't fixed and Venzetti's lawnmower is still stuck in it."

Costello held his hot dog at eye level. Was the wiener actually eating the tomato? "You know, that's the weird thing. Hammerflap circle is sitting in the municipal landfill."

Griz shook her head. "Well, that just can't be right. Hammerflap pretty much looks like a dump, what with Bert Johnson taking up recreational explosives and all. But it's what you call private property and nobody has a dump in their backyard."

Todd looked at everyone with dawning awareness. "Every part of a town has to be properly identified, zoned, to show if it is residential, commercial, industrial, or unrecoverable, such as a dump."

Griz jammed the rest of her hot dog into her mouth and spoke around wiener and mustard. "I'm thinking those Bender boys may have it right about Hammerflap, seeing that Sacco put up statues of his naked dog and wife on his front lawn."

Costello pointed out that dogs were not naked.

"They are when you shave off the fur!"

Buzz was suddenly reconsidering his third hot dog.

Todd watched Griz cover up a mistake under a bottle of barbecue sauce and wondered what kind of monstrous act he had committed in another life that led him to this unusual form of hell. "Oh, right, I drove my car through Amanda's rose garden."

"It makes perfect sense; if you don't want to fix something just rezone it instead."

"You mean they turned Hammerflap into a dump?"

"Actually, they moved the street to the dump, so they don't have to pay for any services. You'd think the people on the street would be bent out of shape about something like that."

Griz handed Costello his fourth hot dog. "You've never met anyone from Hammerflap circle, have you?"

Costello, who was rapidly consuming his hot dog, raised his hand because his mouth was full. "That's not exactly right."

Todd reached over and removed what was left of the hot dog from Costello's mouth. "So what are you saying that Hammerflap hasn't been rezoned?"

"No, what I'm trying to say is that the town has been rezoned."

"You mean the whole town, even my hotel, is now a dump?"

"The correct term is landfill, except for this place; it's listed as a dump."

Griz was seriously annoyed, "Those rotten bastards!"

Costello nodded. "That's about right. By the way, these are really good. Have you got anything to drink?"

Todd and Buzz simultaneously pushed their full glasses of Griz water across the table. "Welcome to Peckersnot."

The next three days were kind of hazy. Of course, things are hazy on both sides of the eyeballs when someone lives under the kind of weather generated by Lamplighter Libation.

It only took one glass and Costello went after the Caribou hanging on the side of Todd's trailer. When he discovered it wasn't going to respond to any form of sexual advances because its body was missing and it was dead. He decided to give Griz's Doberman a seriously good petting, "Here Kitty, Kitty."

So, there it was. The Benders had gotten themselves elected as town council, set up a fake company, relieved the town of every last dime, and then rezoned the entire town into a municipal landfill site so they didn't have to spend the money they stole. The mystery was where exactly the town of Peckersnot was, and where was the long list of civic repairs that were taking place on paper. The Benders had apparently walked away with an entire town and weren't going to give it back.

Ollie returned six days later to a town decidedly the worse for wear. One of Larry Wallace's bean bag bombs had gone badly off course, which was a serious case of ugly on a good day, charting new unexplored territory that took it through the passenger side window of Horace Bender's brand new luxy Cadillac, white on white with matching interior. Larry's indiscriminate sniper attacks had finally come home to roost.

The town was made to pay, until Larry came down off the roof and said he was sorry for trashing Horace's luxy new Cadillac, white on white, with matching interior. Fat chance of that happening, if he wasn't going to apologize to Bert Wallace's Virgin Mary, he sure as hell wasn't going to apologize to Horace, especially after finding out that Horace had slept with both his girlfriend Myrtle, and his mother, at the same time. *HB,* as he was often referred to because he had a lot of lead in the old pencil, was quite the axe man in his youth, still was. There wasn't a sweater puppy in town he hadn't gotten his hands on, except Griz Lamplighters, and he wasn't in any rush to drive out to The Tumbleweed and tell her about it, either.

What really pissed Larry off wasn't that Horace had stuffed Myrtle; it was the fact that Larry was the only one in town who hadn't stuffed Myrtle. The thing about his mother--well, he could go either way on that one. If you lived in a town populated with 6,800 horny jack rabbits with elevated hormone levels, and the only date you could get on a Saturday night was with the palm sisters, and they charged you for it, you can sort of understand why Larry Wallace spent a lot of time on the roof, screaming obscenities and throwing beans at people.

The Benders were not the sharpest pencils in the box, but on the other hand, they weren't lacking imagination, either. A whole new raft of bylaws appeared, such as all of the houses with odd numbers had to be painted green, even numbered houses yellow. The municipal water pressure suddenly increased 20%, which meant you had to wear a bullet proof vest before you turned on a tap. If you didn't own one, you hoped to God that the pipes in the street in front of your house exploded first, or you were off to the hospital to be treated for bullet wounds.

Peckersnot had suddenly returned to its ancestral roots and was only accepting the British pound as currency everywhere, except the library, which would only take German Marks for fines over $50. The library had amassed a substantial collection of really filthy books, magazines, and videos. Within hours, there was a severe run on German currency at the bank.

Todd thought it was Tuesday, but, of course, he couldn't be sure. Come to think of it, maybe it was Wednesday. Fact was he was having trouble remembering what year it was. Buzz was no help. The last time he saw him, he was sewing his name on to every piece of clothing he owned so he could remember it. He was pretty sure Buzz wasn't spelled with two u's and three z's, he wasn't sure it was Tuesday.

Buzz looked up the road one way and then in the opposite direction. "What month is it, anyway?"

Todd gave him a blank, vacant stare. The fact was that time did not seem to have a lot of meaning any more. "Buzz, do you think we'll ever get out of here?

"I am the eternal optimist."

"We're boned! By the way, why are we out here, anyway?"

Buzz looked at his watch, moving it back and forth so his could focus on the dial. "We're waiting for a package with the information on the deal the Benders made with Washington. They said it would be delivered sometime between 12 Noon and 1:00 p.m. today, and it is definitely between 12 and 1."

Todd looked at the sky. "Yeah, but is it today?"

It took a full minute before it registered with both of them that there was something seriously wrong with what he had said.

He looked at the name tag on Buzz's shirt, and then the missing sleeve. "How long have you had that shirt, anyway?"

"About an hour, I'm not sure."

"You didn't actually go into town and buy that thing?"

"I got it out of your closet. I didn't have any clean shirts left."

In the distance, they could hear the sound of an airplane. "Where's that coming from?"

Buzz looked up and to the left. Out of the sun, "I think. There, see it?"

It took a few seconds of searching the sky for Todd to find it.   "Okay, I got it. It's low, maybe they're trying to land."

"Not here. The closest airfield is Cub Run and it couldn't handle something that big."

As the plane got closer, they could see thick black smoke from four engines. As it passed over them, they could feel the heat from the exhausts and the wind from the wing tips trying to pull them off the pavement. The C-130 shrank to the size of a dime, as it made a turn to the right and headed back, without losing or gaining a foot in altitude.

It turned onto a heading that would bring it over The Happy Tumbleweed, with the engines going to full power, 280 knots at sixty feet.

Right over the office, it pitched up and started a rapid and steady climb--an amazing sight for something that large. A wooden box was ejected from the back of the airplane as it reached an angle of twenty degrees.

The box completed a slow, perfect, ballistic arc, tumbling gracefully end over end, as it went through the roof of the trailer occupied by J. Bernard Costello. Standing in the middle of the road, Todd and Buzz could hear screaming.

"You know, Buzz, a helicopter or small plane would have been fine. We didn't need something that big. Where did you get that thing, anyway?

"Sent away."

"We'd better go collect our package."

"What about Costello?"

"Who?"

"Costello, Bernard. The guy we need to figure out the deal the Benders cooked up, the guy who showed up in Ollie's shirt!"

"What about him?"

"We should see if he's alright."

"What for?"

Buzz laughed. "Todd, we really need to finish this and get the hell out of here before we are too stupid to read a map."

Todd grinned. "Amen to that!"

Costello's roof was totaled, along with the dining room table he'd been eating his lunch at. It had been replaced by a large wooden crate, which was sitting on a pile of kindling. "This is my burger and fries! Ten days I have been waiting for that. It actually belongs to all four food groups. What the hell is wrong with you people?"

Griz pried open the box with her crowbar and peered into the box. "Who knew paper could cause that kind of damage. That's coming out of your damage deposit, by the way."

Costello pointed at the crowbar. "Why do you carry that around with you all the time, anyway?"

"Girl's got to keep herself safe, you know."

"Where did you get it?"

"Sent away."

Todd reached into the box, took out some documents and shuffled through them without actually reading anything. "The sooner you can sort this out, Bernie, the sooner you and the rest of us can get out of here."

Costello took out a few sheets and examined them carefully before speaking. "We've got a deal. I help you out and I walk free and clear?"

"Sure, Bernie, we've got a deal."

"It's Bernard!"

"It took a couple of days, but Costello managed to process 4,000 separate documents down to a manageable report that everyone could understand.

"We're screwed! "Doug was amazed that a mere twenty pages could be so complicated.

Buzz poked at a hole that Griz's water had burned in the clean shirt he had gotten from Todd's closet. "We're screwed is a little vague. C'mon, Bernie, what do you really mean?"

"It's simple. The town was given a federal grant to upgrade its government and infrastructure, 28 million dollars, in fact. Peckersnot had thirty-six months to repair or replace 70% of the work. It then needs to submit a legislative report outlining the changes to the town, so it would meet federal guidelines."

"So, the bastards stole the money. I say we iron up, go over to the Benders, and straighten out a few things."

"You know, Griz, you sound just like Elvis when you are into the fiery waters."

She grinned, "Did him, too!"

Ollie was impressed, drunk, but still impressed. "You did the man himself?"

"That I did. The only real woman he ever had! Rode him hard and put him away wet!"

Griz slowly slid backwards off the picnic table and came to rest on her back with the legs hanging on the bench. In a few seconds, she was snoring loudly.

Doug yelled into the office. "Is that true about her doing the horizontal nasty with Elvis, Dave?"

"Yeah, it's true. She did him in the front seat of Gus's De Soto. Griz kicked out the windshield doing it. Elvis went gay after that."

Costello banged the table with his drink. For a second, his left and right eyes got into a dispute as to which way to look, and then sorted it out. "We're talking business here. The Benders did not steal a dime, not a single Dinero. No, Sirree! These guys are good."

"So where is the money?"

He took a deep breath and collected what was left of his brain. "The money is in the office of the Danby Wealth Management Corp, 122 Shaftesbury Avenue, Peckersnot, Kentucky. But we know that already."

Doug was thinking really hard trying to visualize the address. "I know where that is. It is a block past the post office. That's an abandoned parking lot!"

Costello grinned and nodded vigorously. "That's right! There's nothing there."

Doug nodded right back. "No house, no building, and no address!"

Costello waved his stubby finger in Doug's face. "You betcha, no house, no building, no address, no town!"

Doug laughed hysterically, and then stopped abruptly. "No town?"

"That is correcto-mundo! The town is gone, poof. Those Benders are a couple of nasty little munchkins. They steal the cash and then they stole the town, just rolled up the sidewalks right down to the last doorknob, put it in the back of a cheap van, and drove off. For the last two years, the good citizens of Peckersnot have been living in a drainage ditch!"

Costello slid slowly off the picnic table, coming to rest on his back right next Griz. Ollie and Doug stood up and looked over the table at the two of them. Ollie took a long pull on her bottle. "They make a nice couple."

Doug belched and scratched himself. "He was fun."

It took a day for everyone to sober up enough to come up with a plan to return the town to its rightful, but mostly indifferent, owners. The Benders had stolen the town and then rezoned it out of existence, replacing it with a municipal landfill which was an equitable arrangement for majority of the residents of Peckersnot. Town folk weren't so much lazy as incredibly practical. "Am I going to worry about traffic lights, speed bumps, or a two bag limit? I'm thinking a two bag limit."

The plan was simple, but it didn't start out that way. Beginning with going to Congress and the General Accounting Office, the conspirators worked their way down to a civic election to vote the Benders out of office.
They had a better chance of bum rushing the White House and demanding cookies, the crunchy ones with the chocolate in the middle, than getting anyone in Peckersnot to stand up and say I DO!"

"Let's rob the Benders! All those in favor, say I DO!" The logic was that if you actually had the town's money, you owned the town, wherever it was.

"When we are busted for theft over $5000 we'll tell them that it isn't true, that it doesn't even make sense, Todd."

"We're in a town that only sells beans three days a week. There isn't a jury in the country that would convict us."

Buzz scratched himself. "This is true."

"You should stop doing that."
"What?"

"C'mon, let's go rip off those rotten sacks of crap, Buzz!"
"What?"

Doug suddenly got a serious look on his face, or maybe it was just the hangover. "I thought someone said they had invested in the Danby Wealth Management Company. Have I got that right?"

Costello looked down as Griz's dog was trying to remove his right pant leg at the knee. He was surprised and a little alarmed at how the dog's sexual appetite didn't bother him anymore. "They've probably converted it all into stock or bonds. That's a good thing, because we won't have to haul around a big pile of dirty old money. By the way, what have you been feeding this damn dog of yours, anyway?"

Griz smirked, "Love."

Costello looked down at what was left of his pant leg. "It must have cost you a fortune in porn. Maybe you should try feeding it dog food."

"Okay, who is going to keep the Benders busy while we're ransacking their place?" Everyone turned and looked at Griz.

Doug leaned back on his chair and peered at the back of her neck. "Maybe you should clean up a bit, maybe shave a little closer."

"Look who is talking, bean bag boy!"

Doug yelled back at her. "I did not start that, it wasn't my idea to bag Myrtle!"

Griz took a swing at Doug and missed. It would have been a nice left hook if it had connected. "No! She was the only one in town who didn't want to sleep with you, that's why you had to pay for the room,...loser!"

Doug responded with a right jab. He missed. Griz decided to use a leg this time, and she connected. Doug folded like a cheap tent.

Buzz looked at his glass. It was empty. He couldn't recall ever seeing it like that. "What do you think, Ollie? You wanna have a crack at it?"

She belched and scratched an armpit. "I'm saving myself for marriage."

Griz thought that was funny as hell, as Doug staggered towards her with his arms out, like a zombie trying to catch a bus. She backed up too far, tripped over the dog, and landed on her back in a cloud of dust. Doug was trying to laugh through gasps for air, tripped over the dog, and landed on top of Griz.

Griz hollered. "Get off me, you two dollar bag of turds!"

Doug hollered back. "Mangy old cow! You feel like a dirty, broken down old sofa with all the springs busted up by fat people, humping on it all day."

Buzz and Todd watched the show from the table. "You think we'll ever get out of here?"

"Someday, Buzz, someday."

Ollie walked over to the table, carefully stepping over the two bodies, which were now completely covered in dust, road tar, and pooch bombs. "Bernie and I will go and keep the Benders busy while you go about your business."

"It's Bernard, and I'm not going anywhere with you. I don't like you!"

Ollie smiled sweetly and pointed at her over-stuffed shirt. "Oh, yes you will, Bernie. My girls miss you. Your head makes a great sweater puppy." Costello gagged.

Everyone quickly got up from the table. "I guess we'd better get going."

Todd looked at his watch. It wasn't there. "How long do you think you can keep them busy before they figure out what's going on?"

Ollie was uncertain. "No way to tell. But you can be bet it's going to be fun. Come along, Bernard, we have work to do."

Todd walked over to Doug and Griz and dragged them out of the dirt. "Play time is over, kiddies. We've got a bank to rob."

Griz dusted herself off. "I'm not going out like this. I need to clean up and put on some make up."

Doug pulled a chunk of asphalt off her forehead. "You already have."

Griz let loose with a right cross that connected. Buzz suggested they all meet at the truck. Todd picked Doug up off the road again. "Shouldn't that hurt, being knocked down like that all the time?"

"Have I got all my teeth?"

It would be hard to say who had the harder time of it on that fine summer day in Peckersnot. Just to be on the safe side, they decided to take Griz's Doberman and her school bus, because there was no telling what was waiting for them at the Bender place.

Buzz looked back into the darkness for Doug. "Where'd she get the bus?"

"Griz used to do the school run, but it didn't work out. She got fired because she never showed up with the kids. She left them in the liquor store parking lot." Griz said they were a bunch of criminals anyway, and they would probably make a better living shaking people down for money. They were actually doing pretty well until the Girl Scouts put a stop to it."

"Well, they're a pretty righteous group, Todd agreed.

Doug shook his head. "No, they were just cranked because the kids were working their turf."

"Aren't you supposed to be working today?"

"Nope, Wallace is having a bake sale today."

Todd slowly wheeled the bus off the road and into the Bender's driveway. "Are we sure they aren't here?"

Griz nodded. "Trust me; the greedy little trolls are in town thinking up new ways to steal old man Weaver's lawn tractor."

The Benders had quite the spread. "I was out here about four years ago and it sure didn't look like this then. You sure can buy a lot of yard gnomes with 28 million dollars."

"At least a couple of hundred from the look of it," Todd answered quietly.

The front yard was covered with the gnomes, all strategically positioned to make it impossible to stand anywhere, without it appearing that the gnomes were staring at someone stupid enough to set foot on the property.

Griz pointed to a gnome that looked like a large brown rabbit with black around the eyes. "What about that one?"

Doug picked up a stick and was seriously considering poking it. Now, that is one really weird looking gnome. What the hell is it supposed to be, anyway?"

Todd slowly took the stick away from Doug. "I can tell you what it's not,.. A lawn statue."

"How do you know that?"

"Well, for one thing, it's breathing."

Todd was right. The lawn statue was sucking down large quantities of oxygen and staring intently at Griz's Doberman. The dog was well aware of the bunny's exceptional health and was not happy about it.

"You have to admit that stare really hangs on to you and doesn't let go. I've never seen anything like that."

Todd spoke without moving his eyes. "I have.... a cockroach."

Griz, who did not frighten easily, whispered to herself. "That must have been some bug!"

They moved on as a group, walking past the demented bunny and began to check for a way into the house. They looked for open windows, locks, security cameras, and finally decided to kick the front door in.

The place was incredible--expensive and tacky. The Benders had a lot of money, but when it came to taste, the balance in the account was pretty much zero. Doug looked at the furniture in the living room. "This stuff looks pretty old. You'd think they could afford something newer."

Todd stepped around him and looked at the back of a chair. "It's not just old; it's hundreds of years old. This is called Louis XIV."

"I've heard of him. This is actually his stuff? I think he's dead."

Buzz picked up a chair and looked at the legs. "This stuff would have cost hundreds of thousands of dollars each. Too bad they sawed off the legs."

"The place is like munchkin land. Nothing in here is over five feet in height."

Back in Peckersnot, there was dissension in the ranks. Bernard, who'd, had enough of Ollie's sweater puppies and her wicked ways, took a swing at her and nearly broke his hand on her belt buckle.

"Don't do that. You're making me horny!"

She pointed at a dress shop across the street, "F. Delvechio, Proprietor."

"What do you need a dress for?"

"What the hell kind of a question is that? I wear dresses."

In Bernard's mind, he was thinking that she should try the hardware store a few doors down the street, and buy a tent. Of course, he didn't say that out loud.

.   A bell over the door rang gently as they walked in. A voice from the back announced that the owner would be out in a minute.
F. Delvechio appeared a moment later from behind a rack of size eights. Ollie backed up a few steps, displaying a rare moment of surprise.

F. Delvechio, proprietor, was not a middle aged woman dressed in her Sunday best. *She* was an overweight middle-aged *man*, dressed in his Friday night best, which included, but was not limited to, undersized filthy T-shirt, complete with filthy saying. Bermuda shorts, black shoes, and white socks. The ensemble was topped off with a head with five days of stubble, cheap cigar, a nose complete with hairs, and a mustache trimmed with soup. The package was completed with the ultimate sartorial indignity--a really bad comb-over. To be fair, he did have an earring. Nice.

"You wanna buy something, or what?" Costello thought the man needed to work on his sales pitch.

"What do you know about women's clothes?" Ollie demanded to know.

Delvechio took a long pull on his cigar and looked Ollie up and down carefully. "A hell of a lot more than you does."

"You should watch your mouth, buster. That's no way to talk to a lady!"

"What about your little girl? Do you want to get her a dress?"

Costello didn't like him anymore than Ollie did. "I'm a man. I don't need a dress!"

We're talking wrong on both counts."

Costello had enough of the friendly banter. "We're looking for the Benders. Where are they? If you piss me off, I am going to leave you with my friend here. You ever try eating corn with wooden teeth?"

Delvechio objected. "Don't I get any say in this?"

Ollie leaned forward and over him. "No!"

"They're over at City Hall, counting their money, or whatever they do over there."

As they walked out the door, Delvechio suggested a nice blue number. "You want to look nice when she takes you out to dinner."

Unlike Todd and Buzz, Bernard and Ollie had to start on the first floor and wander from room to room to find what they were looking for.

"What kind of place is this, anyway? It's deserted. Maybe it's Saturday."

Costello, who was suffering from the same alcohol induced fog as everyone else at The Happy Tumbleweed, couldn't tell you his shoe size, much less the day of the week.

By the time they reached the third floor, the only thing they'd found was an egg salad sandwich, Oh Henry bar, and what was left of a two-liter bottle of Shasta in a fridge. Ollie sat down heavily in a chair and put a foot on a railing. "Well, this has turned into a wasted turkey shoot. Where are they anyway? Where does someone go to count money?"

Costello had found his way to the judge's bench and was methodically going through the drawers, looking for any kind of loot he could lift. All he could find was an old copy of a less-than-reputable magazine.

Ollie walked around the bench and looked over his shoulder. "You've got it upside down."

Costello silently turned the magazine over. He turned it upside again. "You know, it really doesn't make much difference."

She tapped him on the shoulder, but he wasn't taking his eyes off the photo. She tried again, but Costello continued the mental dance with the picture. Ollie leaned over and whispered in his ear. "If you don't put that away, I'm going to show you what a real one looks like."

He slowly closed the magazine, put it back into the drawer, and pushed it shut. He suddenly came alive and was happy to change the subject. "That's easy. They are in the basement."

Ollie stood up and looked around the room. "Why didn't you say that when we came in the front door, instead of waiting until we got all the way up here?"

"Hey! I'm just following you. I thought you knew were you were going."

"Okay, Okay! Let's go to the basement, find the Benders, rough them up, and take their money."

Costello's face developed a real nasty smirk. "I'm impressed. You're starting to think like a greedy person."

Costello had it right. There was a Bender in the basement and he was definitely counting money. Freddy looked out the door at the people in the hall. He tried to duck back in the room, thinking no one saw him. He was wrong.

"Okay, we know he's in there. What do you want to do?

"What-the-hell-kind-of-answer is that?"

"All right, I've got it all figured it out. We'll make a citizen's arrest. We're citizens, right?"

"A citizen's arrest what-the- hell-kind-of-plan is that? And what are you going to arrest them for?"

Costello had a point. "How about this, we charge them with being greedy little bastards!"

"There's no law against that!"

Ollie screamed at Bender. "You're under arrest!

Freddie dropped the bundle of bills from both of his hands and slowly raised his arms. "What for, what's the charge?"

Ollie, who was expecting him to fold like a tent and plead for mercy, wasn't prepared to provide an answer. Freddie Bender was actually tougher and smarter than he looked. Ollie looked over at Costello, who was over at the desk, running his hand over a stack of bills and carefully examining a counting machine. "You're under arrest for being a greedy little bastard."

A sly look made its way up Bender's face and he slowly lowered his arms. "There's no law against that."

Costello looked at Freddie and nodded in agreement. "I told you that wouldn't work."

Freddie screamed at a movement in the shadows. "Run for it, Horace!"

Ollie pointed at Bernard. "Don't just stand there, go after him."

She quickly turned back to Freddie, who had already moved toward the door. These guys were like squirrels. If you took your eyes off them for a second, they were gone. She closed and locked the door before taking off her jacket.

Out on the street, Costello was discovering that pudgy short people can run really fast, as opposed to tall thin people, who usually can't. Horace was definitely legging it and was going to win the race to the finish line, which, in this case, was Freddy Bender's brand new luxy Cadillac, white on white with matching interior.

Horace Bender who had been chased by every officer of the peace in the country, as had Bernard, slammed the car into reverse and proceeded to chase Bernard around the parking lot, until he found refuge in a compost bin. Bender slammed on the brakes and looked back out the window. "Yep, I still got it."

By the time Costello got back to the basement, Ollie had Freddie singing like a bird. Apparently, the Benders had turned the 28 million into a number closer to 365 million. Most of it was sitting in a Danby Wealth Management fund. "He says all of it is out at their place."

Bernard shook his head. "You can't hide something like that in a house. It has to be in a bank."

"You can if the wealth management fund is a bar fridge."

Costello turned to Freddie in shock and anger. "Danby, you put the money in a refrigerator?"

Freddie nodded silently.

"You are amateurs!"

The only piece of the puzzle missing was the original document, which gave them the authority to receive and manage the money. If they could get their hands on the paper, it would be all over for the Benders, and neither of them was going to give that up without a fight.

"What happened to the other one?"

Costello looked like he had spent the night in a dump; actually five minutes in a compost bin, but the results are pretty much the same. "I lost the little bastard."

Freddie suddenly got his grin back. As long as they had that letter, Horace could cross the border with it, if necessary, and there wouldn't be anything anyone could do about it.

"Well, we still have this guy and he has succumbed to my charms. They've been investing the money in everything but the town. Apparently, they are pretty good at it. They have around a hundred million here in stocks and bonds. The rest is out at their place. But the problem is the letter."

"Where is it?"

"It's at the Bender's place."

Costello pointed to the empty chair. "I'm talking about the greedy little bastard you are supposed to be guarding."

She turned to the open basement window which looked out on to the parking lot and a hub cap from a Cadillac. They could hear the sound of a car door open and closely followed by the kind of giggling a greedy little bastard would make. The hub cap slowly rolled past of the window.

Back at the Bender's, the search had produced very little except for a desire for pastels after three hours of being exposed to red and green furniture. On the third floor, no one heard a car move slowly up the driveway. Griz, who was in a bedroom, wondered aloud why single short guys would need five of them. Doug had stopped at the door. Maybe they're keeping the money in the mattresses."

Griz opened her purse, and rummaged in it for a moment, before taking out an eight inch hunting knife.

Doug was terrified that he was suddenly in a room with her and that knife. "What the hell are you doing with a thing like that?"

"A girl has to have protection these days. There are a lot of angry men out there."

She walked over to the bed and stuck the knife into the mattress up to the handle grip. A geyser of water erupted out of it and hit the ceiling. "They have to be fucking insane!

Back downstairs, everyone was considering the next move.

"There's a bar in the next room. Anyone want a drink?" Nobody said no.

Todd walked behind the bar. It was refreshing to see liquor bottles with names and labels on them. In the corner, a large bar fridge stood, presumably with mix in it. "That's odd. Why would someone tie a fridge shut with rope?"

Doug suggested that maybe the door was broken and they used a rope to keep it shut.

Buzz pointed at the floor. "They sure needed a lot of it for a small fridge."

The rope around the fridge crossed the living room floor and out the door. Todd couldn't figure out how he had missed that. "Oh right, the booze."

The rope suddenly went taught and the fridge jerked away from the wall. It paused for a moment, as if it was taking a breath and then, suddenly, it roared to life. Todd had to climb on the bar as it went by. The sign on the door said "*Danby*."

They got to the front door just in time to see Freddy Bender's brand new luxy Cadillac, white on white with matching interior, pulling out of the driveway dragging the Danby Wealth Management fund by a rope attached to the bumper.

Horace and Freddy stopped briefly to load the fridge into the trunk and tie it down. They worked quickly and had it done in a couple of minutes. They could have taken twenty minutes and still had time for a smoke. They were in no danger of being overtaken by Griz's school bus.

`In Peckersnot, Ollie and Costello were at the gas station, arguing about what to do next, when a car pulled up for fuel. Ollie had her back to the pumps and with Bernard facing her; he could not see the car.

"Hey, he didn't pay for that gas! Bernie screamed as the now fully fueled Caddy pulled out of the gas station and disappeared up the street. Freddy leaned out the window and wiggled his fingers,...Bye, bye."

Understandably, the Benders were a couple of right happy campers with 365 million dollars in the trunk and a town in their back pocket. "Frederick, my good man, what do you say we sell the place to someone as a dump?"

He pulled an envelope with the letter in it out of the glove box and waved it. "Horace, we already did!"

The scales of justice often don't work very well, if at all. But occasionally, fate intervenes and places a finger on the right side of the scale and sometimes it evens out. Once more, the eternal battle was put in motion. Larry Wallace hauled back on a sack of rancid, two-week- old beans, and let fly, screaming, "I hate your guts!"

Simultaneously, Bert Wallace let fly with a sack of Rancid Custard, screaming in pious indignation. "No one screws with the Virgin Mary,... Bucko!"

It was a moment in Peckersnot history that no one would ever forget. There was a statue in the park right next to that guy Bert Johnson. The beans hit the Bender's Caddy on the right side, blowing in the back window and filling the car with rancid beans. The impact spun the car around just as the sack of custard hit the car going in the same window. Every inch of the interior of Freddy Bender's brand new luxy Cadillac, white-on-white with matching interior, was covered in an inch-deep mixture of beans and custard.

Doug ran up to the car on one side and Ollie ran to the other side. They yanked open the doors. For a moment, it was hard tell if there was anyone in the car. Freddie looked like a ginger bread man. He groaned, "Somebody please help me."

Ollie grinned. "Letter, please."

Freddie produced it in a bean covered hand. Ollie handed it to Doug, suggesting that he put on a pair of rubber gloves first.

The town of Peckersnot had been saved. The money and letter were turned over to Judge Hardpecker, who gave it to Perky McClusky, because the Judge was nude and Perky had pockets. The Benders were locked up in the Laundromat because the town still didn't have a working jail. The Benders had sold the bars in the cell for booze money. Considering they hadn't been cleaned up, it was no small feat to keep them from sliding out of the wash tubs. There was a hell of a block party that evening.

"So what would everyone like for lunch?" Doug was back at his job taking orders at Bert's Grill.

Todd looked at the menu and decided on a ham on rye. Buzz went with a burger. Doug laughed. "You want fries with that?"

An hour later, it was close to two in the afternoon, they were back on the street where it all started. Doug held out his hand. "I sure wish you two could stay awhile. It was a lot of fun having you guys around."

Buzz looked up the street in the direction they were heading and shook his head. "Thanks, but we'd better be on our way."

Doug nodded with understanding as he looked up at the dark clouds in the distance, and then turned to Ollie. "Madam, it was an honor to have met you."

. Ollie bowed slightly. "Sir, the pleasure was all mine."

Doug looked up at the sky again and frowned. "Looks like quite a storm out there. I'd better be getting back inside to close things up."

Todd and Buzz shook Ollie's hand. "You know, Bernard's got about 15 million stashed away in accounts all over the globe."

She looked over her sunglasses, "Really?"

Todd pointed in the direction Bernard had taken,...towards Cub Run, "Really."

Ollie smiled. "Well, I'm thinking maybe it's time that he settled down. But first, I'm swinging by Delvechios; he's got a nice little blue number that I really like."

The Harley made a distant rumble as it disappeared in the distance. Buzz and Todd listened, until the sound was gone. They looked back in the direction they had come.

"You ready Todd?"

Buzz handed him the keys to the Corvette. "You get the first leg."

They pulled out and slowly passed the City Hall before accelerating. In a couple of minutes, they were past the service station and the Happy Tumbleweed. Neither of them noticed as the town disappeared over the horizon behind them.

CHAPTER 6
ASH FLATS

"Nothing ruins a good mystery faster than a damn ghost!"

—anonymous

They stood on the bridge for what felt, to them, like an eternity, and watched the freight train appear over the horizon. It started as nothing more than a small star and grew slowly until it reached the bridge where they had stopped for a break. By any standard, it was a monster of a train, a mile-and-a-half long with distributed power, five locomotives at the head and four in the center 7,000 horsepower.

Todd yelled over the thunder. "Where do you think it is going?"

Buzz laughed at the thought and pointed at the car. "Anywhere it wants."

Todd laughed and nodded. "Let's go."

The train that Styles and Murdoch had seen that afternoon had long since come and gone by the time they got to there. It had shed four locomotives and 108 cars, and they wouldn't have recognized train 1417 by the time it was on its way to New Mexico. That's how it was done in Ash Flats. Trains came and went, and not much else.

Sometimes they were bigger and sometimes, they were smaller. In the end, it didn't matter what size they were or what they carried, because the procession was endless, twenty-four-hours-a-day, 365 days a year. There was a constant and endless rumble which had become so embedded in the fabric of Ash Flats, that every hair line crack in a wall, vibrating coffee cup, and wail of a whistle, was just part of the background of life, just like rain and wind. Ash Flats was a rail hub and every mainline road in North and South America passed through it.

How did the citizens of Ash Flats feel about it? All things considered, pretty good. Okay, sure, they could do without the noise once in a while. But crime was low, there was good pay, and plenty of work for almost everyone. People looked after each other and you count the number of strangers in town on one hand. Most of them were rail people on crew change outs, and they pretty much kept to themselves over at the hotel, great breakfast special--no beans. On this particular evening, four strangers came to Ash Flats who had no connection to the town, to the railroad, or to each other.

The man standing in the shadows of the switch shed had been there for over two hours; to hunt well one had to have patience. It was starting to get cold even though it was summer, but he didn't mind, because he enjoyed his work. He reached into his jacket pocket. For a moment, he couldn't find what he was searching for, and then his hand closed over a large cylinder of metal. He smiled. It was going to be a good night, he could feel it. Damn, he loved his work! Leaning around the corner, he heard something that sounded like footsteps on gravel. He waited for his eyes to adjust to the light. There was definitely someone out there, which was perfect for him. It was show time.

It only took one blow and it was nicely done. He put the metal back in his pocket. He'd been doing this for years but never killed anyone, although he desperately wanted to. No matter, the trail of maimed and damaged victims he had left behind was far more rewarding. His was a lifetime of creating living art, the ultimate in graffiti.

A strong man, who could effortlessly dragged his prize, he reached down and grabbed a handful of hair. Three weeks ago he nailed someone to a wall; that was going to be tough to top.

Benny Callistor was also a strong man, although not physically. A man can be strong in all sorts of ways. One thing was for certain, riding the rails was not for the faint of heart, and Benny had been doing it for nearly thirty years, even if eight million pounds of steel was standing still, dangerous,... you bet, and it was a lot more unpredictable now than it was twenty years ago. When he started out, he could walk into a yard, find a boxcar, set up shop, and within a day or less, he would be on his way. The crews and rail police rarely bothered him if he stayed out of their way.

Things were different now. *Hobo's,* as they used to be called, looked after each other. There were camps all over the country where a traveler could get off and rest. Communities, although not all of them, would help most people out, especially if the individual was hurt, and there was no charge for the service. All of that was pretty much gone now. Rolling stock were mostly closed containers, trailers and boxcars loaded and locked. If the traveler did find one, it was usually damaged, out of service for months on a siding, or would move if you took your eyes off it for a second. Even if it was serviceable and empty, it wouldn't stay like that for long. Computers made sure nothing moved very far without something in it. The traveler had to work pretty hard to get anywhere by rail these days.

Except for a few of the old hands the Hobo's were pretty much gone now too. They were replaced by younger, tougher men who looked after themselves first, and this new breed was more concerned about getting their hands on a buck, than where they were going. There were more immigrants these days as well, mostly from South America, with desperation in their eyes and nothing in their stomachs. They were often inexperienced, took unnecessary risks and paid a high price for it. There were broken or missing limbs, or worse. One never got used to it.

Benny Callistor was traveled, experienced, and careful as he checked the last set of rails in both directions before stepping out from behind the grain car. He was looking for a train, not a fist. He never saw it coming.

Ash Flats, Arkansas, Buzz said it out loud as he looked over at Todd. "How did we end up here?"

Todd was annoyed, mostly with himself, because he couldn't up with an answer. "Hey! There's always Peckersnot."

"No!" They both burst out laughing, mostly in relief for escaping that alcohol-soaked twilight zone.

Main Street, Ash Flats, looked pretty much every other small town clean, straight streets with nothing over three stories high except City Hall and the hotel. The town had a number of newer motels in the outskirts, but Buzz and Todd settled for a place on Main Street called The Bell.

The place had been there as long as the town, lots of old wood, worn, heavy furniture in the lobby, and suspended lighting from a wooden beams. The reception desk still had mail slots for guests. When you checked in, you were handed a brass key and in 1948, you were carrying your own luggage up three flights of stairs. Todd wondered why they always put people on the top floor when the hotel was empty.

He had just finished unpacking and was relaxing in an overstuffed chair by the window, when there was a knock on the door. Buzz stepped inside. "Nice! Where are the washrooms in this place?"

Todd reached under the bed and pulled out a bedpan.

"You are kidding? Please tell me this isn't another one of your vain attempts at humor?

Todd just kept grinning.

"I mean, c'mon. Not even you can get down to that level."

Todd just kept grinning. "You want to make sure to get out of the opposite side of the bed from the side where you went to vote."

The food at the Red Signal was very good by any standard. Hot, well prepared, and if there was any fault with the food, it was the size of the meal. It could have easily fed four people. The waitress, short on years but long on personality, spent her time in the next booth doing homework--a science project--when not serving her customers.

"What's the matter Todd? You've been doing some serious brooding in the last couple of days."

Todd shook his head. "No, never mind. I'm okay, just adjusting to the road I guess."

Buzz put his fork down and looked across the table, at what he realized was one of the few friends he had left in life. "We've known each other a long time. Longer than we've known our wives and kids. You don't need to worry about asking a question."

"Thanks. I needed to be reminded."

They finished their meal in silence. When you are enjoying someone's company, you don't need to fill it with conversation.

The waitress, who had gone into the kitchen to take care of some overdue dishes, had done a good job. Todd was putting a good tip on the table, when Buzz got his attention and waved him over to the booth, where the waitress had left her homework. When Todd got there, Buzz pointed to the top page of her notes, and then slowly turned over the page. "You were pretty good at math. Ever seen anything like this?"

Todd whistled slowly. "This is way beyond me, quadratics, expansion in a finite space."

Buzz turned up the last page and the hair on the back of Todd's neck stood up briefly. "How old do you think she is, fifteen?

He put the pages back in order and looked at Todd. Minimum age for part-time work in the country is thirteen-years-of-age.

Todd questioned Buzz. "How much have you got in your pocket?

I've got around $500.00, why?"

Todd took a hundred out of wallet. Give me a hundred, Buzz."

Buzz took another hundred out of his wallet and handed to Todd.

He took the $200 back to their table and left it with what was already there.

They hadn't gotten very far when the owner caught up to them on the street. "Are you guys serious, a $210 tip,... she's not that good a waitress. What are you guys, some kind of philanthropists?"

"No, we're investors."

"What! Who invests in waitresses?"

"We left $210 on the table. You'll make sure she gets all of it?"

The owner agreed and took a twenty out of his own pocket and looked at it. "If it's that important to you, I'll make sure she gets all of it."

They watched him walk back into the Red Signal. "How are you feeling, Todd, everything okay with you?"

"I wonder if we are making any kind of a difference out here. We weren't much help to Herman Spud except to clean up after it was over. Maybe this world doesn't need guys like us anymore."

Buzz took a deep breath. "No, I think the world still needs people who give a damn. I just don't think we're egotistical enough to think we're the only ones out here trying to make a difference. Besides, don't be so hard on yourself. It's been over thirty years and a lot has changed."

"How about I buy you a drink?"

Buzz got a faked, or maybe it was a real, pained look on his face.   "The last time you said that, I spent two weeks drinking Sterno in a junk yard."

Todd pretended he was a demented doctor. "You look much better now, Herr Murdoch. Zee tremors are good now and za rash is gone, ya?"

Buss pretended to ignore him and brushed some lint of his coat. "I liked you better when you were young and obnoxious."

"Yeah, well now I am just young."

"C'mon, let's check out this burg."

"Hell of a plan Gridly. Let's find the nearest watering hole and do some fishing."

Todd deadpanned. "I prefer my libations in an unmarked bottle wrapped in a brown paper bag.

"Down by the tracks, I presume?"

"I prefer the ambiance under a bridge, if you would be so kind."

"Purist!"

The first bar was occupied by rail workers who just wanted a drink before calling it a night. It made you tired just looking at the place. The second place was filled with loud music and teenagers. No joy there. They ended up in front of a place called the Train Wreck.

Todd looked up at the sign. "Well, you have to admit, it's a catchy title."

The inside of the place didn't exactly match the name over the door, a seventies-feel-kind-of-bar occupied by about fifteen regular customers, mostly women. The bartender, recognizing kindred spirits, waved them over to a couple of stools at the end of the bar.

"What you boys need is something to get the dust out of your teeth after being on the road all day."

"What makes you so sure we are from out of town?"

Phil Geters leaned across the bar. At 6' 4 290 pounds, the bar groaned unhappily. Todd and Buzz leaned back in unison. "I have lived in this town every waking moment of my life. I've become one with the place. I can detect the movement of every molecule in its confines. I'm the all seeing eye of Ash Flats! Actually, I just saw you guys come in this afternoon, definitely out-of-state plates. By the way, that is real nice ride you got."

Geters poured out a couple of drinks and put them on the bar without asking what they wanted. He was definitely a good judge of character. Scotch for Todd and Bourbon for Buzz. Todd sniffed his drink and mentally approved. Definitely not house water. "So, you've been here most of your life, and have a good handle on the town."

He shook his head. "I just made that up. I'm from Milwaukee, been here about eight years, showed up after I flunked out of Stanford."

Todd did some mental math. "Aren't you a little on the mature side to be kicked out of school?

"You sir, are absolutely right! I was a brew-master, pretty good at it, too. Good job, wife, kids, nice home. A really solid citizen, seriously secure. Thing was, I just couldn't see myself spending the rest of my life going nowhere, doing the same damn thing. When it was over, they would give me a gold watch-- $100 Timex--and prop me up on the porch wearing Bermuda shorts, white socks, black shoes, and a barbecue apron. Hell of a way to end it all. So, I quit the job, went back to school, and worked like hell to get accepted. I made it, too, not bad for a grade ten dropout. It all fell apart in my second year. The marriage tanked and so did the grades. I got drunk and woke up here."

Buzz raised his glass in a toast. "Good story."

A voice from the back of the bar demanded attention. Geter rolled his eyes." It's going to be a long night."

Todd and Buzz turned on their stools. They could just make out a group of women sitting in the shadows.

"Allow me to introduce you to Hell's Harpies. They come in every Thursday and Friday, single, divorced, and in the low to mid-forties. Actually, they are a pretty good group except when someone has done the table wrong. I had to throw them out of here one night and they were the only ones in the place."

"What does it take to get some service in this place,... menopause?"

Geters grinned and yelled back. "What's the matter, did one of you old bats fall out of the rafters again? That's why guys don't come in here; you're always hanging over the door by your heels and scaring the crap out of them."

Buzz raised his glass and Todd gave it a tap with his own. "It's good to be back, huh?"

"Yeah, it's good to be back."

A couple of drinks later they were back on the streets. "You know something Buzz?"

"What's that?"

"This is the first time I've seen you relax. It's good to see."

"Thanks. It has been a long time. It also helps when you are in a perfectly normal town with perfectly normal people. It's still early. Let's check the place out. It's your call, which way?"

Todd looked in both directions and pointed right. "The adventure says that way."

The direction they took led to the working end of town past an endless series of low buildings, work houses, depots, and finally, the heart of the town, the yards.

The tracks seemed to go on forever, row after row, into the distance. A quarter-mile to the west laid the diesel beds, where locomotives were parked, all sizes and shapes, representing nearly every railroad line in North America--all of them waiting for their next assignment. They were never shut off because it was cheaper to let them idle. Here was over a hundred thousand horsepower, pent up, generating a high energy, low frequency rumble that rattled buildings right down to the nails.

It was amazing that Buzz heard anything over the noise. He yelled, pulling Todd at the shoulder. Todd had a tough time keeping up with him. "C'mon, it's that way!"

When he got to a lane between two buildings, he held up his hand for them to stop. Then he motioned them forward, holding a finger to his lips for silence. Todd nodded, trusting Buzz's instincts. As they moved slowly into the alley, someone stepped out of the shadows and into the light, facing them from the other end. All they could see was a silhouette. It wasn't possible to see a face, but it was clear that whoever was there had turned to look at Todd and Buzz.

It had to be trick of light. The silhouette flickered briefly and vanished, like a piece of paper which had been folded and collapsed to fit in a pocket.

Buzz cautioned Todd. "We'd better have a look."

They walked into the alley to where they thought they'd seen the man standing, not sure what they would find. Todd saw it first, a pair of legs jammed behind a garbage bin.

"I think there's a phone booth back at the gate."

Buzz nodded. "I'll try and get the box off the guy. I'll be alright. The guy who did this isn't coming back."

Even at a run, it took Todd ten minutes to get back to the gate and find the phone. Back in the alley, at 600 pounds, there was no way Buzz could move the bin.

It was close to thirty minutes before they heard the sirens and another hour getting the bin off the man. The combined strength of six men couldn't move it. The yard master was hauled out of bed who got a company forklift to lift the bin and pull the man out.

The EMT's acted quickly when they discovered the man was still alive. A police officer took notes furiously as they prepared the victim for transport. The last thing the officer asked as they closed the doors was if the guy was going to make. One of the EMTs laughed. "You're kidding me?"

The officer was tired and didn't need any humor from a twenty-year-old with a box of band aids. Sorry, officer, what we've got is not so much a man as a sponge. No broken bones but he has been beaten to a pulp. There are multiple dislocations in all of his limbs and he has been subjected to positional asphyxiation for over an hour, judging from the color of his skin, from being jammed under that bin. His chances are pretty poor."

One of the forensics officers tapped him on the shoulder. "We're pretty much done here, Sir."

"What have you got?'

"To tell you the truth, not a hell of a lot that's going to do us any good. We found multiple fingerprints on the bin, which is going to tell us that the whole world has had its hands on it. No evidence was left at the scene. Not even a footprint."

The officer shook his head. "Damn, that is odd."

The investigator turned and walked back to the bin, which had been returned to its original position. He looked at the distance between the box and the wall again, and did a mental calculation." No, not really, it happens. But I will tell you what *is* odd. How much upper body strength does it take to lift a 180-pound body and jam it into a twelve-inch gap, head first up to its knees, without moving a fully loaded garbage bin?"

The Officer shook his head. "You're dreaming in Technicolor. That's not possible."

The investigator looked at Todd. "Did either of you get a good look at the guy?"

"No, the light was behind him, and we only saw a silhouette."

The officer picked up his bag and slung it over his shoulder. "I'm betting, with the light in here and where you were standing, that he didn't get a good look at you two either, which is probably a good thing."

The investigator closed his note book slowly. "We're going to need more information from the both of you tomorrow, 9:30 am, Detective Sergeant Clasp's office. Sorry, gentlemen, but you are going to be guests of Ash Flats for a while."

Todd and Buzz nodded silently.

The officer cautioned them. "By the way, Sergeant Clasp is not a morning person."

They were alone in the alley, again. Buzz jammed his hands in his pockets, "Perfectly normal town, perfectly normal people."

"Well, they were until we got here. Let's head back to the hotel. I don't know about you, but I could use some sleep."

Buzz couldn't argue with that as they walked out of the alley, "A rather exciting end to an otherwise ordinary day."

They had been back at the hotel for over an hour. Buzz was staring at the light in his bedroom as it danced to the sound of the music coming from the bar full of teenagers across the street. He got dressed and went next door. About to knock, he hesitated, doubting that Todd would even here him. He opened the door and stepped inside. Todd's bed, driven by the incredible force of the sound coming from across the street, stopped briefly to acknowledge his presence, before continuing its journey across the room. Its passenger, who was sound asleep with one arm hanging over the bed like a badly damaged curb feeler, coughed briefly as the bed went by.

Buzz took a deep breath and stuck his hands in his pockets. "Thirty-five years and I still don't know how he does that."

As Buzz opened the door to his room and watched his bed trying to get through the washroom door, he wondered aloud if they were ever going to stay in a hotel that didn't redecorate itself every night.

On the other side of town, Detective Sergeant Clasp did not have any loud music to keep him awake. He didn't need any, because he had something better. He had a toothache, the mother of all toothaches. His sister had nagged him for months to deal with it. He hated his sister because her constant haranguing gave him headaches, and now, he had a toothache and his sister. He blamed her for it out of sheer bloody-mindedness.

Aspirins and those drops you can get at the drugstore would dull the pain for maybe thirty minutes, and then it would be back with a vengeance. What fun! The only thing he hadn't tried was the dentist because Ash Flats only had one, and he was on holiday--a month in Belize, bone fishing.

"What the hell was a bone fish, anyway?" He wondered out loud and loud enough for a number of heads to appear from other offices.

Your 9:30 witnesses are here for that John Doe at the rail yard." A bolt of agony shot along Clasp's jaw and cruised up the side of his head.

"The Captain wants it wrapped up and on his desk by Friday."

The profanity trying to get out of his mouth set off another eruption of agony. How was he going to get through the day if he couldn't tell people to fuck off? "It's Wednesday already and he wants it done in two days? Ass hole!"

I guess a blow job is out of the question, huh?"

"Go screw yourself, Hewitt!" The cavity shrieked with joy and make his eyes water.

"Oh I do, Clasp, every night, and if you weren't such a cheap bastard, I'd let you watch."

He shook his head and set off the crater living in his mouth again. "Where the hell does a woman learn to talk like that anyway?"

Down the hall, Todd and Buzz had been waiting in Room 42, a small windowless, and not overly clean, closet. In the corner stood a fan with a bad bearing, which generated a quiet but incredibly irritating whine. When Clasp finally came in, he tried turning it off, but the switch was broken and it droned on. He reached down and yanked out the plug which resulted in an ear-splitting screech which lit up Clasp's jaw like a Christmas tree. He kicked the fan over and then stomped on it. Todd thought this was some new type of interrogation technique. Buzz thought the man was nuts.

Clasp finally sat down across the table from them and quickly ran through the police report and the dossier completed by the night shift. "You guys can smoke if you want."

"Neither of us smokes."

A toothache and now he was stuck with assholes that didn't smoke. He got up, went to the door, and yanked it open, "Smokes!"

A voice could be heard at the end of the hall. "You're a freaking mooch, Clasp! This is the last time. Buy your own cigarettes, you cheap bastard!"

Clasp closed the door and walked back to the table. Reaching into his pocket, he retrieved an ashtray and two cigarettes. He tapped the end of one cigarette on the table, determined to get at least one pleasure out of the day. He reached into another pocket and got out a Zippo lighter, one of those really neat ones with a lid that had a really cool clank when you opened it.   He slowly lit the cigarette and blew out a plume of smoke, which momentarily obscured the "No Smoking" sign on the wall next to the clock. Clasp suddenly coughed violently, ejecting smoke and a dental lozenge to help kill the pain. It hit the table and skidded off a corner, ending up behind the radiator under the clock and the "No Smoking" sign. He yanked the cigarette of his mouth. "Menthol, that rotten fart gave me menthol! That's like kissing your sister. That is low!"

Clasp stuck the cigarette back in his mouth and looked at Buzz. "Let's get down to business, Gentlemen. It says here that you're from Connecticut. I got that right, and you, New Jersey?" Todd nodded in the affirmative without saying anything.

Clasp skimmed through Todd's file, picking out the words from the music and then stopped suddenly at the second last page. He opened Buzz's dossier to the same page. Someone on the night shift was jerking his chain--probably Sheller.

He looked over his glasses and pushed one of the files across the table for them to look at. "Those numbers can't be right? Please tell me that the people on the night shift are yanking my weed whacker"

Todd pushed the files back to Clasp. "They're a bit on the low side."

Clasp leaned back in his chair and took a long pull on what was left of the cigarette. "What are you guys doing in a town like this, at night, on the wrong side of the tracks, in the middle of an assault investigation which could end up being murder?"

Todd shrugged. "We came in late yesterday afternoon. We're just passing through and decided to stop for the evening. We'd been on the road for most of the day and thought it would be a good idea to get some exercise."

"Where are you headed?"

Buzz told him they were headed west.

"West, what part of west?"

"We don't have a specific destination."

Clasp redirected the interview back to the assault. "Says here you heard a noise and ran to find out what it was. Is that right?"

They both agreed that it was correct.

The report doesn't say what kind of sound it was." Help me out on that."

"It was a crushing sound, like someone stepping on Styrofoam or plastic."

"According to your statement, you both ran for about two minutes, which puts you about 100 yards from the garbage bin."

Buzz said that his math was about right.

"I've been down to that diesel bed more times than I can count. You can barely hear yourself think with the noise those machines make, yet you managed to hear someone walking on plastic from 100 yards."

Clasp flipped back four pages. "No description, no height, weight, no distinguishing marks, and you go on to say that the suspect came out from behind the bin and turned toward you before you lost sight of him in the background light, but you managed to hear him from the length of a football field away over the sound of all that machinery. C'mon guys, you're killing me here!"

Todd raised his hands in a gesture of futility.

"Okay, do you think he got past you?"

"No way, he couldn't have done that."

Clasp looked up at the clock--11:30 a.m., two hours, and two crumby smokes with nothing to show for it. "All right, that will be it for now."

As they stood up to leave, Buzz wanted to know if he considered them suspects.

Clasp looked out the door and then back in at them. "Off the record, no, you two just don't fit the profile. But, until this investigation gives me more info, you two are at the top of the list. Make yourselves comfortable, gentlemen, and welcome to Ash Flats."

"Do you mind if we talk to the victim?"

"What the hell for?"

"Maybe we can help and we do have an interest in how this turns out."

"Not going to happen. Do you guys want to be charged with interfering with an investigation, on top of everything else?"

"C'mon, Clasp. Cut us some slack here. We're trying to help this guy!"

Clasp rubbed his eyes because he knew they would just go ahead and do it anyway. "Okay, tell you what I'll do. Lawyer up and I'll send a uniform over to the hospital. The four of you can talk to him if he wakes up. But I'm warning you, if you get out of the zone, you two will be back here looking for bail, fair enough?"

Todd smiled broadly. "Works for us."

Stop smiling. "I hate happy people."

Clasp yanked open the door and screamed. "Okay, you bunch of rotten butt bandits. I am coming out, and I'm going to shove those menthol's up someone's driveway!"

The desk Sergeant called out to Todd and Buzz as they stepped out of the elevator. "Are you the guys who need a lawyer?" Clasp called down and said you needed council."

"Yeah, it looks like we will."

The Sergeant pointed to a bench up against the far wall. "Over there."

"Where?"

"There, over there, sitting on the bench."

Todd followed the direction of his arm to a woman in a business suit sitting with a teenager. They were in the middle of an animated discussion over a piece of paper. It looked like someone's report card was on the wrong side of the bell curve. The Sergeant gestured to them to follow him over to the bench.

The woman, well dressed and in her mid-forties, stood up as they approached. "May I help you?"

Buzz indicated to the two of them as he spoke. "We're going to need legal counsel."

"Sorry, I can't help you."

"You haven't got time for another case?"

"No. I've got plenty of time. I'm just not a lawyer.

She turned, grabbed the paper out of the teenagers hand and walked away. "A million fourteen-year-olds in the county and I find the only one who won't fix a parking ticket!"

A blank face stared up at them from under a ball cap and glasses which were too big for her. A wad of gum moved slowly from one side of her mouth to the other. The legs, which finished an inch short of the floor, swung slowly. The T-Shirt proclaimed that marijuana was, indeed, one of the four basic food groups. "What's up?

Buzz peered over his sunglasses. "You're a lawyer?"

"You bet. Harvard Law, graduated when I was eleven. My dad is a school bus driver. He calls me his little prodigy."

"What about your mom? Buzz asked.

"She drives a truck for the rendering plant."

"What does she call you?"

"My insufferable little smart ass."

Buzz and the girl looked at each other really carefully. "You want a lawyer or not?"

"One o'clock at the hospital. We want to talk to the guy who was beaten up at the rail yard yesterday."

"Oh, yeah, I heard about that. You're the guys who say you found him. Nasty! You shouldn't be talking to him, because you are of interest."

"Clasp has okayed it."

The baseball cap nodded. "They'll want a uniform there so you'll want to be real careful with what's said and heard. Okay. I'll help you out. Hopkins! I'll need a pair of boots at the hospital at one o'clock for that John Doe."

The duty sergeant looked up from his desk and gave her a stern look. "You're mom called. You've got a dental appointment at half past one, remember? You might be a lawyer but you're still a fourteen-year-old young lady.

"Oh, right. I'm getting my braces changed from metal to plastic because my hardware keeps setting off metal detectors at the court house. Better make it for three o'clock."

The baseball cap was delivered to the hospital at half past two by her mother, a woman who would have been a lot happier if her daughter had a paper route.

"Relax, mom, this shouldn't take more than an hour. Todd and Buzz, I would like you to meet my mom, Birch."

"It's Bernice Gardner, call me Birch. You two don't look like the type who beat people up in an alley for chuckles."

Todd laughed at the image. "No, we're not. It just looks like we were in the wrong place at the wrong time."

More like wrong place, right time. If you two hadn't shown up when you did, the guy would be riding the dirt bus."

Birch looked hard at the ceiling for a moment and then took a deep breath. "Why can't you be like other girls, complaining about you allowance, tying the phone up for hours talking to your friends about boys, and spending every last dollar your father makes on clothes."

"I *do* all of that stuff, mom. I'm a girl, it's my job description, except for the clothes, which I don't do all that well. Funny, dad doesn't complain about it, though. I moonlight as a lawyer because I am saving up to buy a car. Sorry, I could have phrased that last part a little better."

"Have you guys considered adoption?"

Buzz shook his head. "Thanks, but we've got or had families of our own."

Birch responded with a perfect dead pan expression. "Not her, me."

"Mom, can I . . . ."

"No, you aunts will be picking you up at four o'clock and you're going to the Piggly Wiggly with that list I gave you, or we will be eating charcoal for dinner."

She handed them a piece of paper and looked at her watch. "Here's our address. Please join us for dinner; better make it before six because my husband is the worst cook on the planet. And you'd better get a move on, young lady. These men are depending on you. You maybe fourteen, but you are still a lawyer."

"Ok mom, let's go talk to the Vic. Cool, huh?"

"You learn to talk like that at Harvard? Todd wanted to know.

"Nope, Matlock reruns."

Birch searched frantically in her purse and pulled out a bottle of aspirins.

Buzz pointed at the bottle. "Do you mind?"

She shook another two out and handed one to Todd and Buzz. "See, I'll even have one with you."

The hospital room was so small there was barely enough room for the bed, much less the visitors. It looked like a scene from Dr. Kildare-old, seriously old. In the middle of the room was a brass bed painted white with side rail. It groaned softly as the occupant moved under the sheets.

The police officer, a man with a drinker's nose and a ruddy lined face, stood at the end of the bed looking intently at the injured man's chart. "So, Herr Doctor, is z patient going to live, hmm?"

He dropped the chart. "Damn, I wish you'd stop sneaking up on people like that. You're scary enough as it is. By the way, how did it go at the dentist, sweetheart?"

She grinned. "Four teeth short of store boughts!"

The officer laughed and gave her a big long hug.

She whispered in his ear. "I'm sorry about Momma Dudley. Parents wouldn't let me come to the funeral."

He stepped back and nodded. "I'm okay."

Todd and Buzz moved over to the bed to give them more time to talk. Buzz pointed to the top and back of the man's head.

"The man is balding."

Buzz shook his head "Not bald,...pulled out."

A look of genuine confusion crossed Todd's face. "Why would someone pull hair out like that?"

"Look at the spot where the hair is missing and then look at the legs and feet. The suspect wasn't after the hair. He used it to drag the man."

The man in the bed suddenly spoke in a slow voice without opening his eyes. For a small man, his voice was surprisingly deep and husky. "I remember that."

"These are the guys who saved your life."

Dudley gently criticized her. "Let the man tell his story, councilor."

She smiled and acknowledged that she knew good advice when she was handed it.

` They listened quietly as Benny Callistor told his story, struggling to get his voice past his damaged ribs. He was close to exhaustion after forty minutes and they still hadn't asked him a single question.

"Did you see anything?"

Callistor shook his head, which caused a large bruise above his left eye to throb. "He hit me with a set of brass knuckles."

Todd wondered if he was sure, which got him a look of disgust from Callistor. "Ask your friend here. He knows how to take care of himself, and what it's like to be hit with one of those things."

Buzz nodded, "I've had personal experience."

The last twenty minutes were pretty much a waste of time. Except for a brief description of being dragged across the tracks, Callistor was mostly unconscious. He had no idea what his attacker looked like, except that he was very strong. After that, he refused to talk and told everyone to get out.

Out in the hall, it was obvious to all that Benny Callistor was as big a mystery as the man who attacked him. Any questions about his life, family, friends, or how he found himself in Ash Flats, were answered with silence.

"How about it, Dudley?"

Dudley lifted his cap and gave his scalp a hard scratch. "This wasn't a problem for the investigation and these fellas didn't get out of line.

"Good, at least now we've got a name to work with. How soon can you get back to me with a report?"

"Cut me some slack, councilor. We can't even make a charge until we get enough evidence to make it stick to someone."

"Dudley, be careful. I represent these men. Don't hand me a mistrial."

He laughed. "Sorry, Gentlemen, she's right. That's not how we do business in Ash Flats. You are going to be here for a while, but the good news is that you have an excellent lawyer."

She smirked. "They haven't paid me yet, and they are coming to dinner."

"Is your dad barbecuing?"

Dudley grinned as he walked away." Gentlemen, you had better hope that your doctor is as good as your lawyer."

Todd tapped her on the shoulder. "Your aunts should be picking you up about now."

She looked at her watch. "Yeah, I had better get going."

Buzz reached out and tapped the crystal. "Impressive. Where did you get it?"

"When we are on family vacation in Texas, my Dad was bugging me to get a watch because I was always late for stuff. My mom loves antique stores and was always dragging dad along. We went into this one place, really huge, with a big case full of watches. So, I had a look. This guy comes out of the back and shows me some watches, but they're all for girls which look really stupid and so small you could barely see the hands. I told him I wanted something different. He said he had some really cool stuff in the back. I had to have dad come with me. What he had was really awesome. Dad freaked when I told him I wanted this one. The guy wanted $9000 for it. Well, dad and this guy had this chat, real quiet like, and when Dad came out, he had the watch. He paid for it out of my trust fund and made me swear never to tell mom what it cost and to look after the watch. No problem on both counts."

They could hear a horn through an open window. "The aunts are at the castle door! I love them but they are, without question, two of the most desperate, love starved, hard up, and over the hill spinsters that ever walked a hotel lobby!"

They were indeed at the front door of the hospital, at the emergency entrance to be exact. The two women were in a heated argument with a nurse and doctor about the fact that their flaming pink Ferrari was preventing an ambulance from completing its appointed rounds. They were having none of that sick people come first nonsense. "If sick people needed to get into the hospital, they could come in the front door like everyone else."

They stopped short of the door and watched the scene going on outside in the driveway. "I don't have to go out there. I have money. I can take a bus home."

Todd shook his head. "No, your mom wanted them to take you to get groceries. Besides, they don't look so bad."

"You're thirty feet away looking at them through a window. They don't do up close and personal well. She took a deep breath and walked through the door.

"Macy! Where have you been young lady?"

"Working, Aunt Bailey. Sorry to keep you waiting."

The other woman slid behind the wheel. "We had better get moving. Your father is cooking tonight and you know how much we enjoy that."

Macy pointed to the two men who were standing back from them at a respectful distance. "Todd and Buzz, I would like you to meet my aunts Bailey and Bridgette."

Bailey stepped in front of Macy, all smiles, and offered her hand to the both of them. "Gentlemen, it's an absolute pleasure to meet the both of you."

Macy was trying to get out from behind her aunt. "They're my clients and mom has invited them to come for dinner."

"Splendid!"

Macy finally managed to get in front of her aunt and spoke to her in quiet voice. "We're late and you are drooling on the pavement."

"For God's sake, Macy, who taught you to talk like that?"

"Harvard."

Bailey stalked off to join her sister in the car. "Your mother should have listened to us and sent you to Bryn Mawr, or Haverford."

Buzz noted wryly. "They seem nice."

"They have more money than they could burn in a lifetime and can still spend a night in a cougar bar and not get a date with a hundred dollar bill."

Macy turned back to Todd and Buzz. "You won't have any trouble finding my parent's place. Just look for the mushroom cloud of black smoke. On a clear day, you can see it for miles."

They watched and waved as Macy climbed up the back of the car and jumped into the space between her aunts. Macy, you are standing on my purse. It cost me $2800 dollars!"

Buzz looked over at the address in Todd's hand. You know, we could be back in Peckersnot by tomorrow morning."

"Don't tempt me Buzz, please don't tempt me. Besides, it's not all bad."

"How do you figure that?"

Well, at least we now know the name of our lawyer. By the way, what was that business about her watch all about?"

"It's an Omega Speedmaster."

"That's a good watch, but I don't think even a new one is worth what her dad paid for it."

"It's only had one previous owner and believe me, Todd, she got a bargain."

"Serious?"

"Oh, yeah!"

An hour later, Buzz eased the car to the curb on a quiet suburban street in a middle class neighborhood. Todd looked at the sheet of paper with the address on it and then at the house. "That looks like the place, all right."

"How big do you think that place is?"

"You mean in square feet?"

"Yeah."

"Well, I'd guess about 1200 square feet and maybe three bedrooms."

"My place in Connecticut is 6200 square feet and six bedrooms."

"Where're you going with this, Buzz?"

"My place never looked, or felt, that good."

"Macy said her dad drove a truck. I think she drives a bus."

"Buzz got out of the car and reached behind the seat and pulled out a bag. Money can't buy happiness."

Todd looked at the rapid darkening cloud coming from the backyard. "It won't get you a decent barbecue, either." When they got back there several of the guests and a few of the neighbors were trying to put out a grease fire.

Birch looked over the top of the barbecue and told Macy to get the fire extinguisher, the big one. She stopped to talk to Todd and Buzz. "I'm glad you could come. Dad's inside changing his shirt, he's looking forward to meeting you."

Todd pointed at the barbecue. "If you don't mind, I'd like mine rare."

"The pizzeria can deliver uncooked."

Buzz rolled his eyes in disgust at Todd. "Where did you get your manners, anyway?"

Todd grinned back, "Sent away."

Buzz handed a bag to Birch who had finally put out the fire. "We couldn't find a human sacrifice so we went to the butcher shop."

Macy poked the bag. "Don't worry. My dad offers up a limb every time he lights up that thing."

Birch opened the bag. "We weren't sure how much to bring."

She looked up in amazement. "There has to be $200 worth of meat in here."

Macy was sarcastic. "That won't even be enough to cover my retainer!"

Bernice looked at Macy and pointed to the back door. "You get in there and find a shirt that your father can wear and make sure it has two sleeves and no burn holes!"

Macy stuck out her tongue at her mother as she walked to the door.

"I saw that young lady!' And just for that, your aunts will be here in an hour, and you will be wearing a skirt tonight."

"That's not fair, those things suck!"

"It's better than having to listen to them giving me a hard time about letting you wear pants!"

She turned back to Todd and Buzz. "Did you guys bring any aspirins? I'm out."

A man in a blackened barbecue apron and soot on his face stepped forward with an out-stretched hand, "Gentlemen, this is my husband, Glen."

"It's a real pleasure that you could come for dinner, but it might take a while though. I think there is something wrong with the gas manifold on the barbecue."

Todd walked over to the open barbecue and poked a blackened unidentifiable lump, which was securely welded to the grill, with a spatula. "Yep, you definitely got a bad burner happening there, Glen."

Everyone nodded. "Sure, Glen, that must be the problem."

Birch put a hand on his arm. "Glen, these are the guys with the car you've heard so much about."

His face lit up. "You mind if I have a look at it?"

Someone stepped forward and took the bag from Bernice. The man had the hands of a cook, a good one. He looked at Glen but spoke to Birch, who nodded in agreement. "I'm sure these fellas would be pleased to show you their ride. We'll try and get the barbecue fixed and get dinner started while you're gone."

Glen turned to the man. "You don't mind taking over for a couple of minutes, Don?"

"No problem Glen, take as long as you want. We'll be fine."

Buzz motioned to the drive way. "C'mon Glen, let's go have a look at it."

"Can I sit in it, Buzz?"

Buzz laughed. "Yeah, I think we can set that up for you."

Birch reached behind her husband and undid his favorite barbecue apron. "Maybe you can leave this for Don to use."

When Glen was out of sight, she handed the apron to Don with two fingers. "You can use it to start the barbecue. You won't even need matches. Just put it in there and I guarantee it will spontaneously combust within a minute."

In the thirty minutes they were gone, Don and Birch had turned the steaks into a really respectable dinner.

"Honey, you should see the car these guys are driving!"

She put an arm around his shoulder. "Shut up and eat, Glen."

"So how long are you guys going to be staying? Glen was asking Todd, but was clearly being coerced by the gestures of his sisters-in-law.

"Dad! You shouldn't be asking questions like that. It could affect the investigation."

Birch rolled her eyes. "Listen to my daughter, the lawyer."

Macy smiled. "I finally got the last word. If the investigation goes our way and if it doesn't hit any big issues, it should be wrapped up in about three weeks."

"Yes!"

Everyone turned and looked at Macy's aunts. "What?"

"What do you think, Buzz? Three weeks in Ash Flats."

He looked around the backyard, at the faces of the kind of people he hadn't known in thirty years-- people like Jessie and Ken.

"How about it Buzz?"

"This will do just fine, Todd."

"Glen, Birch. We've just had the Buzz Murdoch Good Housekeeping Seal of Approval."

"Yes! What?"

Around ten o'clock they said goodnight and headed back to the hotel. "So what are we going to do around here for three weeks, while they attempt to hang a charge of premeditated murder on us?" Todd wanted to know.

"Relax, you know we're innocent and, besides, we've got the best lawyer in town."

"No, what we have is the only lawyer in town and if court runs past eight o'clock, we'll have to get permission for counsel to stay up past bedtime. Seriously, what happens if they decide to hold us over for trial?"

"You're really bothered by this?"

"If you recall, one town tried to hang us without a trial. It won't be the first time a miscarriage of justice has happened in this country."

"Todd, you've got to have a little faith. These are good people. Besides, they'll catch this guy.

"You're awfully sure for a guy that almost got himself shot for making fun of some guy's wife."

"Of course I am, because we are on the case. If they do charge us, I've got a great back up plan!"

"Todd burst out laughing, really?"

"Really."

"Don't keep me in suspense."

Buzz put both of his hands out like he was pretending to be evading police in a really slow car. "We are going to flee like rats."

"'Swell,...we're boned!"

"They'll never catch us."

"How do you figure that?'

"This place only has one police car.

"It only takes one car to catch us."

"We'll flatten the tires before we make a run for it."

"What about the radio? Bet you didn't think of that, did you?"

"We'll break off the antennae."

Todd suddenly looked at Buzz's face carefully. "You brought some Griz water with you and you've been drinking it in the bathroom."

Buzz smirked evilly "There's only five bottles left in the trunk."

"You can't transport hazardous waste across state lines without permits. Let's toss it in the dump."

Buzz shot him a look of disgust. "Shame on you for wanting to throw away such a rare and fine libation."

"Fine libation? The stuff will burn a hole in your shirt. We can't even pour it down a sewer. It'd start a fire and I don't want an entire town on my conscience."

"So, what are we going to do in this place for the next three weeks?"

"Well, I'm thinking, that we should try getting jobs, Buzz"

"I agree with you on that. There's also something else we need to do, find out what Benny Callistor's story is."

"You think?"

Buzz pushed himself away from the dresser he was leaning on. "I'm going to call it a night. See you in the morning."

"How about we try the place next to the Train Wreck for breakfast?"

"See you in the morning. Actually, you go ahead I'll meet you there for 8:30."

"You need the car."

"Yeah, might be a good idea."

Todd tossed him the keys. "Have a good night."

It was exactly 8:30 a.m. Todd looked at his watch as the car pulled to the curb. Buzz Murdoch was the most punctual man on the planet. Todd wondered briefly how someone could be so indifferent to time, and yet, be so good at managing it.

"I thought it might be a good idea to see the scene of the crime in daylight. Our associate is playing very close to the vest."

Todd asked quietly. "Sounds like you have a theory."

"Several of them, none very good, I'm afraid. But I can give you a few solid facts. The first is that this guy is tough and road wise. He's been riding rail for decades without a scratch."

"Okay, so far, so good."

"He got off at Ash Flats for a reason."

"How do you figure that? These guys are like tumbleweeds. They go where the wind takes them."

"I agree, but here's the thing. The train he was on was in the center of the yard on a main line. It was a run-through."

"Maybe he was going to pick up a ride in a different direction."

"That's possible. But he had his back to the tracks and was headed for town when he was hit. If you want a ride, you go to the back of the yard and face the rails; you're looking for trains, not people. He got out of the car and joined Todd on the sidewalk.

"Mister Callistor has decided to join us on our journey. Maybe we should get to know him a little better before we invite him into the car."

They took their time having breakfast before getting back onto the street. "That was a pretty good breakfast."

"That's because we are slowly getting our sense of taste back."

Buzz looked down at Todd's belt, which was running out of notches. "You know, if you got a better dry cleaner, your pants wouldn't be shrinking like that."

"Very funny, you know, your sense of humor has become very droll over the years."

"You like it?"

Todd grinned, "No. I liked you better when you were young, rude, and obnoxious."

Buzz was briefly distracted by an old man with a cane, who was staring at them intently from across the street.

Todd tapped Buzz on the shoulder to get his attention and pointed to a phone booth. "C'mon. I've got an idea."

Stepping inside the booth, he stared at the phone for a full minute, and then stepped out.

"What's the matter, what were you doing in there?"

"You got any change, Buzz?"

"No, I bought breakfast.

"Oh right, thanks, by the way, I'm still going to need some coins for the phone."

Buzz looked over his shoulder into the booth. "You don't need any change. It's electronic.

Just lift the receiver, put your phone card in, and dial the number."

Todd just stood there with a blank look on his face.

"Okay, if you don't have the card, you remember the number. Just give it to the operator verbally."

The blank stare refused to leave Todd's face

"Are you kidding me? Please tell me you're just having fun at my expense."

Todd stood there like some demented Cheshire cat.

"I can't be seeing this. You run one of the biggest digital systems companies on the planet. You guys probably designed this system and you're telling me you don't even have a phone card! How do you explain that?"

Todd was laughing so hard he could barely talk. "Hey, I just make the system. I don't know how it works."

Buzz shook his head slowly." You know, you really scare me when you stop using your brain like that!"

"You have a point there. Seriously, maybe we should have our facts straight before I make this call. Let's go back to the diner and write everything down that we have, including police report, name, and hospital. While we're there, I'll get some change."

Two coffees later, they were back at the phone booth. Todd handed Buzz a piece of paper. Buzz turned to Todd, the phone half way to his ear. "That won't work. It's half a number and a # sign. You sure you've got that right?"

Todd shrugged. "I've never had to use it before. Anyway, what's the worst that can happen?"

Buzz inserted the change and waited for the dial tone. He keyed in the numbers and symbol in the order on the paper. Predictably, the system responded that the number was incorrect, and would he please hang up and try the call again. On the second repetition halfway between the words, "Please hang up", the phone went dead, no dial tone. Even the electronic display had stopped working.

Buzz slowly lowered the phone from his ear. "That's odd."

In a darkened room several thousand miles away, someone watched a number scroll across a computer screen. "You had better have a look at this."

Someone stepped out of the shadows and looked over the woman's shoulder. Steady eyes and a quick sure mind assessed the data and made a decision. He placed a hand on the shoulder of the woman at the computer screen, leaned forward, and picked up a phone on the computer consul. The voice was very Scottish and carried a great deal of authority, "Doctor?"

At Todd's request, Buzz returned the phone to his ear to confirm the phone was still dead. "Mr. Murdoch, I trust that you're well?"

Hearing his name caught Buzz off guard for at least ten seconds. The voice on the other end of the phone was apparently very patient.

`Buzz exchanged pleasantries with a voice that was cool, detached, and pleasant--all at the same time. He was definitely speaking to a woman, but Buzz wasn't entirely sure if he was talking to a human being or a machine. "May I speak to Mr. Stiles please?

Buzz stepped out of the booth. He looked down at his shirt which, despite the fact the temperature was in the mid 60's, was soaked with sweat.

Todd had his turn in the booth for a good twenty minutes. When he stepped out, his shirt was as bad as Buzz's. "At least, it's not just me."

"How did it go?"

"There's a computer at the library we can use. Everything we need will be on the hard drive by the time we get there. By the way, I could use a drink."

"I'm going to regret asking this question. Who was that, exactly?"

Todd put his hands in his jacket and thought for a moment. "Do you know a Ken and Jessie McCullough?"

Buzz nodded slowly. "Yes, I do."

"She promised to look in on them and let them know you're all right."

"You can't help but get the feeling that we're being watched, Todd"

Looking up the street at the library, Todd reflected. "No, I don't think so, but someone has been paying attention to us, that's for sure."

They walked the rest of the way to the Train Wreck in silence, understanding that there were some things that were better left unsaid.

The phone at the computer in that darkened room rang quietly. The Scottish accent answered. "Yes Doctor, we will make inquiries, of course, we will send someone out to Wyoming. We will make the arrangements immediately for our people to spend some time with the McCullough's to see that they, and their grandson, are comfortable."

The man listened intently as he was given a set of instructions, and then hung up the phone. He tapped the shoulder of the woman at the computer and gave her an order. "Pack your bags."

Phil Geter's bar felt safe to Buzz and Todd. No probing eyes, electronic eaves dropping, just a couple of comfortable bar stools. "Coffee! What the hell is wrong with you two, anyway?"

"We're working, Phil. We have to be at the library in thirty minutes.

"If you ask me, and no one has, that sounds pretty damn lame."

"Don't take it personally. We've got some information waiting for us at the library and we should at least show up sober."

Phil nodded. "That sounds fair enough. Maybe we can help each other out here. You guys do your thing at the book barn and have dinner. Be back here around seven. Word has it that you two are looking for short term work. We'll get you set up."

"Sounds great, Phil. What can we do for you?"

"Somebody dissed the harpies and I need somebody to run interference"

"Was it an ex-husband?"

"Nope."

"How about an ex-boyfriend?"

"Still nope."

"That pretty much leaves the milkman, Phil."

"'We're talking the paperboy!"

"Now, that is desperation."

He shook his head, "Oh yeah,...big time! Every skirt in town has been after this kid."

"He can't be more than thirteen!"

"Let's just say he's a legend before his time."

"It gets better. A buddy of mine works for the power company. He was reading one of the Harpies meter. She took a run at him and he told her to try the guy who delivers *The New York Times*. He only checked meters and he didn't get paid enough for inspecting indoor wiring. He also told her he was gay. She screamed back that she knew he wasn't."

"What did he say?"

"I am, now!"

"That's going to be some bar tab."

"Yeah, and you're going to need the house Spaulding."

Phil coughed. "Trust me; they are all bark and dentures. By the way, have you guys ever been to Toot's Shores?"

"Yeah, we both have."

"Good. Don't bring your keys or your livers tonight. If you're not drunk by eleven o'clock, you aren't trying hard enough."

When they were back on the street, Todd made an observation. "Is it just me or has the world gotten a whole lot weirder?"

Buzz looked up at the sky. It was blue. "No, it's not just you.

"You've been doing that a lot lately. What's up there, anyway?"

"Normal." Neither of them said anything as they completed the walk to the library.

It was definitely old school--wooden tables, worn carpet, and rows of cabinets with yellowed index cards. The only acknowledgement to the electronic age was a single computer, an IBM 486, which by computer standards was ancient, on the table next to the stairwell, leading to the reference section on the second floor. The sign, hand- written, and taped over the screen, said "Out of order."

Buzz ran a hand over the top of the computer. "It probably drowned in dust."

Todd pointed to the note. "But you've got to admit, that's pretty nice penmanship."

There were loud voices coming from the second floor, followed by footsteps on the stairs. A woman appeared and she clearly looked like a librarian and she was clearly on a mission to get away from the owner of the other voice, even if it meant sliding down the banister to do it. She looked at Buzz and Todd. What can I do for you two?"

"We're here to use the computer, but it's not working."

"I know, someone poured a cup of black coffee into it."

"That's pretty harsh. Somebody needs anger management."

"You're right! I've been trying to get into a course for over a year."

"Is there another one in the building we can use?"

Everyone flinched as another round of profanity erupted from the second floor. "You can ask the director. She'll be able to help you out. Oh! But I see that you don't have a whip and chair,... rotten old cow!"

Buzz looked up the stairs. "The last time we did this, we found two despicable little trolls. What do think it'll be this time?"

Todd grinned, "A short librarian with a sharpened library card."

"Where'd you get that sense of humor anyway?"

"Sent away."

A woman came out of the director's office, and she looked like a library director, dressed like a library director, but didn't talk like a library director. "What do you two wood whackers want?"

"We're looking for the library director."

"That would be me, Violet Shambles. Now that we've dispensed with the pleasantries and small talk, I'm busy. Fuck off!"

Todd made another attempt at being nice to her. "We just need to use a computer."

"You just can't stop using up my oxygen, can you?"

"Ten minutes, that's all we ask."

"The only computer in this place that is working is in my office. I'm going down the hall to get a baseball bat, come back here and beat it to death, because it isn't working."

"You said it was working."

"You're right. I lied. I'm half way through menopause. If I kill something, it makes me feel better."

"Give us a break here--twenty minutes!"

"You said ten."

"I lied."

"You did that with a straight face. I like that."

"Thanks. We promise not to look at anything important."

She looked over her glasses at Buzz. "Is he brain damaged? This is a library, for fuck sake! What kind of secrets does he think we have here? Twenty minutes, and then I'm taking it out to the ballgame. You don't want to keep my hormones waiting, boys!"

She pushed passed them and marched down the hall "Fucking wood whackers!"

They looked at each other. "She looks serious, we'd better hurry."

Her office was pretty much what they expected a librarian's office to look like. The walls were lined with books and every available surface was covered in papers and journals. On the desk was a surprisingly new computer.

Todd sat down and began to fumble around with the machine. Buzz was amazed. "What's the problem? Don't tell me you don't know how to use one of these things?"

"I haven't got a clue."

"I can't believe this! You have a degree in electrical engineering. You run a company that makes these things. How could you not know how to use a computer?"

"I'm a hardware guy, Buzz. It's called Auto Cad. I can design fifty different circuits with individual tasks, but wouldn't have a clue what they do when they are put together."

"Isn't that kind of dangerous?"

Todd agreed. "Is it ever! And unfortunately, we have seen far too many examples of it in the last fifty years. Now, that is definitely new."

"What's the problem?"

"It says enter your identifier number. That's odd."

"Odd?"

Todd took out of his pocket a piece of paper which had the number they used in the phone booth. He glanced over it briefly and then typed it. He put his finger over the enter key, stopped, moved it off the keyboard, and leaned back in the chair.

"What's wrong?"

Todd responded without taking his eyes off the screen. "This is in plain language."

"I'm not following you."

"Because space and speed are an issue computer statements are always written in short language, what they call *technish*, there has to be a human being at the other end of the wire coming out of the back of this thing."

"What if it's a computer?"

"If it is, its way beyond anything my company could produce and the R&D guys we have are right out on the edge."

Buzz reached across Todd and tapped the enter key. "Let's see if that edge has moved while we've been away."

For fifteen seconds, the screen lit up with a display of technical data that pushed it to its operating limits, went dark briefly, and then followed with three verification questions that scrawled across the screen at a surprisingly slow rate.

Todd entered the answers and hit return. The computer responded to check the printer and sent a request to the both of them to keep in touch. They could hear a printer running in the next room. "I'll get it, Buzz."

The hair on the back of Buzz's neck was standing up straight as he looked at the lines of text on the screen. If Todd had that kind of conversation in a room full of people, it would make perfect sense. But what had taken place here was between two computers, which were thousands of miles apart, with zero time-lag.

"Buzz, you okay?" Todd had returned with a stack of papers, fifty pages in all.

He looked up from the screen. "Yeah, sure,...fine."

Buzz took one last look at the computer as he pulled the door shut behind them. No one was in the room to see the computer reboot itself to the settings established by the library director.

The walk back to the diner was slower than the walk there. Both men kept their thoughts to themselves. As they settled into a booth, the waitress glanced briefly at the papers on the table. They both ordered coffee and waited in silence, until she came back with their orders, before they began looking at the papers they obtained from the library.

"So, what do you think?"

Todd shrugged. "I don't think there are any surprises here. Still, it's fifty pages. It will be a lot of reading."

Buzz riffled through the papers. "Who are these people?"

Todd picked up a couple of sheets and glanced over them. He shook his head in amazement. "'That's pretty tough to answer."

"I'm all ears."

Todd leaned back and rubbed his eyes. "I think this stuff comes from a company that designs and builds computers."

"That's not a big deal. That's what you do."

"We do some pretty interesting work, but we just run a factory. Ninety-nine percent of the stuff we produce you can buy at any electronics store. These guys are different. They build custom made machines, really advanced, leading-edge hardware and software. They contacted us to work on a NASA project with them. That was the first time we'd ever heard of them."

Todd pushed the papers across the table to Buzz. "Making computers isn't the only thing they are good at. There was a rumor making the rounds in the system industry that they'd built a super computer."

"There's nothing special about that either. Everybody's doing it these days."

"Ever hear of HAL 9000?"

Buzz had to think for a moment. "You mean from the movie?"

Todd confirmed. "Yeah, nice voice, fish eye lens."

"They named a computer after something in a movie."

Todd corrected Buzz's conclusion. "No, they built a computer after something in a movie."

"That's not possible. That thing spoke and behaved like it was thinking.

Buzz suddenly remembered the text on the librarian's computer screen. "I think it's time we had a chat with our friend, Mr. Callistor."

"I agree. My coffee's cold anyway."

Buzz got up and tossed five dollars on the table. "So am I."

Macy was waiting for them in front of the hospital. When they handed her the papers, her eyes got progressively wider as she looked at the information. "Where did you get this stuff?"

Buzz smiled, "Not bad, huh?"

"This makes the police version look like the work of a seven-year-old with crayons."

Buzz's smile turned into a big fat grin.

Macy was serious. "This isn't funny. You guys are in a lot of trouble. They're really close to laying charges and you two come up with this. They are going to want to know how and where you got it. And now that you have given it to your lawyer, I'm legally obligated to tell them. There is also that unpleasant business about withholding evidence."

"So, when do we talk to Callistor?" Buzz wanted to know.

She raised her hands in resignation and looked at Buzz. "Okay, I'll set it up for this afternoon and arrange for the police, the DA, and a court reporter to be there. Do you have any more of these?

"No, that's the only copy and it's all there."

Macy waved the sheets. "You know, the law is not a drive by profession. You actually have to practice it the way it's taught."

"You know, Macy, you sound just like your mom when you're like that."

As she stalked off to make arrangements with the hospital, she yelled back at them. "That wasn't nice!"

Callistor looked around at the growing group of people occupying his space. He decided that he hated crowds just as much as he hated hospitals. "Why don't you people get out of here so I can get dressed and be on my way? Where are my damned clothes?"

The doctor at the back of the room had to push his way to the foot of the bed. "Sir, you're not going anywhere. You have torn ligaments in both knees and your hips have been dislocated."

"You can't keep me here. No law says you can!"

"You're right. But you need to walk to get out of here and you won't be able to put weight on your legs, much less walk, for at least six weeks, in a month with luck, so you are going to be my guest until you can."

Macy took the papers out of her briefcase and handed them to Bennie. "I would like you to review this information."

He leafed through the papers briefly, and then held them out to the DA. It took less than a minute of reading before the DA sucked in a mouthful of air. "Where did you get this?"

Macy retrieved the documents from her counterpart. "Relax, we're not bringing this into the house. This is just a fact-finding mission. Maybe Mr. Callistor could take another look at these and help us out here."

Bennie held out his hand and Macy gave him back the sheets. He placed them face down on the bed with his folded hands on top of them. Looking carefully at everyone in the room, he made it clear he had no intention of giving them back until he was ready.

Buzz and Todd looked at each other knowingly. Callistor was a very intelligent man. They had met men like him before, men who read with intelligence and clarity. When they spoke, people listened. Callistor spoke. "What about you? Got any questions?"

He was looking directly at Buzz, who now had to put a suit on. He was dealing with someone who could hold his own in any boardroom in the country. "Is the information correct?"

"You know it is. You and your friend know what you're doing."

Todd was leaning against the back wall. "It's safe to say that we are on the same page with this. But the rest of the people here are going to need a briefing."

Bennie held the papers out to the DA, instructing him to give them to the court reporter at the back of the room for transcription and then ordered everyone but the DA and Macy to get out. "We have a few things to discuss."

They were still in there when Macy's aunts showed up to take her home. They were severely put out when the police officer at the door refused to let them into the room.

When they emerged, the DA made it clear that he was not impressed. "I'm not going to this dance until I know who is on the card. I am going to have this checked!"

Macy watched him walk away. "Man, he is seriously uptight. But he has a point here. Callistor was in Vietnam, four tours. There isn't a uniform made that can carry that many medals. Ever hear of the Congressional Medal of Honor being awarded in camera?" Even her aunts shook their heads.

Macy continued. "Callistor says we're never going to catch the guy responsible."

One of her Aunts suddenly took an interest. "How did he come to that conclusion?"

Macy elaborated. "You can't catch what doesn't exist. He told us to forget the bad guys and save the good ones, which is pretty good advice as far as I'm concerned. Callistor also suggested that things will sort themselves in about three weeks and that you two should settle in and get reacquainted with the real world because he says where you're going, you'll need the practice."

As they walked out to the parking lot, Todd thought that was also good advice.

Macy walked up to the back of her aunt's car and yelled at Todd and Buzz, before bouncing into an empty spot between the seats. "I'll call you in a couple of days."

Her aunt Bridget tried to get Macy's foot prints off her skirt. "Honestly Macy, can you at least try to act like a lady, just once?"

Buzz handed Todd the keys. "Four tours of Vietnam. It doesn't square with a man who ends up in a hospital bed after riding in boxcars for decades. What keeps a man like that out here for that long, living like that?"

Todd hefted the keys in hands and looked out to the horizon. "For the same reason we're out here in a forty-year-old Corvette."

Out on the street, they looked at a sign, which said Harry's TV repair.

Buzz was incensed. "You're not serious. Tell me, this is just another one of your attempts at humor?"

"I was pretty good at this stuff when I was getting started." Todd offered this with a little indignation.

"No you weren't. You're a menace. You could start a fire with a flashlight."

"Oh sure, bring that up again."

The sign also said "Fast Service." The fact was that the neon in the word fast had burned out years ago and Harry, the owner, hadn't been half that in twice as long, or ever, in most folk's recollection.

Buzz and Todd walked into the store. Harry scratched the stubble under his chin, first on one side, and then the other. "Which one of you wants the job?"

Todd raised his hand.

"Got any experience, fell?"

"I have a degree. . . ."

"You're hired."

Harry retrieved a wooden crate from under the counter. "Here you go, Battery Boy. Take these and reload the flashlights in the back. They're for the rail crews."

Todd looked at the pile of batteries in the box. "There has to be at least a hundred batteries in here!"

"What a coincidence. There are a hundred flash lights back there that need batteries."

Buzz patted Todd on the back as he turned and headed for the door. "Welcome back to the real world, Battery Boy."

Later in the day, Harry scratched his stubble as he slowly turned his head, first left, and then right. If Todd had learned anything new about the real world, in the brief time he'd been employed at Harry's, it was that he really liked getting his nails into that bristle. Yes indeed, up, down, and then occasionally, those old nails would go off road and taking a sideways trip just under his chin. That was his favorite part of the journey, when the old cuticles rattled over those old bristles. Todd suspected that Harry never shaved. He just trimmed the hedge with his finger nails.

Harry spoke, observing Todd's glance at a strangely burnt item. "That was a 1956 Dumont Super view."

Todd looked at the blackened hulk sitting on its four thin legs. It was kind of cool the way the scorch marks went symmetrically up both sides of the wooden cabinet. "Well, it was a bit out of date, anyway. I'll just buy her a new one."

Harry found some fresh stubble under his nose and began digging in with a thumb. "No. I don't think Mrs. Rod plaster is going to take to having a new TV in her house."

"Are you sure?"

"Let me see. It must have been back in 1974--that sounds about right. That old Dumont of hers was beginning to show it's age a bit. Picture rolled like a drunken sailor. You know how it is with black and whites?"

Todd nodded agreeably, not sure if Harry was pulling his leg. "Of course, I have one at home, a twenty-one-inch with a rotary dial."

"Suppose it's a Phil co?"

"No, it's a RCA Victor."

"Rich people are always throwing their money around."

"Mrs. Rod plaster?"

"Okay right, got a bit around the horn there for a moment. Anyway, we decided to do her a favor and all, so we brought over a new TV, and picked up the old girl here."

"That was damn nice thing to do."

"The new TV was back here the next day, needing repair."

"What happened, blown transistor?"

"No, she just up and beat the thing to death. Yes, indeed. Old Rod plaster can get right cranky, when the world does not see things her way."

So. what did you do?"

"Oh, we gave her back the Dumont."

"Thought you said it didn't work."

"The screen and power supply were okay. But the receiver circuits were shot and there wasn't any way we could fix that, because they weren't making Dumont's in 1974. So what we did was rig up one of those video things."

"A VCR?"

"Yeah, that's it. We got a tape full of old Jack Benny episodes and set them up on an endless loop. We even put in a test pattern after every third episode, so she wouldn't forget a trip to the powder room. Every couple of months, we'd go over there on a service call and change the tape. Those things don't last forever."

"You've been doing it since 1974?"

"Sure, never had any problems except once. I went over there with the wrong tape, took one of the widow Schmeer's tapes by accident, that she'd left in her own machine when she brought it in for servicing. I was going to drop it off to her, but I kind of screwed up a bit."

"That doesn't sound so bad."

"Yeah, you'd think that. We didn't find out, until a week later, when the town Pharmacist, that would be Herman Bentley, he's a dwarf you know, wonder how he can see over the counter- damn good druggist though--called me up and said that Rodplaster was going through a hell of a lot of Vaseline since our last service call. It didn't take long to figure out that she had gotten a snoot full of the widow's Schmeer's porn."

"Then what happened?"

"Well, you'd have some trouble trying to imagine Rodplaster, after watching three weeks of the widow's procurements, mighty strong stuff. We got her back on track with six weeks of Lawrence Welk. Damn near put her into a coma."

"What about the widow."

"She died."

"Mrs. Rodplaster went after her with her cane?"

Harry shook her head. "No, she just died."

Harry pointed to the TV, which looked like a large blackened marshmallow on four wooden legs. "Except now, we have a problem here that may be tough to fix."

"Sorry about that, Harry."

"Well, Todd, I don't hold you no grudge, what with you having limited experience with electronics. However, you might want to mind where you're poking when you're around those high voltage rectifiers. They can turn on you right quick."

Ten blocks away on the other side of town, Buzz had left the car at the hotel and decided to walk. He stopped on 11th Street and looked up at a sign. Ash Flats Cabs. Well, it didn't get any simpler than that.

He stepped inside. He was a long time away from the days at Able Atlantic. The place was clean and tidy. In the distance, he could make out the voice of a dispatcher and his radio. The woman at the desk removed her reading glasses and beckoned him over. "May I help you?"

It took him a couple of seconds to put the words together; it had been a long time. "I'd like to apply for a job."

Her smile broadened. The lines around her eyes only made her more attractive. "I'm guessing it has been a few years since you have had to fill out an application."

He agreed that it was.

She handed him a form. "Take your time. When you're done, we'll send you in to have a chat with the owner."

Bill Steves offered Buzz a seat before taking his place behind his desk. He looked just like the business he ran--clean, neat, and precise. His handshake was very firm and there was a Rolex on his wrist. It only took him a minute to review Buzz's application. He put it on the desk face down.

"We don't get applicants like you very often. You're not the kind of man who needs a job driving a cab. The town has an excellent golf course and sports facility."

Buzz had to stop himself before he answered. He wasn't directing a board meeting. He was applying for a job. "I'm going to be in town for a while. I was thinking that now would be a good time to put a little back into a world from which I have taken more than my fair share."

Steves nodded slowly. "That's fair enough. It's been awhile since you've driven a flag. Are you up to the hours involved?"

"I'll be fine. It's like riding a bike. You never forget how, or the memories."

Steves stood and held out his hand. "Yeah, something like that. We'd be happy to take you on during your stay. You'll start in daylight, seven to three, so you can get a feel for the landscape. We'll run you onto nights when we're both comfortable. Be here at six tomorrow morning. See the dispatcher before you leave."

He escorted Buzz to the door and then asked his secretary to come in. He closed the door and handed her Buzz's application.

As she read it, her eyebrows moved up perceptibly before she handed it back to him.

"History like that doesn't walk in the door every day, does it?

"Able Atlantic? More like a legend."

Todd was waiting for Buzz outside Harry's place as he pulled up. "So, how was your first day of real work in thirty years?"

As he got in the car, Todd handed Buzz a blackened chunk of metal.

Buzz turned it slowly over in his hands. "This is high voltage rectifier, or at least it was, until someone burned it to a crisp. To be precise, it's what's left of the rectifier out of a 1956 Dumont Superview. They do not react well to being poked with a screwdriver."

Todd was a bit defensive. "Do you have to keep bringing that up? We make integrated circuits, not 1956 Dumont Superviews. Besides, it's bad enough that I have to explain what happened to the owner."

"When are you going to tell him?"

"It's a woman."

"Please don't tell me you trashed a little old lady's TV set.

"She's not exactly little!"

Buzz smirked. "You burned up some nice old lady's TV, on your first day of work."

"Hey, this isn't funny. I can't even buy her a new one."

"Why? Are you too cheap to buy her a new black and white?"

"No, the last time Harry tried to set her up with a new set, she beat it to death with her cane."

Buzz pulled the keys out of the ignition and handed them to Todd. "You have to drive."

"Why? It's your turn."

"Because, I'm gonna start laughing so hard, that we'll end up climbing a tree with the car!"

There was a message waiting for them when they got back to the hotel. "It's from Macy. We're due at a hearing in four days and dinner tonight,... a pig roast. I'm thinking that doesn't sound so bad. What's eating you?' He passed the note to Todd.

"Does the pig know?"

Buzz took the note back. "Are you kidding? The pig is the lucky one."

"I guess we'd better go over there now."

"What's the hurry? The note says we don't have to be there until 6:30 p.m."

"Macy is probably going to want to talk to us. Besides, her dad is going to try and cook a pig. That is going to be one hell of a grease fire."

"Good point, Todd. Should we call the fire department now, or do you think we can handle it?"

"I don't think we have to worry. When word gets around about what he's doing, the Fire Department will be there as soon as he lights a match."

They were already too late. Glen had managed to reduce a 100-pound pig to a five-pound briquette in a fireball. As they stared into the much abused barbecue, Glen's neighbor Don wondered aloud if it was possible to get a whole pig at 4:30 in the afternoon. "Glen, how did you manage to get that thing into such a small barbecue?"

I figured it would shrink when I lit the barbecue starter."

"How much did you use?"

"I'm not sure, maybe a gallon."

"Christ, Glen, you can't put a gallon of lighter fluid into a barbecue!"

He scratched the back of his neck. "Actually, I put it on the pig."

If they were in any other backyard in America, including The Happy Tumbleweed, a comment like that would have been outrageous. "I just never thought jet fuel would burn that hot."

"Everyone slowly turned and looked at Glen.

"I've got an idea, Todd, I'll need the car. Maybe you guys can get the barbecue cleaned up."

"How are we going to do that? We're out of gasoline."

Forty minutes later, Buzz was back with five cases of Spam. "What are we going to do with this, Buzz?"

He handed Glen a can. "What's this stuff made of?"

Glen, Don, and Todd looked at the ingredients on the side of the can. "Well, it's mostly unidentifiable compounds."

Don pointed at the last item on the list. "Is that pork?"

When everyone agreed that Spam was mostly pork, Buzz tossed them a bunch of can openers. "Start opening, boys."

An hour later, they stood back to look at their pig. Glen looked at his watch. "Not a bad rendition and twenty minutes to spare."

Don returned with beers for everyone. As he passed them around, he had to admit that it really did look like a pig. "You know, I'm not sure about those eyes. I don't think pigs have eyes that are red. It looks like it has a hangover."

"No, it's more like it got a snoot full of bad oats. You know, like a sixties stoned- kind-of look."

"What are those anyway, Glen?"

"I think they are ear rings. One of Macy's aunts left them here one night after sleeping one off at the Wreck."

Todd took a drink of his beer. "They must be expensive."

Glen shrugged. "Guess so,…anyone want another beer?"

It was one of Glen's best barbecues, or the only one, depending on who you asked.

Macy's Aunt Bridgette commented between mouthfuls. "I've never had pork cooked so well. It just melts in your mouth, not a single piece of gristle or bone."

There wasn't any jewelry, either. The pig's eyes promptly melted and disappeared in the bottom of the barbecue, thus ending any claims as to their legitimacy.

Buzz excused himself early; he had to be at work at six in the morning. Todd made sure they took the pig's original packaging, some assembly required, with them. The manager of the landfill woke up the next morning, wondering who the hell in Ash Flats would eat 300 cans of Spam in one sitting. After a couple of minutes, he decided, on second thought, that he didn't want to know.

Todd was waiting outside The Bell at eight for Buzz to drive him to work, when Buzz pulled up. "What's this?"

"It's a cab."

"I can see that. What are you doing with it?"

Buzz leaned out the window. "Unlike you, who gets paid to go into the homes of decent, law-abiding seniors and burn up their furniture, I have found gainful and respectable employment."

Todd replied with a dead panned expression as he got in the cab. "That is low."

Buzz put the flag down as he pulled away from the curb. "You want to stop for coffee?"

"Sure, wait a minute! Are you charging me for this?"

Buzz retrieved the ten dollar bill from Todd's hand, when they pulled up in front of Harry's TV Repair Shop. "When are you off?"

"I'm done around four."

Todd got out of the car and remembered that the fare was only six dollars. "The fare was six. I gave you a ten."

Buzz put the car in gear and pulled away from the curb. "Sorry, no change!"

Todd screamed at the car as drove away. "That was a forty percent tip for a ten percent fare, Murdoch. I liked you a lot better when you were a rich bastard!"

Buzz yelled back at him and waved. "You are cheap Styles, cheap, cheap, cheap!"

"Is there a problem, fella?' Harry had come out to see what all the commotion was about.

Todd laughed. "No. I've just been a victim of rampant capitalism. Ten dollars for a six dollar fare."

Harry looked up the street at the receding cab. "You're talking about that new feller. Four dollar tip you say?"

Todd nodded. "Stiffed me for a four dollar tip!"

"My car wouldn't start this morning, dead battery. You got off lucky."

The nasty cab with its shyster driver was waiting for him in front of Harry's at exactly four o'clock. Todd gave the car a nasty look and refused to get in. "How much are you going to charge me this time?"

"Get in. It won't hurt."

"Macy called just after lunch, to remind us about court on Thursday. The judge will rule on whether there is enough evidence to hold us over for trial. The DA is going for a charge of attempted murder."

Buzz gritted his teeth. "That's pretty harsh."

Todd agreed. "Macy figures the judge will reserve judgment and give both sides three weeks to come up with something that will stick. Her best guess is that we will be out of here by the end of the month. She figures the best charge the prosecution has is aggravated assault."

They pulled up in front of the hotel. "It's not my first choice but I can live with it."

Todd got out of the car. "Yeah, so can I."

"Hey, where are you going? I need ten bucks!"

"What for?"

"It's the fare. This is a cab."

Todd checked his wallet. He didn't have any money.

Buzz looked him up and down with disappointment. "Deadbeat!"

Todd went into the hotel and borrowed the money from the desk clerk. As he handed the bill in the window, he looked at the meter. "The fare is $5.56!"

Buzz deftly removed the money from Todd's hand and pulled away at the same time. "Tip!"

Todd watched the cab drive away. He turned to find the desk clerk standing beside him. "Damn fine driver, good head for business, too. He'll go far. What about you?"

"I moonlight as a TV repair man. My day job is to stand on the street and let people fleece me."

The desk clerk gave him the once over. "I'd say you're going to do right well at it, too. I'll put the fifteen dollars you owe me on your hotel bill.

Buzz and Todd quickly settled into a routine that allowed them to get re-acquainted with the real world, which was something they discovered they needed to do. Buzz regained a bit of his youth and remembered that he enjoyed driving a cab. Todd learned a whole new respect for high voltage and began to get fairly good at trouble-shooting circuitry, which was something he had trouble with when he began his career.

Macy was getting a crash course in trial law. She had it right. Judge Crater was short on stature but long on jurisprudence, in his exact words, "The DA was trying to take a crap in a hurricane."

The judge also believed in sharing his wisdom with everyone who came into his court. Macy got a judicial spanking. "Don't come into my court with training wheels on your law degree, Young Lady. Your arguments are as thin as my secretary's coffee. These men are depending on you for more than facts. You are here to argue the law on their behalf!"

Two hours later, the four of them were back out in front of the courthouse. The DA looked at his watch and then down at Macy. He reached behind her to help her get her backpack on. "Well, that was fun."

"We've got our work cut out for us, that's for sure."

"Macy, these guys have got it easy. They didn't have anything to do with the assault. If anything, these two probably saved Bennie Callistor's life."

Macy looked up in surprise. "If you believe that, why keep these guys in the house?"

"Because I have to prove beyond a reasonable doubt that they're responsible and you to prove that they're not, Councilor. He picked up his briefcase and started towards his car."

Macy wondered aloud as she watched him walk to his car. "I wonder what he looked like when he was younger."

Buzz put on his sunglasses and looked at Todd, "Napoleon Solo."

She looked at them. "Who?"

"Bennie Callistor wanted a cab. It was seven in the evening and he wanted a cab. He had been in the hospital for two weeks and he most definitely wanted a cab out front in twenty minutes.

The duty nurse quickly realizing that there was no way she could physically prevent him from getting dressed and leaving the hospital. She went to find a very large, strong doctor. She got Bennie Callistor's doctor, who was neither.

Callistor was ready for the doctor when he stepped into the darkened room. When the lights came on, Callister had a firm grip on the doctor's forearm. When he tried to pull it back, Callistor's grip tightened rapidly. The doctor's hand was starting to go numb. The hand was turning white from restricted blood flow.

Callistor cautioned his victim. "I have an excellent doctor that could help you with that, but I think his arm may be broken."

The doctor winced when Callistor adjusted his hold on the arm. "Do you mind telling me how you get a grip like that, so I can pass it on to the physiotherapist?"

"Easy, steel, cold, hard steel, thousands of tons of it. You learn to hang on tight when it is moving under your hands."

Callistor looked at the doctor's hand. "That must be getting uncomfortable. Maybe you should have the nurse get my cab. Make sure it's the one that belongs to that Murdoch fellow. I don't want any snot-nosed kid who doesn't know how the world works."

Twenty minutes later, Callistor was getting into the back of Buzz's cab. "Doctor, I'll be back in two hours. You have someone here with a wheel chair--that big old nurse with the red hair if she's on duty--to take me back to my room. You might want to put that arm in some cold water, ice don't do no good. It'll take the swelling down some."

"Thanks for the medical advice."

As the cab pulled away from the curb, Bennie leaned back in the seat and took a deep breath, realizing how long it had been since he had enjoyed something as simple as fresh air. He looked out the window, silently watching the town and the sky as it went by. How many towns had he been through and how many sunsets had he seen and not bothering to look at them? Were they all this beautiful?

Understanding what Bennie was experiencing, Buzz took the car in a long circuitous drive through the town for twenty minutes, first up town where the town was lit by the start of the evening, and then, down tree-lined streets, as porch lights competed with the setting sun. "Have you got a destination for me, Sir?"

Bennie answered without turning from the window. "People like me don't have destinations. They just have journeys."

"I'm not sure I understand." Buzz was uncertain as to Bennie's meaning.

"Sure you do. You, and that friend of yours, have been on one for years. If anyone asked where you were headed, you would tell them some town, but it wouldn't mean anything, nor would it matter. You were driven on, not knowing where you were going, by a force you couldn't understand.

Buzz just shook his head. "I've never believed in anything like fate. It's just a road trip for us."

He could see the look in Bennie's eyes in the rear view mirror. "You're here aren't you? So am I."

Of course, they did have a destination that evening, the diesel bed. It was surprisingly quiet.

There were only twenty units in the bed and except for a distant rumble, it could hardly be heard.

As Buzz helped Bennie out of the cab, he pointed to the east across the switch line. "We've got to cross over there.

It was fifteen minutes before he asked to stop. Buzz's shoulder was aching from Bennie's grip for support. "Is this where it happened?"

"Yeah, I was headed in that direction, back the way we came."

"Was there anything in this part of the yard?"

"The train I was on was a run through. Except for a few hopper cars behind me, it looked pretty much like this. It was a lot louder, though."

Buzz looked behind him and then down. The yard lights would have been behind him and too high to cast a shadow. He wouldn't have seen anyone coming from behind him. There was a lot of machinery here that night. "You may not have heard him."

"You'd think that. But when you have been around these things long enough, you learn to hear the sound of every locomotive, flat car, boxcar--everything right down to a switch changing, and those things are bloody quiet. You're life depends on it. I would have heard someone, if they were out there."

"So who hit you?"

"Not who, what."

Buzz was a pragmatic man and he refused to say, or accept, what he was thinking, without proof.

Callistor smiled and put his hand on Buzz's shoulder. He was getting tired, but he was determined to continue. "Ever see a monster?"

"No. I can't say I ever have."

Callistor's laughter was almost deafening. "Sure you have. You just don't want to admit it. But you know."

In the distance, they could see the long shadows of the track shed where Bennie had been beaten. "There, I need to sit. We've still got time."

Both men, lost in thought, barely noticed that the sun had set. Buzz struggled for the word to describe for the color of the sky. Indigo? "We should start back. It's starting to cool down and you don't need more problems."

"Relax. Bennie whistled a few bars of a tune and looked at Buzz.

"Sentimental journey?"

Bernie nodded with approval. It went back and forth, just the line and then the guess. "There!"

Buzz looked out into the dark as far as he could see. The only thing he could identify was the tops of the tracks reflecting what little light was out there.

"Help me up."

Bennie slowly stood up, putting his hand on Buzz's shoulder for support. With his other hand, he pointed into the night. "You see that floodlight, third from the left, the farthest one? Watch the base of the pole real careful."

Buzz found the pole and let his eyes travel to the base. His eyes focused on an area of shadow caused by the base of the lamppost. Briefly he thought he was focusing too hard and his eyes playing tricks on him. It was almost like the shadow was starting to fold and pinch in on itself.

Callistor took his arm off Buzz's shoulder and squared his own. "He's taking his time, he's not stupid. I'll give him that."

A shadow that had detached itself from the base of the pole, and started moving towards them.

"Don't move. Make him come to us."

It felt like hours but it was less than five minutes. A silhouette, that stubbornly refused to give up the shadow from the pole, it stopped less than ten feet away.

It seemed to consider briefly. Then, the shadow dropped away to reveal a solid structure with features. It took several steps forward, not into direct light, but enough to be seen clearly. The man was impossibly nondescript and certainly didn't look like a threat to anyone. Buzz had no doubt that within an hour, he wouldn't be able tell anyone if the man in front of him was five or ten feet tall.

The man looked at Bennie from side to side and nodded approvingly. "Good to see you again, Bennie. You're healing up nicely."

Callistor was utterly fearless and never took his eyes off the apparition in front of him. "Sorry to disappoint you."

"Oh need to apologize. I badly underestimated you."

In the distance, they could hear a car. "I let my guard down. I won't make the same mistake again."

The man nodded. "Let's just say we both played the hand badly. But you don't have to worry. I won't be seeing you again, and it seems the world is a better place with you in it."

He continued. I feel sorry for you, though. You and I are a lot alike. We live on the edge, feeling the rock move under our feet and stepping back at the last second. These people have stepped forward, pulled you back, and cleared the path, paved the road. That's no way to live, for people like you and I. If you decide to come back to the cliff's edge, I'll be waiting. You and I--it will be a glorious battle."

Headlights were visible now. Looking at Buzz, he calmly remarked. "That will be your associate, Mr. Murdoch. Sorry we didn't have the chance to chat this time and I shouldn't keep you waiting. *Tick, Tock.* Mr. Murdoch. *Tick Tock.*"

The man took a step back and into the shadow he brought with him. In the time it took to blink, the shadow and the man were back at the base of the lamp post.

Callistor rubbed his left arm. "You're right. It's starting to get cold."

The Corvette appeared out of the dark as bright and as real as the brain could absorb. It felt good to be back in the real world. Todd joined them in front of the car. He jammed his hands in his jacket pockets to ward off the chill. "What the hell is going on? I got a call from your dispatcher. He's been trying to get you on the radio for the last forty-five minutes."

Bennie responded calmly. "Sorry to get everyone bent out of shape. Old Buzz and I were enjoying the evening and just up and lost track of time."

Buzz looked at his watch. They'd only been out here for a little over an hour and ten minutes. "We've got to have you back in fifteen minutes, Bennie."

"I think I can make my way back to the car okay. I'll wait for you there."

They watched him until they were sure he was going to be safe.

"You okay, Buzz?"

Buzz took a deep breath before looking at the sky. His eyes dropped to the shadow at the base of the pole. He watched intently, it didn't move. "Yeah, I'm okay. We both are."

"What happened out here?

"The best answer I can give you is that we went out to the edge, took a good look, and stepped back."

Todd looked out into the yard pausing at the shadow at the base of the pole. "It's a hell of a view from out there."

"That it is, my friend. That it is."

"I guess the Dispatcher is pretty cranked. I'll have to smooth some waters."

"No, they didn't care about you at all. They just need the car back to clean it for the evening shift."

The doctor, Bennie's nurse--she was sneaking him chocolate bars against the dietitian's orders--and the wheel chair were waiting for him at the curb. "You two look like hell. What did you spend your last ten bucks on, the best whorehouse in town?"

The doctor gave the nurse a hard look which just bounced off her.   "Where did you learn to talk like that, anyway?"

"A whorehouse."

Bennie extended a hand to Buzz as he was helped into the wheel chair. "Thanks. It was a good ride."

"The pleasure was all mine."

Judge Crater had been in his office most of the night, jacket off, sleeves rolled up, and his robes hanging neatly on the coat rack. He suddenly had a judicial epiphany after finding out about Murdoch and Callistor's trip to the rail yard. The wheels of justice were grinding far too slowly for his liking. He decided to move things along. He picked up the yellow note pad, looked at the clock, and started to read. "Damn! He was a good writer. It was a shame to waste it on that bunch of goobers out there. When he retired, he was going to write one of those 'Tell all books'. He was going to name names. Yes, Sir! When everyone sued him, he would get them all in court, and brother, was that going to be a party!" Maybe he'd buy his own island with the settlement.

Dropping the pad on the desk, he reached for the bottom right drawer of his desk, stopping to look suspiciously around the room and the door, especially at the door, because his executive assistant used it to get into the room. Executive Assistant! Who the hell came up with that title, anyway? She was a damn secretary! He pulled out a bottle of bourbon and a glass. The glass was half way to his mouth when there was a banging on the door.

"Court, ten minutes!"

"Damn! How does she do that?" She has to have the place wired, he thought to himself. "I'll be out in twenty minutes."

'Ten!"

"Twenty and you can't make me. I'm the damn judge!"

"You get that rotten, wrinkly old butt out here and dispense some law!"

He pushed the glass aside and took a long pull from the bottle. Using his left foot, he cleared a space on the desk, which was occupied by some important legal documents and put his feet up. The judge wondered, briefly, about those important legal documents which had fallen on the floor. He returned to the case at hand. He decided he was going to dispense some good old-fashioned American frontier justice. Too bad they wouldn't let him bring his gun into court anymore, bunch of pansies. His thoughts wandered briefly again. The fish were biting like crazy up state. The nasty banging on the door returned.

His secretary got up and blocked his path as he came out of his office and tried to brush past her. Without a word, she straightened his tie and adjusted his robe. "There was a time when I was one hell of a lawyer."

"You still are. Go make your secretary proud."

The court clerk had pretty much come to the conclusion that Crater had gone off his rocker when he dispensed with a month's worth of legal proceedings in two days. In one case, a senior New York stock trader from Lehman Brothers was arrested for relieving himself on a parking meter outside the Train Wreck

The stock trader's lawyer unwisely argued with the judge's decision. "With all due respect, your honor, two weeks for my client is unduly harsh. At best, this allows for a fine."

The judge countered. "Three weeks!"

"It was a parking meter!"

"Four weeks!"

"For the love of God your honor, why?"

"I don't like his tie. It looks cheap!"

"You can't jail someone because you don't like his tie."

"Where are you from anyway?"

"New York. I represent the accused in all his legal matters and I am licensed to practice in this state. As I said, you can't jail someone in Arkansas because you don't like his tie."

"Where'd you get that tie, Councilor?"

"Los Angeles, on Rodeo Drive, I was visiting there when my client requested representation."

"I don't like it."

"Your Honor, I ask the court to stay focused on the issue of my client's inappropriate use of a parking meter."

"Six weeks."

"What? Your Honor, do you know anything about the law?"

"Sure do! Watch this. Bailiff throw the learned council and his client in jail for six weeks and put them in that nice cell next to Mr. Weedwacker, Warren."

"On what charge?"

"Tacky Ties and contempt of court!"

Crater banged his gavel down on his bench "Next!"

"Case 21286, Judge Crater presiding in the matter of assault." Crater cut him off before he could go into his spiel. "How about it, Councilor, have you got enough to go to trial?"

"With all due respect, Your Honor, the court gave us three weeks to prepare."

"Tough! Now you don't have three weeks. Are you ready?"

"Justice Crater, three weeks would have been manageable, but we're talking eight days to properly prepare a case that would normally take eight weeks."

"Where's the plaintiff, Councilor? You know the guy who complains?"

"He's still in the hospital and isn't well enough to attend court."

"Bull! He was well enough to spend an evening joyriding in a cab driven by one of the defendants. You know, the guy who is being complained about."

Crater leveled his gaze at Macy. "Help me out here, Councilor. What do they call that thing when the complainer stands in one corner and the complainee stands in the other, and they can't talk to each other?"

"Expartite, Your Honor."

"See! There you are. I knew there was a name for it. Now, what the hell is going on here? C'mon, people, you are making me look bad. "

Macy looked down at her notes and then walked out in front of the bench. She addressed the judge. "My clients are innocent, Your Honor."

The DA groaned as the judge leaned back in his chair and peered over his glasses at her. "Four years of Harvard law and that's it? You're not exactly selling me here."

She consulted her notes. "The time line doesn't support these men as the assailants.

Crater was having none of that. He leaned forward abruptly and glared, frightening Macy enough to make her take a step back. "You are a lawyer. Let's you and I make some law today. To hell with the facts, put you notes down and argue with me!"

Her voice shook for the first couple of words, but she got it under control. "We're here to determine if there is enough evidence to hold these two men over for trial for attempted murder. I submit to the court that they are innocent because they are still here."

"Objection!"

"Shut up! I am not seeing a destination here, Councilor."

Your Honor, these two men are collectively worth about seven billion dollars. They show up in a backwater Arkansas town in a forty-year-old sports car. They checked into a hotel which they could purchase out of petty cash. They end up in court, facing a felony charge that could put them in prison for the rest of their lives because they came to the aid of a vagrant."

"Objection!"

"What did I tell you to do?"

"Shut up, Your Honor."

"Then, why aren't you doing it? This is my last warning. Get somewhere, quickly."

"Your Honor, these men could be anywhere in the world, but they are here and they are still here. They could have dropped the most expensive and brightest legal minds in the country on us, and been out of here in forty-eight hours. This town does not have the legal resources to hold them."

"You're going to have a hard time convincing that nice man from New York and his lawyer, Councilor."

Macy tried deepening her voice for effect. "With all due respect, Justice Crater. The nation's best jurists don't go to Rodeo Drive to buy their ties."

Crater leaned back and nodded. "Not bad."

Macy pointed to Todd and Buzz. "Here they sit with a lawyer, who was sitting on a hospital bench sorting out a parking ticket. They could have had any lawyer in the country, but they settled on a fourteen-year-old, who carries her legal briefs in a backpack."

Crater banged his gavel down so hard the light shook. He raised it again and pointed it at the DA. "Everyone is going to be in my chambers in one hour. If you would be so kind, as to extend the invitation to Mr. Callistor."

Precisely one hour later, everyone was standing in Crater's chambers. The judge saw a man, who hadn't been in court. "Who the hell are you?"

"I'm Mr. Callistor's doctor."

"I hate doctors. They're always nagging me to lose weight, stop drinking and smoking."

"You should."

"Where's that damn court clerk?"

A hand came up in the back of the room. "Here, Sir."

"What the hell are you doing back there?"

"There are no chairs left."

"Sergeant, take the doctor out and have him shot."

The DA coughed up a lung. "Your Honor! You can't do that!"

"Is that right, Sergeant?"

"I'm afraid so, Justice Crater."

"Damn."

The judge turned to Bennie. "Nice of you to join us, I trust you are being looked after at the hospital?"

"I can't complain."

"Ever been in a judge's chambers before?"

"No I can't say that I ever have."

"How do you like it so far?"

"Not much. Ever been in a boxcar?"

"Yeah, just after the war, couldn't afford the bus fare to school, so I hopped from New Mexico to New Jersey."

Bennie was impressed. "Not bad. How did you like it?"

"Not much."

Crater reached behind him and picked up a file on Bennie Callistor. He thumbed through a couple of pages. He stopped at one page, and examined it carefully before looking up. It would appear from this report that your integrity is beyond reproach."

"That's good to hear."

The future of these two men depends on what you have to say."

"I know."

"Did these men attack you?"

"No, they did not."

Judge Crater, pointed to the DA and cautioned Bennie. "He's going to shoot that full of holes, that you were hit from behind. You didn't regain consciousness until you were in the hospital. I would accept that argument."

Bennie looked around the room. His eyes stopped at the fishing rod resting discreetly behind the judge's robe. "I could say that I saw his shadow just before he hit me, and that he was left handed. Both of these men use their right hands. I could also say that he was at least an inch shorter than these two men, and that he had chunk of metal in his hand to increase the power of the blow, which means the knuckles take a beating. That takes a couple of days to heal. If someone does that frequently and over a long period of time, the hands start to look like they have been hit repeatedly with an iron. They are broken and flat. However, in here, what I say doesn't matter. It only counts out there in that court of yours."

"What are you going to say when I ask you in my court?"

"You'll have to take my word for it."

Crater took a long look at his fishing rod and then told everyone but Macy to get out. When everyone was gone, he handed her Bennie Callistor's military file. "One of the few privileges of being a judge is that you get to see the cool stuff first."

He stopped her before she could begin reading the file. "Don't bother. See to it that Mr. Callistor gets it, because it belongs to him. I've made my decision."

"Is this why you asked me to wait?"

"No. Your dad came to me when you decided to go to law school. I told him that you'd never make it as a lawyer and I refused to sponsor you. My opinion hasn't changed. But I will tell you one thing. Your parents would have been proud of you today,... and so am I."

When court began, the court clerk called everyone to attention.

"All rise, Judge Alexander Crater presiding."

"Sergeant, is everyone present?"

He looked around the court and indicated to the Bailiff at the door to open it. He escorted Macy's parents to a bench at the back.

Without looking up from his notes, the judge ordered the Sergeant. "The front of the court."

Crater looked up when he saw that Birch and Glen were in the seats right behind Macy. The Sergeant instructed everyone to take their seats.

"In the matter of the state of Arkansas versus Messer's Murdoch and Styles in respect to a finding in support for a trial of attempted murder: the state is required to prove that sufficient evidence exists to guarantee a conviction. It rests with the defense to prove that there is reasonable doubt for a verdict of innocence. In this instance, neither the state nor the defense has succeeded in proving to this court that there would be a reasonable chance of success. The failure here is substantial. A crime has gone unpunished and someone has escaped lawful justice. Mr. Murdoch and Mr. Styles, stand up. In accordance with the laws of the state of Arkansas, until evidence is produced to the contrary, this court sees no reason to proceed. You are free to go."

The DA held out his hand to Macy. "Well done."

Macy's mom pushed open the gate separating them. "Mom, you can't come in here."

"Tough! I'm your mother. I'm proud and I am going to hug my daughter."

Bennie Callistor reached across the barrier and patted Macy on the shoulder. "What's in the file?"

She had forgotten. Mr. Callistor, "Judge Crater asked me to give this to you. It's yours."

He took it without looking at it. "Thank you. Would someone mind taking me back to the hospital?"

The DA raised his arm. "I'll take you back."

Bennie put a hand on his shoulder for support. "Appreciated, why don't you stay and have dinner? It's steak night.

The DA gagged. "Eat at the hospital? Christ! We'll go to the steakhouse, it's on me. Besides, we've broken just about every rule in the book, and one more isn't going to make any difference."

Todd spoke for Buzz and himself. "Macy, you did a terrific job. Thank you."

Macy shook her head and looked at Crater's now empty chair. "I don't think I earned it."

"What makes you think that? Of course you did."

She reached into her backpack and pulled out a copy of Callistor's file which Crater's secretary made for her. She handed it to Buzz. "It's an impressive read. It covers a lot of the material you provided, but in far greater detail."

"Macy, what do you want us to do with this?"

She shrugged. "Crater was seriously Expartite on this. If the DA knew I had this, he would have been screaming obstruction, withholding evidence, and demanding a change of venue. All of us would be here until hell froze over, so who knows why he gave it to me."

Todd gave her a look of mild reproach. "Did he say anything else to you?"

She chose her words carefully. "To check if anything got missed so I could learn from this."

Buzz looked at Macy with understanding before speaking. "Do you mind if we hang on to this for a bit? Maybe we can clear up a few loose ends."

Buzz and Todd were alone on the steps of the court house--no judge, no Macy, and no obligations, except for saying good-bye to their employers. Todd was going to miss the TV repair business, but after having nearly finished off Harry's business with a rectifier hiding in the back of an old short wave radio, he was ready to call it a day. Buzz, on the other hand, had delivered the inebriated teenage daughter of the Governor's sister home safe and sound. He was rapidly reaching folk hero status. They could feel the wind urging them to move on. I guess we need to be here for a few more days."

It took at least a couple of days for them to come up with a plan, which was easy. The issue was Bennie Callistor. He was already making plans to leave. The problem was not where, but how, because a man like Callistor didn't have a fixed address. As soon as he was capable, and when he had finished whatever business had brought him to Ash Flats, which was still an unanswered question, he was going to be looking for a boxcar. According to Bennie's doctor, "This wasn't going to happen."

Todd and Buzz paid Bennie a visit on Sunday to see how he was getting on. When they came into the room, he was pulling on his shoes, slowly. Todd asked him about this. "A little early to be checking out of the hotel, isn't it?"

Bennie looked up at Todd and laughed. "I'm getting out of here before they hand me a bill."

"No worries. The tab has been covered."

"I know and it's appreciated. They're letting me out of here for a couple of hours a day to get some exercise, physiotherapy. This is my first day."

"How are you feeling so far?" Buzz wanted to know.

"Like a bucket of loose bolts. If I bend over too far, I can feel my arms in the shoulder sockets. Feels like an electric shock."

"Sure you want to try this?"

"Got to, sooner or later, I'm going to have to catch a train."

"You mind if we join you?"

"No skin off my nose."

Todd commented on this to Buzz. "Well, his sense of humor has certainly improved."

It was slow going. In one block, Bennie was struggling, in two blocks, he was tiring, and after three blocks, he was exhausted. Todd stopped. "I'll get the car."

Bennie grabbed Todd's arm. There sure as hell nothing wrong with his grip. "No! I've got to see this through. Let's stop for coffee at that place across the street."

When they got settled at a table, Bennie began to relax a bit. "I take my coffee black."

The waitress suggested waiting for a fresh pot.

Bennie shook his head. "I'll take what you've got in the pot."

"The stuff is three hours old. It's asphalt oil."

Bennie tapped the table where he expected his cup to appear.

The waitress looked at Todd and Buzz. "What about you two? Wanna wait for fresh, or are you going for the road tar like your friend here?"

"We'll wait for a fresh pot."

She looked at Bennie and muttered as she walked away. "Jesus."

"My kind of woman."

When she came back, she placed the cup on the table and slowly pushed it across to him. "There's a phone at the counter when you need to call an ambulance. The number is on speed dial."

"What is it?"

"666."

Bennie tested the coffee and nodded with approval. "Gentlemen, in my line of work, you don't want to get used to being comfortable. You try to stay safe, clean, and dry. A warm summer night, a clean empty boxcar, and a hot cup of coffee are luxuries."

For the next half hour they compared notes on life and shared some stories.

"So, why did you get off here? You could have stayed on the train to just about anywhere." Todd suddenly asked the question, needing to know the answer.

"I think I'll take you up on that ride back to the hospital. Your friend, Buzz, can keep me company until you get back."

Todd got up and dropped some change on the table. "I'll be back in fifteen minutes."

"Take your time. I'm not going anywhere."

When he was gone, Buzz turned back to the table. "That was harsh. It was a fair question."

"Your friend's a college boy. He won't understand the answer."

There was an edge to Buzz's voice. "Don't make the mistake of underestimating him. He has excellent street smarts."

Callistor conceded the point. "He's a good man, true enough, and he's right. I got off that train for a reason."

"What was it?"

"Not yet. I need more time to get my strength back."

"It's going to be weeks, maybe months, before you're strong enough to get anywhere, and you know it."

Callistor leaned forward and spoke softly and with some menace. "I haven't got that much time and neither do you."

There was sound of a horn, and Todd was back with the car.

The wheelchair and the nurse were waiting at the curb when they pulled up. She lectured them. "He shouldn't be riding in a car like that. He can barely get out of his chair."

Bennie was going to respond with something rude, but Todd gave him a look that said, "Don't go there."

Bennie eased himself into the chair. "Eleven tomorrow, we'll do lunch."

"Sure, we'll be here."

Bennie looked up, and then, putting his head squarely on the nurse's chest. "Ever do it on a trampoline?'

She swatted him across the back of the head. "I can't believe you actually put food in that mouth, you dirty old man!"

The next day was surprisingly cool, but what wind there was brought a little heat with it. However, weather was not what concerned Buzz and Todd, as they stood in front of the hospital. They recalled Bennie's words." I haven't got that much time and neither do you."

"You feel it?"

"Yeah, and it seems to get stronger by the hour."

The nurse appeared with Bennie. "I see you got a proper car this time. Make sure he's back in three hours."

Bennie did a little better, but in the end, it was only another block and a half farther. They had him back in less than the three hour time limit which the nurse gave them. They repeated the process for another four days. Bennie went a little farther each time out. As he settled into the chair, he looked up at sky. "The wind is starting to change. Tomorrow will be last the day."

They watched him go into the hospital. Todd was concerned. "We are way past our due date on this one, Buzz."

"I know."

When they pulled up in front of the hospital the next day, Callistor was already out front. The wheelchair and the nurse were nowhere to be seen.

"You're a changed man. We're impressed."

"With a little help from the Doctors procurements. We need to get started.

Their walk took them along the same route, but his time, they didn't stop at the diner. They kept on with Bennie getting stronger with each step. He stopped at the cemetery gates. They were old, iron, and high. He reached out and slowly grasped one of the bars on the left gate. "God, I love the feel of iron."

Stepping through the gates, he looked back at his companions, who intended to let him have his privacy. Bennie motioned them to follow him. "You've come this far. It's only right that you see it through to the end."

It took him some time to get his bearings before he started up a gentle hill. He was breathing hard when he got to the top. "There."

The headstone was definitely military, and it identified the occupant as Lt. D. Sills, KIA, An Soc Bridge, 16 August 1965."

The stone offered no memorial.

"You two ever have any contact with the Klan?"

Todd spoke for the both of them. "Once, it was long time ago."

"Well, Lt. Sills here was a card carrying member."

"You knew him?"

"Of course, you have to remember what it was like back then. It was hatred, on both sides, that went right to the bone. We were the same rank but different services. He was Air Force, I was Navy. We ended up in the same company together providing Intel support for the Army. It didn't take long before we got into it. The company Commander was a real sadist. He was taking bets to see which one killed the other first. That's why he tasked us to do a recon on a group that was getting a real bad reputation, even for the Viet Cong. Everyone called them the green men because of the outfits they wore. They were assassins who weeded out informants. The VC were tough, but these guys were really over the top."

"A Forward Operating Base squad on a patrol found the site of a village they had obliterated. They killed everything and everybody, including the pets, and then burned the buildings down on top of the remains. There was nothing left but scorch marks. We'd been out for hours, and had just cleared a village, when they jumped us--just one hell of a cross fire. We fought our way back to the village. We cleared with two of our men wounded and kept them pinned down for another two hours, but it was just a matter of time before they got reinforcements. Two of the villagers walked two miles and managed to get back to us with a couple of trucks. We took everyone, and I mean everyone, including two old folks who were dying. No one was going to be left behind to those bastards. We fought our way back to the An Soc."

"A mile from the bridge, a kid fell out of the truck in front of us. The boy was right in the middle of the road. The VC opened up on us with everything they had when we stopped. Sills looked at me and said, with that good old boy voice of his, "that just ain't right.""

"He went out to get the boy and I used up two mags, giving him covering fire, there and back. It was worse when we got to the bridge. They had regrouped and were waiting for us. Sills and I took the point and cleared the way across. Seven men and forty-nine villagers made it with only one casualty. Sills was hit by a round that cut the femoral artery in his left leg. He died during the evac. His last order was to call in air support. When they blew bridge, almost all of those green men were on it."

Bennie handed a small box to Todd. "This is why I got off the train."

Todd opened the box and then handed it to Buzz. "You can't do this; it's the Congressional Medal of Honor. It belongs to you."

"It might have my name on it but it belongs to the both of us. He's earned the right to have it."

Buzz closed the lid. "We can arrange a capsule for it and have it properly buried here tomorrow, if that's what you want."

"Put it right up at the base of the stone for me."

"We'll see to it."

In the distance, they could see a cab pull up to the gate. "I took the liberty of planning ahead. Can I offer you gentlemen a lift?"

Buzz and Todd declined the offer. "If it's all the same, we'll walk back."

"You're right. It's a nice day and it would be a shame to waste it."

Buzz and Todd were alone on the hill. "I can barely remember Vietnam, Todd."

He looked down at the Stone. "What do you think Sills would've said?"

I doubt if he would have said anything. But I have a good idea what he would have done."

Todd looked up. "What do you think it would have been?"

"He wouldn't have let Bennie Callistor walk down that hill alone."

Murdoch and Styles were important men, but they still had to wait their turn, so it took another week to make arrangements at the cemetery and also to finish their plans for Bennie Callistor.

"I've never been in a Caboose before. What would be the crew compliment?"

Buzz thought about it for a moment. "They don't use them much anymore, but I think it is about three."

"That should be more than enough for one man and a palace for a man like Bennie Callistor."

Todd looked at his watch. "You'd better get going. I'll meet you at the yard."

Macy, the DA, and Todd were at the tracks when Buzz pulled up with Bennie, his doctor, and the nurse. The doctor jumped out and ran over to the tracks. "I've never been down here before."

Everyone looked at him in amazement. ""Is he kidding?"

Macy turned in the direction of a whistle and then looked back at Bennie. "You know, you are not going to be able to do this."

Bennie spoke softly so only she could hear him. "You're right, but I have to try. It's the only life I have."

Buzz stepped forward. "Bennie, ending up under a train is a lousy way to die. So, Todd and I may have come up with a solution for you. All we ask is that you give it a chance."

Everyone stepped back as it crossed the switch and on to the siding. At sixty feet, 4400 horse power, and 387,000 pounds, the locomotive was hard to ignore. It was an impressive piece of technology that literally blocked out the sky. Gliding to a stop, the brakes barely made a sound.

The conductor climbed down and made his way up the platform. He stopped in front of the group and looked at a clipboard. "Which one of you is Mr. Callistor?"

Everyone stepped aside, silently identifying Bennie. "Sir, would you sign here, please?"

Bennie read it carefully. "This must be a mistake."

The conductor shook his head. "No mistake, unless you're not who you say you are."

"I'm Callistor."

"Then, I will need your signature. I have a schedule to keep and you are holding me up."

He took a step forward and came to attention. "Sir, one vet to another, I would consider it an honor if you took a ride on my train."

Bennie slowly signed the documents and handed them back. The conductor checked the signature and then his watch. "Maybe my watch is about five minutes fast. I'd better have it checked."

They all walked to the end of locomotive and looked up at the caboose. Bennie turned and looked at Todd and Buzz. "Why?"

Todd shrugged, "Because it's the right thing to do."

Macy extended a hand. "I looked after the legal end of it as my last official act as lawyer."

Bennie was clearly bothered. "Why would you do that?"

She waved a hand. "Don't worry. I have decided to go into physics. You can blow stuff up."

"Like what?" The nurse was curious.

Macy grinned evilly. "Lawyers."

Todd handed him an envelope after everyone shook Bennie's hand one last time. "These are instructions and contact numbers. Everything is taken care of. You can go anywhere you want."

The locomotive whistle sounded. The nurse stepped forward, hugged Bennie, and whispered in his ear. "I have done it on a trampoline, you dirty old man."

She let him go as the train started to move. Bennie stepped smoothly off the platform and on to the steps of the caboose. He waved one more time before the caboose made its way on to a main line and disappeared.

Macy raised her arm against the sun. "He didn't even have time to say good-bye."

The DA looked at her. "He didn't need to."

She looked at everyone. "My dad's barbecuing tonight."

The nurse thought it was a great idea. "I've heard about your father. I could use the practice treating burns."

The DA feigned hurt. "Oh, sure, don't invite the lawyer."

"Oh, of course you must come. How could anyone resist the opportunity to poison the District Attorney?"

It was a terrific party. Glen was prevented from getting to the barbecue by at least twenty people who kept feeding him drinks. It was great evening with good people, good food, and a beautiful sunset.

Around 11:30 p.m., Todd and Buzz said good night to everyone. They found their way back to where it all started, in the diesel yard. Even at that hour, a few rays of the long setting sun were still visible.

Todd took one last look around, trying to take it all in one last time. "It's time."

"It's time, Todd."

No one was on Main Street and no one saw the taillights of their car, as it disappeared into the night.

CHAPTER 7
MCCOOK

"There are those among us who create monsters, with love and care they send them out into the world to create great mischief

Oggie Briggs shifted his weight on the bar stool. It groaned in protest, a lot. He didn't seem to notice, or care for that matter, about the damage he was doing to the furniture under him. Big men sometimes don't notice the small things around them, and Oggie Briggs was a big man. At six foot three inches and 340 pounds, he was more planet than man, but what really set him apart was his strength. He was born strong and his strength never stopped increasing. At the age of twenty, he was terrifying. The deltoids in his shoulders were half way up his neck, despite the fact he'd never done a lick of exercise.

Of course, with great strength comes great responsibility, and Oggie exercised that virtue about as much as he physically exercised, which was never. Put simply, the man was a brute and no one would ever know, or dared to ask, why brutality was so central to his being. Was he reacting to something, a slight, an injustice? Had he come to a fork in the road of life? The answer to both was no.

He was fifteen in 1955 when he made a decision. It was a hot summer in McCook, Nebraska, that year. Oggie had spent most of May and June doing odd jobs in the hope of learning a trade, because as his father, bluntly, pointed out, "it don't make a whole lot of sense sending a stump to school every day to sit at a desk made of wood."

Gainful employment wasn't his strong suit, either. Of course, he could do the work well enough when he wanted to, but it was not much of a challenge. He sure wasn't being paid much for his time, the way he saw it. But you had to have money to live, and on a particular evening in July of 1955, Oggie Briggs wasn't doing a lot of living.

He succeeded in getting himself fired from a machine shop job, when the lead hand saw him deliberately break a lathe, in order to get off work early. It was ugly. The man called him some right ugly names, and if Oggie had learned anything in his short life of fifteen years, it was that he didn't like being called names. He also learned that day that he liked the look and feel of fear in people. Oggie didn't hit the man, but when he threatened him, the lead hand backed up. Oggie had never really seen fear before, but he liked the power it had over people and he found that it could be very useful.

His education continued that evening in a liquor store parking lot. Oggie walked a lot back then, because he liked the outdoor smells. He also walked because he didn't have a car. A man coming out of the liquor store had two bottles under his arms and another quart under his belt. At fifty-four years of age, he'd seen his share of hard living as a coal miner, a good steak and a drink were as good as it got.

He wasn't surprised to see find a snot nosed kid standing in front of him demanding his fire water. Kids just didn't have any respect for their elders these days. He politely told Oggie "to go fuck himself."

They were both surprised at what happened next. The first punch caved in the miner's rib cage. The second, following rapidly, broke his left eye socket. Oggie stood over the man, fists clenched, not believing what he had done and how easy it had been. He reached down and took the bottles, started to walk away, and stopped. He looked back at the man who was trying to get to his feet, while at the same time, trying to stem the flow of blood from what was left of his eye. Oggie walked back, looking at the label on each bottle of bourbon and whiskey. He decided he liked whiskey better. Taking the bottle of bourbon by the neck and swinging with everything he had, Oggie caught the man square in the face with it. The force of the blow lifted the man off his feet and on to his back. Oggie could still hear the screaming a block away.

His work was very clumsy, but he was learning. He understood on that very hot night that he had a gift and that he'd never have to work again.
He made that very clear to the town's only police officer who tried to arrest him a few days later. "You can't take me on, no one can, and there ain't a cell that can hold me." The police officer reached for his gun and, for his trouble, had his left wrist broken so badly he would never have full use of his hand again.

The bar stool groaned. He was forty years older and eighty pounds heavier, but the muscles under his skin had only gotten stronger under a layer of fat. Oggie had quickly settled into a comfortable life. He didn't vote, work, or run for office. He just took what he wanted, and no one dared to object, *ever*. McCook, Nebraska was his in everything but name. No fear or want for anything-- except once.

It was a long time ago and he'd dealt with it. He'd made an example of the man at the liquor store. No one had any doubt as to what would happen if someone mouthed up. But the fear had been there, just that once, and he'd felt it. It was not the outcome; that was never in doubt. It was the way the man hit him, the blows actually hurt. But it was the look in the man's eyes that really scared Oggie. *No fear*. It was a long time ago. Oggie heaved himself off the stool and threw some change on the counter. It didn't matter if it was right.

`It was hot out on the street. He liked the heat, because it made it easier to smell things. He loved smells. Oggie had a secret he'd never told anyone. His sense of smell was well above the range of most humans. In fact, his sensitivity was higher than most dogs. To Oggie, smells were like colors. Everything had odor. Skies were green to him, not blue, but the desert was. Women were always yellow, and not even perfume covered that. Fear was orange. Everything and everyone had a smell and he never forgot any of them.

He took a deep breath, drawing in all of those pretty colors and cataloging them in what there was of his cerebral cortex. It tasted so good he took another breath, but this time, it was different. Oggie knew every odor in the town. Now there was something different in the air. It was very, very faint, but it was definitely there. His third breath was even deeper. There was no doubt this time, there was something out there. He knew this smell. It was familiar. But the smell must have been from a long time ago, because he could not associate it with anything. Oggie had no sense of distance. He only knew that it was still a long way off. He shrugged and stepped into the street. Whatever it was, it was almost forgotten.

Oggie didn't get twenty steps. He stopped and froze like a statue in the middle of street. It was something he knew from a long time ago, and it was coming back. For the first time in his life, he felt a real disquiet come into his world. He slowly turned and looked up the road out of town. Something was coming. It was old and real, and fear was coming with it.

People can get off the path of their lives, for any number of reasons--because they want to, or because they don't. Sometimes, it's a detour, or they just get lost. There are times when they are pulled off the journey for reasons they don't even understand. Often, they don't even know it's occurring.

That's what was happening to Todd Styles and Buzz Murdoch. They hadn't planned to change direction. They had been to more places than they could possibly remember in the sixties. They had good and bad memories of hundreds of towns.

McCook had been long forgotten by both.

Sometimes, forces which were at work are difficult to explain, and those forces were bringing them back to McCook.

Todd looked over at Buzz, who was behind the wheel. "You've been uncharacteristically quiet the last couple of days, anything wrong?"

The puzzled look on Buzz's face changed to a smile. "No, just lost in thought, I guess. When we were out here the last time, did we have a plan? Did we ever stop and say we're going somewhere?"

Todd leaned against the door and looked at the passing countryside for a moment before answering. "I don't know if we had a game plan. It was a long time ago. If we did, it probably wasn't a very good one."

"How do you figure that?"

"If it was any good we'd have finished the trip."

"Well, this time we've got it together, although I'm stumped as to why we're headed in this direction."

"Is that what's bothering you?"

"As a matter of fact,...yeah. I know we have a lot of ground to cover, but this leg has got me thinking."

Todd moved his gaze out over the hood of the car and watched as the road pass under the Corvette. "Well, whatever's out there, we're a lot better prepared for it than the last time. We were pretty green."

"Uncharacteristically,... you've been reading the dictionary again, haven't you?"

"Just the really filthy words."

It was mid-afternoon of the next day, when Todd suddenly pulled off onto the shoulder.

"What's the matter?" Buzz was concerned.

Todd got out of the car and walked across the road without saying anything. Buzz waited a second before getting out and following him. They stared up at the sign, understanding now what brought them to this spot. The lettering, barely visible after more than fifty years of inclement weather, announced that you were leaving McCook County, that there was nothing worth seeing between the sign and New York, and to come back soon. "It's been over thirty-five years. He can't still be alive?"

Buzz turned and looked up the road to a town still a half day away. "If that sign is still here, so is he."

Sometimes, people become so comfortable and familiar with each other, that it's possible to say as much with silence as it is words. Neither man spoke at all for the next two hours.

Buzz spoke, finally. "There's a hotel a half mile up on the left. Let's stop there for the night and go the rest of the way in the morning." Todd nodded silently in agreement.

The Roadside Motel wasn't exactly five stars, but it was clean, comfortable, and had a small diner that offered home cooked meals, even though there wasn't a house within a hundred miles of the place. The owner was about as old as the hotel. Florence Walker was a thin woman with a care-worn face and blessed with the firm belief that everyone was nice, until proven otherwise.

The two men standing at the counter seemed to be another matter, altogether. They had stood there for a full minute without saying a word. "May I help you, Gentlemen?"

Todd suddenly came out a trance. 'Yes, we'd like a couple of rooms for the night."

Reaching under the counter Florence retrieved two keys and a receipt book. "That will be $38 a night." When she completed the receipts, she handed over the keys and paperwork. "The diner is open until eight. If you don't feel like a sit down, let me know before seven and I'll make you some sandwiches."

They thanked her and stepped outside. "Did we just have a flashback?"

"Oh yeah, big time!"

"Well, she certainly doesn't look like Greta Gebauer or Gloria Lamplighter."

Buzz suddenly got a serious look on his face. "It ain't dark yet."

"Droll, Murdoch, really droll."

"Don't worry. I'll put a bucket of garlic outside your door. That should keep that nasty old Florence Walker away, provided you don't stick your head out the window."

"Where'd you get that sense of humor anyway?"

"Sent away."

Buzz was leaning against the car, waiting for his turn to get his luggage off the rack, when Todd asked a question. "Did you ever stay at the Grisemont?"

He scratched the back of his neck and tried to recall the location. "Griesmont? That's about ten blocks up from the Empire, close to the Battery. Is it a Brownstone?"

"Yeah, that's it."

"No, can't say that I ever have. Why do you ask?"

Todd smiled to himself and shook his head. "No reason."

Forty-five minutes later, they were in the diner, studying the menu board. "So, what do you think?"

"It doesn't look half bad."

There was an enormous bang and then, every light in the place went out. Florence's voice rattled off the walls. "God damn it, Wilson, the lights are off again!"

"What?"

"The lights are out! Are you blind?"

"Yes,... I am!"

"Oh, right."

The lights came back on with an uncomfortable flash. Todd was surprised to see a strange hand resting comfortably on Buzz's shoulder. He was even more surprised that he had one on his shoulder, too. They turned around to find Florence smiling up at them.

"What's the matter? You two look nervous, afraid of the dark?"

She laughed and stepped between them on her way to the kitchen. No worries, boys.

Old Wilson is harmless and couldn't find his way out of a paper bag with a flashlight."

They sat at a table next to a window that faced west. The view was spectacular. The sun was orange and about fifteen minutes off the horizon. In the distance, they could just make out an abandoned farm house with a windmill. An endless line of telephone poles marched behind the farm and disappeared over the horizon.

Florence had suddenly appeared at the table and handed them menus. "What can I get you fella's?"

They took quick glances through the menu's, handed them back with their orders, and returned to the view out the window, both lost in thought about what lay ahead. Florence was back in about five minutes with Todd's order. He thanked her without taking his eyes off the view.

"Todd?"

"Yeah?"

"Your dinner is here."

Todd just wasn't going to let go of that view. "Hmmm?"

Buzz picked up his fork and tapped it on his glass for emphasis. "Your dinner is on the table."

Todd reluctantly and briefly turned his head. Something out there was pretty damned interesting. He glanced at the plate and started to turn his head back. Then, he did a double take. His dinner, exactly what he ordered, was indeed on the table. Stacked up, one on top of the other, was the pork chop on the bottom, with a large clove of un peeled garlic sitting on a piece of toast that was perched, precariously, on the top of a mountain of mashed potatoes. Where are the peas?"

"They are on the side of the potato mountain."

Todd leaned over so he could see under the toast. "Okay, I see them. At a distance, they kind of look like trees."

"Yeah, except they're rounder and farther apart."

"What did you order?"

"I went with a burger and fries, pretty tough to mess that up."

Todd picked his fork. "Well, you'd think that. Where do you think I should start?"

"Eat the trees."

Buzz's order arrived a moment later. Todd, picking trees off his mountain, looked at Buzz's order. "Well, at least the hamburger part is in the right place."

At a distance of twenty feet in a dark room, it did look like a hamburger, but not up close. The buns were upside down with the tomato, relish, onion, and mustard sitting on the outside. "You want some of my garlic?"

A clove of garlic seemingly out of nowhere, but probably from the kitchen, hit the window and ricocheted back onto the table next to Buzz's plate. 'Thanks. I'm okay."

Buzz picked up what looked like a French fry, and tapped his plate, breaking off a corner.

Todd picked one off Buzz's plate. "That's something you don't see every day. Who would have thought you could get breading to stick to a machine screw?"

"What are they?"

"You didn't get fries, you got the fry maker."

Todd broke off a piece of breading. "Not bad. I should have ordered this instead."

Florence suddenly reappeared out of the woodwork with another order. She picked up Buzz's plate, dumped the fry cutter parts into a bag, dumped the real fries onto his plate, and then dropped it back on the table with a bang that lifted the utensils. She strode back to the kitchen, stopped halfway, returned to their table, picked up the bolts that Buzz was still removing breading from, and marched off to the kitchen--all without uttering a single word. In the kitchen, they could hear a large heavy machine start up.

Todd picked up a piece of garlic toast. *"Bon Appetit."*

Dinner done and back outside, Todd took a deep breath. The air was cool and clean. "You want to talk about it, Buzz?"

"No, not yet, let's get squared away for the evening first."

Todd opened the trunk and pulled out his travel bag and a bottle of Griz water. "See you in a couple of hours. We can sit out back and have a drink."

Buzz took the bottle out of his hand "How about coffee tonight?"

Todd took the bottle from Buzz and put it back in the trunk. "That sounds like a better choice. I'll get some from the diner before it closes."

"See you out back around eight."

Todd unlocked the door and stepped inside. It took a few minutes of fumbling to find the light switch. The fluorescent light in the ceiling flickered to life. "Charming?"

He dropped the bag on the bed and began to unpack, taking out a change of clothes for the next day. As he searched in the bag for a pair of socks, his hand closed on a hard object. He pulled it out and turned it over in his hands. It was a small photo album he hadn't seen in years, and he certainly couldn't recall packing it.

Sitting down, he slowly opened it. The pictures were old. The kids weren't even teenagers. He remembered that Marcie had put it together to cover one year, two pictures for each month. Turning the pages slowly, Jan and David seemed to age with each passing month. Todd stopped at one picture and laughed. Jan, feeling she was not getting the correct amount of attention, had picked up a large chunk of David's birthday cake and proceeded to jam it up his nose, just as Todd took the picture. Marcie was visible in the background with a horrified look on her face. She really gave Todd a going over for that one.

"Nice timing, Todd! You couldn't just take the picture?" He never said a word when she gave him the photo book for his office on his birthday. The picture was on the first page.

He took a deep breath and looked up at the room. He was a thousand miles from home. The loneliness was crushing. He would give everything he had just to have his family back for five minutes. Todd closed the book firmly. There would be plenty of time for this when the journey was done. He had work to do.

There was a knock at the door before Buzz stepped inside. He looked down at the book in Todd's hand with understanding. "I was beginning to think I was going to be stood up."

The alarm clock announced that it was ten after eight. "Sorry, I lost track of time. If we hurry, we should be able to get coffee before they close up shop at the diner."

Buzz waved a thermos and a couple of mugs. "We are covered! Good Sir, the sunset awaits us."

They found a couple of battered chairs behind the motel. It promised to be a spectacular evening. Buzz handed Todd a cup and poured out coffee for both of them. He took a drink and looked at Todd in shock.

"What's the matter? It can't be that bad."

"You aren't going to believe this stuff!"

Todd drank a mouthful, rolling it around on this tongue before swallowing, and then he looked into his cup. "That's the best cup of coffee I've ever had. Whoever made this should be given a medal."

"Wilson made it."

"Wilson's blind."

Buzz held his cup and saluted the setting sun, "To the blind!"

"To the blind!"

They watched the sun set in silence. It was quite a while before one of them spoke. It was just three days and a long time ago. "We can't blame ourselves for how it turned out."

Buzz shook his head. "We screwed up,... I screwed it up."

"It wasn't our first foul up, our last and you know it wasn't our worst."

"We shouldn't have turned our backs and ran, Todd. That's what really bothers me, and it still does. We're better than that."

"No, it wasn't about running. We won the battle. We just couldn't finish the war. You gave as good as you got, but you were hurt pretty badly in that fight. If we'd stayed, it could've been a lot worse, and we bought that girl the time she needed to get out."

Buzz knew Todd was right. But it didn't lesson the pain or fear of the man, if you could call him that. "Well, we all have to come back to face our demons, eventually."

"That we do, Mister Murdoch that we do. We have lived to fight another day." On that note, they decided to call it a night.

Back in his room, Buzz pulled out a small album of his own. He stopped at a picture he took of Molly, when they were on a holiday in Baia Dos Tigres off the coast near the horn of Africa. They had planned the vacation for over a year. He'd decided to surprise her with a complete package that included England, France, Germany, and Italy. She was ecstatic and asked if she could make a few changes to the itinerary. A week later, she presented him with the amendments. No England, France, no Italy. Germany was still there, if you planned to holiday at the airport. There was only one destination and he couldn't even find it on a map, until she pointed to a dot in the Pacific. When he asked why it didn't have a name, she told him they hadn't come up with one yet. The way she saw it, if they were going to travel halfway around the world, they should see the parts that really mattered.

It was one of the best times of their marriage. They went to every back lane in every backwater that they could find. Molly shopped, shopped, and shopped some more. There wasn't a street bazaar that escaped her. People who thought they could take advantage of her considered themselves lucky to get away without paying *her*.

He'd taken the picture at one of those bars that lined the beach where they stayed. Molly was at a table with three bottles in front her, all of which were made from a home brew made by a local named Winer. The stuff was as smooth as silk and had the alcohol equivalent of someone dropping an anvil on your head. The bartender was determined to wave Molly off when she ordered a bottle of the stuff. Molly was just as determined to get her hands on it. "Winer not drink for lady. Ginger Ale is for nice girls like you!"

Molly politely asked him if he would like the nice girl to punch out his lights, which he, fortunately, misunderstood to mean it was too bright in the bar. He decided it was easier to serve what she wanted than to translate weird American English.

With the men in the bar watching in stunned silence as Molly manned down three bottles and made it out the door under her own steam. It shortened the night considerably--no harm, no foul. But damn, did she snore! The manager accused Buzz of tuning a motorcycle in his room all night. Buzz rubbed his eyes, closed the book, and put it back in his suitcase. He lay awake for a while in bed and chuckled at how thin the walls had been in that place. He reached over his head and tapped. These walls were even thinner. As he drifted off to sleep, he thought it was good thing history did not repeat itself in hotel rooms. Of course, history *is* a notorious repeat offender and on this particular night, there was some serious offending going on in Rooms 18, 19, 20 and 21. That's how legends are made.

It started around two in the morning, when the occupants of Room 20, names withheld although no one was innocent, decided to have sex. Starting with the subtle tell-tale squeak of bed springs, it progressed, over the next two hours, into tub thumping, window rattling, flat-out mindless rutting. That would have been acceptable, understandable, and even admirable. But no, the occupants of Room 20 decided it was more fun to do it in a mind numbing, endless series of increasingly violent sessions, which lasted twenty minutes, followed by silence. There was no predicting when they would start again.

By three in the morning, both Buzz in Room 19 and the Oliver H. Schmedlapps of Rhode Island in

Room 21 could tell within a foot where the occupants of Room 20 and their bed were at any given time. The occupant of Room 19 was asleep.

Buzz rolled over and looked at the alarm clock. The numbers were hard to read because of the vibration coming through the wall behind his bead. The motion was giving him a headache. In fact, he was starting to get a little sea sick.

He was debating whether to get up and talk to his neighbors, when he heard the voice of Mr. Oliver H. Schmedlapp of Rhode Island, over the moaning, groaning, and thumping. "FOR THE LOVE OF CHRIST!!! FINISH HER OFF!!!" In a melodramatic touch, the love monster stopped halfway between finish and off.

Mrs. Oliver H. Schmedlapp, also of Rhode Island, gently chided her husband. "Herman, keep your voice down. You're going to wake up the entire motel."

"Wake everyone up! Holy Crap, Myrtle! Our neighbors back home can hear those two doing the carpet nasty!"

"Don't be silly, Herman. Bill Gavin is seventy-five, and he is deaf as a post."

Mr. Schmedlapp had a little trouble fielding that one. Mrs. Oliver H. Schmedlapp of Rhode Island was good at derailing a conversation. "Oh yeah! What about that blabber mouth wife of his?"

In a patronizing voice, she reminded him that Bill Gavin's wife was dead.

"Really, you sure?"

"You should know."

"How do you know that I should know?"

"You were the one that embalmed her, Herman."

Herman suddenly had a flash back that generated a totally evil and filthy grin on his face.

"Oliver,... Oliver! What's the look on your face? Have you done something?"

"No dear, of course not ".Of course, he'd done something,...really naughty, but he sure as hell wasn't going to tell his wife what it was. He decided that now would be a good time to take his evil, filthy grin out for some fresh air.

"I better go next door and talk to the neighbors. I am going to ask them to try and keep the noise down."

"You know you can be a bit grumpy after eight in the evening, if you don't have your Cocoa, so do try to be nice. They are just young and don't know to keep the music down."

For Buzz, sleep was now impossible, and when he heard the Schmedlapps door open he decided to get up, just in case things got ugly, and generated more noise. The Schmedlapps were already outside when he got there. Philip Schmedlapp was a short, balding man in his fifties with a bad comb-over. His wife was an exact duplicate of him, except for the comb-over and housecoat. Philip Schmedlapp, Rhode Island, extended a hand to Buzz.

"Buzz Murdoch, Connecticut."

That's my wife over there with her head plastered to the window. You'd think with it moving like that she'd have a pretty big headache by now, but far as I can tell, it's mostly bone."

Buzz tried to be pleasant under the circumstances. "She's a very attractive woman. You're a lucky man."

"What, are you on crack? God damn it, Myrtle, show some manners and introduce yourself."

"Yeah, sure,...hi." Trying desperately to see through the blinds, Myrtle wasn't letting go of that window without a fight.

The two men had now forgotten about the occupants of the hotel room and were watching Mrs. Oliver H. Schmedlapp, Rhode Island drag her face back and forth over the glass, until the shaking blinds finally relented and let her get her eyes on the action. "Holy Crap, look at the size of that thing! Now, that is some kind of pork sword he's got going there. You can grease my hinges with that thing, baby!"

"God damn it, Myrtle, you're getting that window all sticky!"

Myrtle pried her face off the hotel room window, and ran back to their room. "I gotta get the movie camera. The girls in my bridge club aren't going to believe this!"

Oliver Schmedlapp immediately pulled the door to the room shut, went to the car, and got a tent rope out of the trunk, tied one end to door knob and the other to the bumper of his car.

Myrtle Schmedlapp made it pretty clear that she was annoyed. "Oliver, open this door, you fat sack of crap!"

"Shut up! You are going to wake the neighbors."

"They already are awake. That's what I got the camera for!"

The only thing that prevented her from dragging the Schmedlapp's 1958 Buick Roadmaster through the motel room door was the fact that it was in park.

"Was she always like that?"

Oliver scratched his chin. "No, she's usually been pretty damn boring, except that time when she went after a gopher with the car. "Fella at the Texaco station got the windshield cleaned up right nice. I'm thinking it's all this fresh air that's making her nuts. We don't have a lot of it back in Rhode Island."

"Air?"

"Oh, we got lots of that, just none of it's fresh."

Buzz watched the Schmedlapp's car rocking back and forth as Myrtle Schmedlapp tried to simultaneously open the hotel room door and tear the bumper off the Buick. "So, what are you going to do now that you can't get back in?"

"I'll sleep in the car; the extra weight will help hold the car down."

Oliver Schmedlapp said good-night and crawled into the back of his Buick. Buzz was left standing alone in the cool air that can only be found at 3:00 a.m. in McCook County, Nebraska. It was definitely good air. There were big challenges coming, and for the first time in many years, he felt ready to face them. He stopped on the way back to his room and looked at the door to Room 18. Todd hadn't made an appearance. He couldn't possibly sleep through this. Buzz raised his hand to knock, changed his mind, and just opened the door. A blast of sound hit him in the face. It was even worse here, two rooms away.

Todd's bed, and just about everything that wasn't nailed down, was moving to the rhythm of the hump-a-thon taking place two walls away. Boom! The room inhaled. Scream! The room exhaled. The medicine cabinet door in the bathroom swung like a metronome, spitting out a bottle on every swing. In the middle of the sonic chaos, Todd lay face down, with one arm hanging over the side of the bed, like a weird curb feeler. He was sound asleep, oblivious to the energy raging around him. Buzz slowly closed the door, not that it mattered. He could have thrown a grenade in there and it wouldn't have made any difference.

The climax finally came an hour later, the big enchilada. Buzz pulled the sheets over his head. "I hope I live through this!"

"Here it comes, baby, the big one, the fucking dreamliner coming right out of the big apple!"

The impact and acceleration was unbelievable as the energy from the love bugs in Room 20 drove their bed through the wall, striking the headboard of Buzz's bed, and rocketing him across the room and into the wall on the opposite side. As it struck the wall, Buzz pulled the sheets tightly around this head and wondered what was on the other side. His brain reminded him that he was going through a wall in a bed at ten-miles-per-hour. "Who the hell cared?"

Todd rolled over and looked at his alarm clock. "What time did I put in that wake call for?" He rolled over and scratched the top of his head before sitting up. There was a draft coming in from someplace. Maybe he left a window open. "Hey, Buzz."

Two rooms over, he could see two people he didn't recognize, waving at him from their bed. "Hi. How are ya?"

It took about thirty minutes for Buzz and one of his neighbors to push the beds back through the walls. Todd decided to go back to sleep and was unavailable. The process was slowed by the fact that most of the walls were on the floor and the female half of the *sexathon* refused to get up. She liked the idea of being pushed around in a bed by two men.

"She always was like this?"

The man nodded ruefully. "I'm running out of bullets."

By the time they got back to Todd's room, he was sleeping soundly. "That's amazing. How does he do that?"

Buzz shook his head. "It is truly one of nature's great mysteries."

"I'm thinking you may be right."

Buzz said good night and started for the door, when the man coughed and pointed to the wall. "Oh yeah, right."

As they stepped through the wall, both men turned for a final look. "You know, your friend should cough up a couple of bucks for a new pair of jammies."

The sun rose over the Roadside Motel right on time, just like it did at the Ocean Grove Hotel and the thousands of others like them all over America.

Florence looked at the two of them speculatively over her glasses. "Sleep all right?"

Todd reported that he slept like a baby.

She looked Buzz up and down. "What's your problem? You look like crap.

The room was a little drafty."

"Next time, we'll give you a blankie. Hope to see you again on your return trip."

They loaded the trunk and secured the luggage rack before climbing into the car. Todd was reaching to put the car in reverse when he looked up. He tapped Buzz on the shoulder, who was trying to recover some sleep, and pointed through the windshield.

The two doors in front of them opened simultaneously with the Schmedlapps of Rhode Island, emerging first. They waved at Todd and Buzz and looked at the adjoining door as two hands appeared on the door frame.

"You know them?"

"Shchmedlapps, Rhode Island, nice people."

A man in his high forties appeared in the other door. Balancing himself carefully on the door frame, he looked down and made a couple of attempts at stepping out the door, first with one foot, and then with the other, without success. The four-inch drop was beyond the mobility of his damaged hips and limbs. In desperation, he turned his back to the open door and proceeded to step down backwards, never loosening his grip on the door frame. When he was on the sidewalk, he slowly gave up his grip on the door frame, like a drowning man letting go of a life buoy.

He slowly shuffled the three feet to the hood of the car, grabbing the ornament. From there, he worked his way along the fender until he got his hands firmly on the door handle. Carefully pulling the door open, he stepped around it and discovered he could not lift his legs over the door sill. He backed into the car, sat down and pulled his right leg into the car, and placed it on the accelerator. He was reaching for the other leg when a voice erupted from the hotel room. "Honey, I'll be out in a minute. Have you paid for the room yet?

He panicked, presumably in attempt to get away in the car, and slammed the door, forgetting that his left leg was still out in the parking lot. He grabbed the steering wheel in agony.

Mrs. Schmedlapp of Rhode Island was anchored to the sidewalk as her husband tried to drag her to the car. She had paid to see a train wreck and no one was going to deprive her of the show. "Don't you want to see what she looks like?"

"No, I do not want to see what she looks like, Myrtle. Now, get in the damn car!"

"Oliver!"

"I don't want to be within hundred miles of this place, in case she decides to have a 'God Damn' flash back!"

Their car disappeared in a cloud of dust with Myrtle Shmedlapp of Rhode Island, hanging out the window, with one hand holding on to her hat and the other hand holding a camera.

Buzz looked over at the terrified man sitting in the car next to them, and then at Todd.

"Todd, Todd!"

Todd suddenly came out of his trance and looked down at the shift lever and at the open hotel door.

"Reverse, Todd. We are going to need reverse."

The car responded with a reassuring thump as the transmission engaged and slowly moved out of the parking space. As the car pulled out on to the road and accelerated, Todd burst out laughing. "Can we pick them, or what?"

Buzz looked at him with a perfectly straight face. "Three rooms destroyed in a motorized orgy and we still got our damage deposit back. We are living the dream."

They laughed well into the drive to McCook, knowing there would be little to cheer about in the days and weeks to come.

A wiser person than this narrator has proven that time is a river. True enough, it has eddies, currents, and hidden dangers. Like a river, everyone is carried along with it, subject to its whims and moods. People, like time, seem to speed up and slow down, picking up some things and dropping others. The one thing neither is supposed to do is stop. Todd Stiles and Buzz Murdoch were going to learn very shortly that time, for the citizens of McCook, had indeed come to a halt and they were paying a terrible price for the privilege..

Todd pointed to the left. Buzz steered the car across the street looking for oncoming traffic, not that it mattered, there was nothing moving as far as the eye could see. He pulled into a parking spot and looked down at the gauges. The tank read almost full. Buzz leaned against the door and turned off the ignition. As soon as the engine quit, a wave of silence seemed to rush in from all directions and flood the car. The sign on the store front announced Arnold's Groceries.

Todd got out of the car and took a deep breath. Even the air was thick and stale, like the smell of old sweat. He walked out into the street, not bothering to look for traffic. He waited for Buzz to join him.

Buzz handed him the keys to the Corvette. "Still think he's dead?"

Todd answered, looking up the street, and then back to Buzz. "No, he's still alive. You can see it and feel it. There is real fear here."

"Worse, they're terrified. There has been no progress here in over thirty years. None! These people are too frightened to even paint a wall."

Todd nodded and pointed at the sign. "Let's see if the prices are still thirty years old."

They stepped into the store and waited until the door shut behind them. The place was as quiet as the street. Buzz picked up a basket and walked down an aisle to get some groceries. It looked like they were going to be in town for a while.

Walking over to the counter, Todd looked for someone to provide service. He stopped short, looked down, and slowly moved his foot over the floor. Spots, they looked fresh against the dirt on the floor.

"Just juice from some meat I sold a customer. I should have cleaned that up already."

Todd looked up at the man, who was in his early fifties. He had appeared from a room in the back behind the counter. At first impression, he looked fairly normal, except that he appeared to be anchored to the floor like a statue. "How may I help you, Sir?"

"We just need to pick up some groceries."

The man replied slowly. "You'll be staying at the Cameron McGregor Hotel, then?"

"I suspect we will."

"The Cameron has kitchens in the second floor rooms, which should do you fine. We have everything you need here. When you're done, just holler, and we'll get you settled up."

Todd thanked him as he turned and returned to the back room. He could hear a woman's voice.

"Who was that out there? I don't know that voice."

"Just customers, don't you pay any never mind. You know you shouldn't be getting up until you heal right."

"Those voices are different."

"A couple customers, some folks passing through, is all."

"My God, you got to tell them to go, while they can!"

"Woman, curse you and that mouth of yours!" The door closed cutting off the voices.

Buzz appeared from an aisle. "How did you make out?"

He handed Todd a package of sandwich meat and pointed to the expiration date.

Todd whistled slowly. "Is it all like this?"

"Worse!"

Buzz looked at the closed door. "Getting acquainted with the citizenry?"

"If that's what you want to call them. Let's just take the dry goods".

Buzz reached for his wallet. "Don't worry about it, Buzz, let's take what we need and get settled in at the hotel."

"Seriously?"

Todd reached over the counter and retrieved a grocery bag. "That's why no one ever leaves. Everything in hell is free."

The owner stepped out of the room. "Did you find everything you need?"

Buzz told him what was in the bag. "That comes to $9.00, Sir."

They watched as he wrote a bill. He asked if there was anything else they would like.

Todd looked at the bill, and handed it to Buzz, who glanced over it and gave it back to the man behind the counter. "We're friends of the Mayor. Send him the bill."

They went back to the street. "You remember him?"

"No. He must have gotten here after we left. Did that bill look a little light to you?"

Todd reached into the shopping bag and pulled out the sandwich meat and pointed up the street. "Not if you were living in 1966. Let's hope we can get out of here in less than a week."

"You're quite an optimist."

Todd tossed the package of meat into the street. "If the food in this town doesn't kill us, we'll starve to death."

Back in the store, Bill Schwartz sat down on the edge of the bed and looked down at his sister. He had cleaned up the wound, put a fresh bandage on her shoulder, and pressed down gently. She winced. The infection was almost gone. Using some of the books from the doctor's office, he'd done a good job, but the wound kept opening because he couldn't do stitches, no one in town could. All he could do was keep it bandaged and control the bleeding until it closed.

"Those voices, you said they were customers?"

He looked down at her, smiled, reached over and placed a hand on the bandage, encouraging her to keep the pressure on it. Getting up, he walked over to the window, put his arms on the sill, and looked out. A nice day? He couldn't remember the last time he asked himself that question.

Without taking his gaze away from the window, he finally answered his sister's question. "No, they weren't customers, Sis."

"Well, who were they, then?"

He smiled for the first time, in a long time. "They were angels, sister, angels."

"You'll be in my bed tonight."

His smile disappeared. "No. Not tonight. You know it ain't right!"

"Don't care. I'm afraid."

The Cameron-McGregor was clean, at least in the lobby, which was not difficult, when you consider that the place didn't see a lot of walk-in customers. Buzz tapped Todd on the shoulder and pointed to an old grandfather clock ticking purposefully in the corner of the lobby.

He nodded that he remembered it. "It's hard to believe that it's still running."

At the reception desk, a guest book lay open. Buzz slowly thumbed through it while waiting for the desk clerk. He stopped. "Todd, you're going to want to have a look at this."

He quietly closed the door on the clock and joined him at the front desk. Buzz tapped the book and pointed to the sixth entry on the page. Aug 1962, Stiles and Murdoch. Beside each name was their signature.

Todd turned the page. There were four more entries. The last one was 11 Sept 1966, "Four people from 62 to 66."

"And no one has checked in here in over thirty years."

"Can I help you?"

They looked up from the book to find a man, in his seventies, standing on the stairs. "We're going to need a couple of rooms."

The man continued down the stairs. He looked like he was over seventy, but he didn't move like it. Back ramrod straight and footsteps solid on the floor. He walked past without giving them a second look, opened a small door, and stepped behind the counter, making sure it was properly closed. "I'm the proprietor. Welcome to the Cameron-McGregor Hotel. How long will you be staying?"

"We aren't sure but it shouldn't be too long." The answer seemed to agree with the man behind the counter.

"I should think a week should be sufficient."

Buzz looked at the man steadily. "That should be more than adequate for our needs."

The proprietor relaxed slightly and looked briefly at the register before pulling it off the counter, putting it in a drawer and retrieving a couple of cards. "We don't use the register any longer. Just fill these out. We only take cash here."

He picked them up, read them over and looked at Todd and Buzz. He gave no indication that he had seen either of them before. The cards went into slots nine and ten. "Here are your keys; both rooms are on the second floor."

"You don't need a damage deposit?"

"You two look like a couple of safe bets. Enjoy your stay."

His gaze never wavered as he watched the two men climb the stairs to the second floor. When they were out of sight, he removed the cards, leaned against the counter, and re-read them. Hell was coming back to McCook and this time, everyone was going to pay for the visit. He slowly put the cards into his pocket.

Buzz pushed in the key, turned the lock, and opened the door. The room was surprisingly large. He hadn't stayed in this room the last time he was here. It had a bar, fridge, stove, and a small fold-out table built into the wall for a place to eat. He turned as Todd entered the room.

He watched as Todd slowly inspected the room. Todd ran a hand across a table and opened the drawers at the end of the table, before settling into a chair.

Buzz laughed. "What are you looking for, microphones?"

"Anything is possible in this town. Is that thing working?" He pointed to the fridge.

Buzz held up two glasses with ice in them, poured in some ginger ale, and handed a glass to Todd, "Just barely."

Buzz took a mouthful and grimaced. The drink was flat.

"How are you enjoying the stay so far?"

He put his drink down. "Not very much, did you recognize him?"

Todd nodded slowly. "Not the face, the walk. That's hard to forget. I don't think he was working at the hotel, but he was definitely in McCook the last time we were here. You?"

"I remember him. He wore a suit and a Fedora, but nothing beyond that. Where do you want to start?"

"Let's begin with moving the Corvette off the street. It's like waving a flag. There should still be a parking lot behind the hotel. When we've got that covered, we should try and find some food that isn't forty years past its due date."

Buzz waited for him on the street while Todd parked the car. He handed Buzz the keys. "Tops up and the doors are locked."

He pointed to a restaurant in the distance. "I guess we'd better get used to being on foot for a while."

It wasn't a pleasant walk. The sun was high in the sky, but the air felt cold. They only saw three people in the fifteen minutes it took to get to the diner. Two of them they passed on the sidewalk. They had their eyes down, no acknowledgement. One other was across the street. He was an old, ancient looking black man sitting on a bench, wearing a dark suit and straw hat. He was staring intently in their direction. "You remember him?"

Buzz replied softly, even though there was no way the man could hear him from across the street. "No, the face does not register, at least not at this distance. From the look of it, he's blind."

Todd didn't say anything, but he didn't think the man was blind because he was definitely looking at them and his head moved as they walked. When Buzz stopped to tie a shoe lace, Todd looked directly across the street at the man, making eye contact. The man sat intently for a full minute, and then he suddenly smiled. The teeth were white and very straight. From across the street, they looked like piano keys embedded in his face.

The man stood up and turned to the bench, groping for something until his hand closed on the intended object. Standing as erect as the owner of the hotel he began to walk away in the opposite direction, the white cane in his right hand gently feeling its way along the sidewalk.

When Buzz stood up and looked across the street, the man was nowhere to be seen. "How long did the guy who runs the hotel say we would be here?"

"About a week."

"I'm thinking we should make it less than five days."

It took ten minutes to get to the restaurant. They didn't bother looking for a sign. The place didn't have one, never had. They remembered it as soon as they stepped in the door, not a single thing had changed. It was like it had been frozen in amber, right down to the rivets. On the left, a florid man in a booth, in his late 60's, sat with the owner of the hotel. The back of the head of the other man belonged to someone younger. On the right, two women were drinking coffee. The one facing them had a cup of coffee halfway to her mouth, when it froze in recognition. Farther back on the right, in the shadows, a movement caught Buzz's attention. He watched it intently. Whoever was back there had moved deeper into the darkness.

Todd walked over to the lunch counter and turned a menu around so he could read it. The man behind the counter was cleaning a spill. He turned to serve Todd, and then, he stopped in his tracks. There was eye contact and immediate recognition.

"Two grilled cheese sandwiches and coffee. Does that work for you, Buzz?"

The man behind the counter suddenly discovered his legs and slowly moved to the kitchen door without taking his eyes off Todd.

They sat down in a booth so Buzz could see the shadow at the back of the place. It was like watching a trapped animal trying to find a way past a predator, and the animal was becoming more agitated as the sunlight shrank its ability to hide.

The sandwiches and coffee arrived. The waiter placed the food on the table and backed up a few steps. Todd took the top from the sandwich and inspected what was two pieces of toast with chunks of cold, old cheese in it. The coffee was hot and bitter from being on the burner for hours. They ate without saying a word as their waiter scurried away. The little animal in the corner was now having trouble staying put.

A woman appeared with a piece of paper.

"Where is our waiter? Is he too afraid to come out of his hole?" Todd asked the woman, sarcastically.

She answered quietly and with a hint of rebuke in her voice. "Can you blame him?"

The nasty critter in the corner suddenly moved, causing her to jump. "I got to get back to work. Just leave your bill and money on the table."

Todd watched her run back to the safety of the kitchen. "I'm surprised she didn't leap over the counter."

Buzz dropped five dollars without checking the bill. "That be enough?"

Todd hadn't looked at the bill, either. "Who cares?"

When they stepped out onto the street, Buzz pushed Todd off to the side and indicated that they should wait. Less than a minute later, the little animal hiding in the shadow in the back of the restaurant burst out of the diner. He really looked and behaved like an over sized weasel. He was just over five feet tall, with close set eyes, greasy hair combed back. The only thing missing was a coat of fur.

"Hello, Gilly.

He stopped and spun around as Buzz stepped away from the wall. There was immediate recognition followed by a feral grin, which displayed teeth as greasy as his hair. "Well, well. Welcome back! About time, I was wondering when you two chicken shit cowards were going to return and cleanup some unfinished business."

Buzz hit him in the solar plexus with a left jab that lifted him off the pavement. Gilly landed on the pavement like a folding chair.

Todd picked him up off the sidewalk and slammed him against the wall. "You've gotten a lot more arrogant in the last thirty years, Gilly. Too bad you still haven't gotten a set of balls to back it up!"

"Fuck you! You think you are going to make a difference this time! You should see him now. There ain't no police or doctor here anymore to carry you out, no need. There won't be anything left when he gets back and finds you here!"

Todd grabbed Gilly by the throat. "We are going to save him a trip. Where is he?"

Gilly gasped for air. "You are not going to die easy, Pal."

The waitress from the restaurant joined them on the street and looked hard at Gilly. "He goes out of town every couple of months, but God only knows where he goes or what he does. Not even this little rat knows. What I can tell you is that he goes down to the operator and makes a call. The telephone building has the only working phone left in town. Oggie had all the others ripped out.

Buzz tightened his grip enough for Gilly to start gagging. "When was his last call and how long has he been gone?"

The waitress grabbed Buzz's wrist. "Don't kill him, not yet. He does it random so people can't predict when he goes or comes back, but he made a call this morning. He is usually gone for about a week."

Gilly gave her a wicked look. "You're getting pretty brave, bitch. I'm going to ask him to let me watch when he takes you to the fun house."

The two women who had been drinking coffee in the restaurant came out to the street. The waitress looked at the women, and then back at Gilly. "Hand over the keys."

"I'm not giving you squat! What do you think you're going to do?" Gilly spat in her face.

Without hesitating, one of the women stepped forward and with everything she had, kicked him. This time he landed on his back with his hands between his legs. They could hear his scream a block away.

"You have to admit, Buzz, it's pretty hard to tell him from the pavement when he's down there."

The waitress bent over Gilly and reached under his shirt. She held up a long brass chain that was attached to a belt loop. "He keeps the keys and his wallet on a chain."

One of the women from the restaurant grabbed it and yanked, ripping off the belt loop, causing Gilly to scream. "You bitch! That's theft!"

"I'll bring the car around front."

"Get all the rope you can find."

The waitress looked down at him with open hatred. "This has gone on long enough. The flats south of here are as bad as a desert."

The other woman nodded. "We'll let you know when we're finished."

The waitress shook her head. "No. When it's done, keep going. This is your chance to get out. Don't waste it."

"They're going to come looking for us. We might as well come back and face it here with everyone else."

She looked at her friend with sadness. "By the time this is done, there won't be anything left to come back to."

Gilly's car pulled up to the curb. The two women reached down and grabbed Gilly. When he fought them off, one of them stomped on him hard, taking the wind out of him. They tried again, dragging him to his feet and over to the car. One of them opened the passenger door, shoved him in, and then got in next to him. Gilly was now learning to understand what terror really felt like.

The waitress looked in the car window. "Can you handle this?"

They nodded. "We'll deal with it. Jesus, Beryl, come with us."

The man who was behind the counter came running out of the restaurant, just as she was stepping off the curb, as the car pulled away. "Beryl! What the hell are you doing? You're going to get us killed, you stupid broad!"

She turned on him with white hot hatred. "Nineteen years! Nineteen years, that animal used me and you did nothing. He rode me like a dog! There isn't an inch of me that isn't scarred."

"What did you expect me to do? Say no, that's my wife?

She slapped him across the face. "He didn't ask. You gave me to him to save your own hide, so you could keep the diner from being burned to the ground!"

She turned and waved Todd and Buzz over. "Have you met my husband? What woman wouldn't be proud to have him?"

They looked at him with disgust.

Beryl pushed him away from her and turned to Todd and Buzz. "You'd better get down to the town office. That's where the operator station is. Put it out of business before Janice Hollis gets wind of this. She's got rats everywhere and she's related. It's on the first floor on the left as you go in the front door, move!"

Twenty minutes later, they were standing at the back of the town building. "You're the electrical guy, Todd. How do we do this?"

Todd reflected. "If it's the system I think it is they are still using one of those plug stations where you plug a jack in to connect a line."

Buzz laughed. "Like in those old movies, where there is a woman who says, Operator, how may I connect you? You've got to be kidding!"

Todd nodded. "Sure, that's the way it was done. Today, all of it happens from a pier station on the street. You've seen them, those little grey boxes on the curb."

"So, what do we do?"

"Well, with the old system they have here, there will be a single line out of the building. We'll start by cutting it, if we can find it."

When they got to the back of the building, Todd pointed up the wall just below the second floor window. "There!"

"We can't reach that, Todd."

Todd pointed at an outside receptacle on the wall. "You're right, but electricity can. I'll be back in a couple of minutes."

Buzz looked up the wall and at the receptacle. "This is going to be interesting."

Todd returned with two ten foot lengths of clothes line. "Okay. This pipe on the wall is what they used to bring power into the building. They ran the phone line to it at the top of building to anchor it. Now, the wire that is wrapped around the outside of the phone line helps support the wire and acts as a ground. It runs to the bottom of the pole, and you can see it anchored to that steel rod in the ground at the base."

Buzz stuck in his hands in his pockets. "I'm listening."

Todd took one length of wire and exposed a foot of wire at one end and a couple of inches at the other. He repeated the process with the other.

He then took one wire and wrapped the long exposed end to the ground wire on the pole. He took the other wire and attached it to the pipe on the wall. "All we have to do is plug these ends of the wires into that receptacle and complete the circuit."

Buzz pointed to the ground. "What about that?"

Todd looked down at his foot. "I guess I missed that."

"I guess so."

Todd rolled the bra up in a ball and tossed it back over the fence. "Okay, now we're ready. You wanna do it?"

Buzz didn't say, "No." He just shook his head.

It was pretty impressive. The phone line just didn't melt. It exploded like a roman candle. Buzz finished looking up at the carnage.

"Was there anything you learned in college that didn't involve property damage?"

"Built a solar powered still. It was pretty cool."

"People party at night."

Janice Hollis was on the phone with what she considered to be her current love interest, explaining to him that it was in his best interest to date her. After all, he wasn't getting younger, and if he didn't make her real happy, he wasn't going to get any older, either. The phone suddenly went dead. She was banging the phone on the table furiously, when two men stepped into the room. She stared at the two men for a full minute. "Who the hell are you?"

"We're friends of Oggie. We're looking for him."

"What for?"

"We have unfinished business. Where is he?"

She sneered. "Don't worry, you'll be seeing him soon enough."

Todd walked over to the operator station, pulled it away from the wall, and looked at the cable at the back. "Keep her here until I get back."

"No problem."

Buzz pointed to a chair. "Make yourself comfortable."

She didn't move and he took a step towards her. "You can do it with your teeth or without them. It's your call."

She laughed, but she did sit. "When he gets back here, he's going to kill the both of you, and anyone who even looked at you. By the time he is finished, the only thing left will be your teeth."

Todd returned with a fire axe. He pulled the station out as far as the cable would allow, and then he swung it, cutting the cable off clean at the station. He repeated the process at the wall. He picked up the cable, tossed it on a table, and then turned the axe on the station. In a short ten minutes, it was reduced to a pile of kindling and broken wires. When he was finished, he surveyed his handiwork. "Not bad."

Janice stood up and walked over to what was left of the station. "You two really know how to sign a death warrant!"

Buzz grabbed her by the arm, dragging her through the building, and out onto the street.

Todd started after them and stopped. "Does she have a purse?"

"Go check. She may have something she can use."

When Todd came out, he pulled the door closed, and made sure it was locked, so that she couldn't get back in. He held the bag up to Buzz. "Do you want to do the honors?"

Buzz laughed. "No, I'm betting she has a rat trap in there."

Todd turned the bag over and dumped the contents into the street.

Janice yanked her arm free and tried to stop Todd, but it was too late.

"Well, how about that Buzz!" Pointing at the contents of her purse.

Buzz picked up an almost new two way radio and turned it over in his hands. "I wonder what the range is on this."

He handed it to Todd, who looked at Janice carefully. "This is a very nice piece of hardware. It's definitely not your dime store radio and you're not bright enough to just go out and get something like this on your own. Come to think it, neither is that retard, Oggie. Where did you get it?"

Todd's comment drove Janice Gilles insane with anger. "No one talks about him like that. Fuck you!"

He turned the radio over in his hands and looked at the specs. "I'm thinking that with the right receiver and weather, this could get an effective signal out 500 miles."

Buzz looked out into the distance. "The only thing between here and the border was a mine. Was it the Ridge Mine?"

"That sounds about right."

Todd dropped the radio on the pavement and stomped on it, cracking the case wide open. He then ground the electronics under his heel, until it was totally destroyed.

Janice went nuts, again. "You two are not getting out of this town alive! When I get to another phone, you two will be done like toast!"

Buzz stepped up to her, his fists clenched. Todd put a hand on his shoulder. The message was clear. He reminded Buzz that they were different. "As bad as this could get, we will never get down to that level." Buzz stopped, briefly, and without words, remembered how important friendship was. His fists relaxed.

Todd stepped up to her and whispered in her ear. "Can you hear me?"

She nodded without saying anything. Buzz had scared her badly.

"That's real good. First, you aren't going to be calling anyone from this town. All the lines go through what's left of that switchboard of yours, and you know it."

Janice recovered some of her arrogance. "No problem. In less than an hour, someone in this town will be taking me out to Oggie. When I get there, it won't take him long to get back."

Todd scratched his chin. "Well, now, you see that's the second thing. Right about now, Gilly, that would be your ride, is out in the desert digging a grave. When it's deep enough the two women who took him out there are going bury him in it."

Buzz grabbed her before she could take a run at him. Janice was defensive. "I don't need him. He was a weasel. Oggie was going to do him anyway. I'll just wait until he gets back. It will be more fun that way."

"Now, that is your third problem. You're alone in a town with 1,500 people who hate your guts. The sun is going to be down in a couple of hours, and it will be a long, long time before Oggie gets back here. That's going to be a long, long, *long* time in the dark, alone

Buzz let go of her arms and pushed her out into the street. "C'mon, we've got work to do."

Oggie had been sleeping, or as close as he could get to it, on a stack of rail ties used for shoring in the mine. It was no longer possible for him to have a normal sleep cycle. Over the years, his other senses, except his eyes--which had even begun to fail a bit-- had begun to catch up with his sense of smell. As a result, he was in a constant state of sensory overload in sound, touch, and smell. He coped with it by cat-napping. It didn't matter where he was or what he was doing. He would suddenly stop and drift off into a light sleep, until the riot of sensations drove him back to consciousness. When it was important, he could go for weeks without stopping, until he was forced to shut down. But even after three weeks awake, the longest continuous downtime he'd had in the last fifteen years was twenty minutes.

He woke with a start, and looked sharply in both directions. This recovery was different. He stared malevolently at the two men who were watching him from ten feet away. They were too close. He didn't like it when people were too close, when his eyes were asleep. He didn't like that all, not one bit.

Heaving himself off the ties, he decided to beat the man on the left. He took a few steps and stopped in his tracks. What the hell woke him up? His brain struggled, but whatever it was, it danced around inside his brain, just out of his grasp. It ducked and weaved and then lashed out with violent imaginary-- blows that felt real and hurt. It was as though he was trying to fight a shadow on a wall.

Oggie worked at the Ridge mine, when he felt like it, because he liked to have some change in his pocket--not that he needed it. He could barely count past twenty, anyway. The mine owner employed him to keep the immigrants under control. This was also something he liked doing. He grabbed the man by his left arm lifted him off his feet. It always surprised him how light they were. Maybe it was because they were full of air. With his other hand, he turned the man left and right, and then thought of something he'd never tried before. He grabbed the man's jaw, yanked open his mouth, grabbing the lower part of the jaw in his fist, and crushed it flat. Oggie continued to grind the bone until it was pulverized. When he was done with the lower half of the man's face, it was a bloodied sack with a couple of teeth embedded in it. There wasn't enough of the face left for the man to scream with. He dropped the man in the dirt, and without looking down, stepped on him as he walked to the equipment shed. There was work to do, but that nagging shadow followed him.

Five hours away in McCook, Jasper McCain's jaw was receiving similar treatment but he was luckier. He could still breathe through his mouth. He looked down, and saw two of his teeth looking up at him from the floor of the Lazy Rider Bar. When he was sure they were his teeth he looked up at the man who put them there. "You broke my fucking teeth!"

Jasper's brain erupted in stars from another blow. This time, the teeth, instead of joining their friends on the floor, ricocheted off the roof of his mouth and disappeared down his throat. He gagged and staggered back, hitting the bar hard. Screaming and spitting blood on the floor, he yelled. "What the hell is wrong with you? You got any idea where you are?"

Todd stepped out from the shadows. There were a lot of dark places in the town. He joined Buzz. "We sure do, Jasper! We're in the Lazy Rider Bar, a fine drinking establishment in a fine town. Isn't that right, Buzz?"

"It is."

"Now, why don't you step back there and serve us up a couple of drinks and we'll have a chat, and catch up on old times. Does that sound like a good idea, Buzz?"

"It does."

The memories hit Jasper harder than Buzz's fist. He was never going to admit to anyone that he had never been more terrified in his entire life than he was at that exact moment. It was thirty years ago, but it felt like yesterday, when a beaten Buzz Murdoch was carried out of the bar. Everyone had been cackling and cheering at what Oggie had done, those thirty years ago. Then that damned blind Negro just popped up out of nowhere, for the first time, with that snicker of his, and spoiled it all.

"You think this is finished, Vendor? No sir, not done at all. Your debt is gonna come due, with interest, Vendor."

"God damn!" He hated being called that, and the man had been coming in here like clockwork to remind him. Every Thursday at exactly eight in the evening, one shot of Bourbon, neat. Last week was different. He was on time and put his money on the bar. Jasper poured his drink and put it in front of him, like always. The man didn't touch it, just stood there showing him those pearly whites of his.

"What's wrong, my booze not good enough for you?"

The man laughed in his face. "You've been watering my glass for years. You've been refueling the same bottle for as long as I've been coming in here. It doesn't matter none, anyway. I'll be leaving soon. My time is up here."

Jasper remembered that last part clearly. The words were still ringing like a bell in his head. "You ungrateful Negra, I treated you more decent than most folks around here. You should be giving me some respect, or your time will be up lot sooner than you think. Oggie will see to you right proper."

The man laughed even harder, picked up his cane and banged it on the bar for emphasis. "Oh, you are most definitely right, Vendor. I am well and truly done here!"

The voice suddenly got deathly cold, so cold you could almost see his breath, as he turned and walked out the door. "And so are you, Vendor. Your debt has come due."

The old man stopped at the door and looked back at McCain, smiling with those pearly whites of his. "*Tick tock*, Vendor, *Tick tock*!"

McCain was back in the present. He grabbed the bar from behind to hold himself up and to control the shaking. "What do you want?"

Todd pointed to a bottle. Jasper began to shake violently. That was Oggie's booze. It was the only thing he drank, J&B whiskey, and the only legitimate bottle of booze in town. "You don't want that. It's garbage."

Buzz grabbed him and dragged him across the bar.
"How many teeth you think you got left?"

He let Jasper go with a shove. Put down two glasses and that bottle for my friend of mine."

Todd interjected. "Three glasses, where are our manners, Buzz? I know our friend Jasper would be pleased to join us. We'll even pick up the tab."

Buzz nodded slowly. "Excellent idea, can't think of a better way to get reacquainted."

McCain slowly produced the bottle and three shot glasses.

Todd swept the glasses off the bar. "We'll have real glasses, Sir. Don't you agree, Mr. Murdoch?"

"I do."

When the glasses were replaced, Buzz grabbed the bottle from Jasper, before he could pour. He held it over a glass, filled it to the brim, pushed it over to Jasper, and then moved it over the next glass. "Where is he?"

McCain knew he could refill the bottle and get away with it, remained silent.

Buzz began to fill the second glass to the top and stopped. "Again,… where is he?"

When McCain stood there and smirked, Buzz started to pour again and the glass overflowed on to the bar. This time, the whiskey wasn't going back into the bottle. "I'm getting tired of asking."

Buzz moved to the third glass and started to pour. This time his aim was off and the whiskey missed the glass and began to cover the bar. Jasper let out a screech.
"Where is he?"

"Honest to God! I don't know. He's going to kill me for that booze. He knows how much is in there to the ounce!"

Buzz started to pour again and McCain screamed. "Okay! It's a work camp at the mine. They process lumber and rail ties for shoring. Oggie goes up there every couple of months. The owner uses immigrants for the grunt work. He hires Oggie to keep them in line."

"When did he leave?"

Jasper rubbed his sleeve across his mouth, leaving a smear of blood. "About two days ago."

"You remember anything about a camp, Buzz?"

"No. But he can't drive, so someone has to come here and get him. He wouldn't let Gilly take him because he needed him here to watch the town."

Buzz turned back to Jasper. "I don't hear anything coming out of that mouth of yours. Maybe your teeth are getting in the way?"

Todd suggested that maybe he needed a drink. "I'm not touching that. It's Oggie's stuff."

Buzz grabbed him, dragged him across the bar on his back, and smashed his elbow into the top of his mouth, splitting Jaspers lip and breaking off his two front teeth. Buzz finished by pouring the glass into Jasper's mouth, face, and shirt. When Buzz let go of him, Jasper shot off the bar, holding his mouth. He screamed. "There was no call for that!"

Buzz picked up the bottle and started to pour again. Jasper grabbed at the liquor on the counter like a man reaching for the last drop of water in the desert, and then watched it slip through his fingers, and crying. "He's usually gone for a week, but he could come back at any time so he can catch the people he's looking for. His sister calls the camp regular to let him know who's misbehaving. It's always been at night. Folks have to keep their doors unlocked so he can come in and get them."

They'd heard enough. Buzz grabbed him one final time, this time with both hands. "Three decades! You bought your safety at the expense of the lives of the people of this town. Now you are going to pick up the tab!"

Buzz hit him square in the face with a blow that drove Jasper up against the liquor cabinet with a crash. He rebounded, with both hands covering his face. His hands filled with blood.

Todd picked up Oggie's bottle of whiskey as they turned to leave. Back out on the street, they each took a deep breath. For the first time in years, the air in McCook smelled clean.

"We need to come up with a plan quick, Todd."

"I figure we've got a least three or four days to have something ready."

Buzz looked up the street. "No, it's not days, hours. He'll be back tonight."

"How can you be so sure? There is no way he could know something is wrong so soon."

"Trust me, Todd, he knows."

Todd looked down at the bottle and hefted it in his hand. He couldn't count the number of times that his life and friendship depended on Buzz's judgment.

Buzz looked back at the bar. McCain was right. "There was no call for what happened in there."

"Don't be too hard on yourself, Buzz. This place does tend to bring out the worst in people.

Todd stepped off the curb and threw the bottle. It landed in the middle of the street. In the quiet of the late afternoon it sounded like a gunshot.

There was screaming coming from the direction of the phone building. When they got there, Janice Hollis was trying to take the car keys away from another woman. "What the hell is wrong with you people? You know who I am! Give me the damn keys."

She stopped fighting with the woman when she saw Todd and Buzz coming. "Well, look who's coming, the cavalry! They want to die at their own Little Big Horn."

She turned to the woman who was holding on to the keys. "Take a good look at them because they are going to die tonight. When Oggie is done, those men will be stains on the pavement. You are going to watch, and then, you are going to join them!"

Buzz stepped between Janice and the woman, and he spoke softly. "You've got a car?"

She shook her head. "For what it's worth, Oggie only lets me have a couple of gallons of gas so I can deliver mail after Gilly checks it."

"Reading the mail is more like it." Someone in the group yelled.

"She can get gas for it and was going to drive to the camp and get Oggie. It's about 180 miles out at the end of County Road 9."

They each took Janice by an arm and dragged her over to the car. How about we get some that gas?"

It was close to dusk when two cars pulled over to the side of County Road 9, halfway between McCook and the Ridge Mine work camp. Buzz opened the back door and let Janice out. She walked over to a sign without saying a word.

"Sit down!" She sat in the dirt with her back to the post.

"So, how do you want do this, Todd?"

"We don't want to stop him. We just want to slow him down."

"That sounds good. Let's start by disabling the car in the middle of the road, so that he will either have to move it, or go around it by driving into the ditch.

It took them about fifteen minutes to get the car into a position, which made going into the ditch impossible to avoid. When they were done, Todd looked at Hollis, who hadn't moved from the sign. "Her?"

"She looks way too comfortable."

"How do you figure, Todd?"

Without a word, he crossed the road to her. She got up as he approached. Hollis had developed a healthy fear of both of them. She smiled slowly. "Having problems, boys?"

Todd looked at her carefully and before she could react, grabbed the bottom of her dress and yanked it over her head. Even Buzz was surprised. "That's a new approach for you. Maybe you should go back to that line you used to use?"

"Do you come here often?"

"That's it."

"It never worked."

Todd let go of her dress. "You son of a bitch, you can't treat a lady like that!"

"You're right. I can't and I wouldn't."

Todd looked at Buzz. "No pockets?'

Buzz replied, "and no purse."

"I'll check the car."

It took a while to find it, she'd a done a good job of hiding it under the front seat. Buzz joined Todd at the hood of the car, looking back at Hollis. She had returned to sitting at the post, but she was no longer smiling.

She had quite a haul in her purse. Cigarettes, six chocolate bars, a flask of whiskey, and a fully charged hand-held radio.

"This one is on the same frequency, but has a lot less power, maybe thirty miles. She probably planned to call him as soon as she got in range."

Buzz held up a Harley Davidson solid silver signature "Zippo lighter, very nice."

"Have we still got a full can of gas in the trunk?"

Buzz grinned. "Even better than mere gas, six bottles of Griz water!"

Todd burst out laughing. "Jesus, Buzz, we just want to torch a car, not the state! Let's do it."

Buzz watched him run back to the car, thinking he was enjoying this part way too much. He yelled after him, "Just one bottle!"

He looked over at Hollis and waved at her to come over. When she got to the car, he gave her instructions to put everything back in her purse, except the chocolate bars, and to put the purse on the front of seat of the car. Hollis protested. "I need that."

Buzz started working on one of the radios. "No, you don't. You have a long walk and you don't need to be carrying any extra weight."

Todd had returned with the bottle and checked on how Buzz was making out. "Okay, Todd. I've taken the battery out of this one."

"Good. Give her the radio and the batteries. She'll put them back in when we are out of sight. It'll take her at least a couple of hours on foot to get in range. That will give us until midnight, or possibly one in the morning, before she can contact him and he can get back to McCook."

She whined. "You can't just leave me, there's all sorts of crap out here. At least, give me a flash light."

"I'll see if there is one in the car, Todd."

He returned with the one out of the glove compartment and handed it to her. "It works but the batteries are almost shot."

Todd held up the bottle and the lighter. "It's show time!"

"I'll move the car off to a safe distance."

Todd looked at Hollis. "You don't want to be within a mile of here when I put a match to this stuff."

Janice was shocked that he would even consider doing something that drastic. "You're actually going to burn a car right in the middle of the road!"

She watched as he poured half the bottle into the front seat and on her purse. He then proceeded to pour the rest in a circle around the car. When the circle was complete, he poured out the remnants onto the hood and put the bottle down next to the small puddle of Griz water.

He turned to Hollis. "You've got the flashlight, phone, batteries and chocolate?"

Giles held up both hands that were now full to show him that she had everything.

Todd suddenly felt sorry for her. When Oggie found out what'd happened, she was probably not going to survive the night. He took off his jacket and put it around her shoulders. She didn't thank him, but pulled it closer over her shoulders. It was probably the only time anyone had ever shown her any compassion. "I'll give you a couple of minutes to get clear of this stuff. When it goes off, it will incinerate everything within two hundred yards."

By the time Buzz had returned from moving the car, she could barely be seen in the approaching darkness. He didn't ask where his coat was. Is everything ready?"

"We're just giving her time to get clear.

They waited another two minutes. "It's time, Todd."

He agreed. "You're right. It's time."

They took one last look for Hollis and couldn't see her. They walked around to the side of the car closest to the Corvette. Todd lit the Zippo.

Buzz looked down at the oily film on the pavement left by Griz's fire water. "You sure this will work? It looks like the stuff has almost evaporated. Maybe we should get the gasoline."

Todd dropped the lighter. It was instantaneous and it was spectacular. They had to run to stay ahead of the heat. Buzz could barely hear him over the concussion. "I think it's working okay, Buzz!"

As soon as the lighter hit the pavement, the Griz water ignited in a brilliant white flame which raced around the car in less than a second. It climbed up the hood and ignited what was left in the bottle, turning it into a rocket which went through the windshield, igniting the interior of the car. There was an explosion which literally lifted the car off the pavement, and then, dropped it with a bang.

"It's a good thing we don't smoke!"

"Okay, drop me at the substation. I am going to blackout the town, except for the area where the bar is. While I'm looking after this, I'll need you to cover as much of the town as possible to make sure everything is off."

"I'll start with the hotel. I'll clear out our rooms and pack the car. When do you need me back?"

"I can't give you more than thirty minutes."

"I'll be back here by eleven."

Buzz was waiting for him when he stepped out of the substation at 10:45 p.m. "The power is off except for the east end, where the bar is. How did you make out getting people to turn things off?"

"You are not going to believe this. There isn't one person out there."

Todd looked in the direction of town. "Are you serious?"

"Have you ever seen 1,500 people trying to hitchhike at once?"

"You saw it?"

"They're out on the highway, on foot; the line goes on for miles."

Todd looked back the way they came. "We'd better get back into town."

Buzz turned the car around. "We still have a little time. Drop me off at the bar. Take a drive around and see if you can find any stragglers, meet me back at the bar around midnight."

As Buzz got out of the car, Todd stopped him. "It ends here, Buzz. We can't leave them to that monster a second time, whatever the cost."

Buzz agreed. "Let's wrap this up tonight and get the hell out of here. First stop will be burgers and a beer."

"Just don't go nuts on the onions, okay?"

Buzz gave him a thumbs up and walked into the bar. He listened. The place was deserted. McCain would have been one of the first to run. The place was utterly silent except for the occasional squeak from the ceiling fan. Buzz took an inventory of what he had to work with. There was a set of brass knuckles, a baseball bat, and a loaded pump action twelve-gauge. He wondered what McCain would use it against. Probably on himself, when he knew the end was coming. He doubted if Oggie even knew it was back there.

Buzz walked into the kitchen and helped himself to some coffee, which was still warm, and used the time to think. He remembered what Oggie looked like when he was in his twenties. He then tried to imagine him thirty years down the road. Oggie didn't have a lot of weak points. His eyesight wasn't great and he had no skills as a boxer. He could throw a punch well enough with either arm, but made no effort to protect himself. He was lazy and relied on his strength. He'd never gone the distance because he didn't have to. Now he was older, heavier, and slower. Buzz stopped himself. That was a dangerous assumption. Oggie was surprisingly fast for his size and Buzz didn't think that had changed.

Oggie whirled when he heard the sound of the car explode. He didn't know what it was. It just made him angrier and he had been in a foul mood ever since he had come out of his last eyes down. Whatever had gotten him up so fast was back again, gnawing at the wiring in his head. And that damned smell was back, it was stronger,...closer.

It was just past dusk. Oggie was explaining to a laborer that working harder would guarantee the continued use of his arms and legs, when a truck pulled into the yard at high speed, coming to a stop against the fence. A crowd was gathering around the driver, wanting know what was happening. Oggie pushed the crowd aside and grabbed the man by the throat. "Talk!"

The man gasped for air, making Oggie loosen his grip so the man could talk. "The train man saw a car blocking the road from the track as he went by. It had a great fire inside it."

Oggie tightened his grip again. "What kind of car?

The man at the end of his arm was beginning to die from the choking. Oggie loosened his grip again and asked the question again. "Train man says it was dark. But it looked like the kind the mail lady uses."

Oggie finished the job, crushing the man's neck throwing him away, like a piece of paper. The body landed face down, fifteen feet away. Oggie waited until everyone had fled. When he was sure he was alone, he turned to toward McCook, and took a deep breath. It was like being slapped in the face. The smell was now overwhelming.

The years came roaring back with so much force, that he rocked back on his heels. There was the taste of blood in the back of his throat. Rubbing a hand across his mouth, he looked down. The hand was clean.

The second blow that his senses was even stronger. Oggie lashed out at the wind, there was nothing there. But in his mind was a face, and for the second time in his life, he felt fear, real fear. Then, the anger came.
"My town!"

He wheeled and walked back to the center of the yard and screamed. "Ride!"

The half-ton flatbed truck which took him to the camp appeared in less than a minute. Someone put a step down at the back of the truck so that he could climb up. When he got in, he walked to the front of the flatbed and grabbed hold of the rail. With his head just above the top of the cab, he had a commanding view of the road.

"Drive!"

The man who brought the steps was watching the truck leave, when a man appeared beside him with a bottle. "What is this for?"

The man help up the bottle, took out the cork, took a drink, and handed it to him. "Two man dead, one man maimed for life, it has been a good week."

The man with the steps took a drink, "A good week."

The unfortunate driver, the only one on the site besides the owner who had a license to drive, had been hit four times by Oggie on this visit. He had a broken collar bone, his right eye was pretty much closed, and he could barely see through the other one.

At the same time that Oggie's driver was able to see something in the middle of the road and jam on the brakes with both feet, an officer with the Nebraska State Police was encountering his first mass exodus, 1,100-plus people, all the citizens of McCook, walking on the side of the road. They were carrying flashlights and everything they owned. The officer had been on this patrol route for just under eight months. His jurisdiction ended twenty miles short of McCook's town limits. He hadn't stopped a single car in over three months. There wasn't anything out here but dust, dirt, bush, and coyotes. *"Not tonight."*

In the distance, on the opposite side of the road, he could see lights. They looked like fireflies in the distance, lots of them moving, slowly. In a line going on forever, they looked like ghosts that suddenly appeared out of the night air.

He had parked the car on the side of the road, with the visibar on, no one even bothered to look at him.

The officer reached for the microphone and then stopped. How the hell was he going to explain this? Seriously, what the hell was he going to tell the dispatcher? One thing was certain, he had to do something.

He got out of the car and walked into the center of the road. They ignored him and kept on walking. He summoned his best law enforcement voice and yelled. "Can I see your driver's license and registration, please?"

"A woman in her fifties and pushing a shopping cart, pulled out of the line, and walked over to him. "That's a dumb ass thing to say. What are you, some kind of a retard?"

The trooper pushed his back Stetson and looked down at her. "Oh, yeah, look who's talking, Lady. You're out here in the middle of the night, in the middle of nowhere, pushing a shopping cart full of groceries."

"So?"

"So, it ain't normal now, is it?"

"How do you know that I'm not going to visit my sister?"

"You don't have a sister."

"How do you know?"

"Your rap sheet says you were busted in 1976 for running a whorehouse. My dad was there."

"Your old man arrested me?"

"No, he was there when the cops busted the place."

"He was one of the regulars?"

He said you overcharged."

An old man with an old leather suitcase stepped out of the line and crossed the road to where the officer and the woman were standing. "He looked down at the officer's gun. You only got eight bullets, Son. You can't shoot all of us.

The trooper looked down at his hand and back up at the man. He slowly took his hand off the butt.

The old man smiled gently. "Smart Boy."

The driver of Oggie's truck wasn't enjoying the night much, either. He was already driving too fast in a truck that shouldn't be moving at all. To make matters worse, he was relying on one headlight that bounced and shimmied on a rusted fender. He only had a few seconds to react, when he saw *something* on the road. The truck bucked and weaved as he tried to control five tons of steel with the wheels locked. For a moment, there was silence as the brakes overheated and let go, followed by a bang and cracking under the wheels. The truck traveled another 150 feet before it came to a stop. In the distance, he and the other man in the front seat could just make out the glowing embers of the car Todd and Buzz had destroyed.

The man sitting with the driver grabbed the flashlight off the seat and started back up the road. In the distance, it looked like he had hit a deer. When he got closer, the outline of a body started to form. It was turned away from the light. It was a woman. The wheels had gone over her legs and hips. It was bad. What was she doing out here?

He walked around the woman and slowly raised the light to the face. The face reacted and turned toward the light. When recognition set in, a scream rose from his throat. Some terrors go on forever. He dropped the flashlight and fled into the night. With that final image in his mind, he would be running for the rest of his life.

Standing in the back of the truck looking out into the dark, Oggie yelled for the driver. "What's this all about? Get my steps."

The driver appeared with a set of folding stairs that were always in the truck. The suspension screeched as Oggie's weight came off the truck.

"I've got another flashlight in the truck. I'll get it."

Oggie grabbed him by the neck and roughly shoved him forward. He didn't want another disappearance in the dark." I don't need it. Go that way. Walk!"

In a minute, they could see the glow from the other man's flashlight on the pavement. In another minute, they were *there*. Some terrors can't be stopped and others you can't run from. The driver began to shake violently. He'd had run down Oggie's sister. He was going to pay with his life, one bone at a time. "Honest to God, I did not see her!"

Oggie didn't say a word as he picked up the flashlight and shone it in her face. With his left foot he shoved her over on her back. She screamed in agony.

He grabbed the driver by the shoulder that was already been broken, causing another cry of pain, to add to his sister's scream. He wasn't going to kill the man, not yet anyway; he needed him to drive the truck.

"Let's go."

Walking back to the truck they could hear the woman pleading between screams for her brother not to leave her.

The driver's own compassion overrode the pain Oggie's grip was causing him. He stopped and turned. "We can't leave her out there like that. Only a bad person could do such a thing."

Oggie's hand clamped down hard on the shoulder, causing a break in the skin around a broken bone, as he dragged the man back to the truck like an old blanket. The man's eyes watered as the pain shot all the way to the jaw. "I can always get another sister."

Any thought of escape vanished as Oggie squeezed into the cab of the truck. With Oggie's arm over the back seat, the driver knew he wouldn't be able to jump or wreck the truck fast enough before that arm killed him. It was going to be a long night, he thought morosely.

The trooper looked at the slowly moving line of humanity stretching into the darkness in both directions, and would certainly agree with the drivers' assessment. "Would somebody tell me what the hell is going on here?"

"The old man put his bag down. Why, not at all. You are looking at the residents of McCook, Nebraska."

"What are they doing out here?"

"Well, isn't it obvious? They are leaving McCook."

The trooper rubbed the bridge of his nose in frustration. "Why are they leaving McCook, Sir?"

The woman with the shopping cart answered that one. "Oggie Briggs is coming back to McCook and hell is really coming with him this time."

They proceeded to tell him everything about was going on in McCook--how everyone was leaving in fear of being tortured and killed and that two strangers from the past had come back to confront a monster in a darkened and empty town.

The trooper listened, overwhelmed by what he was hearing, before finally stopping them. "I had better make the call."

There was a Sergeant on duty in the dispatch office when the trooper placed his call. It took a full ten minutes to make the report. He noted that the Sergeant didn't ask him a single question. At one point, he had to stop and ask if there was anyone there. There was. He ended the report by stating that he would hold everyone where he was, until back up arrived.

The Sergeant pinched the bridge of his nose in frustration, leaned into the microphone, and held down the button. "There are 1,500 hundred people out there. How the hell are you going to do that? You let those people walk. They've got food and water and the temp is in the low 60's. Stay put out there, in case someone needs medical help. We'll start making arrangements for transport, medical services, and a place to put them."

Sergeant, I'll start a running escort up and down the line to make sure everyone's okay and keep traffic off their luggage."

"Good work, young man." .The sergeant leaned back in his chair and looked out the window. He'd been in uniform a long time. At best, he had been average. Thirty-six years carrying the badge and he'd never done anything wrong. At least, not serious enough to get anyone's attention, but he didn't stand out in the pack, either. He was a plodder, a man who made a career out of putting one boot down in front of the other. After a while, you stop noticing the people who pull out and pass you on the career track. On the other hand, he didn't have the screaming demons that they had, the demons that made your personal life a wide-awake nightmare, the demons that quit bothering you when you decided to clean your gun in the garage at two in the morning. Sergeant Gardiner Stanislov only had the one, and he wasn't going to need a gun cleaning to get rid of it. He looked down at the pencil he was turning slowly in his hands. Stanislov held up his left hand and turned it slowly. Decades and the wrist still looked swollen and misshapen. He tossed the pencil on the desk, reflecting on many of the things he'd been through in his career. He stopped the train of thought, realizing that it was a big number. "Someone get in here and take over dispatch. I'm going out."

Stanislov walked down the hall and out into the back lot. He took a long pull of air. He loved the smell of night air. He had been doing this a lot in the last couple of years. Looking looked down at his watch, he realized that didn't he have a lot of time left. The guys in the detachment and that young man out on the road had no idea what was really going on in McCook, but he did. Stanislov knew who was responsible for it and he knew exactly what a 1962 Corvette looked like.

For a moment, he debated going back to the dispatch office and doing his job, with no one the wiser, except for himself and his demon. He'd taken a step back forty-one years ago. He was getting a second chance and this time it would be a step forward. He walked back to the building, yanked open the door, yelled for his deputy to join him outside, and held the door open till he appeared. Iron up. "We're going to McCook."

"That isn't our jurisdiction Sergeant."

"It is when the town can't or won't respond to civil authority."

"That would have to be a riot or something they can't handle."

"What do you call an entire town fleeing for their lives in the dark?"

"That's pretty funny. I can't wait to see the desk report when it's done"

"Wait till you see the dispatch log. Get a detail together and have it start rounding up medical, transport, and accommodation for 1,500 people. When you get that done, get a patrol car, the shot guns we took off those Nazi's from the bust two weeks ago, and the beast."

"The beast, what the hell do we need that thing for? Is there a rhino loose in the town?"

"Worse. Saddle up, Corporal!"

"Yes Sir!"

Stanislov stopped as he pulled open the door. "Son, you're going to want to get a grip on those handlebars. It is going to be rough ride."

By the time he had cleared through dispatch with his instructions for the corporal, the keys and shotguns were waiting for him.

The duty Sergeant handed him the papers for the sign out. The weapons have been cleared. The case has been closed, but they are still evidence."

"Tell the corporal I've gone ahead. Tell him to follow in the beast as soon he gets back. No Stops. I'll leave the other shot gun for him and make sure he's got 200 shells with him."

"Gardy, what the hell is going on that you need that damn thing for? The thing weighs eighteen tons with six inch armor plating. We've only used it three times and two of them were in a parade. Those guns have pump action, and are long barrel, twelve-gauge Winchesters, with chokes. The only thing they're good for is blowing the doors off the beast. What are you expecting to find out there?"

Stanislov took the guns and keys. My demon."

As he pulled out on to the road, he took a final look at his watch. It was going to be close if he was going to make it to that bar in time.

McCook looked every bit the ghost town it had become as Oggie's truck turned on to Main Street. It pulled over to the curb and came to a stop, with the one headlight aimed at a window across the street. The engine sounded like a demented animal in the still night air.

Oggie got out, dragging the driver with him. His town was supposed to be totally lit--streets, stores, houses. There was no dark in his town. If he wanted something, he would just come in and take it. He didn't like dark in his town. He walked over to the hardware store. Like everything else, the lights were off and the door was locked. There were no locked doors in his town.

Running back into the street dragging the driver along with him, Oggie let loose with a roar which echoed off the buildings. "This is my town. No one touches my things"

The only reply was silence. Out of the corner of his eye, Oggie saw a brilliant flash of white streak across the darkness and strike his wrist. It felt like an electric shock, followed by violent pain. His hand sprang open, releasing the driver's arm.

The man took a step back in shock at the sight of Oggie holding his own wrist. A voice in his head suddenly screamed,"Run!"

Oggie made a grab for him and missed. He tripped over something on the pavement. Picking it up, even in the darkness, it shone like fire. It was a white cane. It belonged to that damned blind Negro. From a distance, he heard the man's voice. With the cane still in his hand, Oggie wheeled, but the voice seemed to be coming from everywhere and nowhere. It was as though the dark had suddenly learned to talk. *Tick Tock*, Fat Man."

Oggie turned on his heels again, and again there was nothing out there to get his hands on. "You're pretty brave in those shadows! But don't you worry. I'll put some light on you and then I'll have your skull in my hands. There's no way out of here, Old Man!"

Oggie could hear the voice again, but this time it was barely there. Even with his exceptional hearing abilities, he had to strain to hear it. *Tick, Tock, Tick, Tock.* Times up, Fat Man.

Oggie knew the voice was gone for good and he was alone in the street. In the distance, light flared to life in the bar. As he started down the street, his wrist began to ache. Having no experience with pain, he shook the wrist thinking that hurt could be forced to fall off. The ache turned into real hurt, and now, that maddening smell was back, swirling out of the bar with a vengeance.

Something brought him to a stop. Holding up both hands, Oggie suddenly realized he did not have that old man's cane. Did he drop it? He knew he had it in his left hand a few moments ago. Oggie looked around him on the ground. It wasn't there. The damn thing had vanished, just like that rotten old Negro.

He turned back to the bar, the light coming from inside almost hurt his eyes. He started to walk again, pushing his way through garbage in the street. His anger increased with every step. For all of his faults, the one thing Oggie couldn't stand was dirty streets and now his town not kept proper. His property was hiding from him. When he got to the bar, he stopped in the middle of the street facing the entrance. Taking another breath, the smells coming from inside the bar now seemed old and familiar, but the images they generated were like shadows on a wall, clear and distinct, but faceless.

Something cracked under his foot. It was broken glass. He took a step back and looked down. In the dim light, he could make out a patch of white. When he bent over, the smell hit him like a fist in the face. It was JB Whiskey, *his* whiskey, out here in the street. Until this moment, he had never experienced real and uncontrolled rage. No one had ever dared to do something like this to him before, not only touch his stuff, but actually break it. He felt like he was on fire.

Oggie took a step forward and stopped. For a brief moment, his emotions were interfering with his motor functions. He took another step, as though he was relearning the process. The next steps came quicker, one after another, until he was doing something he hadn't done for decades. He was running.

Propelled by blind fury, he made no attempt to slow or brace himself as he hit the doors. They exploded inward in a shower of wood, and his momentum removed the door from its frame. At 340 pounds, the force carried him the length of the room. At the last moment, as he struggled to maintain his balance, he raised his arms against the impact of his body as he hit the bar, driving it back to the wall. The air in his lungs was blasted out. He hung on to it as he struggled for breath.

When he looked up, he saw his face in the bar mirror. A jagged crack ran through his reflection. He never cared much about his appearance, but this frightened him. He shoved himself away from the bar and the pain in his wrist shot like fire up his arm. He held it up to a light. The wrist was swollen and blue. Oggie knew what broken bones looked like. He pulled his fist tight. The hand stayed closed. That was all he needed. He let his arm drop and slowly turned in the room. The silence from the street seemed to flood in and wash over everything like a wave.

He brain struggled to sort through the chaos. In the past, when Oggie started to get confused, he would take a deep breath. Smells--they always cleared his head. They were simple and easy to understand.

Taking a deep breath, it was like an aphrodisiac. Then, it was there, in the corner, deep in the shadows, the smell that had been harassing him for days was right back there, in the dark. "Hello, Oggie."

Oggie wheeled in the direction of the voice, confused that a smell could be in two places at once, another voice, in another shadow. He caught a movement out of the corner of his eye and turned back to where he had been looking. The darkness moved, twisted in on itself, and a figure slowly stepped out into the light.

Oggie held his position, looking slowly up and down at the man in front of him. The man looked back at Oggie, totally relaxed, with his hands in his pockets. There was no fear on the man's face, or in his eyes. He had seen this man before and knew the smell of him, but it was from a long time ago.

Suddenly, his brain figured it out. The odor was in two places because it belonged to two people. The shadow produced a second figure, and like the other one, he was completely relaxed, also with his hands in his pockets.

"Good to see you, Oggie. It's been a long time."

Oggie took a step forward to get a better look. It was coming back to him. It was here, thirty years ago, that he'd fought this man and won. He relaxed and laughed out loud. If he was responsible for all the damage, this was going to be an easy fix. In fact, this could work out just fine. He was going to make an example out of this guy and no one would ever get out of line again, as long as Oggie lived.

"I don't recall the name but I do remember that they carried you out of here on a board."

Buzz nodded. "That is correct."

Oggie smiled. "At the moment, there ain't anyone about to carry you. Don't matter none anyway, what with you going to be dead, but don't worry. There's a canvas sack in the back that I keep around for special occasions. I'll use it to carry out what's left of you and your friend. Its waterproof, no stains on the floor."

Buzz smiled back as he saw Todd reach behind a pole and retrieved McCain's shotgun. "We'll just have to see how things turn out, won't we?"

Oggie's smile slowly disappeared. "I think you already know."

Buzz stepped into Oggie's range and spoke slowly, deliberately, and softly. "Time's up Oggie. *Tick, Tock.*"

The rage that had ebbed in Oggie suddenly returned like a flood. He took a step toward Buzz without even bothering to lift his arms. The blow was unbelievably fast and struck him square in the face. Oggie merely rocked back and forth slowly. It had the effect of a flash bulb going in his face, but nothing else. "Is that all you got?"

As Buzz stood there looking at his face intently, Oggie was puzzled. The man was not reacting right. There still wasn't any fear in him. Oggie felt something on his face. He rubbed his mouth, thinking it was sweat. He sweat a lot more these days. His hand came away from his face, causing him to inhale rapidly, blood. For the first time in his life, when Oggie looked down at his shirt, there were two red streaks. "Big mistake."

When he looked up, he didn't even have time to blink. Five straight arm blows struck. The first three didn't have much affect, but the fourth broke a molar on the right side of his jaw, and the last one drove him back a step. No one had ever gotten this far with him, ever. Oggie finally reacted with a round house that barely missed caving in the right side of Buzz's skull. Both men had learned a great deal since their last encounter.

Oggie had learned that you could do as much damage with a well-executed punch as you could with brute strength. Buzz had learned that great strength requires great energy, and if you weren't careful, you could run out of both very quickly.

Buzz leveled a blow to the solar plexus that reflected his fist back with no effect. Oggie responded with one to the rib cage. Buzz rolled away, but the glancing blow sprang a rib, and he gasped for air.

Oggie smelled success and pressed home his attack. Grabbing Buzz by the wrist, Oggie yanked him forward, and got Buzz into a bear hug. He lifted Buzz off the floor. He didn't hear, and wouldn't have cared if he did, the sound of Todd jacking a shell into the shotgun. "I think we are done here, fella, any last words?"

Buzz gasped for air as his rib cage began to crush. With what was left of his strength, he brought both arms back as far as he could and then brought them together as fast he could, slamming his palms against Oggie's ears.

Oggie shrieked in agony and dropped Buzz. The pain was excruciating. The hammering in his ears overloaded all of his senses. He yanked at his ears, trying to pull them off his head.

Buzz had landed on his knees, gasping. Every breath felt like fire in his lungs. He looked up at the monster that was clutching his head, oblivious to everything around him. He didn't have a lot of time.

He got slowly to his feet and closed this distance between them. As soon as he was within range, he hit him with everything he had. Oggie shook like he had been hit by lightning. Buzz continued hitting him in the face. He was going to keep it up until he ran out everything he had.

Oggie kept falling back and the blood continued to flow from him nose and mouth, covering his jaw and shirt. He hit a beam and bounced off. Buzz shoved him back and the beam cracked. Buzz hit him again; Oggie's head hit the beam and bounced back into Buzz's fist. Buzz could feel something in his shoulder give with a snap.

Oggie took a step forward, and blinked a couple of times until his eyes refocused. The look in his eyes said it all. This was far from over.

"That will be enough, Gentlemen."

There was a state trooper standing in the door with a really big shotgun. He looked at Todd. "Sir, you're going to want to put that Winchester on the table, real slow."

Todd had no problem with that and put the gun down slowly, butt first.

The trooper nodded with approval. Smart man."

Stanislov stepped into the bar and surveyed the damage. "You two have been busy little beavers."

He separated the two men with a wave of his gun. Buzz was clearly on the wrong end of the fight. "Can you walk?"

Buzz nodded without speaking.

"There's a doctor and ambulance outside."

Oggie took a step forward and Stanislov raised his gun at him. Oggie sneered. "I'm not done with him."

Stanislov ignored what he said. "What about you, need a doctor?"

"What do you think?"

"You're right. What you need is a lawyer."

Oggie laughed. "Are you serious? Look at me. Do you think anything will stick to me? You'd need someone in McCook to testify and I'm thinking you're going to find that real difficult. You can't touch me and no jail can hold me.

This time Stanislov took a step forward and looked Oggie right in the eye. "I know. You've already told me."

Oggie smirked. "I know you."

Stanislov pinched the bridge of his nose. "I guess you're right. We'll just take you in to the detachment, get a statement, and send you on your way.

Out on the street, the doctor working on Buzz stopped to watch Oggie being loaded into the beast. Stanislov climbed into the cab alone and pulled the door shut. "That's odd."

The EMT who had accompanied the doctor wanted to know what was wrong. "Prisoners are never transported in that thing without a least two officers."

The doctor spent another twenty minutes examining Buzz and bandaging his ribs and adjusting his shoulder. "It's not broken, just dislocated. Try to avoid breaking furniture over people's heads for at least three weeks."

When Todd was satisfied that Buzz was going to be alright, he asked him if he wanted him to get the car.

Buzz looked up at the night sky for at least a full minute. "It's really something out here at night, isn't it?'

Todd looked up the road in the direction they were heading. "Yeah, it is"

"Todd, I think it's time to go."

When Todd left to get the car, Buzz asked the doctor about Oggie's sister.

EMT got to her about thirty minutes ago. "She's alive, but she'll never walk again, from the sounds of it."

Twenty minutes out of McCook, a patrol car flagged down Stanislov, and pulled him over to the shoulder.

"Chief, what the hell are you doing out here?'

"I thought I would pull down a little overtime."

Stanislov nodded, it was the Chief's right. "With all due respect, shouldn't you be at home. What with . . . ."

The Chief cut him off. "Cancer? Relax, Stani, all that Chemo is making me as frisky as hell. I'm wearing out the old ball and chain. I thought I would give her a break tonight. "

"That was right decent of you, Chief."

"Wasn't it? Here, you need to sign off on these. Transfer of prisoner."

"Transfer?"

"Sign!"

Stansilov reviewed the documents, made a small correction on the time, signed and handed them back.

The Chief looked them over to make sure the signatures were all there and handed him his car keys. "Take my car back to the detachment."

Stanislov looked at the armored car and back to the Chief. "Good night, Sir."

"Did you make sure all your weapons are accounted for?"

"One side arm, two twelve-gauges out of the lock up, one in the beast and the other with the Corporal."

"You're going to make one hell of a chief.

When Stanislov got into the Chief's car, he saw that the shotgun was missing out of the rack.

Todd pulled up beside the ambulance and got out. "How are you feeling?"

"Not bad for a man who's been playing tag with a bus."

"I've got the cure for what ails you."

What's that? "The doctor wanted to know.

"A burger and a beer."

The doctor made a note on a prescription pad, tore it off, and handed it to Buzz.

Buzz looked at it. "That's very funny."

He laughed. Trust me. I'm a doctor."

As they walked out behind the ambulance, an old black man with a cane was standing between them and the car. *Tick, Tock*, boys. The widow's waiting. *Tick, Tock*.

As quickly as he appeared, the man took one step back and disappeared into the darkness. Buzz took a step forward to where the man had been standing and looked down, rubbing his shoe on the pavement. "I wish people would stop doing that."

"Hey, what about that burger and beer, Todd?"

As they got into the car, Todd asked how Buzz was feeling.

"It only hurts when I laugh."

"I'll only tell you jokes that aren't funny."

Buzz smirked because that didn't hurt. "All of your jokes aren't funny, so that should work."

If you were standing dead center in McCook looking east, you would see a line of lights two miles long and heading into McCook. If you looked west, all you'd see was one set of taillights going out.

CHAPTER 8
ALAMOSA

So here's the *thing* about roads. They intersect--on ramps, off ramps, merges, in intersections, and all kinds of stops. They're all part of the rules of the road. They all have a part to play in the grand scheme on the nation's asphalt arteries, and the bigger the artery, the bigger the role. Well, not *always.* Some really small intersections can be pretty damn important when someone is trying to get from Point A to Point B, and there's nothing in between. And then, there are the intersections that no one wants to talk about. They're out there. It's always something, like, turn left. But don't ignore that second side road and look for county road six before you turn off."

The Devil's T is like that. Everyone tries to ignore it, but it always manages to get up front and center--right to the head of the lineup for the movie. Of course, it's not on anyone's map and if you asked anyone where it leads to, you're just going to get a blank stare and I don't know.

On the other hand, if you ask anyone how it got its name in the first place, you will, most definitely, get an answer. They will also tell you where the road "*lives,*" not where it *is*. You'd think that they had misspoken on that, but you don't want to go correcting the good folks of Mesa Verdes County.

The Devil's T just sits out there on the edge of the Colorado badlands, for days on end, sucking oxygen out of the air, which is bad enough. But Lord Almighty, you don't want to be out there when it exhales.

"Hogwash!" That's what Sheriff Alvin T. Carr says every time he hears one of those crazy stories, not his exact words, you understand. He'll tell you that the intersection of Highway Eight and Center Road is ten miles south of Monte Vista.

Sheriff Carr leaned back in his chair and reached around the back of his head, giving it a nice good scratch. He liked doing that and there sure wasn't a hell of a lot of anything that he enjoyed much anymore. He brought his chair up right, and stopped to rub the top of his head, before checking his watch. It was 3:30 in the afternoon.

Looking out the window at the sun heading for the horizon, he knew it was time to go. He would get his coffee for the evening patrol at Whistlers and be on the road by four. By the time dusk hit the pavement, provided he did not actually have to enforce the law, he could cover his entire patrol area up to Creed and be back at Whistlers for a late dinner. After that, he'd spend the night on general patrol. He was pulling a double shift patrolling Alamosa. It would be another four hour's tomorrow morning, cleaning up paperwork, and then it was a week off, fishing with a couple of his buddies. Of course, that was a lie, straight up. Not the part about the fishing, just the part about his buddies. Fact was there were no buddies. In fact, there never were any buddies. He just told his wife that little lie, so that she wouldn't worry that he was fooling around on her.

Alvin T. Carr, Sheriff Mesa Verde County, was going fishing for two reasons. The first reason was he didn't care for people's company, at least not in a mean way. He just liked being alone, always had. Truth be told, he wasn't sure he even liked fish all that much, either.

Of course, he was married, with three good kids. Carr had been a good husband and provider. His kids, all girls had grown up right, gone to college, and now lived lives of their own. His wife was a fine woman and he always tried to treat her right. The only disappointment, at least for her, was that she hadn't given Carr a son. When he told her that it didn't matter, he really meant it, although he may have led her to believe that it did.

Carr wasn't perfect. He had a short temper, and was lousy at small talk, but he did his best. In the end, he wasn't motivated by love, devotion, or anything like that. He considered his personal and family life a civic duty. Marriage was like handing out a speeding ticket. It was important, but in the end, it was what expected of him, just another job.

The second reason he was so determined to get out of Dodge was the letter, dated for three days from now. It was this weekend, and legacy or no legacy, there was no way he was hanging around so destiny could screw up a nice weekend.

Carr had been with the Mesa Verde detachment for close to nineteen years, six of them as detachment chief. Four men had ridden the chair with the letter on their watch. His predecessor, Dave, T-Bone, Bomba, was a short timer in the chair after thirty-nine years of bad food, bad booze, and bad women. He had been sidelined with an Alomasa Blue, code word for big time coronary. He had been posted up from Creed for his last fifty-two months of duty before mandatory retirement. The word was that he was quite a firecracker back when he had a stride in his boots. He had hit the jackpot with full disability and pension and still got all of the grab-ass he was able to handle, except now, Doctors orders, he actually had to do it horizontally instead of vertically in the backseat of a patrol car. The coronary didn't turn him into mush like it did some men. Not soft. Thoughtful would be a better word, and this was a rare quality for a policeman.

Bomba called Carr into his office on his last day. The only thing left on his desk was the letter. That was another thing about the Mesa Verde detachment, unlike others where the outgoing chief opened his door, everyone had a drink and some tall tales were told. Here, the outgoing chief would clear out his desk and his last official duty would be to hand over the letter.

Bomba picked up the envelope and turned it over slowly in his hands. The edges were turned up and yellowing now. Bomba looked up at Carr, put it on the desk, and pushed it across to him. "This is my last official duty. I've enjoyed every minute of it, but like everything in life, the ride eventually has to come to an end. It's your time in the chair, now."

Bomba stood up, took his coat off the back of the chair, walked around to the front of the desk, picked up the letter, and handed it to Carr. "This makes it official. The detachment is yours."

Carr remembered the confusion from that moment." That's it, no briefing, no paperwork, not even a good luck, Fella. ."Just hand over an old letter, with no explanation, and an Adios."

Bomba gave him a hard look, shook his head, and turned to leave. "Do not take that thing lightly. Three men have spent more than four decades guarding it. There's a date and a safe combination on the back. Make sure to memorize it before you put it back."

Carr stopped him at the door. "What's in the damn thing?'

Bomba put his hand on the door frame before he answered. "I have no idea, but you'll know in six years."

Carr sat up in the chair with a start. The memory was so fresh, he expected to see Bomba still standing in the door. He checked his watch and was ten minutes behind schedule.

An hour and change later, as dusk chased the wind across the Colorado plains, a single car crossed the intersection of Highway Eight and Center Road. The temperature had been going up steadily all day and had suddenly dropped fifteen degrees in the last three hours. At the current rate, it would be well below zero by midnight. Of course, there was nothing out there that would have noticed either the car or the temperature. Anything that could was long gone or a day away.

Carr rolled up the window and turned on the heat. The car shuddered briefly as the speedometer dropped 18 miles per hour. He wondered aloud if the engine had started to miss. He squeezed the accelerator and the car slowly recovered the speed it had lost. In the rear view mirror, the intersection was five miles back and out of sight.

The waitress at The Salindon Roadside Diner had opened at 7:00 and now, it was a bit past four in the afternoon. She was still on the first pot of coffee as the sports car pulled in. She poured herself a cup and put on a fresh pot. From the look of the two guys in the car, they were going to need it.

The driver got out and filled the car with gasoline. When he was done he leaned over the driver's door and spoke briefly. The man on the passenger side nodded slowly and got out. The driver of the car held the door open for his companion.

She motioned them over to the stools at the counter. "Trust me the food is better over here.

"How's that?" Buzz wanted know.

"I don't have to carry it as far."

Todd ordered a Burger and coffee.

"How about you, Fella, what's it going to be?"

"Coffee for me, black."

She tapped the menu pad slowly in her left hand as she looked at Buzz carefully. "The food isn't that bad."

"Thanks, but just the coffee will be fine."

After she left to fill the order, Todd asked Buzz how he was feeling.

"Not great. I've had broken ribs before, but they never hurt this bad. I'll be all right."

Todd put a hand on his shoulder. "I just need to know where to send the flowers."

The waitress came out from the kitchen with their orders and put them in front of them on the counter. "So, where are you gentlemen headed in that fancy little ride of yours?

Between bites, Todd told her that they were headed west.

She picked up her towel and walked out from behind the counter to clean some tables. In two swift moves, she grabbed Buzz from behind, yanked him off his stool and pulled his shirt over his head.

Todd came off his chair and tried to get between her and Buzz. "What the hell are you doing?"

With one hand securely holding Buzz's shirt over his head so he couldn't move or see she used the other one to push Todd back, at the same time pulling Buzz towards her. "Who put this bandage on?"

Buzz's voice came through the shirt. "I got it from a doctor yesterday."

"What doctor, where?"

"He got it in Nebraska, in McCook."

She looked at Todd steadily. "You two were in McCook?"

Todd confirmed that they were.

"Christ Almighty! My purse is behind the counter. Bring it over here."

"What does it look like?"

She gave him a "That's a stupid question" look. "I'm the only woman in here."

When Todd brought the purse, she told him to take out a bottle of pills and an address book. "The doctor's name is Hills. There's a phone in the kitchen. Call him, tell him to get his ass over here, and don't take any crap from him about it being late. If he wants to stay up all night playing poker, then he can stay up all day being a doctor."

When Todd had gone into the kitchen, she helped Buzz out of his shirt and handed him two pills out of the bottle, "Tylenol Three,

These won't stop the pain, but they'll at least slow it down. I'm going to loosen the bandages. Put your hands over your head. This is going to hurt like hell for a few minutes, but the pain will ease up fairly quickly. You'll be able to breathe easier.

When she loosened them, it felt like the ribs had come loose in his chest, and she was right. It hurt. He sucked air in violently. "Damn it. Stop breathing long enough so I can re-tape the ribs properly.
The pain eased as the bandage took the stress off the ribs. When she had finished and he put his arms down he was already starting to feel more comfortable. "Where did you get that bedside manner of yours?"

She extended a hand. "The name's Margaret and I got my bedside manner in the Army. Thirty years, Korea and two tours in Vietnam."

"How long were you in Korea?"

She answered softly and with strength. "All of it."

When Todd was back, she told them their food was probably cold. "I'll put another order together for the both of you this time."

The diner door opened and an incredibly unkempt man, barely out of his twenties, stepped inside. He was wearing badly battered Bermuda shorts, sandals made from a couple of old tires, and a T-Shirt which hadn't spent a lot of time in a working washing machine. The wardrobe was topped off by long hair and a beard that was dirtier than the shirt. "Someone in this place had better be dying!"

"Gentlemen, I would like to introduce you to what passes as a doctor in this county."

"That's very funny, Margaret. I see that you are still happily trying to murder the motoring public with that food of yours."

"You didn't have any trouble eating it yesterday, Mister."

"I am aware of that and you had to get me drunk first. What am I doing here?"

She pointed to Buzz. "Have a look at him."

"The name is Stanson. Show me."

Buzz turned around and raised his shirt. The doctor pulled Buzz's shirt up, first examining the exposed bruising and then the bandage. He instructed Buzz to raise his arms as high as he could and then the doctor pulled the bandage down far enough to see the bruising and swelling, repeating the process on the sides and front. When he was satisfied he repositioned the bandage and checked the tension. "You can pull your shirt down. Good work. Margaret. Now why don't you tell me a bedtime story?"

Margaret cut them off before either of them could get started. "They were in McCook."

Got any beer left in this dump?"

"Sure. You want to wash it down with food for a change?"

"Yeah, and while you're back there, bring some for these two and yourself."

For a while, they ate silently, with a few pleasantries and talk about the weather. When they were finished, Stanson wrote Buzz a prescription, and asked Margaret a question. "You got any room in that bug infested trailer of yours?"

Margaret mocked him. "Sure. What is wrong with your bug infested trailer?"

"I really do have bugs in my trailer."

She laughed, reaching into her pocket to retrieve a set of keys, and handed them to Buzz. "You can't miss it. It is on the left, a mile south. I'll be along this afternoon to set you up with towels and whatever else you need. By the way, you don't want to get too close to that other trailer. It's a beat-to-crap, mud-flap of a dirt hole that looks like it was painted by a drunken reprobate."

Todd had been listening in awe. "That was amazing. Who lives there?

Stanson smirked and pointed. "Margaret does."

By six, Buzz and Todd had gone. Margaret was ready to close. "I'm going to clean up and call it a day."

Stanson helped himself to coffee. "I'm going to need your car tomorrow. I'm on coroner duty this month and I've got a call."

"No problem. How long do you figure you will be gone?

He wiped his face with a napkin. "This could take longer, five days maybe.

"Sure, no problem, give me a hand with the dishes. I'm opening late tomorrow and I don't need these waiting for me when I get here."

Forty-five minutes later, they pulled up in front of the trailers. She handed him the car keys before she got out. As he walked to his trailer, she stopped him with a hand on his arm. "Where are you going, anyway?"

"McCook."

"No wonder you didn't tell them."

Margaret's trailer was large, clean, and she was an excellent cook. The next day, Buzz was up earlier than Todd. Buzz gave Margaret time to put on a new bandage on and to show him how to do it himself. Margaret observed his progress. "You're looking a lot better than you did yesterday."

"I'm much improved, thanks to you and your hospitality."

Todd put in a brief appearance and wished them a good morning before heading for the bathroom. "Where'd you get those jimmies, out of a dumpster?"

"I'll have you know there were very popular in the sixties!"

"No they weren't."

"You're just jealous!"

"No, I'm not."

Buzz drove Margaret up to the diner after breakfast while Todd cleaned up the dishes and packed. She was seriously enjoying the ride in the Corvette by the time they pulled up to the diner. "I've always dreamed about being in a car like this. That was an awesome ride!"

Buzz took a deep bow and winced. "The pleasure was all ours, Madam."

"So, where are you going from here?"

That was a good question, and up to now, no one had asked them. It took a bit of time for him to respond. "I can't give you an exact destination, but we seem to be headed southwest as far as Solida, for sure."

She looked at him with understanding. "Just be careful, a lot has changed since the last time you were out here."

Buzz decided that he liked Margaret a lot. "Mind if I give you a hug?" Without saying a word, she stepped up to him and held on with both arms for a full minute before walking away. "She didn't look back.

Todd was waiting out in the driveway when Buzz got back. "Did you say good-bye and thanks for the both of us?"

Buzz looked back up the road in the direction of the diner for a very long time.

"Buzz?"

He suddenly turned back to the car. "Yeah, it's all taken care of. We'd better start putting some asphalt under us. You mind if I take the first leg?"

Todd got in on the passenger side and pointed to the location on the map. Buzz nodded and put the car in gear. As always, they never looked back in the mirror. What was behind them was part of the past.

200 miles southwest, Sergeant Bailey Goldstein was not a happy woman. She was not happy because her boss, Alvin T. Carr, was not a happy man. Someone had gotten in the way of his stupid fishing trip and she really wanted him to go fishing. Actually, she couldn't care less where he fished, as long as it wasn't here in the office. Instead of spending four hours in the office before leaving, he was going out on combined patrol with the aerial detachment. The officer normally assigned to the duty had the poor grace and timing to get into a bar fight with a bouncer at the Dirty Spur and got himself a free trip to the Mesa Verde hospital with a broken nose and jaw, which put him out of action for three weeks. When he got back, Carr was going to assign him to the worst duty on the planet for the rest of his natural life--night shift on the north side of Alamosa. It wasn't violent like the east side. In fact, it wasn't anything. The only things on the north side were two warehouses and sixty-square-miles of scrub, dirt and cactus,... purgatory indeed. As far as Carr was concerned, it served the guy right for marrying her.

Carr would still be putting in the four hours. But he could control paperwork. Being out on the highway looking for stupid people was another matter. Carr stood up and yelled out the door at Goldstein. "I'm going out. I'll finish up that paperwork when I get back."

"That's wonderful. I'll alert the media!"

As he left, he wished he had a back door so he didn't have to walk past her desk. "Can't you ever be nice to people, just once?"

"No! If I had to be nice, it would make me unhappy and I would have to start murdering people gratuitously."

"You're already as mean as a badger with its nuts caught in a door."

"Ain't nobody dead, so you see, it's working."

Halfway to his patrol car, she yelled out to him that he'd forgotten his Stetson and threw it out into the parking lot. "You don't want woodpeckers going after your brain, again!"

He walked over to the hat and picked it up. She'd stomped on it. The woman was just plain nasty sometimes

After a coffee run at Whistlers, Carr finally pulled over to the side of the road at the set up point. Despite his best efforts, he was still early. He got out of the car, looked up the road into the rapidly growing morning heat, and then checked his watch. It indicated in no uncertain terms that it was exactly eleven minutes after nine in the morning. He should be out here for another hour. By 10:00, he'd been out there for close to an hour, and he hadn't seen or heard a single thing. From where he stood, he was slightly more than thirty miles from the Devil's T. In the distance, he could see things moving out there on the desert floor. Of course, there really wasn't anything really there, just mirages from the rising heat.

Hearing the radio squawk, he returned to the car and reached into it. It was getting too hot to sit in the car for any length of time. He pulled the mike off the cradle. He pressed the button and then released it for a second to get his head around what he wanted to say. "Dispatch, 25, what's going on? Is anyone coming to this dance or what?"

The dispatcher was fresh out of college and seriously unapologetic. "That's what I'm calling about. The helicopter can't fly because it has a stuck switch or something."

Carr put the mike down on the hood and took a deep breath, because he didn't want to blow a gasket while he was holding the button down. The radio dispatcher waited quietly until he was ready. Carr was ready. "Are you sure you got that right; how can a button stop a helicopter from flying?"

"Well, they told me it was a switch, not a button so there must be a difference. Anyway, that what's they said. Also the Seline detachment wants to know when you are ready to synch the radars."

Carr cursed and put down the microphone. He hadn't even started to set up the equipment. Forgot was a better word for it. "I'll be ready in ten minutes. Let me know when the chopper is on its way."

It took longer than the ten minutes he promised to set up the tripod, the radar, and to hook up the power from the car. He skipped a step by running the up-link with the other radar sixty miles away and the diagnostic at the same time. When the helicopter finally showed up, the process would be repeated again among all three of them, until all of the units were on the same page.

After a short interval, his equipment announced that it had found its counterpart on the side of the road sixty miles away. For the next five minutes, they had a silent dialogue at the speed of light. When they were both done, they chimed again to indicate the process was complete and then they asked for max and min speed setting. Carr entered them into the keypad as did his counterpart. There was another brief electronic conversation, which indicated that the electronics were deciding if their human masters knew what the hell they were doing.

The helicopter roared over his location, letting him know that it was there. A call on the radio would have been just fine, as far as he was concerned. The helicopter had enough fuel on board to stay on station until noon. The radars repeated the synchronization once again. When this step was completed, Carr, the Seline officers, and the helicopter crew carried out a radio check. That was it. Now, all Carr had to do was wait it out until the end of his shift.

Walking out into the center of the road, he looked both ways. Three hours. How bad could it be? A couple of tickets at worst and he was done. Carr could almost hear the answer coming out of the light wind, which had suddenly come up. "You wish!"

Way down deep, he knew it wasn't going to happen. That fishing trip might as well be on the other side of the moon, for all the difference it was going to make. In about an hour, he would feel and hear it in the sudden intensity of the radio traffic. Even now, as he looked out into the morning sun, he could see the changes in the mirages, trading the look of ghosts for harder edges and color. The T was waking up.

Buzz pointed to the sign in the distance and Todd nodded silently. He eased the car off the road and pulled up in front of the pumps. Todd leaned across and looked at the gauge. It read three-quarters of a tank. "Do we need gas?"

Buzz rubbed the back of his neck. "Out here, it's not a bad idea to have a full tank when you can get it.

"You okay?"

"Sure. You know why I bang my head against the wall?"

"You got me. Why?"

"Because it feels so good when it stops."

Todd responded with a really good W.C. Field's impression. "You're starting to worry me, Boy. I'll get us some coffee to go."

As Todd crossed the island between the pumps, he glanced briefly at the car on the opposite side, which was four pumps up. It was a dark brown Corvette. It was built in the seventies but he wasn't sure what year. Todd was back in five minutes with the fuel receipt and the coffee. He hadn't noticed that the other Corvette had left.

As they pulled out on to the road and accelerated, in the distance they could just make out the other Corvette approaching the steadily thickening mirages. Todd looked down at his coffee and frowned. It was sitting rock steady in the cup as if there were no forces acting on it.

Somewhere out there, Sheriff Carr was waiting to finish his shift and go fishing. He looked down at the clock on the dash. Ten minutes after eleven. He debated starting the car, but he knew he would never hear the radar over the air conditioning. The heat was all in his mind. Actually, the heat was right outside. He just told himself that to feel better. Actually, what he refused to admit to himself was that the temperature had been dropping steadily and he could feel that too.

He half-listened to the chatter back and forth between the chopper and the Seline detachment. The conversation was mostly about baseball scores and a marital indiscretion. It was all flagrantly non-regulation. They were from the same detachment. Carr was all but excluded, which was fine with him.

A comment between the pilot and co-pilot about having to make a pitch compensation change because of a difference in the air temperature caught his attention. "Wait a minute. I got something. Is it the pitch again? No, it's the radar."

Carr sat up in his seat, reached for the microphone, and then stopped. "I'm getting some weird readings up here. The numbers are all over the place."

Seline answered back. "Yeah, we saw that, but the guy is down to about six over now.

One of the Seline officers rechecked the radar display indicator. "I've never seen anything like that. The gauge has to be massively screwed up. Maybe it is caused by the heat."

"It can't be the radar. The chopper is getting the same numbers."

The radar readout bounced from fifty to seventy-miles-per-hour several times before settling back to sixty-eight-miles-per-hour. "Look at the distance indication, Charlie. It should be decreasing but it's stuck at twenty-one miles. The thing says it is not moving. But velocity says it is.

"Maybe we should contact Carr."

"It's still too far out for him. He won't be able to see anything yet."

"Do it anyway, Charlie. He has a right to know."

For a full minute, the target, or whatever it was, refused to physically move, despite indicating forward velocity of sixty-eight-miles-per-hour. The distance indicator suddenly dropped from twenty-one miles to sixteen miles, and then to zero. The speed indicator followed suit by jumping to seventy-four-miles-per-hours, and then to zero. When the Seline and Chopper radar failed, they restarted a recalibration. "We've had a radar drop out up here. As soon as he passes under us, we will do a visual and hand him off to you."

The man running the equipment on the chopper looked at his radar. It was still in recalibration. He then looked out the door to confirm visually. "Okay, Charlie, we see him now. He's about ten miles past you."

Charlie had thirty years in. The young man standing behind the radar didn't have his first year completed yet. "Ask him to repeat, Son."

"Say again, Chopper."

"Target now eighteen miles from the Devil's T, speed is seventy-eight-miles-per-hour."

They both turned and looked out onto the road, one with a lifetime of experience and the other one with only weeks, but both with the same question. "
"The car didn't pass them?"

The radar operator in the helicopter, wasn't taking his eyes off his screen now that it was going haywire, watched the car down on the road creep up slowly from behind. The helicopter was flying straight up the center line of the road at 110 knots, which was keeping it well ahead of the car. He switched on the recording camera. The car was now in the center of his screen, holding steady at seventy-eight-miles-per-hour.

He took his eyes off the car for a second to silence a calibration alarm and turned back to the screen. "What the hell is going on down there? He is right under us!"

The pilot jumped in his seat. "What the fuck are you talking about? He's ten miles back!"

The radar operator screamed. "He's at 94. No, that's not possible. Damn! Everything has gone off scale high!

The pilot got a flash of light off a piece of chrome in his eyes, and then, all hell broke loose. In his right hand, the control stick began to vibrate, followed by the helicopter suddenly starting to yaw to the left.

"What's wrong?"

The pilot was starting to fight the controls. He had to yell over the noise. "It feels like a shock wave, from behind us."

The radar operator yelled back. "At this altitude, that's not possible!"

Carr got out of his car and walked out into the middle of the road. His radar was reading zero when he got out and started to climb as he got to the center of the road. He ignored it. He knew that he could not stop what was coming, but whatever happened, the automatic recorders on the radar and the car would probably survive.

With each passing second, the radar counted up. It chimed when the target reached fifty miles-per-hour, and two seconds later, it maxed at seventy-eight-miles-per hour. Carr didn't move. There wasn't going to be any fishing today.

Buzz glanced down at the speedometer, sixty-five-miles-per-hour. He looked over at Todd, who was lost in thought. The car jerked slightly

"You feel that Buzz?"

"Yeah, it didn't feel like an engine miss. It felt like it came from behind."

Todd looked over at the speedometer and then turned in his seat and looked out over the back of the car. There was nothing back there. "Like being pushed, or pulled."

He nodded and took a little pressure off the accelerator. The car held steady at seventy-miles-per-hour. He lifted his foot completely off the accelerator and rested it on the brake in preparation to stop. The Corvette accelerated to seventy-nine-miles-per-hour. Buzz yelled to Todd to put on his seat belt.

Buzz began to apply pressure to the brakes and to move the car to the shoulder. He could barely hear Todd scream over the wind. "Don't!"

He now realized that he was no longer in control of the car. He couldn't move it because the steering would not respond and he couldn't stop. The car just continued in the middle of the road with the center line passing right under the center of the car. It suddenly rocketed forward to ninety-one-miles-per-hour!

Todd managed to get one final sentence out before the wind drowned out his voice. "You might want to buckle up."

They couldn't see Carr standing in the middle of the road thirty miles away, but everyone out on that road on that hot summer morning was experiencing something they were never going to forget. The human mind is an amazing thing. Even when it is experiencing something that defies all the senses, something impossible, it just keeps on processing.

Carr removed his Stetson and rubbed a hand across his forehead without taking his eyes off the road. His hair, hand, face, and hat were soaked with sweat. Almost simultaneously, he saw a flash of light in the distance, the only thing everyone would be able to agree on. Then, the first alarm sounded, indicating that the target was accelerating beyond the maximum programmed speed limit.

The second alarm followed immediately after the first. The target was now moving at more than eighty-miles-per-hour. Carr did a mental calculation. The minimum was set to fifty and the maximum was at seventy-eight. There had been about five seconds between them and about a second for the next two. Whatever was out there had accelerated from fifty to eighty-miles-per-hour in about six seconds. The third and final alarm came three seconds later, indicating velocity off the scale high. Carr turned to look at the radar. This was no longer about a fishing trip. It was about whether a tomorrow was even possible. In the distance, he could hear a deep boom and see the ground shimmer as a shock wave ran through the heat. The radar gave a loud shriek and went silent. He envied the machine, its electronics fried. It wouldn't have to face what was coming. Carr looked down at his feet, willing them to move, but they didn't. He laughed out loud. "Where the hell am I going to go?"

The chopper pilot would have given an arm to be in Carr's shoes, because from where he was sitting, he was in way over his head. The last thing he could recall was that the car they were tracking was right under them when the turbulence, or whatever it was, hit the back of the helicopter.

Every alarm in the cockpit had gone off at once, as something tried to drive the helicopter it into the ground one second and then onto the roof the next. On top of everything, the torque overload warning alarm was screaming that the blades were being driven beyond limits. He tried reducing the collective and pushing the nose over. The machine refused to respond. None of his inputs made any sense. He yelled at the radar operator. "Man, I hope you are still back there!"

He could barely hear the operator over the howling of the turbine and blades. "Where the hell am I going to go?"

"Lock everything down. I'm going to put this thing down!"

"Are you nuts? You don't even know what's going on down there."

"Well, I sure as hell know what's going on up here! Grab something and hang on!"

He took one last look around the cockpit to make sure everything was secure. The radar operator had his hands fastened firmly between his legs. "Smart boy!"

The leading edge of the shock wave had finally reached Carr. It was like being hit in the face with a fist. He could hear the radar being the blown off the tripod onto the hood of his patrol car. He managed to stagger forward one step before the shock wave slammed him face down onto the pavement. It shrieked and howled, trying to pull him off the pavement. Then there was silence.

It seemed like the darkness that came with the wind lasted for hours. In the distance, he could hear a familiar sound, the wind in the telephone wires. Then, something different arrived. When he looked up, he had to wipe the grit out of his eyes to see. It was the helicopter. It hit the pavement hard enough that it didn't even bounce, but not hard enough to check its forward momentum. It slid sideways down the road, sparks flying from the landing skids.

Carr got up in hurry and started running with one thought going through his mind. "This is one seriously screwed up day!

Carr wasn't sure how far he got before he tripped and fell on some debris on the road. He grabbed his Stetson and pulled it down over his head, thinking he was going to die looking like Gomer Pyle. He lay there for what felt like hours, waiting for the helicopter blades to carve him to pieces. He felt a slight tap on the soles of his shoes.

He rolled over slowly, and raised his head to look at his feet, where the skids of the helicopter were resting comfortably. Above him, the blades were slowly winding down. His eyes drifted to the windows of helicopter. The radar operator slowly raised his hand and waved.

When Todd and Buzz saw the flash and heard the boom generated by the shock wave, Buzz yelled. "Todd we are no longer in control of this car!"

Todd leaned forward and covered as much of his head as possible. Buzz crossed his arms over his face and leaned on the steering wheel. The buffeting came first, followed by silence, and then a roar as they encountered violent winds coming from every direction at once. The car whip-sawed violently from the right to the left, and then back into the center of the road. Everything in the car that was not secured--paper, glasses, maps--were sucked out enough force to turn even small objects into missiles.

Buzz looked up over the wheel. The car was still holding position in the middle of the road. The speedometer read seventy-miles-per-hour. They were in a fog even though the sky directly above them was clear. The temperature in the car felt like it was barely above zero. He looked sharply at Todd. "You okay?"

Todd leaned back in his seat. There was a small cut on his forehead from something ejected from the car. He rubbed the cut, and there was a little blood on his hand. "Yeah, any crash you can walk away from is a good one."

"No argument on that one, Todd. Did we crash?" A simple question, except the car was still moving.

Buzz raised his foot and placed it on the brake and slowly applied pressure. The car slowed about five-miles-per-hour, followed by a loud metallic bang from the back end. The brake peddled reacted instantaneously and traveled almost to the floor before the car began to slow again.

"Have we got anything, Buzz? It sounded like we lost the rear brakes."

Buzz sat up in the seat and pushed the pedal to the floor, "Barely."

They both looked at the speedometer. Even with the brakes gone and the power off, the car should have come to a stop in 500 feet. At the rate they were bleeding off speed, it would take over a mile just to get down to thirty-miles-per-hour. In the distance, the fog was clearing and they could see objects in the middle of the road.

"We are out of time, Buzz. Use the gears if the engine is still running."

"We've got power but just."

He slowly worked the car down from fourth gear to third, losing another twenty-miles-per-hour. From third to second, the car only gave up four-miles-per-hour.

Buzz shook his head. "We've got one gear left. If we use it, the engine will red-line and we'll probably lose the drive shaft." He placed both hands on the wheel and looked at Todd, who nodded silently.

Buzz put his right hand on the wheel, raised both feet, jammed down the brake, and then reached down and yanked hard on the emergency brake. Chunks of metal blew out from under the back of the car as it finally started to give up speed. As the car passed forty-miles-per-hour, they could now see a helicopter and at least three police cars in the middle road.

At the last possible minute, Buzz yanked on the wheel and put the car into a skid. Smoke poured out from underneath as it thundered down the road. The speedometer was no longer registering and the engine had quit. Todd and Buzz put their heads down, to prepare for the crash. The Corvette scattered police officers in every direction as it came to a stop less than ten feet from the helicopter. From behind, a Seline patrol car screamed to a stop, blocking their exit.

Todd looked up first, seeing the helicopter blades directly above them. He put his hand on Buzz's shoulder, to reassure himself that he was all right. "You might want to cut back on the melodrama a bit there, fella."

Buzz rubbed his eyes to get them clear. "I do enjoy my work."

For a full minute, no one moved. Not the police on the road, or Todd and Buzz in the car. And there wasn't a hell of a lot left out in the desert making noise, either. Finally, an officer stepped out of the ditch. He took off his Stetson and examined it carefully; brushing off the dust, before placing it squarely back on his head. The man squared his shoulders. It was the slow, steady walk of a weary man. When he got to their car, he looked it over carefully from left to right, before taking off his sunglasses.

Todd looked up at him and smiled. It wasn't returned. "You want to see my driver's license and registration?"

"Driver's license and registration! Gentlemen, I've got three broken radars, a patrol car that is going to need a new windshield, a two-million dollar paper weight stuck in the middle of my road because its electronics are fried, and now I can't go fishing! What I want to do is throw your freaking asses in jail!"

Buzz leaned back in his seat and looked at Todd. "Did he say he wanted to throw our freaking asses in jail?"

"That's what the man said. Not his exact words though, except the part about jail. That part was pretty clear."

"Well, that's new, isn't it?"

"Not really. There was Ash Flats, and Peckersnot."

"I don't think Peckersnot counts. They were parking tickets. And we did run the mayors out of town."

"That's true."

Carr motioned to an officer. "Take Martin and Lewis back to the detachment."

The officer pointed a patrol car. "This way gentleman, which one of you is Lewis?"

Carr grabbed is head in agony. "How old are you?"

"I'm twenty-two, Sir."

Buzz raised his hand. "I'm Martin."

Todd gave him a dirty look. "That's no fair! You always get to be Martin."

"That's because I'm cooler than you are."

Carr didn't have much of a sense of humor at the best of times. "It's not good when I don't like people. Please don't make me dislike you two anymore than I already do, which is a lot."

The officer escorted them to the car and put them in the back seat.

When Carr was sure they were gone, he yelled at the helicopter pilot, who was examining the Corvette. "Can it be driven?"

"About as much chance as my flying my chopper out of here, which is zero. The brake drums are missing."

"What are you talking about? That's not possible. Have another look."

"Go look for yourself, Carr. There is nothing there but the front plates where the wheel bolts go through the drum. It looks like the drums were blown off. Even the shoes are gone."

Carr had to get down on his hands and knees to see under the car. "Someone get me a flashlight."

When he was handed one, he returned to look. The pilot was right. The drums and shoes were missing. There was brake fluid all over the back end.

He shone the light farther back under the car. Everything looked normal until he saw the differential. He yelled out from the car. "What's the temperature?"

The pilot looked at the officer next to him. "What did he say?"

"He wanted to know how hot it is."

"Why the hell would he want to test the temperature under a car?"

The officer just shrugged. The pilot asked why it was important.

Carr pulled himself out from under the car. "Well, what is it? Just give me an answer."

The pilot yelled at the radar operator and pointed to the chopper. "Check the temperature."

"I'll have to put power on to do that.

"Well, what the hell do you think the electricity is for? Just turn the stupid thing on. You can't damage it any more than it already is!"

They waited for him to get a reading. "What's the weather report for?"

Carr handed him the flashlight without saying anything. He climbed under the car.

Have you got it yet?"

The radar operator waved. "The ambient is 72 degrees."

The pilot yelled out from the car. "What did he say?"

Carr told him what it was.

"Well, what did you expect? We are in the middle of the desert. His voice suddenly trailed off and he pulled himself out from under the car.

"What would it take to do that?"

"You ever see liquid oxygen up close?"

Car shook his head.

"It might be able to do that. But you can't handle it without protection and it is as explosive as hell. The only way to move it is in a special tank."

"Out here, in this temperature, something like that would evaporate pretty quickly."

"Instantaneously--you'd see ice fog for miles."

Carr took the flashlight back and handed it back to the owner.

"What do you want to do with this thing?"

He thought about it for a moment. "Tow it back to the police service depot and have the mechanic start fixing it."

"What about that blender of yours?"

"The electronics are cooked, but if it starts, all I need is air speed and altimeter to get it back. The rest I can do visually. If I get off the ground, Call the air field and tell them that I am coming back without a radio."

It took close to two hours to get all of the equipment packed up and to retrieve the radars and recorders from the helicopter. Carr watched as the rotors slowly built up speed. The machine shook violently for a couple of seconds before settling down. The pilot gave him a thumbs-up and slowly lifted it off the pavement, turned, and disappeared into the early afternoon sun.

Carr got in his unit and drove the rest of the way until he got to the Devil's T. He turned the car around at the intersection facing home, pulled over to shoulder, shut off the car, and got out. It was like nothing had happened. As he climbed back into the car, he felt a short cool breeze, as though the earth had exhaled.

The radar tech was walking through the police garage when the tow truck with Todd and Buzz's car arrived. The tech had used the washroom in the service bay because he didn't want anyone to see how airsick he had been. He'd spent almost all of the time out there in the ditch and hadn't come out until almost everyone had left. He nearly ended up being left behind.

He stopped the truck and pointed to the Corvette. "Charlie, where did you get this?"

"It's the car that crossed the T. You should know. You were there."

"I was in the ditch coughing up a lung when it appeared."

The tow truck driver got out and joined him at the back of the truck. "This is one, sweet piece of iron. It must be tricked out or modified to reach the kind of speeds they said it did."

The radar tech just kept staring at the car without listening, as the driver rattled on about horsepower and value, before the tech cut him off with a short sentence.

"That's not the car."

There was dead silence in Carr's office as he was asked to repeat, for the third time, what he had said to the tow truck driver.

"Sir, I can repeat a hundred times, but it won't change anything. The car you've got in the garage is not the one we were tracking."

"Are you talking radar or visually?"

"Both, Sir."

Carr looked at the patrolman who was looking after the Seline equipment. "What about you? Is that the car?"

The man was unsure. "I was in the middle of a recalibration when it went through the radar trap. But there may have been another one, because at one point, I was getting a return with velocity but no distance."

Carr threw his pencil down on the desk and rubbed his eyes. "This is nuts! Did somebody cancel the laws of physics and not tell me?"

Nobody had an answer to that one.

"Okay, let's wait until we get the data out of the radars and cameras."

"What do you want to do with the guys who own the car? We can't just leave them in holding until we figure this out." The desk Sergeant was adamant.

Carr nodded slowly. "Have the judge issue a bench warrant to hold them in Alamosa for a week."

"On what grounds, you know the judge is going to want a probable cause, what do I tell him?"

He exploded, "For screwing with my fishing trip!"

The Sergeant gave Carr a look that suggested he should consider seeking professional help. He then walked back to his desk in the hallway, where all the normal criminals and lay-abouts were hung around.

Carr sat at his desk. He was finally alone, looking out the window and trying to lose himself in thought, which had nothing to do with work. He finally took a deep breath, sighed and admitted defeat. There was no escaping this.

Carr picked up his phone and dialed two numbers. Normally, he would have just yelled out the door for help. Goldstein gave him a hard time about yelling, just after he took over, telling him that his own phone was there for dialing. He told her he enjoyed yelling at people. She answered on the second ring. "Talk to me."

"Do you still have the combination to Bomba's safe?"

It was a stupid question. Goldstein never forgot anything. "Sure. What do you want out of it?"

Carr thought *that* was a stupid question. "What do you think? There's only one damn thing in it!"

"Will there be anything else? This is the only time you have actually used the phone in the six years you've been in there. I don't want to cheapen the experience."

"Sure, call Smitty's Bar and have him bring over a bottle of brandy and one of those big cigars."

"You want a Panatela? That's what Churchill smoked."

"Name doesn't ring a bell; did we book him for something?"

"He was the Prime Minister of England."

"He was?"

"It was in all the papers."

Carr struggled to put a face to a name. "What's he doing now?"

"He's dead!"

"Oh, right. Sure a Panatela and brandy will be fine."

"Will there be anything else, Chief?"

"How long will it take to get everything out of the data recorders and cameras?"

"You're not going to see it today, that's for sure."

He looked at his calendar. "How about setting up the meeting for Wednesday at 11:30 hours?"

"That will work."

"Make sure those guys in holding are released, put them on ice at the Biltmore. No walky, no talky, and extend an invitation for the Wednesday get-together."

An hour later, Goldstein was putting a bag on his desk, and in her other hand was the letter. She turned it over and looked at the date on the back before she held it out to him. "Bomba wasn't a great boss. He was arrogant, and had a problem keeping his hands to himself. You're a good man Carr, not perfect, but you've always treated me right proper."

He leaned forward and took it out of her hand. "You ever do any fishing, Goldstein?"

"No, can't say I ever have."

Coming from Carr, it was a riot of emotion. "That's too bad."

Buzz pushed open the door to the room for which the good citizens of Alamosa had graciously paid. Todd looked over his shoulder. "Cozy, isn't it?'

"Bunk Beds, what kind of a hotel has bunk beds? Why can't we, just once, stay in a normal hotel?"

"Shotgun!" Todd leapt on to the top bunk with a crash. He gave Buzz a victorious smirk just as the springs let go with a loud metallic twang. The mattress descended through the frame, closing to within an inch of the bottom bunk, and folding like a fig Newton with Todd in the middle.

Buzz went to his luggage, took out one of Oggie Briggs bottles, looked at the label, and nodded approvingly. He tapped the mattress and asked it if it wanted a drink. The mattress said it would be delighted. Buzz filled two glasses and handed one to the hand sticking out of the top. "Have you noticed that we spend a lot of time as guests of the police?"

The mattress agreed that there was a lot of merit in Murdoch's conclusion. Todd and Buzz spent the hour discussing their current situation and what they should do, once the car was fixed. They concluded with Todd wanting to know if Buzz was going to help him get out of the mattress.

"It's only going to happen if you promise not to wear those stupid jammies."

The mattress remained silent for a moment to consider the proposal. "I make no promises."

They repaired the springs with coat hangers to support the mattress. Buzz gave the repairs a once over. "Not bad work, Todd. You haven't lost your engineering skills sitting behind a desk."

Todd shook his head. "I'm an electrical engineer. You know a hell of a lot more about real engineering than I ever will."

Buzz stopped what he was doing. "You want to talk about it?"

Todd motioned to a couple of chairs and sat down. As Buzz joined him, he took a drink before speaking. "Look, Buzz, I owe you an apology. I had a bio put together before I contacted you."

Buzz listened without saying a word. When he was done, Todd apologized again for prying, saying that at the time, he thought it was the right thing to do.

Buzz leaned back and turned his glass in his hand, "You?"

"I've got two kids, a boy and girl."

"Your wife?"

"I lost her three years ago to Multiple Sclerosis."

"Damn! I'm sorry Todd. I've seen what that can do to someone. What about your kids?"

Todd got up and went to the window, looking out briefly. "Janice has gone into law. She'll be completing her Masters this year and is on the *Harvard Review.*"

"She has to be pretty bright to swim in that pond."

"That she is, Buzz, that she is."

"You have to be pretty proud."

Todd turned back to the window. "I haven't seen or heard from her in three years, at her mother's funeral."

"And your son?"

"David. He's taken over company operations in California. He's a great kid!"

"I bet he is."

Todd leaned against the window, took another drink, and wondered aloud how their lives got so train wrecked.

"Maybe that's why we're out here, Todd."

"How do you figure that?"

Buzz was thoughtful. "Well, something got you fired up enough to go looking for someone you hadn't seen in thirty-five years."

"I was driving out to the plant for meetings. I started day-dreaming, or at least, it felt like it."

"What was it about?"

"I was back out here. You remember what those old asphalts looked like when they were new?"

"Sure, they looked like black ribbons with edges so sharp you could shave with them. The country was covered with them back then."

"Yeah, the oil coming out of them when they were new would reflect sunlight."

"I remember that."

"This was different, though."

"How so?"

"This road went right out beyond the horizon."

Buzz looked at him skeptically. "Past the horizon?"

"I'd hired a young fellow to drive for me, Eddie Gluck, a good kid. I must have scared the hell out of him. He probably thought I was nuts."

Buzz got up and joined him at the window. "Just for the record, Todd, I would've done the same thing.

"Thanks."

"And you might be right; the horizon may be a lot closer than we think."

"Are you hungry?"

As a matter of fact, yes."

When they reached the door, Buzz stopped him. "Did you have the brakes serviced before we left New York?'

"Sure, in Buffalo. I had them adjusted when they were replacing the water pump. Why?"

"The guys who looked at them said that the drums were completely gone. How much heat does it take to shatter that much steel?'

Todd shook his head. "Heat doesn't do that. They'd melt, not shatter. As they got hot, they would expand to the point where the shoes would lose contact with the drums. Even if the shoes could stayed in contact with the drums, there's no way they could reach the 1800 degrees required to melt that kind of steel."

"Not heat, Todd, *cold*--if the steel in the drums got down, to say, 100 degrees below zero, and then got hit with a lot of heat."

"Like standing on the brakes?" Todd offered.

"Right. That much all at once would cause them to fracture and break apart from centrifugal force."

"Okay, that makes sense. They have that problem on spacecraft. Environmental control is a big issue. Electrical equipment will freeze solid in absolute zero. If they suddenly got hot from use, they would explode. So, they have heaters to warm hardware before it is powered up. But we are talking spacecraft, not brake drums."

Buzz pulled open the door. "I'm not sure about that anymore."

They had a late lunch at a diner two blocks away. The food was plain, but good. The service was excellent and the place wasn't hit by a forty-pound sack of rancid custard. When the waitress wanted to know what was so damned funny, they told her about Larry Wallace's diner.

She listened for ten minutes with a face made of stone. When they were done, she stared at them, and then put the bill on the table. "Who the hell left the door open and let you two pecker heads in here?"

Back on the street, they were momentarily at a loss for something to do. "You know, she did call us a couple pecker woods."

"Not pecker woods, Todd, she called us pecker heads."

"Well, that's all right, then."

Buzz looked at a car rental sign down the road and pointed. "Maybe we need to get out of town for a couple of hours."

Todd reminded him that they weren't supposed to be getting out of any where, because their car didn't have any brakes, and was currently in the good care of the local constabulary. "Sheriff Carr won't be a happy camper."

"Sheriff Carr never had to deal with a couple of guys who have a trunk full of Griz water before."

"Good point. Let's go see what they have on the lot. Maybe they have something really fast and expensive."

"We're not made of money you know."

Todd argued. "Yes, we are, we just don't have any of it."

"Do you want to call your secretary and ask her for your allowance?"

"Noooo."

"Not to worry, I've got a plan."

"That's making me feel a whole lot better."

"Welcome to Cadillac and Rolls Car Rentals, Gentlemen."

"The sign says Rent a Wreck."

"We're under new management."

"We'll take a Cadillac."

"We don't have one"

"You said welcome to Cadillac and Rolls Car Rentals."

"That is correct, Sir, but I didn't say we actually have them, did I?"

Buzz told the owner that they would like to rent a car for a couple of days.

"Excellent! We can provide you with a fine vehicle to suit your every need during your stay in Alamosa. How far will be you be traveling with the car?"

Todd looked at Buzz and then shrugged. "Couple of hundred miles, I suppose."

"Well, that will make selecting a vehicle for you much easier."

Todd could see into the car lot through the window behind the counter. "You haven't got a car that will last more than 200 hundred miles?"

"Sir, we have a wide selection of the finest automobiles from all over the world. Our maintenance program and facilities are second to none. Unfortunately, you have arrived just as our fleet has come due for servicing. We can't have you going out in a poorly maintained vehicle. Can we?"

Todd responded. "We will take whatever you have available. I have no doubt it will suit our needs."

"Good choice, Sir!" .He smiled, unctuously, pushed some forms across the counter like he was poking a dead weasel, and then turned to the window Todd had been looking through.

"Arthur,... Arthur!" A head appeared behind an open hood.

"You got that fire out yet?"

The head smiled, no teeth. "Yup, sure did!"

"Get number eight."

The smile disappeared, "What for?"

"It's going out on a two day rental. Bring it around front."

"Do I have to drive it? I got the tow truck right here."

"Of course you have to drive it! It's a car."

"Is not!"

The owner slammed the window, cutting off the stream of profanity coming from under the hood of the car. The voice was complaining about being unfairly treated. The voice was halfway between something about workplace safety and employment equity when the window cut it off. "Your car is being groomed and will be here in just a moment. It will be $250.00 plus taxes.

Todd took a credit card of his wallet and stopped. "That's pretty steep for two days."

"And that will be cash only."

Buzz looked surprised. "Cash only?"

"That is correct, Sir, cash."

Todd and Buzz looked at each other. "How much have you got, Todd?"

Between the two of them they could only come up with $116.

Todd looked down at the cash on the counter. "That's all we've got Buzz. We'll have to try another rental agency."

He looked back at the counter to retrieve the money but it was gone. The rental agent smiled greasily and handed him the keys. "That will do nicely. Enjoy your stay in Alamosa.

Todd looked out the window at the car. "Of course, if there is a problem, we can call you."

The owner gave him the, "I've got your money smile." "Absolutely, we are on call twenty-four hours in order to meet your servicing needs, if you have any problems."

When they got to the car, Todd walked slowly around it. "Have you ever seen a car like this before?"

Todd stopped at the front and looked down at the grill. "Well, it's got a name."

Buzz pointed to a letter missing between "B" and "N". "That would have to be a vowel missing,… Trebant?"

Both of them looked at the two heads watching them through the blinds of the rental office. One of the heads stuck a couple of fingers through the louvers and waggled them. "Why do I get the feeling that I've seen these guys before?"

Buzz got in the driver's side. The car was small, smelled weird, and the driver's window was up. Several attempts to adjust the seat were futile. On Todd's side of the car, his seat was so far back that it was up against the back seat and had every intention of staying there. Todd pulled his door shut and the arm rest came off in his hands.

"Are you going to roll down your window? This thing is like a toaster with wheels."

"The window doesn't work."

How do you know that? You haven't even tried it."

"I'm an engineer and I know when something isn't going to work!"

"You're an electrical engineer and you don't know anything about windows."

"Sure I do. Where do you think power windows came from?"

Buzz slammed his door and Todd's window exploded outward into the parking lot in a shower of glass. "There we go!"

Todd opened his door and slammed it. Buzz's window shook violently and disappeared into the door with a roar and exploded. It was pretty clear that it wasn't coming back. Buzz looked out the hole and could see the pock marks that the glass had made in the metal.

"You ready to go Buzz?"

"Absolutely!"

Buzz slowly put the key in the ignition and turned it. Nothing happened. He breathed a sigh of relief.

Todd grinned. "Try it again."

As he turned the key, Todd slammed a fist on the dash. The car roared to life, blowing a quart of oil and gasoline out of the tailpipe.

"You, Sir, are an evil man!"

Todd smirked and pointed to the grins smiling at them through the blinds. "No, that is evil."

The car rental agency owner slowly reached up and turned the open sign off. He and his assistant, like a couple of demented .jack-in-the-boxes disappeared into the darkness at the back of the office. They could hear a door slam at the back, and laughter was followed by the sound of a car starting. A bright white Cadillac exited a gate in the back lot and disappeared in a cloud of expensive dust.

As they pulled out on to the street, Buzz wondered who made Trebants. Todd was pretty sure it was built in Germany, like the Volkswagen, so it had to be a pretty good car. The odometer made it to 666, and stayed there, as they finally got to the first set of lights.

It was a long day getting out to the desert with three stops--two for water and one for oil. Buzz pointed out the hole where his window used to be. He pulled over to the side of the road and the car sputtered and quit. "This is it."

They got out and looked both ways up the road. "Not much chance of being run over out here."

Buzz nodded. "It's quiet, that's for sure."

Todd looked out into the desert. "That's the problem. It's too quiet."

Buzz pointed up east. "Let's walk that way. The intersection should be about a mile. If we are going to find anything, that's where it will be."

It took about twenty minutes in the late afternoon sun. The Trebant was now just a light blue smudge in the heat rising off the pavement.

"Let's give it another ten minutes and then start back. It's getting seriously hot out here."

"Agreed."

They had covered another ten yards. Buzz pointed to something on the pavement.

Todd reached it first--a blackened chunk of metal. He picked it up and juggled it from hand to hand because it was hot.

Buzz took it and turned it over a couple of times quickly. "This is definitely off the Corvette."

Without thinking, he put pressure on the metal and it broke with a loud crack. "Damn."

"Well, I got to tell you, Buzz, that is going to be one for the metallurgists!"

In the next ten minutes, they collected enough debris to account for one complete brake drum, all of it as delicate as glass.

"We've got enough. Let's start back."

He looked around at the intersection twenty yards away. "Yeah, I can feel it, too. Let's go."

They were just on the other side of the intersection when Todd stopped. "What's the matter?"

"That is definitely not supposed to be there."

"I don't see anything out there."

Todd walked off the road, making his way across the scrub, sand, and rock. Buzz yelled at him to get the hell back on the road. When he realized Todd wasn't going to turn back, he cursed and followed him. It took a close to seven minutes to reach Todd.

It looked like a tombstone sticking out of the sand. "This is one strange place to bury someone."

"It would be if this was a tombstone. It's the right hand roof panel off a Corvette."

"You sure?"

"I'm sure. Go get the car. I'll wait here for you."

"I'm not crazy about that."

He put a hand on Buzz's shoulder. "I'll be fine. I'm not going anywhere."

As Buzz walked back to the car, Todd wished he could be certain about still being here when Buzz got back.

It was a long drive back to Alamosa and it wasn't because of a car made out of cardboard. Neither Todd nor Buzz said a word from the time they loaded the roof panel and debris into the car until they got back to the hotel. When they pulled into a hotel parking spot and turned off the car, Todd rubbed the back of his neck. "We are in deep on this one, Buzz."

"That we are."

Todd looked out the window. "We have the money and resources. We could be out of here by four o'clock tomorrow. We'd be gone before they knew what hit them."

Buzz looked at the broken metal and plastic in the back seat. "You're right, we could. But leaving is not what this all about. We aren't back here to walk away again. We've done that. This is about going this distance this time!"

Todd nodded. "Thanks for reminding me."

"No problem. Don't forget that it's your turn to take back the car."

"Just for that, I'm going to drive it between two trees and tell them it was your fault!"

"They'll probably give me a medal."

When Todd opened his eyes the next morning, the first thing he saw was the roof panel they found in the desert leaning up the wall staring back at him. He got out of bed, picked it up, and turned it over to look at the interior side.

Buzz came in with groceries and placed them on the table. Todd looked into one of the bags. "Are the best before dates in this decade?"

"Even better, some of the cans have these really neat pull tabs, so we don't even need a can opener."

Buzz gestured to the collection of parts on the floor and the panel Todd was holding. "What should we do with this stuff?"

"I'm thinking we might try taking this stuff to a lab. Maybe we can find out who owned the car."

Todd put the panel back against the wall. "I don't think we'll get anything from that. Those panels are not serialized to the car. If I remember correctly, they are actually considered accessories. I was wondering what kind of force it would take to pull one of these off. By the way, you'd better get it together. Carr wants us in his office by ten."

Carr was thinking the same thing. He was thinking that the only thing he hated more than being around people was meetings, because they always involved people. That meant he had to hang around them with no way to stop hanging around them.

Goldstein looked over her glasses at the two men sitting on the bench and then checked her watch. Carr would sit in his office till hell froze over rather than come and ask if anyone was out here. She hadn't bothered to call him and tell him they were here. The meeting was supposed to have started at ten and it was now twenty-five minutes after. The only thing that pissed Carr off more than people was waiting for them. "What fun!"

The sounds of drawers slamming and swearing could now be heard coming from Carr's office. Goldstein slowly put her pencil down, pushed herself away from the desk, stood up, and went to the office door. "He's ready to see you now."

When she opened the door, the sound of swearing coming from the room blew papers off her desk. Actually, it was a breeze, but it was a nice special effect.

Todd stopped and looked her up and down. "I know you. I've seen women like you before."

She smiled sweetly. "Aren't I just the cutest, most adorable thing you've ever seen?"

"No."

She grinned evilly. "Offer me some candy. I dare you!"

Ten minutes later, she could still hear Carr screaming that as long as he was the Sheriff in this town, people were going to be on time for meetings or he would throwing their sorry asses in jail. She loved it when the windows rattled, and brother, they were singing a song this morning, "Silly bunch of pud-knockers."

Buzz and Todd stood there and watched, patiently, as Carr's rant slowly exhausted itself. "Are you feeling better now, Sheriff?

Carr shot him a dirty look. Buzz elbowed Todd and gave him a look that said.
"Be nice."

Carr walked over to the coffee machine and held up the pot. The stuff looked like used motor oil. "You two drink coffee?"

"Yeah, sure."

He retrieved a couple of badly stained cups from a drawer and handed them to Todd and Buzz. "Good!" Buzz was going to run a finger around the inside to see if it was clean, but he decided to take a pass. He didn't want to lose a nail.

"I brew my own, because the stuff that Goldstein makes will burn a hole through three inches of steel. I'm convinced the woman is trying to kill me."

Carr filled their cups and his own. Buzz sniffed and took a mouthful. He raised an eye brow. He couldn't remember having a better cup of coffee.

Todd tried a mouthful. "This is pretty decent. What are you using?"

Carr walked back to his desk, sat down and motioned to them to join him, "Coffee."

He watched the two of them carefully for a few minutes before saying anything. "You two have been out there a long time."

"Not as long as you'd think. Let's just say we are getting back in the game."

He nodded with understanding. "That sounds about right. Okay, let's do some business here. We are still waiting for all the data to be processed, but to be frank I do not have anything on you two, except speeding. The best I can do is hold you for forty-eight hours and only if I threaten the judge for a warrant, which I am prepared to do. So, why don't you two support your local sheriff and hang around on your own recognizance for a couple of days? In the interest of justice, you understand."

Todd made the observation that it was a lot of time and effort for thirty miles over the limit. Carr leaned forward and watched them carefully. "You would be right, if speeding was all there was to it. What year is your car?"

The question caught them by surprise and they looked at each other briefly before Buzz answered. "It was built in 1962."

Carr looked at Todd, "You the owner?"

"I am."

"The car was a built with a fuel injected small block 283."

"That's correct."

"You haven't made any changes to it?"

"No, it's the original engine. It's never even had an overhaul."

Carr showed surprise at that. "The speedometers on that make and model maxes out at 160-miles-per-hour. "You think it could get there on level ground under ideal conditions?"

Todd shook his head. "I've raced it a couple of times. Even modified, it couldn't do it. You seem to know a lot about Corvettes."

Carr stretched walked over to the window and squinted. He preferred the afternoon sun, because it wasn't as hot. "I don't know a damn thing about Corvettes, or any car, for that matter. But what I do know is how to do is ask the right questions."

He took a drink of his coffee, running it around the inside of his mouth briefly. "That car of yours couldn't get anywhere near 160 or the speed the men out there say they recorded, which means there had to a second car,"

"There was."

Carr turned slowly and looked at the both of them. "Now, how would you know that?"

"We have a piece of it in our hotel room."

Carr put his cup down on the window sill and rubbed his eyes. "You two are making my case before the judge a lot easier. Withholding any kind of evidence is a felony."

Buzz protested. "We're not withholding anything."

"Where did you find it?"

"Yesterday afternoon."

There was real exasperation in Carr's voice. "How do you think a judge is going to react to that when he finds out you had it for twenty hours? Were you going to get around to turning it in sometime today?"

Todd conceded that he had a point. "We didn't handle that well. We were going to send it to a lab for analysis."

"Did you find anything else?'

"Just some pieces of the brake drums off our car."

"Okay, I believe you two. I'll send a car around to pick that stuff up. We'll follow through on your idea of sending the stuff to a lab for analysis. As for you two, I don't want any more goddamn freelancing!"

"Don't worry, you don't need to sick the judge on us. We are going to see this adventure through to the end."

"Just promise that when this is over, you'll take me with you."

As they were leaving, curiosity got the better of Buzz. "So, what exactly have you got on the judge, anyway?"

"Drunk in a public place, driving under the influence, grand theft, assaulting a peace officer, and being pulled over for being totally wasted. While the trooper was writing up the summons, he was punched in the nose and had his patrol car and pants stolen."

"His pants?"

"His pants!"

"Man, that is some kind of judge."

Carr laughed, "Not the judge, his wife."

"She must have been quite the firecracker at the high school prom."

"They named a ditch after her. She can get right snarky when she gets a snoot full!"

Back out on the street Buzz pulled out a packet of gum and offered Todd a stick. "You didn't tell him everything."

"You remember us stopping for gas at that station an hour out from where it happened."

"Sure, we were only down a quarter of a tank, but I thought it was a good idea to fill up any way. Why?"

"I'm positive that the car they are looking for was sitting on the other side of the pumps."

"How can you be sure? There has to be more than one 1970's Corvette between here and the coast."

"The panel matches the color and year of the car and the left hand panel was stowed and the right was on the roof."

"If you are that sure, why didn't you tell Carr?"

"Well, they already have a good idea what they are looking for, and I didn't think it would make any difference, anyway."

Buzz agreed with him. "Now that you mention it, I don't think he's putting all his cards on the table, either."

Okay. When Buzz Murdoch talks, I listen. But you might be reading more into this than is really there."

I'll admit that I have nothing more than a hunch, but I'm thinking that this doesn't have anything to do with a couple of sports car. Something happened out there and Carr knows, or suspects, what it was."

"Well, one thing's for sure. Carr knows how to play the game. All he has to do is write a report in his log and attach supporting documentation. The guys upstairs will bury it as soon as they read it. Problem solved and Carr survives the blow back by offering to keep the investigation open. Everyone does the duck and cover. The problem goes into a drawer in the basement."

"You're right, if the problem is over."

"Of course it is. It was just a lot of high wind, dust, and bad visibility."

"What about the brakes?"

Todd struggled with an answer. "It's a forty-year-old car. It was metal fatigue."

"Trust me on this one, Todd. It wasn't metal fatigue, dust, or wind! Something did happen out there. All that's left of a two thousand pound car and its driver is a thirty-pound chunk of fiberglass. This is definitely not over and Carr wants someone to ride it out with him."

"And that someone would be you and I?"

"It's all about trust, Todd. It's been a long time and it's overdue, but there are only five people on this planet that I trust. Buzz held up only one finger.

"What happened to the other four?"

Buzz pointed east. "They are part of the past."

"And the one left?'

Buzz pointed at Todd and then west.

Todd smiled. "Well, I can't ask for better than that! C'mon. I'll buy you breakfast."

: Not up to your usual culinary standards, I hope?"

"Of course, I have a lot of class. All of it low."

"What about that trust I was talking about?"

"Unfortunately, it does not include breakfast."

A police officer dropped a copy of the lab report at their hotel late in the afternoon. Todd skimmed through the ten pages, picking out the words from the music in the mathematics. He pushed the report across the table to Buzz and drank some coffee. He waited until Buzz had read through it slowly. He stopped on the third paragraph on the fourth page.

"This can't be right, can it?"

Todd remained silent and continued to drink his coffee.

It took Buzz another twenty minutes to finish reading. He slowly put it down and looked out the window, trying to convince himself that it really was the sun out there.

Todd picked up the report and put it in his pocket. "We'd better go over to that lab and pick up the stuff that the police dropped off. Carr is going to want it back first thing tomorrow morning."

Johnson Scientific was a small, independent analytical lab, on the out skirts of Alamosa, occupying four abandoned Air Force Quonset huts, most of which were filled with junk. The sign, hand painted, indicated analytical services in metallurgy, water, soil, and a number of other obscure tests. The sign had seen considerable editing over the years, as things were added or removed. "Morris Block, P. Eng., Proprietor."

Buzz got out of the car and tossed the keys to Buzz. "You sure this is it? The place looks like the Happy Tumbleweed."

Todd hefted the keys to the Trebant. "I'm sure. You know, I don't mind riding shotgun."

He chuckled and cut him off. "Nope, it's your turn."

"I thought you were my friend."

"I am and it's still your turn."

When they stepped inside, they had to wait to let their eyes adjust to the darkness, to avoid tripping over the incredible amount of clutter lurking everywhere. Todd reached for a switch next to the door, it didn't work. Mr. Block is not big on electricity."

When Buzz's eyes adjusted enough to move safely, he could see benches lining the walls. They were filled with bottles, tubes, and dismantled machinery of all sizes and composition, hiding in corners and under tables.

Todd walked over to a bench and picked up a small device which looked like an over sized pepper mill. He held it up to the dim light which was coming through a dirty window, whistling softly, as he turned it over slowly. "Ever see a device like this before?"

Buzz, recognizing that it was a delicate instrument, handled it carefully. On the sides were a series of slides. On the top were matching windows in which numbers were displayed. "This, my friend, is a calculator."

"No kidding?"

` "It's called a Curta. Thanks, Gentlemen. I've been wondering where I put that."

They turned to see a short balding man, almost as wide as he was tall, wearing a leather apron with a large number of burn holes. There was a welding helmet on his head, also with a large number of burn holes.

He stepped into the room, extended a hand, and waved to the debris surrounding them. "Morris Block, owner, proprietor, and sole participant in man's quest for knowledge. Or, to be brutally honest, I own the dump. You two must be the guys that sent me the wreckage from the T."

Buzz extended a hand. "Buzz Murdoch"

Todd did likewise, "Todd Stiles."

"It's a pleasure to meet you. You guys are definitely not from the neighborhood, so it's not a surprise that you don't know."

"You're right on both counts."

"That intersection you went through at Highway Eight and Center Road, the Devil's T as folks like to call it is not just another chunk of asphalt. Things have been going on out there for decades."

"What kind of things?" Buzz asked.

Block took off his dirty glasses, pulled an even dirtier rag out of his pocket, and proceeded to try and clean them. "Fact is I've spent a lot of time out there, arrived just after Nam. Now, mind you, I don't necessarily agree with ninety-nine percent of what is said and done around here, but I do have a certain degree of local loyalty. You just don't hang your laundry, or your curses, in the front yard for everyone to see."

Buzz told Block that he thought he was being fairly evasive for a man of science.

Block had no problem agreeing with him. "Okay, I'll try and fill in some of the blanks in that report. You got a copy?

They eventually worked their way back to Block's equally cluttered office. He dusted off a couple of chairs with the rag he used on his glasses. He had them sit down before squeezing himself into the space behind a desk. He forced himself down into an old wooden chair which didn't like him sitting on it. It was painful just to watch.

"You're biggest problems with that report are pages four and six".

Todd pulled the report out of his pocket and thumbed through to page four, and then, six. "Okay, I see it. It's the magnetics."

"The polarity has been changed in the metal, or to be precise, there isn't any, which in Ferris metal is impossible, unless you run it through one hell of a magnetic field."

Todd reflected on what he was reading. "That would be on the scale of rocks in the earth's crust that reflect changes in the planet's magnetic field."

Block looked at him over his glasses. "You're an engineer?"

Todd nodded. "I am."

Block looked at Buzz. "How about you Sir?"

"I'm old school, made my way up through the trades."

"Excellent. I admire people like you, real problem solvers. Sir, hand those papers to our friend here. I have no doubt he has the answer."

Todd handed the report to Buzz, with it open to page four.

"Now, while our friend is solving this mystery for us lowly engineers, let's have some coffee and chat."

They talked amicably for about twenty minutes about college, comparing stories about courses, exams, professors, and women, mostly ones that got away.

Block suddenly interrupted Todd in the middle of a description of a particularly filthy bar. "It appears that our wise mentor has solved the riddle. Don't keep us in suspense. Fill the room with your knowledge."

Buzz looked up from the report, frowned, and handed the report back to Todd.

"It's the magnetic field?" Todd looked down at the page and back to Buzz.

Buzz pointed to the spectra analysis at the bottom of sheet. "There's no oxygen in the metal, and what there is barely at the observable level. I didn't think that was possible."

Todd looked at the graph. Buzz was right. It was a very good find. "That would explain the brittleness of the steel. When oxygen is taken out of steel rapidly, it creates carbon monoxide that out gases and blows holes in the steel."

Block beamed. "Sir, Mr. Stiles and I are Captains of industry. Men like us decide the look and feel of science and technology. We are, so to speak, in command. But it is men like you who own it. It would have been an honor and privilege to work with you. Now let's get back to our little investigation here. What would it take to get that much oxygen out of hardened steel?"

"A hell of a lot of heat."

Block waved off Todd's theory. "Not heat. All the metal would do is melt before it got hot enough to out-gas. *Cold.*"

Buzz figured it would take a lot of it.

Block agreed. "Temperature would have to be close to absolute zero in fact, but why just the brakes and not the axles, differential, and drive shaft? Did either of you feel anything?"

They did say that there was frost on the differential and there was definitely a sharp drop in temperature. But it didn't last very long."

"But nothing even close to what it would take to do this." Block picked up a piece of brake metal and broke it in two with his hands.

"What about the roof panel?"

"I looked into that. It's off a late 1970's Corvette. From the photo's I have of that make and model, it looks to be a pretty aerodynamic car. But a car like that would come apart long before it got close to the speed required to pull off something like that."

Block looked at his watch. "Gentlemen, I have another appointment, so we will have to continue this discussion at a later date. There is a box in the other room you can use to carry your evidence. By the way, can I have that copy of yours for a moment?"

Todd handed to over to him. "What about page six?"

Block held up a hand, asking him to wait, as he reached into his desk and pulled out a stamp, which he inked with gusto. He quickly skimmed over page four and then slammed the stamp down on it. Flipping to page six and back to the cover page, he repeated the process, adding three extra blows to the cover page. He then signed each of them before handing the report back to Buzz.

Todd looked at the front page, which was nearly covered in stamps. "You know, one stamp would have been enough."

Block repeated the process, in reverse. "I'm an individual who really enjoys his work."

As Block escorted them out, Todd stopped at a large metal cabinet with a microscope bolted to the side of it. "What is this thing?"

"Ah, good eye!" It's an electron microscope."

Todd was understandably amazed. "You actually made one of these out of spare parts?"

"Pretty neat, huh? It plays hell with the electricity bill, though. I got drunk and left it running, spent an entire night playing what's inside. I had to sell my car to pay off the bill. Carr thought I was growing dope out here."

"Were you?"

"Hell no! I don't have any truck with that, no Sir. I make a decent shine, though. Want some? It's on the house."

"Thanks--but if it's all the same, we'll take a pass."

What are these slots for?" Buzz wanted to know.

"That's where the bread goes."

"You use this thing as a toaster!"

"Sure do. It has a fifty-watt laser that intersects the beam to super heat samples to improve resolution. It's a bit slow what with waiting for the vacuum to set up. But the toast is awesome!"

When they got out to the Trebant, both of them were trying to figure out if the last ninety minutes made any sense. "You have to admit that we've had a very different experience, Buzz."

Sure, so is *The Twilight Zone.* But that doesn't mean you should vacation there."

"This is true."

On the drive back, Buzz leafed through the report, stopped at page four, and burst out laughing.

"What's so funny?"

Buzz handed him the report. Todd took his hands off the wheel and looked at the page. It didn't make one bit of difference to the Trebant that he wasn't steering or looking out the window. The steering was so bad on the car that half of the time; it pretty much went where it wanted anyway.

They both had their heads down looking at one of three Morris Block's 3' x 4' bright red stamps, as the car plowed under a detour sign.

Todd looked up briefly. "You hear something?"

"Nope, see look at the note he made under the stamp. Metal fatigue!"

Todd thought that was the funniest damn thing he had ever seen. "This guy is good!"

"I think there is something stuck under the car?" Todd continued to ignore the road and steering wheel. Turning in his seat, he put both hands on the door and leaned out the hole where the window used to live. Buzz repeated the process on his side.

"I'm seeing a lot of blue sparks over here, Todd."

"They're red over here."

"Drive faster, and maybe that will make them the same color on both sides."

Carr was now three days older. He was still sitting in his office, looking out his window, and wishing people would go away and stop bothering him, especially the six people sitting in his office. He slowly closed his eyes and tried to make them go away. When he opened his eyes they were still there. What the hell was wrong with them anyway? Cars were vanishing all over the place, why not this bunch of pudknockers. No, Sir, they just remained solidly glued to the furniture and refused to disappear. He wondered, briefly, if there was some kind of cream or spray that he could use. He turned his chair around and stared balefully at them. Maybe he could take out his gun and shoot them. No, too much paperwork.

He turned to the police analyst. "OK, Sherlock, tell me a bedtime story."

Goldstein cleared her throat. Public presentations were not her strong suit. The data suggests that there were two cars involved, and not one, as we originally thought."

"Bullshit! I was there, flying in the chopper and it's not the one sitting in the garage."

"Hey, put in a sock in it, Chuckles. You wouldn't recognize the Pope if you had your head up his ass! I'm the one who analyzed the telemetry and visuals and it shows a brown car, not a red one, under the chopper."

Goldstein pointed to a map on the wall, picked up a pin, and stuck it in. "That's the point where the target was when the Selina radar acquired, 10:57 hours, eleven miles out, at sixty-eight- miles-per-hour."

Everyone agreed that the numbers sounded right.

"Approximately thirty seconds later, the Selina radar operator reported a drop out on the return."

"That's right, the thing went to zero and then to seventy-four-miles-per-hour, but it seemed like it was lot longer than thirty seconds."

"Your radar started a recalibration with Sheriff Carr's radar at 10:57:10. Right?"

Both of the men at the Selina's radar were beginning to wonder if anything they saw and heard was right. "Yeah, sure, I guess."

She picked up another pin stuck it into the map right on top of the Devil's T. She turned to the helicopter crew. "That is where the target was when your radar acquired it at 11:01:04, velocity ninety-four-miles-per-hour. How far was it from your radar to the intersection?"

"About thirty miles."

Someone said it softly. "That's thirty miles in less than three minutes."

"At 11:01:44, you reported that it was directly under you, followed by a flash of light, possibly off chrome, and then you were hit by turbulence And then, five minutes later, a red and white Corvette, not a brown one, stopped sixty feet short of the road block."

The chopper pilot stood up and stared at the line of pins. "Almost ten-miles-per-minute, 600-

miles-per-hour. Anybody know what the top speed of a Corvette is?"

"Modified, it's about 120 under ideal conditions."

She picked up two more pins. She stuck a brown one next to intersection. "   That's where you saw the brown Corvette. This pin, for the red Corvette, I am going to put it here at the road block where you landed."

The rookie officer who was at the Selina radar breathed a sigh of relief. "So everything makes sense, except for the speeds, which could be just equipment failure."

The helicopter pilot scoffed at that. "On three radars simultaneously, give me a break!"

"It could be a solar flare. They can really mess up electronics. I went through one about six years ago. It was bad enough to cause sparks in phone and power lines."

Goldstein pointed to the pin for the brown car and then the pin for the red one and ran her finger along the line marking Highway Eight. "There wasn't any solar flare out there."

Carr leaned forward and pointed at the map. "Then, what the hell is the problem? Let's wrap this up and go home."

She walked to his desk and put the last pin down on his blotter. "You're missing a car, Chief."

This time, Carr got up from his desk before turning to the window. "Why don't you give us couple of hours before you show us the visuals and the readouts from the recorders? We'll meet back here at five."

All of the officers gathered around the map. A few poked speculatively at the pins. Someone spoke for everyone. "I mean, how is any of this possible?"

"Well, we were all there. It's not like we're making this stuff up."

"That's too bad. At least, we could explain that."

Goldstein wondered aloud. "Is it even possible for a car to travel that fast without coming apart?"

Buzz got up and stretched. "There are cars, if you can call them that, capable of speeds in that range. They are basically jet engines with seats strapped to them. But even they can't reach those speeds in the time we're looking at here."

Carr decided that the people in his office were really starting to get annoying and politely asked everybody to get the hell out. He stopped Todd as he was leaving. "Wait, I want to talk to you."

Todd looked out into the hall before closing the door and told Buzz he would be along in a couple of minutes.

"I ran a background check on you and your buddy. You two just don't add up. What are you doing here?"

"We're just passing through."

Carr burst out laughing, "Just passing through! Two guys with enough money to buy the state show up in an old car, and all hell breaks loose. Try again."

"Sorry, Sheriff, that's my story and I'm sticking to it. I don't have any answers for you. You were there, just like I was."

Carr stopped him as he opened the door. "Accelerating to ten miles a minute in seconds, no one can survive that much force."

Todd looked out the door, and then back. "That's about forty G's of force. It's possible, theoretically."

"And the car?"

Todd shook his head. "It would disintegrate long before it got even close to that speed."

Buzz was waiting for him on the steps. "There's nothing I enjoy more than a good mystery, how about you?"

"Sure, if it's stuck to the pages of a cheap paperback novel."

"I know what you mean. I'm starting to miss Peschersnot and Ash Flats."

"Yeah, and the Ocean Grove Motel is beginning to feel like a long time ago."

"C'mon, let's get something to eat. It's going to be a long day."

It was just after five in the afternoon when everyone was back in Carr's office to see the last and most vivid part of the mystery. Carr was back behind his desk facing his window, taking in the last of the day's sun. His fishing trip was now a long time ago. "We all know why we're here. You might as well play it."

Goldstein coughed briefly before speaking. "I've edited the tape so that only the key five minutes are shown. If anyone wants the whole thing, I can arrange a copy."

She gestured to someone to push the play button on the recorder. The screen flickered and came to life. The officers at the Selina radar appeared in the camera of their patrol car. The clock and radar data ran silently in the lower right corner. Everyone watched in silence as the men set up their equipment, and laughed as one of them disappeared out of sight briefly for an unidentified reason.

The tension in the room increased as the clock slowly counted up and the radar began to react to something. The clock indicated 10:57:40. The image split briefly into three to include Carr's and the helicopter's cameras.

Everyone jumped at the sound of the Selina officer's voice when the camera switched back to their car. The readings were now off scale, high at 11:01:10. There was the sound of high winds buffeting the car and someone yelling to forget the equipment and go to the ditch.

The screen jumped violently and then the view was back in the helicopter. It seemed suddenly calm and almost surreal to see the road passing slowly under the helicopter. In the corner, the clock marked time normally as the radar data jumped and fell between sixty and eighty-miles-per-hour. For a brief second, it acted normally. Then, it instantaneously jumped to ninety-four-miles-per-hour. In the corner of the screen, an object suddenly appeared on the road as nothing more than a smudge, and in matter of seconds, it appeared clearly under the helicopter. It held its position for a couple of seconds and then the machine began to count up again with the tenths of a second becoming a blur. The radar tech's voice erupted from the speaker, indicating that the car was almost under them. In the comfort of the office, the tech was surprised at how terrified he sounded.

The image jumped violently and recovered, as the first wave of turbulence struck, showing the car passing under the helicopter. There was one last clear image, barely a frame, because the car was accelerating away faster than the camera could move to track it. It was brown, a Corvette, with the left panel off and the right one in place. The driver was clearly visible behind the wheel; he was wearing a yellow golf shirt. The car seemed to freeze for a second, followed by a violent flash of light off the chrome roof rail, and then in the next frame, it was gone, leaving a distorted image of the road before the camera failed in the turbulence.

She pushed the stop button. "The rest of it is the data from Chief Carr's radar and camera. Does anyone want to see it?"

: Can you back up the tape to the driver?" Everyone turned and looked at Buzz.

"Do what the man asked." Carr ordered.

The tape rolled back until the car backed into the center of the screen. "Can you back it up another tenth of a second?"

"That's pretty precise, but I think so."

She adjusted the controls and the car moved back imperceptibly. Buzz motioned Todd over to the screen, speaking barely above a whisper. "Is that the car?"

"Yes, it is."

Todd tapped the screen, calling Buzz's attention to the drivers' right arm. Does that look like a man who's in trouble?"

"No, it doesn't it. Either he was fully prepared or it had happened so quickly he didn't have time to react."

Carr interrupted their conversation. Gentlemen, there are no secrets in this room."

Buzz turned to the group. "His left hand is on the steering wheel. His right is on the center console. He doesn't appear to be reacting to anything."

"So, what you are saying is that whatever he encountered hit him so fast, he didn't even see it coming."

"In a word, yes."

Carr got up and turned off the television. "I can't adequately express the joy you people have brought into my life. Get out and don't come back till tomorrow at 11:00."

"Why eleven?" Someone asked.

"Two reasons. I want to have one decent cup of coffee before you people show and ruin my day."

"That's only one reason."

"I don't like you!"

As everyone filed out slowly, Carr slammed the door violently on Todd and Buzz as they were about to leave. "The garage says the parts are here for your car. They should have it fixed late tomorrow."

"That's good to know, but they don't have to put in overtime to fix it."

"I told them to put in overtime"

"Are you trying to get rid of us, Sheriff?"

"Like a relative at Christmas! And from the sound of it, Morris Block is going to be burning midnight oil as well. Seems he has a project that is keeping him up late these days. When they've got your car back together, let him have a look at the drive line, differential, and axles for cracks. I'm guessing he will need it for a couple of days to finish his work. He's as strange as the day is long, but he's a good man."

"That works for us."

Carr kept his hand on the door to make sure it was shut. I have no doubt that he will have a report completed the following morning. Read it thoroughly and follow up on any recommendations he makes."

"You want us to bring you a copy?"

"That won't be necessary, I'll already have one. By the way, word has it you got a car from Rent-A Wreck over on Bleecker Street."

"Sure, it was the only game in town."

"What did those two bandits give you?"

"Number Eight. Why do you ask?"

Carr let loose with an impressive string of profanity, calmed down long enough to return to his desk to write a set of instructions, and then, put them in an envelope.

"These are the instructions for returning the car. Do not open them until you get back to Rent-A-Wreck and follow them to the letter. You two got that? When you have returned the rental, you can pick up your car."

"Is that all?"

Carr pulled open the door. "Good-bye, Gentlemen."

Buzz stopped on the steps and looked at his watch. "Are you hungry?"

He stood up from tying a shoe lace. "Sure, you bet. Got a particular food group in mind?"

"Come to think of it, I haven't done Chinese in a while."

"Now that you mention it, neither have I. There's a place a couple of blocks over."

Buzz frowned. 'Are you talking about that hole in the wall we saw on the way into town? I think that was a Laundromat."

Todd pointed to the evil metal troll squatting at the curb. "There's only one way to find out."

They couldn't get the doors open. The damn car was just not going to let them in. "Can you believe this? It's like the doors have been welded shut."

After another fifteen minutes of pulling and cursing, the doors still refused to budge. At one point, with the both of them pulling on the driver's door, they dragged it sideways. "We could just climb in the windows, Todd."

"I am not giving the rotten thing the satisfaction."

Exhausted, they stood there staring at the car. "One door I can understand. But we are talking both sides here!"

"It's the heat. The doors are made of metal and the stupid thing is expanding at different rates."

"Well, that is just nuts; half the car is made of cardboard."

He stuck his hands in his jacket pockets. "You got a better idea?"

Buzz rubbed the back of his neck. "No? Neither do I. One thing I am sure about is that when we open Carr's instructions, it will say we have to drive this metal munchkin through the front door of the place.

"Still, that does not solve our immediate problem. Todd walked over to the car and gave the rear quarter panel a good swift kick.

The car rocked slowly on its rusty leaf springs, emitting a high pitched squeak as it moved back and forth. It suddenly stopped, rattled violently, stopped again and both doors popped open with a bang. They stood there and watched the car for two full minutes just to make sure it wasn't going to explode.

Buzz walked around the car and got behind the wheel. He lost the toss and he had to drive. His door closed without a sound. Todd was not taking any chances, standing on the curb, moving the door back and forth slowly. The handle came off in his hand. Buzz leaned over the seat. Why don't you just get in?"

"Why?"

"Because you can't ride on the roof."

"Why not?"

"No roof rack."

Todd got in and put on his seat belt.

"You know, that isn't going to do you any good, the ends aren't bolted to anything."

Todd yanked on the two belts and they were indeed not attached to anything. He tossed them out the door and tried to pull it shut. The door wouldn't move an inch and no amount of pulling and cursing was going to convince it otherwise.

Buzz watched the contest of Todd versus machine for a couple of minutes. When he was satisfied that it was a stand-off, he got out of the car, walked around it, and slammed the door shut.

When Buzz got back behind the wheel, Todd just sat there and stared at him. "You realize that this car likes you and that can only lead to no good."

Buzz grinned. "Don't worry. I know she's a no good cheap tramp and I'm going to dump her at the next bar."

"Are you going to stiff her for the bar bill?"

"Absolutely!"

"Good man."

As the pulled out into traffic, Todd stated the obvious. "We could have saved a little time if you had just let me get in on the driver's side."

"You didn't ask."

Ten minutes later, Russia's contribution to motoring mayhem pulled to a stop in front of a clean, white, and very narrow store front. A small oriental man with a thick accent was sweeping the entrance. Todd leaned out the window. "Is there a Chinese restaurant here?"

The man stopped his sweeping and walked over to the car. "Yes, you have come to the right place."

He looked at Buzz who shrugged. Buzz looked back out of the window. "How come your sign says Laundromat?"

"Because it's a Laundromat, how do you think the silverware gets cleaned?

Buzz looked out the windshield. There was a crack that he was sure wasn't there when they left the police station. "Well, I haven't got any better ideas, Todd."

"Neither do I. By the way, I'll get out on your side."

From the street, the owner of the Laundromat watched patiently as the two men extricated themselves from the Trebant.

"That's a pretty crummy car. You sure you guys can pay the bill?"

They looked at each other for a moment. "We should be good for a meal and desert."

The owner poked the car with the broom handle. "My grandmother was big on Karma. She was always going on about how it would always be following you around through different lives and crapping on you if you did something bad. You guys must have been chain saw operators who kept bringing work home with you. On the other hand, who am I to turn down a fast buck? C'mon."

Decor was not high on the owner's list, but the place was pretty decent. The menu was in Chinese. Buzz looked at the other side of the menu looking for a translation. There was no doubt that the place was a real Chinese restaurant.

Todd put his menu down. "Go for 36 or 49."

Buzz looked up in surprise. "You can read Chinese?"

"I understand enough to get my face slapped in a bar."

"Where'd you learn Chinese?"

"In a bar."

About fifteen minutes later, their orders arrived, hot, well-prepared, and identical.

Buzz looked over at Todd's plate. "They look like the same thing. Is that what we ordered?"

"How the hell should I know?"

"You don't even know what's on your menu?"

The owner or waiter, depending on where he was standing, threw his order pad on the table. "Do I look like a guy who speaks Chinese?"

"Well, as a matter of fact, you do."

"Isn't that typical? A guy looks just a little bit Asian and everyone thinks you know confusion!"

"You mean Confucius."

"Yeah, whatever."

"And what's with the made-up Mid-West accent?" Todd wanted to know.

"It's not made up. I'm from Baltimore, third-generation American. The last time I tried to use chopsticks; they had to hose the place down."

"Baltimore isn't in the Mid-West."

"Okay, so I can't read a menu and my geography sucks. Anything else you want to complain about,...how about the service?"

"No, the service is pretty good."

He held his arms over his head and yelled," Praise the Lord!"

"So why bother with a Chinese menu?"

"That's for the cook. He only speaks Mandarin, or that other one, Cantonese. I forget which it is. All sounds the same. It doesn't matter because he can only cook one thing, anyway. He just sprinkles something on it to make it look different. Nobody notices most of the time."

A look of recognition crossed his face. "Hey, aren't you the guys who came in the other day after that big explosion on the highway?"

They both nodded. "Yeah, the Devil's T."

He smiled. "Is that what they are calling it these days?"

Buzz poked his food carefully. "You know something about what goes on out there?"

The restaurant owner/waiter decided he liked these guys and stuck out his hands. "The name's Francis. Why don't you move over to that round table where we can have a chat? As a matter of fact, I'll get something to eat and join you."

"It looks like it's reserved."

He reverted to his fake Chinese accent briefly. "It would appear that is so."

The cook screamed something in Chinese.

"He's over filled the blender again. I'll be back in a couple of minutes." On his way to the kitchen, he grabbed the reserved sign off the round table and tossed it on the floor. He was back in ten with a hamburger, fries, and a Schlitz beer. "How's the food?"

Todd and Buzz indicated that it was pretty good.

Francis sat down and took a drink. "I've been in this place for eighteen years and not once have I been through that intersection. I came in from the southwest, the same way you are heading."

"How did you manage to avoid it?"

"I'd have no problem crossing the place, but I just never had a reason to go that way."

"A lot of people would envy that."

"Fact is I've never given the place a lot of attention, though maybe I should. The road has had a lot of names over the years. *Hell's Back Door, Salem's Porch,* different names, same results. People go in one side of the angle and don't come out the other, and that ain't just some intersection."

Todd pushed his plate away. "I'm not following you. The problem is everyone thinks the road is haunted."

"You guys ever hear of a place called Whitney?"

Neither of them had.

"Southeast of here, you can see radars all over the place. Air Force used the area to test stuff. They closed the place about ten years ago."

Buzz raised his eyebrows. "Military closes bases all the time. That's not a big deal."

"They don't do it in three weeks with no notice."

"That's hard to believe. Politicians would go nuts over that."

"Not a word."

"Why, what happened?"

"They started losing aircraft in the test range, wouldn't say how many, but it must have been a lot."

"It could have been a run of bad luck. It's a risky business."

Francis shook his head. "Rumor's started getting out about a couple of the really big fighters chasing something into clouds. I think they called them Phantoms."

"What happened?"

"They never came out the other side."

"They didn't find anything?"

"That's what started the base closing. Two weeks later, they found six feet of fuselage of one and the wing tip off the other."

"So, it's happened before,...since you've been here?"

Francis laughed. "Man, you are giving me too much credit. This has been going on as long as there has been a road out there, probably longer."

"Okay, what's been going on?"

"You should know--you were there and lived to tell about it. You cross the T at the wrong time and, poof; you are down the rabbit hole. Except, this time it was different."

"What's different about this time?" Buzz wanted to know.

Francis held up his beer, "You are! I'm in honored company. You two are the only ones to make it across the T while it was awake. That's why everyone is so bent out of shape this time."

"We got lucky. There was someone ahead of us. It doesn't look like he made it."

Francis took a pull from his beer. "Whatever is out there doesn't play favorites."

Todd leaned forward and pointed with a chopstick. "You're playing awfully close to the vest."

"That I am. I also know that old Morris Block is going to look at your car and do some kind of report."

"You are well informed for a man who runs a Laundromat.

"Morris is a smart man. But he won't be able to figure it out."

Buzz wanted to know how he came to his conclusion.

Francis held up his bottle. It was empty. "Either of you want a toad?"

Both of them declined. "Well, I do."

When he got back to the table, he waved the bottle under his nose. "I just love this stuff. Ever had Chinese beer? The stuff really sucks."

"You were saying something about the road."

"You were on the east-west run of the T, the top of the letter, so to speak, which is not the problem."

Todd and Buzz looked at each other, not sure where the conversation was going.

Francis raised his voice in emphasis. "It is an intersection! Cause and effect; didn't you guys ask about the north-south leg?"

"No. We didn't check to see where it went because what we hit was going east-west."

Francis burst out laughing. "What makes you think that what you hit was going in the same direction you were?"

Buzz conceded that he had a good point. "Okay, if whatever was out there was following the other road, where was it headed?"

"He's right; Buzz, we should have checked to find out where Center Road goes."

Francis took a drink and put his drink down. "You'd be wasting your time, gentlemen."

"Why is that?"

"Center Road doesn't go anywhere. Twenty-five miles out, it just stops. There are no barricades, no signs, *nothing*. The pavement just drops off as sharp as the edge of a knife."

"For someone who has never been there, you seem to know a lot about it."

"It's amazing what you can learn from a trip to the library.

"The road was supposed to connect to county lines. According to the records, the project was a real problem child from the get go. Lots of weird stuff, like things breaking. They called it metal fatigue. Things in tool boxes there one minute, and then gone the next. Just odd stuff they could not explain. And then they got to mile twenty-five.

"It was the third or fourth truck of the day delivering asphalt. They used dump trucks in the 20's, so things didn't happen too quickly in those days. Anyway, the driver gets the signal to back up and prepares to unload. He looks in his mirror for the flag man to give him directions, but all of a sudden, he can't see him. Things get real quiet all of a sudden, way too quiet. So, he gets out of his truck and what does he find, absolutely nothing."

Todd hit him with a skeptical look. "You mean the guy wasn't there."

"No, what I meant was that there wasn't *anything* there. Twenty men and all of their equipment were gone, in the blink of an eye. Of course he panicked, drove off, and left a pile of asphalt in the middle of the road. When he got to Alamosa, he went right to the police with his story and they thought he was crazy. They didn't even bother going out to check until the next day, when the families and relatives reported the men missing. When the police arrived, they didn't find a thing, not even a candy wrapper. Even the four tons of asphalt the driver left in the middle of the road was gone. Everyone decided that the crew just up and took off with the equipment and sold it upstate. The fact that the driver of the asphalt truck was locked up in a nut house didn't prevent anyone from thinking that he was involved in it.

In a couple of months, the fear factor falls off and they are back out there trying to finish that damned road. A survey crew goes out to reset the grades and everything is fine for the next two weeks. Everyone is just one happy bunch of campers driving stakes into the desert. They go back out on a Friday to reset some of the grades that were damaged due to winds, so they can restart the road work on the following Monday. The crew did not report back at 2:00 p.m., as was customary. The construction supervisor goes at 3:30 to see what they are doing and all hell breaks loose. The next thing you know, every ambulance, fire truck, and police car in three counties are out there. The site looked like a war zone. Every piece of equipment is burned and shot full of holes. Not from bullets, but from electricity. They found the survey crew hiding in an excavation. All of their clothing was shredded and burned. The doctor who came with the ambulance, who had been in the First World War, said they looked as though they were suffering from shell shock."

"Did they ever figure out what happened?"

Francis laughed. "These guys weren't rocket scientists. They concluded that they were attacked by a bunch of First World War veterans with an axe to grind."

Todd reached into his pocket and took out a handful of shell casings and put them on the table. "These are 303 caliber rounds. They used that kind of ammo in the First World War. Did anyone ever talk to Morris about the story?"

"Sure, lots of people. He even went out and looked for himself. He didn't find of any of this, though. Morris is a scientist, and it's all about the numbers. Because the numbers don't make any sense, he can't bias them. And his numbers are right.

Francis reached out, picked the shell casings out of Todd's hand, rolled them around in his own hand, before pocketing them. "Creates a bit of a problem, doesn't it?"

Buzz suggested that the place was an old First World War firing range that was abandoned and forgotten.

Francis grinned. "You aren't going to explain it away that easily."

Todd looked at his watch. "We'd better get going, Buzz."

Francis picked up the plates. "I'll bag this up for you guys. Maybe you'll get your appetite back later."

When Francis entered the kitchen, the cook started screaming again. Buzz and Todd didn't have to be Chinese to know it was something really filthy. When he got back with the food, they both had a feeling that Francis' cook was annoyed.

"That didn't sound very nice."

Francis handed them there food. "I'm pretty sure no one husks corn like that and I am absolutely sure your mother wouldn't do it."

Buzz hefted the bag as they walked out to the car, "That was a pretty wild story. Sounds like something you'd see on *The Outer Limits* or heard in a Bermuda Triangle story.

"Yeah, but in the middle of the desert?"

Buzz put the food on the roof of the car and opened the passenger door. "I'm having trouble believing his story."

"He's right about one thing."

"What's that?"

"Something is going on out there and we have the brake drums to prove it."

Todd pulled on the driver's side door and it refused to move. He tried again with more force and the door handle came off in his hand again.

Francis appeared on the street. "Tell you what. You give me twenty bucks for the food and I'll help you out with the door."

"I'm sure I'll manage okay, but thanks for the help anyway."

Francis stuck his finger in the hole where the handle used to be. The door gave a reassuring thump and popped open. "You got that twenty?'

Todd handed him the money and got behind the wheel. It took Francis less than a minute to walk back to the car. He leaned in the window, making sure not to touch the car, just in case something vital like a bumper or the motor fell off.

He reached in and shook Todd's hand. "I figure you'll be on your way soon enough so this is good-bye. Remember, you'll want to be going out to the southwest. Take care of yourselves."

"Thanks for the info, Francis. It's appreciated,"

"No problem. By the way, I forgot to pass on a message."

"What's that?"

"*Tick, Tock*. Time's flying and people are waiting". Francis gave them a wave and disappeared back into the Laundromat as quickly as he'd appeared.

As Todd steered the car out into traffic, there was silence in the car for quite a while before either spoke.

"Buzz, we're getting close to the point where we stop reliving history and start making it, aren't we?"

Buzz nodded slowly, took a deep breath, and looked out his window. "Yeah, we're almost there, and they know we're coming."

"Let's see how they are doing with the Corvette."

The police mechanic was installing a new set of brake shoes on the right front wheel when they came in. "You the guys who own the car?"

Buzz pointed to Todd. "He's the owner. I just hold down the right seat."

Todd got a chuckle out of that. "Let's just say the car lets us both drive it."

Buzz walked over to the right wheel and looked at the work. "It was good. I thought all the damage was in the back end."

The mechanic cleaned his hands with a rag. "It was, but we still had a complete set of shoes that fit this car, so I thought, what the heck! We're never going to use them, anyway."

"Thanks. It's appreciated."

"No worries. That part is on the house. They are only going to bill you for the back end. Besides, you're lucky. This is one sweet piece of kit."

"When do you think it will be ready?"

He grinned. "In a few hours, of course, I'll have to road test it, just to make sure it's done right."

"Sure, that's okay with us."

"Terrific. You can pick it up around three."

Buzz suddenly remembered something. "Isn't Morris Block supposed to have a look at it?"

"You mean the fat weird guy with wires hanging out of his pocket that has that land fill site just outside town?"

"Did he have pocket protectors, Todd?"

"Don't recall."

The mechanic took off his hat and gave his head a good scratch. "Been here, done that. He left about an hour ago. He was here all morning. He had a bunch of boxes with blinking lights and dials on them. He said something about going to some kind of meeting.

"Did he say anything about the car?"

"Yeah, he did, something real strange about the front of the car being newer than the back end of it. But said it was all right to drive though."

"Okay. We'll be back at three for it. Enjoy the road test."

They were just pulling out of the parking spot when the mechanic came running out of the garage after the car. He ran up to passenger side and handed Todd a brick.

"What's this?"

"It's a brick."

"I can see that. Why am I getting one?"

"The Sheriff said to give it to you. When you turn the car in you'll need it."

He handed it to Buzz who hefted it in his hand. "What did he say it was for?"

"The cruise control."

Todd suddenly remembered the instructions that Carr gave them. "Hand me that cruise control, Buzz. I remember how to install one of these. I'm thinking it might not be a bad idea to check out of the hotel before we return the car."

"You want to check out of the hotel before we unload the car?"

" No, let's do the car first and take a cab back for the Corvette. That way, we will be packed and ready to go."

The afternoon sun was hazy from winds blowing up dust as they pulled over to the curb down the street from Rent a Wreck.

Todd handed Buzz the envelope which Carr had given to them. "Open her up and let's see what's behind door number one."

Buzz burst out laughing and handed him Carr's instructions. "You are not going to believe this!"

He read the two sheets carefully. "I have always wanted to do this."

Todd carefully folded the papers and put them in the glove box.

"Why are you putting them there?"

"First rule of business put the evidence in the trunk."

Buzz finished the sentence, "and then torches the car."

"You got a plan, Todd?'

"Absolutely, I have a plan!"

"Will it work?"

"Absolutely, I have a plan!"

'Are we are going to regret this?"

"Absolutely, I have a plan!"

They made ropes out of wire from under the dash, which did not seem to affect the way the car ran, and ran them through the fire wall, which had plenty of holes. When they finished, they parked the car in the parking lot directly across the street from rental office.

Todd opened the hood and tied the end of one wire to the manifold and then got in the car and held down the clutch, as Buzz tied the other end around the clutch pedal. They repeated the process with the gas pedal, tying the end of the wire to the frame instead of the manifold.

"You're sure this is going to work?"

"Trust me. I'm an engineer."

"Yeah, I know, but is it going to work?"

"Guess so."

"What about the brick?"

"Leave it on the dash. It won't go anywhere."

As Todd and Buzz stepped through the door of Rent-A-Wreck, the two men who rented them the car from hell stood behind their counter and gave them the "Welcome back, and now we are going to screw you out of your damage deposit smile."

The owner pushed the rental agreement across the counter. "As soon as you enter the mileage, fuel, and other particulars, and sign here, we will do the damage inspection and you will be on your way."

Buzz looked over the papers carefully. There was an unusually large amount of fine print. "Isn't the inspection done first before signing?"

The owner helpfully pointed to paragraph eleven that specifically said signature first.

Todd looked over Buzz's shoulder and thought he was writing rather slowly. Todd looked at his watch and told him that time was up. He pulled Buzz away from the paperwork. "We've been on the road all day and I need to find a bathroom, how about you?"

Buzz declined. "I'm okay, you go ahead."

Todd grabbed Buzz and pushed him down a hallway that lead to the back door. "No, you're not!"

While they were inside the agency, the manifold heat from the red lined Trebant engine finally burned through the wire holding down the clutch.

When they burst out the back door, Buzz came to a sudden stop. "Holy crap, Todd, we forgot to tie off the steering wheel. The damn thing could go anywhere."

"Who cares? Let's get the hell out of here."

The rental rep grinned as they disappeared down the hall. "That's just perfect. Go get the car and let the screwing begin."

Arthur went to the door, opened it, and stood there for at least ten seconds before slamming it shut.

"I thought I told you to go get the car."

"Don't have to."

"Of course you do. Now go out there and get the car."

"Don't have to."

"Go get the damn car. It won't drive itself here."

"Wanna bet."

The owner walked around the counter to the door, glared malevolently at Arthur, and pried the blinds open with his fingers. His eyes darted left, then right, and finally straight ahead. He pulled his fingers quickly out of the blinds and they closed with a snap. He turned to Arthur, after casually brushing some dust off his shirt. "Holy freaking crap!"

He turned and ran for the back of the building like a rat off a sinking ship, leaving Arthur alone at the door. Arthur started to follow his boss, stopped, went back to the door, and locked it. He hesitated for a moment before walking over to the window, just as the Trebant removed the door, most of the wall, and continued its journey through the counter. The car hesitated, appearing to be losing traction on the linoleum. Arthur slowly raised his arm and pointed to the back of the building, indicating to the car which way the owner went. Arthur reached up and turned the *Open* sign in the window to *Closed* and followed the car.

The Trebant continued its journey through more rooms, and ended up sticking half way out the back wall, before exploding and burning down the building. In one final act of revenge, it spit the brick out the windshield which, in an act of cosmic harmony, which went through the windshield of the milky white Cadillac, as the owner was trying to make his getaway.

Standing safely across the street, Todd and Buzz watched as the Rent-A-Wreck rental agency finally adhered to the United States code of advertising. "You know something, Buzz? The Russians really know how to build a car."

Buzz looked at his watch. We'd better get back. We'll grab the first cab that comes along."

"To tell you the truth, I could use a walk."

"You're right, so could I."

When they got back to the garage, it didn't take as long as they thought, Todd stopped at the door. "You got any money on you?"

"How can you be out of money?"

"I wasn't out of money until we took the car back."

"We lost the damage deposit."

"Yeah, but you got admit it was worth the price of admission!"

"It was also the price of a hotel room. Anyway, you can use your bank or credit card."

"I'm sure they take Discover cards in Alamosa."

Buzz looked first at the sky and then at the sidewalk. "No one in forty-nine out of fifty states takes the Discover Card. What have you been doing? Using what you had in your wallet since we left New York?"

"Pretty much."

"How the hell do you get through a day?"

Todd just shrugged and grinned. "Money does that to you. Meals cooked cabs and flights arranged. The more money you own, the less control you have."

Buzz nodded in agreement. "You forget that simple things are the most important. Let's checkout and then see if we can find a bank and get back some of that control we've lost."

"Thanks for picking up the tab for the room. The next one is on me."

"You don't owe me anything, Todd."

"You have to let me pay you back."

"Are you crazy? I'm not paying for a room in this flea bag, no star dump. We're skipping out on the room."

"You've got to be kidding!"

Todd, that's another thing about money. When you have too much of it, larceny and theft under $500 isn't any fun anymore."

"It also means we don't have enough to pay for the car either."

"Okay, so we steal the car and then tell them the cheque is in the mail."

"Cool!"

It's surprising how fast people can pack when they are running out on a hotel bill.

"That's amazing, Todd. We're done in less than ten minutes. Did you get the towels?"

He stopped with a luggage strap. "What?"

"Did you get the towels?"

"Sure, of course I did."

"What are you looking so guilty about, they're only towels."

"I know that. I've got them right here in my suitcase."

Buzz pushed him aside and opened his suitcase, "The hotel Bible!"

"Well, it's not like anyone actually reads them."

"You lifted a hotel bible. That is a new low, even for you."

"Well, your suitcase is full of towels, too."

"It also has a bible. But at least, I stole it out of the room next to us."

Buzz pulled open the drapes, exposing the fire escape outside the window. "C'mon, let's blow this fire trap. We'll use the fire escape, just like the old days."

"We've never used the fire escape."

"Are you sure?"

"You bet! We just fled out the front door when no one was looking."

The fire escape was designed for people fleeing a burning fleabag hotel in the middle of the night, while they're in their underwear, and not for a couple of guys with their luggage, fleeing a fleabag hotel bill, fully dressed, in broad daylight that isn't burning. Steel, narrow and rusty, the fire escape creaked and groaned as they made their way down eleven sets of stairs and landings.

A woman, in her late 50's, with red hair sat in her window, and watched as they dragged their luggage down the fire escape. She braced herself on the sill with one hand and took a long drag with her cigarette with the other. "Afternoon, Boys."

They stopped and regarded her for a moment. "We're fine, thanks."

As they started to squeeze by her on the landing, a very well-heeled stockinged leg slowly extended itself across the landing, with the heel locked firmly in the railing. "I'll bet you are."

She dropped the cigarette on the landing and ground it out with the other shoe. "Well, isn't this a fine day, Sun shining, birds singing."

"Ma'am, if you don't mind, we'd like to get down to the parking lot to pack our car before we check out."

She lit another cigarette and looked out at the setting afternoon sun, which was now just above the skyline. "That's the problem with people these days. Everyone is in such a damn big hurry, and they can't take the time to admire a beautiful day. What a waste."

Reaching back into the window, she retrieved a glass. "You two look like scotch drinkers."

Buzz put his bag down and looked over Todd's shoulder at the very well-preserved, and admittedly, impressive leg. "I guess we've got time to stop and chat."

"Smart man."

She stood up, which was even more impressive. "Toss your bags in and I'll follow you."

Todd looked at her blocking the landing. "We're not going to run out on you."

She reached out and gave his cheek a pat. "No, you're not."

When she climbed through the window, she picked up one of their bags and tossed it on the bed. Without asking, she unzipped and opened it. "Well, I see you already have one."

She took the bible sitting on the night stand and dropped it into the bag, closing it. "On the other hand, you can never have too much religion; there are a couple more glasses on the dresser."

She had dropped a couple of cubes in their glasses and filled them, Buzz took a drink. It was very good scotch. "My compliments to the house, this is very good."

She raised her glass. "I'm honored. It's been a long time since I've had real gentlemen with good taste up to my room."

Todd held his glass up to the light. "We rarely see women of your caliber, either, these days."

"Knowing how to talk to a woman properly is an art. You two have been well-trained."

She got up and handed Buzz her drink, before stepping behind a screen to change. "Let's see if I've got this right. You dropped off that Russian fire wagon you rented, picked up your car from the garage, and were planning to skip on the hotel and repair bill."

They were surprised. "Mind telling us how you know all that."

Her head appeared above the screen. "Easy, word is all over town about how you got here. Everyone was taking bets on how many street signs you were going to knock down with the Trebby. By the way, they want to give you a medal for how you handled the damage inspection at Rent-A-Wreck. The guy who repaired your car is a friend of mine, great mechanic, too."

"We're glad to hear it."

She gave them a hard look. "He's a good man."

Buzz apologized and she relaxed as she stepped out from behind the screen, "How do I look?"

They had to admit she looked pretty good.

"Here's the deal. I get you out of here and you get to take a classy broad out to dinner."

"That sounds like a good deal. Just give us a couple of minutes to get down to the car."

"You won't get past Guido. He practically lives at the bottom of the fire escape, so he can catch people going out the back. So, why don't you two go over to the window while I make a phone call?"

Buzz picked up the bags and tossed them out on the landing. "Okay. We're ready."

She casually picked up the phone and waited till the operator answered. "Gloria? Yeah, everything is great. He's at it again. Drunk and naked as a jay bird, Oh, and he's into his phantom pisser routine.

Thanks, Gloria, and don't forget to alert the media, just for laughs."

"That's some story!"

"Oh, he's here alright. After all, the place is a brothel. Okay, I can hear the sirens. Guido's out front by now, trying to block the door. Pick me up out front."

It was one of the best evenings they'd had since leaving New York. They were the guest of the redhead and a friend of hers, both of whom could hold their own in easy conversation and serious debate.

"Well, Ladies, we thank you for a great evening."

Buzz's date bowed. "The pleasure was all ours."

As Buzz handed the keys to Todd, the women looked at each other knowingly, at the ease Todd and Buzz had when deciding who was going to drive. The redhead put her hand on Todd's shoulder and looked at her friend. "Do we want to see the dash lights?"

"Yes, we do."

Buzz reached into the car pulled out the switch and stood back so they could see the dash."

They stood together and leaned in to look. That is the most beautiful thing I've ever seen."

The redhead reluctantly stood up. "I'm always going to remember that, and you two had better be on your way before we change our minds.

As they pulled away from the curb, Buzz looked back and waved one final good-bye to the two women standing on the street. "Are we sure we should be walking away from this one?"

Todd had both hands on the wheel and was working really hard at not looking back in the rear view mirror. "No, I am not."

Sheriff Carr got up from his desk and stretched. His back was sore. He hadn't kept track, but he must have been sitting for hours. He walked over to window and opened the blinds. The sun was setting rapidly. The town silhouette sat right dead center in the sun's halo. It really was an incredible sight which he thought was wasted on his window.

He sighed, knowing he should have been home hours ago, or at least, he should have called his wife to let her know he was going to be late. She'd be worrying. Of course, she never really did, and that always hurt a bit, but he wasn't surprised. He'd never called once, in all the years they'd been married. It wasn't that he had started deliberately not calling, and maybe she had cared--years ago. But he never asked and she neither did she. He rubbed his eyes and looked at his hands.

Carr turned away from the window, walked back to the desk, pulled out a key, and then, picked up his travel bag. Ten minutes later, he had changed into his civvies in the hall washroom. The place was deserted except for the dispatcher, who was on the far side of the building. Everyone else was on patrol or running all over the hotel, trying to corner the Mayor.

He stopped and looked briefly at Goldstein's desk. He could of think of a lot of things he could have or should have, said to her over the years, to let her know how much he valued her being out here. He walked back into his office and took a key out of his pocket, unlocked a drawer in his desk, took out a shoulder holster, a box of shells, and an American Eagle 44-calibre revolver. When he put on his wind breaker, he shrugged his shoulders to straighten the holster.

As he reached down to close the drawer, he saw the letter. Carr reached in slowly, took it out, sat down, and put the letter on the desk. Even in the fading afternoon light, the envelope seemed to glow against the old, coffee-stained desk blotter. He picked it up, turned it over in his hand, and looked at the date written on the back. The writing covered the flap, so it made it impossible to open and reseal. The ink was clearly from a fountain pen. People hadn't used those things in years. The date was still clearly legible.

Carr picked up the phone and dialed his phone at home. It rang fifteen times before he hung up. This time, he dialed his neighbor's number. A woman answered on the third ring. She was surprised to hear his voice. "Alvin?"

"Is Della there?"

"No, she left about an hour ago, said she needed to do some shopping for Jackie when she got home from Europe. Della said she got her Ph.D. You must be real proud of her, Al.

He was silent for a moment, trying to remember if Jackie was the oldest. "Of course, she's done well."

"Of course you are. You and Della brought the kids up right."

Carr suddenly needed to change the subject. "Sarah, I'm going to be working late tonight. Can you tell Della that I love her?"

He didn't have to see the look on the woman's face to know it was there, or to see her briefly hold the receiver away from her face and look at it. Her voice came back with concern. "Is everything alright, Alvin?"

Carr hadn't taken his eyes off the letter during the entire conversation. "Sure, every thing's fine. I just have to work late, that's all, and I'd appreciate it if you would pass on the message for me."

"Of course I will." She wished him a safe night and hung up.

He placed the receiver back on the hook, stood up, and placed the envelope in his shirt pocket. When he got to the door, he took one final look around the office before he stepped out and closed the door behind him.

On the other side of town, an extremely blood-shot eye opened, moved from the left to the right, and decided it didn't like what it saw. It closed again. "Leave me alone and let me spontaneously combust with dignity."

Buzz and Todd had found Morris passed out behind his desk, after they stopped in to say good-bye. Buzz picked up a bottle lying on the floor. "How did Morris get back there after drinking all this?

"I didn't think they even made this stuff anymore."

"They don't. It was banned as a war crime."

Todd gave him a poke with a broken broom handle. "You look like hell, Morris."

"Of course I do. I'm a scientist. We live for adversity."

"I don't remember adversity looking this bad."

Without opening his eyes, Morris placed both hands on the desk and tried to push himself into an upright position. The desk refused to move an inch. However, the shelf of books behind him was willing to accommodate him and it collapsed on top of his shoulders.

Covered in dust, books, and what was left of the shelving, he got up off the floor and dusted himself off. "Of course you don't. You are far too young. I, on the other hand, invented it. Hand me that jar behind you."

Todd handed him a jar of instant coffee.

Morris poured some into a really dirty cup, took out a bottle of equally dirty rum, filled the cup, and emptied it in one long stiff drink. "Gentlemen, let us toast the gods!"

Buzz took the cup from him and looked into it. "Morris, the gods have been dead for years, and for good reason."

The concoction seemed to have an invigorating effect on Morris Block. He rocked violently from side to side and suddenly popped out from behind his desk like an overweight and demented jack-in-the-box.

"The fixings to make a respectable thermos of coffee are in the first aid cabinet in the hallway. Give me twenty minutes to make myself, once again, a productive member of society, and then I'll meet you outside."

They were sitting at a picnic table next to a pile of old transmissions when he finally appeared. While he was still a long way from society, he was at least back to where he was when they first met.

He picked up the cup and swished it around in his mouth. "Definitely not up to the standards of a physicist--perhaps a mechanical engineer. But, nevertheless, a very respectable first try.

Morris put the cup down and sat on an old barrel next to the table. He sighed heavily because he didn't want to spoil a beautiful evening. "Gentlemen, take a look out there," pointing to the sunset. "Tell me what you see."

Todd responded that it was just a sunset.

Morris looked at him with disappointment and turned to Buzz. What about you?"

"I'll have to go with my friend on this one. It's a sunset."

Block smiled slowly. "Once again we come, hat in hand, for your wisdom, Good Sir."

Buzz frowned as he watched the sun vanished with a last flash of solar rays. I remember reading, years ago, that Einstein was asked if it was possible to explain music mathematically. He replied that it was possible but the answer would be meaningless."

Block slapped the table. "Well done! He did say that and that's what's happening out there. As beautiful as that it is, it is totally without beauty mathematically. The world runs on differential equations and that is the ultimate in the practical application of mathematics. But it is meaningless without us here to see it."

"I'm not following you, Morris."

"It's very simple. Everything runs on mathematics. Physical laws obey the laws of mathematics and so do we.

Buzz pointed out that his logic made perfect sense. "If the laws broke down, there would be chaos."

Morris looked at the both of them carefully. "So, what do you would think would happen if something got outside the zone of compliance?"

Todd and Buzz looked at each other. "That isn't possible. You can't turn the physical laws on and off like a switch. That's science fiction."

Morris pointed out to where the sun had set. "And it wouldn't be very beautiful either, would it?"

"How do you explain what you've experienced here?" Block asked patiently.

Todd answered for the both of them. "We can't. But you can't expect us to believe what you are implying, either."

Morris looked back at the horizon. "What is that color? It has a name, but I've forgotten it."

"They call it indigo."

"It's the most beautiful color I've ever seen."

He stood up without taking his eyes off the sky. "Gentlemen I'm going to need your help. Do you think the three of us and some food can fit into that car of yours?"

It was about 10:30 when Morris asked Buzz to pull over to the side of the road. They were about eight miles from the Devil's T. It was a perfect night and the temperature was right where it was supposed to be for the time of night. At his request, Todd got out of the car so that Morris could get out after him. "Do you mind?"

Buzz reached behind the passenger's seat and pulled out a bag of food.

Morris put the bag down on the hood and took a flashlight out of his pocket. "I'd like to thank you both for giving an old man a new lease on life."

"We're not too comfortable leaving you out here alone, Morris. You know what this place is like."

Morris laughed. "Believe me, I'm not alone. Besides, I thought you didn't believe in this stuff."

Todd shook his head. "You're right. But that doesn't mean the place isn't dangerous."

Morris shook Todd's hand and reached across and shook Buzz's. "Relax, I'm sixty-eight-years-old and my dues are paid. The ride I'm taking tonight is on the house. I had better get going before it leaves without me."

He picked up the bag and walked into the darkness. Just as he reached the outer range of the headlights, he yelled to them. "The first interchange on your left will take you southwest and back on your journey."

There were three sounds on that road that night that mattered. The tick of foot-steps as Sheriff Carr turned to see Morris Block appear out of the darkness. The soft whistle wind makes over a windshield. The ping a radar makes when it acquires.

CHAPTER 9
DUSTY

He, who does not punish evil, commands it to be done.

—Leonardo da Vinci

Dusty, New Mexico, sits on the plains of St Augustine. It's a town of about 6,500 people, incorporated in 1840. Its principal industries, mostly ranching, some light industries and oil fields, are now very long in the tooth. The only airport, and not a large one, includes a runway which is close to 9,000 feet. Dusty has a rail line that's still in use but passenger service had ended years ago. There's an abandoned station still there, just to prove that people actual got off the train back then. If you're behind the wheel in New Mexico, you're either looking for Dusty or you aren't.

The fact is Dusty is a right decent town to look at it, with clean streets, houses and yards kept up. People go about their business with purpose. Every 4th of July, the town has a parade.

Every effort is made to maintain the image of that kind of small vibrant town for which America was famous. Of course, if you weren't paying attention, you'd pass through, from one end in the southeast and to the other end in the Northwest, and miss the place altogether. However, if you did take the time to stop at that diner on the north end for lunch--Weezits--you would get a burger that was spectacular and a spotless washroom in where you can get rid of breakfast. You could be across the plains in about four hours, and then, check into The Halona Inn in Vanderwagon by five. There's a lot of great history in this Inn, inside and out. The locals are fond of saying that George Washington never slept there, nor Lincoln, Taft or Coolidge, but damn near everyone else has, Truman stopped for gas in 1932. The town has a local band that can pull nails out of a hardwood floor with a rendition of Rawhide on Friday nights.

If you decide to stay in Dusty, there was a pen and a smile waiting for you at The Checks Inn. The food in the hotel restaurant is half decent with good size portions. After dinner, you can go for a walk, stop at few store windows, and if there is a little wind on the street, you can watch the dust devils.

As dusk settles in Dusty, New Mexico, visitors find their way back to their hotel room, not driven or forced, but more likely escorted by an old friend or memory. The cable in the room was pretty decent and the night skies were spectacular, if you were on the west side of the hotel. By 11:00 p.m., the only lights to be seen on most Fridays were the ones coming from televisions in living room windows, the basement of the Ratepayers Association building, or a big ochre-colored house up on what's called Spyglass Hill. Folks just called it The Spyglass.

The house on Spyglass is old. It would be difficult to find anyone in the town who'd even dared to guess its age. On this Friday, there were three dim lights on, two up and one down, on the main floor. Over at the Ratepayers, two lights were on in the basement.

Someone appeared at the downstairs window in The Spyglass. The figure pulled up the shade to allow a face to peer out for a moment into the darkness, before closing it and retreating back into the darkness. A moment later, the door opened and a man stepped out onto the porch. The shadows and the light coming from inside made it impossible to describe his appearance, except that he was old and moved slowly. He responded to a muffled voice from somewhere in the house and went back inside, closing the door.

He stepped into the living room, which is almost completely dark, and waited patiently. It's nearly impossible to see the woman sitting in a wheelchair by the fireplace. The only light in the room was coming from a dim table lamp on the far side of the room.

"Are they on their way?"

"They are."

"Are the lights still on over at the Ratepayers?"

"They're burning as bright as a furnace at midnight."

She shifted to the left in the chair to make herself more comfortable. "Can't say I blame them, terrified,... going to get what's coming to them."

Without another word, the woman in the wheelchair turned away from the fireplace and moved farther into the darkness.

The man standing at the door, sure that he was alone, whispered softly to himself. "We all are."

Todd and Buzz were a day out of Alamosa, when Buzz saw the car behind the oncoming semi pull into their lane. At two miles, it looked like it had plenty of time to pass. Buzz hit Todd's shoulder, whose head was down looking at a map. "Damn! That was quick."

Buzz yelled back that the guy had run out of time and wasn't going to make it. He waited till the last minute to make sure that the driver of the oncoming car was going to stay on the pavement and then took the car to the shoulder. Todd ducked as gravel came over the door and into the car. It was over in seconds. The truck and the car still beside it were rapidly disappearing in the rear view mirror.

Buzz leaned back in the seat. I could use a cup of coffee."

Todd agreed. "Better make it a double. By the way, who taught you to drive like that?"

He laughed. "Your Dad did."

The coffee was terrible, but it was hot and black.

Todd took a second swallow of the coffee, to make sure he wasn't hallucinating, that the coffee in the cup, and dirty road sign announcing fresh ice cream, were both the same color. In the distance, he could see a picnic table. He took Buzz's cup and went inside to get refills. When he returned, he handed Buzz his cup and pointed to the table.

They sat for thirty minutes before either of them said anything. Buzz finally broke the silence. "It's tough putting it into words."

Todd was looking up at the sky. It had been getting steadily grayer. There was thunder coming from somewhere in the distance. "We were going to have to pay for it, sooner or later."

Buzz turned briefly to look at the clouds in the distance. "Maybe it isn't even there anymore. It's been known to happen."

"I wish you were right. But trust me, it's still there, as large as life."

Buzz turned back to the table. "A lot of things were said and done that I wish I could take back.

"Sorry, but you can't take words back once they are said, and neither can I. For what it's worth, we both have to answer for what happened. You don't have a monopoly on regret."

"This isn't about us or what has brought us back here in that car. It's about fixing a mistake that we made over thirty years ago."

Todd reflected for a moment. "Have you ever wondered what our lives would have been like if we'd gotten it right or if we managed to fix it?"

"To tell you the truth, I'm not sure it was possible. But we would've been on our way within an hour. It would've been less than a memory in the rear view mirror, in less time than that."

Todd got up, stretched, and walked out to the road. He picked up a piece of asphalt broken off the road shoulder, and hefted it in his hand before handing it to Buzz. "It's time, Buzz."

Buzz nodded. "It's time."

Walter Slezak was the man who'd been keeping those lights on late in the basement of the Ratepayers Building. A balding, heavy set man in his mid fifties, his suit hung on him like a tent and the collar was a tad too tight. A man born with a permanent five o'clock shadow, his face was the picture of mean small-mindedness. The picture was completed with a couple of bushy eyebrows which failed to hide an extended brow.

Standing in front of the building he was joined by a much thinner man who had close cut hair and wire-rimmed glasses. The other man gave the impression of being frail and shop-worn, until he raised an arm. Muscles moved effortlessly under the sleeve of his jacket.

Slezak looked down at the sidewalk with distaste before speaking. "This town needs a proper cleaning, making it right for decent folk."

The thin man smirked, and corrected Slezak, "Right-thinking folk."

Slezak carefully checked his watch, he was near sighted. "Well, that time is coming soon, true enough. This town has been waiting over thirty years for another chance. This time, it's going to get done right. Anyone who doesn't understand the message won't want to be here after dark. When it's done, I am going to go up the Spyglass and settle a personal score."

"What's going on with you, Walt? You've been wrapped around the axle about something for the last couple of weeks."

Walt turned and laid a vicious slap across the thin man's face, which immediately raised a welt. "Keep that mouth of yours shut! You're not smart enough or important enough to have an opinion. That's why I tell you what to say, when to say it, and when I need to hear from you."

The man sucked in a deep breath. "Jesus, Walt!"

"Did you make the call to the district and tell them what I needed?"

"Sure I did. They wanted to know why, I told them exactly what you told me to say, which was because you said so."

Slezak looked at him with loathing. "See how easy it is when you don't try to think and do as you're told? You got that list I gave you?"

The man shook his head slowly.

"Well, it ain't going to get done with you standing here. Times flying, Perch! *Tick, Tock.*"

The man turned and quickly left, grateful to be able to put distance between him and his tormentor. Slezak watched intently as Perch walked away, pleased that he had stomped on the man. Walt stepped into the street and looked hard into the distance, focusing on a spot on the horizon. Without thinking, he reached up, loosened his tie, and unbuttoned the collar on his shirt. There was nothing out there to see, not yet.

Walter Slezak had never met Oggie Briggs, although he had heard plenty of stories and hearsay about the man. He never believed any of it. But one thing was for certain. He could certainly understand what Oggie experienced that day when he had looked up the road. For the first time, Walter realized that something was out there. Something, most definitely, was coming. The only difference here was that there was no mystery for Slezak, no wondering what it was.

To him, it was the culmination of decades of waiting and preparing, the final period in a game which had started decades ago. He stared hard up the road, willing it to come, to make it happen faster. This time, there would be no mistakes. *Tick, Tock*!"

Todd suddenly pulled the car over to the shoulder. They were six hours out of Dusty, New Mexico.

"Hell of a time to get cold feet." Buzz immediately regretted
saying it.

Todd didn't even notice. "When was the last time we saw the coin?"

First surprise, and then concern, crossed Buzz's face. "Damn!"

Buzz got out of the car as Todd joined him at the door. He elbowed him aside and knelt down on the gravel, reaching under the seat frantically searching for it. After a couple of minutes, Buzz tapped him on the shoulder to let him have a look. He got the same result. "It should be there."

"Maybe it was the mechanic in Alamosa?"

Buzz didn't think so. "Good man. I doubt it."

Todd slid the seat all the way forward and reached in from the back, searching from memory. He smiled and stood up. The coin exploded with light in the morning sun. Buzz nodded with approval, took it out of Todd's hand, and walked to the front of the car.

"Go ahead and give a toss, Buzz."

It shone like a star as it descended to the hood. It bounced twice before coming to rest upright on edge of the hood, and dead center in the middle. Todd reached for it and stopped. "Is the car is still running, Buzz?"

"Sure, you can hear it. Why?"

"It's upright and rock steady with 700 pounds of machinery running directly under it."

Buzz grinned. "So, what do you think of the odds?"

"We have a chance, Sir. We have a chance."

Todd picked up the coin and put it back under the seat. "We have waited long enough. Let's get it done."

"700 miles away in Taos, New Mexico, Gus Brubacher finished signing off on the documents on his desk. He was the manager of a bank. He was a man with a high school education who had worked his way up from teller to retail banking, the old fashion way, with hard work. He was the last of the old guard in the organization, and he was definitely old school. So were his beliefs.

Brubacher had two jobs, the one that paid bills and the other one, which was his passion and way of life. As the head of the district, he was responsible for a group of men and women who wanted to turn the clock back to a time when there were rights for decent folk. In other words, they wanted a nice, clean, "white" country. He was also no fool. The old ways wouldn't work now. He had no problem with having legs broken or arranging a convenient fire, but the days of a boat anchor and a ride on the river were gone.

It'd been ten hours since Brubacher had been in contact with Dusty, and that was never good. The men in Dusty were a bunch of ignorant loose cannons and bad for the cause. But what really pissed him off was talking to Slezak's pet monkey, Perch. The SOB hadn't even bothered to speak to him directly. It was disrespect, plain and simple. Slezak wanted control of the district, but he had to get past Brubacher to do it, and that wasn't going to happen.

The real issue was why the call happened. Slezak wasn't going to admit to a grudge over a battle that was lost three decades ago. Brubacher reluctantly admitted that they came close. If they had pulled it off, they would've owned the town, and probably the state, by now. It didn't turn out that way.

Slezak's people had held their ground and a fraction of the town still supported him; however, the last three decades had been a stalemate. Two groups were bound together, going through the motions of civility, with a river of hatred and distrust running just below the streets. Brubacher had been to Dusty on a number of occasions. He could almost feel the tension and anger thundering under his feet. Despite the occasional flare ups of over the years, as people aged, they'd come to terms with the situation for the betterment of the town. They had learned to live with their penance, for something that happened over three decades ago. Now, Slezak wanted to bring it all down on their heads, again.

Brubacher was in a tough spot in this one. If he said no, he would take it in the teeth. There were still people, plenty of people, who supported Slezak, although more didn't than did. On the other hand, the jackass was probably going to a start a war up there, just when the cause was starting to enjoy the benefits of mainstream support. Of course, Brubacher would take the hit for that, too. If he said yes, it meant that the people of Dusty were going to answer for their sins.

It would be ugly and it wouldn't matter which side of the fence you were on. It was always the innocents who got caught in the middle and ended up as casualties. Those were the people the cause wanted to protect to get their support. Brubacher wanted the same thing as Slezak. The difference was that Brubacher wasn't prepared to burn a town to the ground to accomplish it. Slezak already had fifteen men and women, half of them worthless. He told Perch he'd send seven more for a week.

Personally, he hoped that this time, Slezak would succeed. Brubacher was one of the officers detailed to secure the bridge in Selma in 1964. They had won the battle but lost the war. With luck, Slezak would get himself killed for the cause.

In a few short weeks, the citizens of Dusty were going to get a history lesson. It wouldn't matter about the outcome. Justice was coming to Dusty and hell was coming with it.

The two men in the Corvette were again silent as the road and hours passed under them. These men were not lost in thought any longer. These men were focused, very focused. The road sign on their right announced their destination. Dusty, New Mexico 50 miles. Todd tapped Buzz on the shoulder as the sign was passed. He had to yell over the crosswind which was hitting the car.

"The weigh scale?"

Buzz nodded and pointed forward and down to the odometer. He was thinking that Todd was a lot more optimistic than he was. He doubted that the man was still there.

The road to and from Dusty was not on an interstate or even a primary road, so no one was ever sure why the New Mexico Department of Transportation decided to put a truck weigh scale thirty miles from a town of 8,500 people. But there it was one day, and that was that, forty-one years ago. Nine months ago, the New Mexico Department of Transportation discovered that they really didn't need one there after all. The Department announced that weigh scale 21L was going to be closed in eighteen months.

Mark John James, a short wiry man in his sixties, was the sole, last, and only officer at 21L. Mickey John, as everyone called him when anyone ever actually saw him, had read the dispatch informing him of the closure, without the least bit of surprise or regret. He'd been there the day they dropped the converted mobile home here for the temporary station forty-one years ago. He was going to be here when they hauled it away, along with the temporary weigh scale they were going to use until the permanent one was put in the ground. Forty-one years and the temporary scale was still out there on cement blocks, weighing everything that moved, for forty-one years. You had to hand it to those fellows up there in Santa Fe. They sure knew how to make things happen, "Yes, Sir."

He got up from his desk, and stretched. His back made as much noise as his chair. Looking down at his watch, he decided that now was as good a time as any to be outside. It didn't really matter whether he was inside or outside anymore, as he was fond of telling anyone who would listen usually, no one did-- as long as he was somewhere.

He retrieved his baseball cap from the coat rack and walked to the door. He whistled a tune with the words Times Up! *Tick, Tock.* He froze for a moment, wondering where that had come from-- maybe a TV commercial or something. It had been popping into his head a lot in the last couple of months. Mickey John shook his head sharply a couple of times and the tune disappeared. It was a catchy little ditty, though.

Stepping out into the late morning sun, he figured he didn't have a lot to complain about. The State had paid him a lot of money to sit out here, every day. He was retiring, and he had plans that didn't include hanging around this dump. He watched intently as an object approached. It broke into two, and slowly grew to be a couple of semi's. It was time to do the daily calibration on the scale, not that it mattered anymore.

When the first truck was close enough to see him, he gave the driver a signal, allowing him to pass without a weight check. The driver waved back and the truck slowly accelerated. As the second truck approached and began to slow, he gave the woman driving a thumbs up and a wave through. She smiled and accelerated to catch the first truck. They would, no doubt, pass the word up and down the line that Mickey John had decided that it was a nice day and that he had better things to do than bother people about how much their trucks weighed. And it didn't make sense to go to all that trouble of calibrating something that wasn't going to be used, anyway.

He turned and started to walk back to the station. He didn't get ten steps when something stopped him. His feet had suddenly decided that he wasn't going anywhere. That silly tune from the TV was back. Not so fast fella. *Tick, Tock, Tick, Tock.* Something moved under his hat. He removed it and looked at the inside. It was full of sweat.

There was a sound coming from a distance, the sound wind makes when it goes through high tension wire, except there weren't any wires out here. He looked in the direction of the sound, but there wasn't anything out there. When he tried to look away, the same force that held down his feet kept his eyes focused on a spot in the distance. Slowly, something began to move across the horizon.

Mickey John suddenly felt a rush of excitement and fear, all at the same time. His feet suddenly became unstuck and he moved toward the object, even though it was still a couple of miles away. When he saw the flash of light reflect off chrome, he knew immediately what was out there. All he could do was wait, his mind trying to deal with the impossible and the inevitable, at the same time.

The car slowed and pulled off the road. It was just as he remembered it. It drifted effortlessly across the parking lot, found a spot, and stopped. When the engine quit, the lack of sound was almost deafening. For the longest time, the occupants didn't move. The door on the passenger side opened first. The two men slowly got out. Mickey John thought to himself, "Thirty-three years and they've barely changed."

He walked past them without a word, reached out carefully, and put a hand on the left rear quarter panel. The body of the car was cool to the touch even though it had to be absorbing ten watts of heat from the sun. It was a good minute before he said anything. "Murdoch,… Stiles?"

Todd nodded. "Mickey John?"

Good memory. It's almost noon. You two ate anything yet?"

Buzz indicated that they hadn't.

"Let's have a drink first."

Mickey John was the first in the door and put his hat back on the coat rack. He removed a bottle and glasses from the file cabinet. He filled three glasses and handed two to Todd and Buzz. "It's called Metaxa" Todd told him that it would do just fine.

Buzz looked around the cramped trailer. "I've seen a lot of these."

"I'll bet you have."

Mickey John sat down and directed to them a couple of chairs. He slowly turned his glass in his hand. "I hope you're not expecting to be welcomed with open arms?"

"We're surprised that the place wasn't burned to the ground."

"It damned near was, you two set quite a fire, and left those people with half a bucket of water to put it out. But here is the damnedest part of it. You'd be surprised to know that a lot of people were on your side, and still are, because you tried. What got them all up and pissed off was what happened between you two. You guys gave ass hole a bad name!"

"And the other half?"

Mickey John laughed at the obvious question. "It's a hate that is still white hot."

Todd shook his head in amazement. "All those years, how long can a hate like that last, anyway?"

Mickey John banged down his glass in exasperation. "It can go on forever when it's a hatred that goes right to the bone. That's why I got myself a place a couple of miles from here and moved out of town."

Buzz put a hand on Todd's shoulder as he tried to get up. "It's all right, Todd. Listen to the man he knows what he's talking about."

Todd slowly returned to his seat. "Sorry."

Mickey John retrieved his drink off the desk. "The bitch of it all is that everyone thinks that it's that bunch of sheet riders in the basement of The Ratepayers that got it all started again. It's actually those nut cases on the hill. They are the ones that are really cranked about this and gotten everyone riled up, again. When you two bailed out, the widow ended up being the plug in the dike, and was the only thing that prevented the place from going up in flames like a Roman Candle."

"Or like a card game waiting for someone to turn up the last hand."

"Worse! The money is on the table, as are the cards, and everyone is still in their chair. Then, someone suddenly decides to get up and take a leak, and never comes back."

"And everyone's still waiting? Todd asked.

Mickey John nodded. "Everyone has been waiting three decades for you two to come back, to sit down, and to turn up your cards."

Buzz suddenly remembered the name to go with the face. "Slezak?"

"Yeah, you never forget a name like that, and now he has a nephew to carry it on."

"How does he fit into it?"

"The nephew's name is Terry. The kid is smart enough, but his uncle knows how to push his buttons. For a while, it looked like he was going to fall farther from the tree, but now that may not happen. He's been getting into it with a colored kid from the south side of town. I don't know much about him, the word is that the both of them are looking to get the hell out of here and are competing for the last college entrance spots."

"What about his mother, where does she stand?" Todd asked.

"She vanished a couple of months after he was born, like dust in the wind."

Buzz finished his drink. He needed it. "This doesn't add up, to just sitting on a powder keg. Why didn't they just go up the hill and get the widow? He certainly had the manpower and the support from the town."

Mickey John poured himself another drink. He needed it. "You two remember the widow?"

"Barely, went to the house once, visit only lasted a couple of minutes."

"Very few have lasted longer. Everyone's terrified of her, that's why they never took her on. Just ask Slezak."

"He's seen her?"

"Oh yeah, it was about a year ago, a command performance, and a private audience no less."

"What was the reason for the meeting?"

"Slezak wouldn't say, still won't. But within hours of it happening, the whole damn business started up again with a vengeance. He's been on a mission ever since. Everything is on the table, including his nephew, to get it done. There is going to be a race war here and it is going to make Alabama look like a Norman Rockwell painting."

Todd got up unsteadily and walked over to the window. It was a long time before he said anything. "I've never regretted anything more in my entire life! We left these people in a dark room, locked the door, walked away, and forgot about them for three decades. How the hell do we answer for a thing like that?"

Mickey John polished off his second drink. "It's not all your fault. It would have happened, anyway. You may have even prevented it from being worse. People are just pissed off because you made it personal between the two of you, and they paid for it."

Buzz got up and joined Todd at the window. "Todd, I'm damn sorry for all of this, and the fact that it brought us back here after all these years. This didn't need to happen."

"We're both to blame, Buzz. We both went in different directions for the wrong reason. This mess belongs to the both of us."

Buzz put his hands on the window sill. "Let's get this fixed. Then we can say the words. That's when it will mean something."

"Well, there is one good thing has come out of this."

"What's that, Todd?"

"I got my best friend back."

"Gentlemen, I hate wasting good booze."

When they returned to their chairs, Mickey John reached into his pocket, took out a set of keys, and tossed them across the desk. You can use my place, its two miles to a side road on the left, and another three-quarter of a mile from there. It's a mobile home. No one will bother you out there and it's a hell of a lot safer than staying in town."

"It's appreciated. But we don't want to drag this into your living room."

"No problem. They're finally shutting this place down. With my banked holiday and sick time, I could have left six months ago. Now's as good a time as any to punch my ticket."

"You'll need to pack a few things and file papers for pension." Todd pointed out.

Mickey John laughed. "Everything I need is in that bag over there. When you two are gone, I'll cut the power off and disable the generator. It will take months before anyone knows I'm gone. Pick up the keys, get yourselves squared away, and head into town. I suspect the widow will want to see you at your earliest opportunity."

"I suspect she'll be surprised to know we are back." Buzz replied ruefully.

"No she won't."

How can you be sure of that, Mickey John?"

"Because she already knows you're here."

Mickey John stopped them as Buzz opened the door. A couple more things, that car of yours is like waving a red flag at a bull. I'd hate to see it damaged. There's a car in back of the trailer. Don't let the look of it fool you. It can get right nasty if you twist its tale."

"And the other thing?" Buzz asked.

"Good luck, Gentlemen."

Mickey John pulled out a pad of paper from the desk drawer and wrote down a forwarding address on it, followed by "I'm retired!"

He looked at it with satisfaction, retrieved his ball cap off the coat rack for the last time, locked the door, and then tripped the main breaker on the wall. As he walked past the desk to the back door to put the generator out of action, he stopped and took a last look at the place he called work for 41 years. He picked up the pad, considered for a moment, and then wrote another sentence. As he walked out to the generator shack, he thought. "Up Yours,… Asshole!" was a fitting epitaph.

Todd Stiles and Buzz Murdoch had nothing to say as they slowly walked back to the car. Buzz pointed in the direction they needed to go. Todd nodded silently and slid behind the wheel.

It took longer than they thought to find the trailer, because it was farther back from the road and so covered with dust, it looked more like a rock that a double-wide. They went past twice before they actually saw it. Todd eased the car off the road and across a small bridge, which last saw water under it when Truman was President.

They pulled up in front of the trailer and stared at it through the windshield. Todd spoke first. "He actually lives in this."

"No, I think he lives in his car and just has his mail delivered here, you know, just to keep up appearances."

Todd got out of the car and looked at the thing from one end to the other, and finally down at the stairs. "Tell you what, Buzz. I'm thinking we should take our chances in town. When my time comes, they can say he died with indoor plumbing and wallpaper."

Buzz looked down at the track left by what appeared to be a very large and well-fed snake. The track ended under the stairs. He looked at Todd, tossed him the keys, and smiled, "Watch where you step."

Todd opened the door and stepped inside. Buzz remained outside, considering his options. He could stay out here and die in the heat, or he could face whatever was inside. He wasn't crazy about either option. He decided on door number two. As he walked up the stairs, he looked back to see if he was being followed.

Buzz stepped inside and then looked back out the door, just to make sure he was, in fact, entering the same place. He could see Todd in the kitchen inspecting the fridge. "Well, we are not going to starve."

Buzz picked up an envelope off the dining room table and turned it over in his hands. It contained two sets of keys and a note. He read it and passed it to Todd. The other side was blank.

"Don't get comfortable. *Tick, Tock.*

"I'm thinking we just got our marching orders."

"I'll get the luggage and pull the car around back."

As he turned to leave, Todd handed him the keys. "Mickey John was right. They knew we were coming."

"I'll put the top up. We may not be using it for a while."

"Good idea. It will be full of dust in an hour and no telling what we'll find under the seat."

When Buzz had left, Todd continued his tour of the trailer. Mickey John had spent a lot of money on the place. There was wood-paneling everywhere and it wasn't cheap, marble counter tops and recessed lighting. When he turned on a tap, it produced a stream of clean water. From a distance, he heard a pump running. There had to be a very impressive filtration system somewhere. He didn't bother turning on the switch on the wall. If there was water, there was power. Four bedrooms and a den-- the place was impressive from front to back. He was wondering how all of this could fit into a forty-foot double-wide, when he heard Buzz come back in.

Buzz was standing in the doorway with the bags and a huge grin on his face.

`Todd asked, "What?"

"You're going to have to see this for yourself."

"It better not be another Russian wonder."

Buzz held open the door. "Trust me. I'm you best friend."

"You are?

Buzz's smirk got even more evil. "I heard you say it."

Todd followed him around the back. It was a short walk that added to the confusion of perspective. It felt a lot bigger on the inside of the trailer. He looked in a window but the glass was dark and seemed to reflect the light back. He followed Buzz around the corner and stopped. The car provided by Mickey John was sitting or squatting, depending on your perspective, next to the Corvette.

He walked around it, careful not to get too close. When he got to the far side, he yelled to Buzz. "What the hell is it?"

Buzz laughed. "If I am not mistaken, it is called a Pacer, built by American Motors. The company went out of business about a decade ago.

Todd looked in a window. "And it's a damn good thing, too."

Buzz opened the passenger door for Todd. "Don't let the thing fool you. It's a lot tougher than it looks. Let's lock the trailer and go into town."

He got in the driver's side and looked out at Todd. "What's the matter?"

"I'll go lock the trailer."

When Todd got back, the car was still there and the door was still open. "Are you going to get in, or do we strap you to the roof?"

Todd slowly eased himself into the seat. He was clearly having a Trebby flashback.

"You going to close the door?"

Todd reached out and slowly pulled the heavy door shut. It closed with a solid thump.

Buzz pulled the shift lever forward in the column.

Todd asked him why he wasn't going to start it first.

He looked down at the dash to confirm it. "It's already running."

Buzz moved the selector to drive and the car moved forward with a barely perceptible shudder. He stepped on the brakes to make sure they were working.

Todd looked down at the floor and across to Buzz. "Okay, I'm mildly impressed."

"I have a feeling, that by the time this is over, we are going to owe this thing a serious debt of thanks."

"Buzz, I believe it is time to put this show on the road."

The drive into Dusty took about twenty minutes in real time and three decades in memories, all of it compressed into that short drive. Past and present would be one and the same until it was over.

As they entered Dusty, they knew exactly where to go.

The Wasteland Diner was two blocks up from the gas station on the right. They pulled into a diagonal spot next to a battered pickup with Arizona plates. When they got out, Todd looked up at the sign as Buzz looked up the street. "The place is still a dump."

"There isn't enough paint on the planet to change that, Buzz."

Three blocks away, Walter Slezak put his pen down as Perch stepped into his office. "What did I tell you about coming in here?"

"You told me to knock first, Sir."

Slezak leaned back in his chair and looked at Perch with disgust. "Knocking is pretty complicated, it requires brain cells. From now on, try yelling through the door. You think you can do that?"

Perch said he could.

"What do you want?"

Perch stepped forward and put a phone message on Slezak's desk, making sure it was placed so that it was within his reach.

Slezak reached down and picked it up without taking his eyes off Perch. He read it slowly, folded it, and put it in his shirt pocket.

"It's from that fellow that looks after the widow."

Slezak's face turned crimson. "I know who *or* what sent the damn message!"

Perch jumped and then, moved quickly back a step.

"Get out!"

Perch didn't have to be told twice. When he pulled the door shut after him, Slezak leaned back in his chair. He was going to enjoy seeing Perch disposed of, for the cause. Slezak was going to use him as fuel to set a really big, healthy, and cleansing fire.

On the hill, the man who made that call to Perch slowly put the phone down and looked into the shadows that lived permanently in the living room. "Why call him instead of Slezak?"

The voice that lived back there in those shadows wasn't interested in idle conversation. "Was it done?"

"It's done."

"Good. Meet him outside. He knows the drill. I don't want him in here. He stinks."

The wheel chair rocked slightly. "What?"

"Why do we keep sending messages through that guy? He's as dumb as his name."

"You remember your bible teaching? The meek shall inherit the earth."

"Yeah, sure, I think it's in the bible."

The voice responded with disgust. "The meek aren't going to get it, the stupid are!"

The wheel chair retreated into the shadows and then stopped. "Why are you still here?"

Todd and Buzz stepped inside the diner and pushed the door shut behind them. You want the counter or a booth?"

It was a long walk to the counter as voices trailed off and eyes followed, as they crossed the floor. Todd pointed to a couple of chairs and sat down. A waitress appeared, placed a couple of menus in front of them, and walked away.

Todd picked one of the menus. "I'm starting to get used to the silent treatment."

Buzz thumbed through his menu and pointed out something to Todd with contempt. He then tossed it on the counter. "Three decades and they haven't changed a thing."

The waitress returned to take their orders. When she saw the discarded menus, she slowly put her order pad away.

"We'll have coffee, black."

"That's it?" She asked sarcastically.

Buzz leaned forward on his stool and repeated the order.

"What's the matter, the service not good enough for you?"

"Make that paper cups, to go."

"You're going to be paying the table charge. Enjoy your five dollar coffees!"

"Shelley! That's no way to treat guests." The sound of the voice in the diner was almost explosive.

Two men had come in and taken up a position in front of the window. Even in the light coming from behind, the man was instantly recognizable even after thirty-plus years.

"Slezak". Todd spoke softly.

` The man who came in with him was black and well over six feet. The suit he was wearing did a poor job of hiding muscle.

"Do we know him, Buzz?"

"No."

"Well, aren't you going to come over here and say hello, because me and my friend here are sure as hell glad to see you! "

They got up and walked over to the two men. Buzz and Todd ignored the outstretched hand. The man with Slezak didn't even bother taking his hand of his pocket. Slezak just smiled and lowered his hand. "Shelley, rustle up some sandwiches all around and bring them over to that table." The four men sat in silence as Shelley served Todd and Buzz their coffee.

"So, what's everyone having?"

When no one answered, Slezak ordered sandwiches and Iced Tea for Todd, Buzz, and himself, ignoring the man who accompanied him.

Shelley turned to the man with effort. "What do you want?"

The man, who had been expressionless up to this point, smiled suddenly. "I'll have a steak sandwich, complements of Walter."

"You want watermelon with that?"

Slezak roared with laughter. "Damn! You are good, Shelley."

In the less than a second, Buzz had his hands on Slezak's tie and yanked him forward across the table. Slezak's face rapidly turned crimson. He grabbed at Buzz's hand to pull it off and Buzz slapped him hard across the face. "We're here on business and you don't want to be wasting our time."

Todd ignored Slezak's gagging and directed a question to his companion. "Do we know you?"

"John Smith. I'm the nephew of Antrim Weeks."

"The widow's brother?"

"That's right. He died two years ago."

"Did you know him?"

"Only by reputation."

Buzz let go of Slezak's tie and shoved him back into his chair, which result in a loud bang. "Does she know the kind of company you're keeping these days? She'd be disappointed."

Shelley had returned with their orders. On Smith's plate were two neatly cut slices of watermelon. Slezak didn't find it funny this time. Smith picked up a slice and ate it before speaking. "Not bad. You've had practice cutting watermelon proper."

Speaking now to Todd and Buzz, he continued. "While my associate is recovering his voice after that well deserved throttling you gave him, I'm sure he won't mind if I speak on his behalf. It may surprise you to know that we both have a common goal and agree on the way to achieve it. It's only the outcome where we have a difference of opinion."

`   Buzz told him to continue.

"Walter's people and mine want to resolve our problem once and for all. We have been waiting quite some time to finish what you started, and now that you're here, we're anxious to get it done."

Todd pushed the food aside. "It was a god damned injustice and your people did nothing to stop it. We did. You know what would've happened if we stayed.

Smith laughed in his face. "Of course we know! Look around you. You should eat, the food is good here."

Slezak took a drink of water before speaking. "As Mr. Smith so delicately puts it, you deprived us of, shall we say, a meeting of the minds."

"What we did was deprive you of a race war between two rotten bastards, neither worth a dollar bet, waiting for the bell to ring, and still waiting."

Slezak looked at Smith. "Do you believe these guys? They still don't get it."

Smith put down his food. "We didn't care, on both sides, if that girl lived or died. We still don't. Hell, our people didn't even care who won or lost, and still don't. Look around you. This place is a cesspool.

Slezak and the rest of his rats can have this sewer. We just wanted to get out."

"You had a chance! You could have walked anytime and you didn't need us to finish it."

Slezak chuckled. He was back to form. "No one walks away from a war, there always has to be a winner and a loser. It was a little delayed, but now it's going to happen."

Buzz got up first, and then Todd. "We deprived you of carnage and you can spend an eternity locked together in your own personal hell. We saved a life that night. It cost us big time. But it was a price we were glad to pay."

Smith yelled to them at the door. "You ought to take a drive up to the psych ward in Vanderwagon. Stop by and see her. Watch you don't step in the drool."

Buzz took a deep breath of fresh air as they walked away from the Wasteland Diner. "That was fun."

They turned when they heard Shelley from the diner pursuing them. "I want $11.30 plus tax for the coffee and sandwiches or I'll call the cops!"

Todd looked at her and then at Buzz. "What do you think? We came back and we can walk away. Stiles and Murdoch have done their bit for the country and the road."

Buzz agreed. "But we still have to answer for what happened. I say we give them what they want and let the place burn."

"Agreed, what's the next step?"

"We drive to Vanderwagon and pay our respects. I doubt if our apology will be worth much, but at least we can make sure she's being cared for."

Todd pointed to Shelley, who was standing with her order pad in one hand and the other one extended for the money. "You want to pick up the tab?"

"Nope."

"I'm not paying for it either."

Shelley shrieked. "You two are going to pay big time for this!"

Todd rounded on her so fast that she jumped. "Listen, you racist tramp! You tell everyone we're back and by the time we're done, everyone in this town is going to pay, and this time hell is not going to come cheap!"

They could still here her yelling a block away.

Buzz frowned as they continued to walk. "Racist tramp, where'd that come from?"

Todd shrugged. "This place just seems to bring out the worst in people."

Buzz could find no argument with that.

Back in the restaurant, Slezak finished his sandwich and looked up as Shelley returned. She told him that they had stiffed her for the bill and that she was going to call the cops.

Slezak turned to Smith. "This is it! We're finally going to get this thing done."

Smith picked up a menu and thumbed through it briefly before speaking. "It's going to be messy, that's for sure."

"But, it'll get done, and the winner will be able to move on."

Smith looked at him in surprise. "You're dreaming in Technicolor, Slezak! There will be nothing left of this place when it is over. This town is going to burn right down to the pavement."

Slezak picked up the menu, opened it, and showed it to Smith. "Shelley, how big is that number six, anyway?"

She yelled from the kitchen. "The steak is sixteen ounces with trimmings, and it comes with apple pie and ice cream."

"That sounds pretty good, Walt, that sandwich was pretty light. Tell you what. Let's do it and we'll split the desert."

"Excellent idea Shelley, we'll have two sixes medium rare and one desert to split."

It was just after three in the afternoon when Todd and Buzz pulled into the hospital parking lot and got out of the car. Todd retrieved the directions they got at the service station five miles back. "This can't be right, Buzz. This is a Navy Veterans hospital."

The place was clean, antiseptic, and the halls, floors, and walls were painted a soft white. The hospital was also very quiet. They were directed to Hospital Receiving by a lab technician that looked as young as Macy McCallister.

"Yes Sir. Miss Parsons is here." The Ensign answered without referring to her computer.

"How did she end up in a military facility?" Buzz asked.

"You understand, of course, that at that time, the hospital in Dusty would never admit her and Vanderwagon didn't have one, so the only place they could bring her was here. We are required by law to treat anyone who is in need of critical care in an emergency. That's the condition she has remained in and she just never left. Everyone who's been assigned to her over the years has come to love her. In the seventies the Navy stepped up to the plate and assumed guardianship for her estate and granted her permanent palliative care. We're all kind of proud of her because she was breaking down barriers way ahead of all those other folks. And, she did it from a hospital bed."

Ensign Keith stood up, offered her hand, and pushed some documents across the counter. "You'll have to fill out some paper work and give us about a half hour to get her ready for you can see her."

"Is she that bad?"

Miss Parsons had virtually no cognitive function left when she was admitted, just eye movement and some limited vocalization. She slipped into a vegetative coma about twenty years ago. I'm afraid there's not much left, except for the eyes. We just try to make her remaining time as humane and as comfortable as possible.

She stopped when she noticed Todd staring. "Is there a problem?"

Well, I didn't think women were still required to wear skirts in the military."

She laughed. "I'm impressed you noticed, and no, it's not a requirement any longer. However, I'm a woman and an officer in the United States Navy and I can do both equally well."

Keith pointed to a couple of chairs. "Make yourselves comfortable, Gentlemen. I'll be back when she is ready to see you."

Todd watched Keith as she walked down the hall. "How do you feel about your country, Buzz?"

Buzz put down the magazine he was reading, and followed Todd's gaze, "Proud to be an American and for all the right reasons."

"Yeah, so am I."

Keith ushered them into a room that was in partial shadow from the blinds over the window. There were lines of light across the floor and walls. The room had the look and feel of a church on a Saturday afternoon. They didn't hear Keith close the door behind them.

"It happened in 1963, when she was attacked by the Klan. When they were done with a woman, they lynched her."

Buzz quietly cut her off. "We know. We were there."

"I'm sorry, I didn't know."

"It's all right, so are we. We're grateful for what you've done for her."

She nodded. "She's breathing on her own. She's having a good day. I have to get back to work. If you need anything, the attendant pull is on the wall. You're welcome to stay as long as you like."

When she had gone, Todd pulled off his jacket, put it over the back of a chair, pulled it over to the bed, and sat down. Buzz went to the end of the bed, removed the chart, and took it over to the window where the light was a little better.

Todd watched her hands resting on her chest, as they moved slowly with every breath. "She's barely breathing."

Buzz looked up from the charts. "She'll be fifty-nine this year."

Todd rubbed his eyes slowly.

"You okay?"

"No,... we need to offer some measure of justice for this. Let's make sure she gets the best medical care possible."

Buzz handed him the charts and gestured to the door. "She already is, but have a look at page seven."

He thumbed through to the page and reviewed it carefully. "I'm not a doctor, but it looks like she was making progress until 1966. Then, she had a relapse, due to progressive oxygen deprivation, as a result of cardiac arrest."

"Can you make out the name of the attending physician?"

"It's your standard medical signature. Even if we could decipher it, the thing was written over twenty-five years ago. The man is long gone, if he's even still alive."

Todd got up and put the chart back on the end of the bed.

Out of curiosity, Buzz opened the closet door. "Her clothes--the ones she was wearing on the night she was attacked--were just as they were when they were removed. On the floor was a pair of black and white shoes. Todd picked them up and turned them over. They were covered in dirt. He put them back and closed the door. "We'd better go."

As they passed her bed, Buzz stopped and pulled the blanket over her exposed feet.

It was a long, quiet walk back to reception. Ensign Keith looked up at the sound of their footsteps. "Thank you for coming. I'm sure she was glad to see you."

"Ensign, how many visitors has she had since she's been here?"

She reached behind her, retrieved a book off the shelf, and placed it on the counter. After a couple of seconds of searching, she found what she was looking for.

"Well, you're the first since I have been here. But she had four names in the sixties and one in 1974."

Buzz pointed to two of the names in 1968. "Does that match what is on her charts, Todd?"

"Pretty close."

He turned the book back to Keith and pointed. "We know who these are, but maybe you could help us out with the other two names."

"I can't help you with the one in 1974, but I do know, from a patient briefing when I first arrived, that these two men were here for a competency review, which is standard procedure. The second name belongs to a doctor, but that's all I can tell you."

Todd pointed to the signatures. "Can you do us a favor? Don't let this man back in here and if possible, find out who that doctor was."

"That's a tall order. This is an open base and I don't have any control over civilians. I can't prevent anyone, with a legitimate reason, from coming in here."

Todd was going to say something when she cut him off and picked up the phone. Her voice echoed off the walls. "Petty Officer Watts,... reception."

A few moments later, a uniformed enlisted man appeared in the hall. At a distance, he looked big. By the time he got to the desk, he was immense. Petty Officer Watt was a military police officer and the 45-caliber side arm he was carrying was loaded. "As you can see, the Petty Officer is clearly not a civilian. If he is given a lawful order by a senior officer, he will obey it. Who is the senior officer on duty at this facility, Petty Officer Watt?"

"You are, Ma'am."

Buzz took out a piece of paper out of his pocket and made some notes.

Todd looked at the man's medals. "Time overseas?"

"Three tours in the Middle East."

"Ever had any flashbacks?"

The Petty Officer smiled slowly, "When I'm really motivated."

Todd took a step back slowly.

Buzz finished writing down instructions and handed the list to Keith. "Purchase a new outfit for her and arrange to have her clothes and shoes cleaned. Did she have any other personal effects with her?"

"She had a watch, which was broken, and her wallet. She didn't have any money with her."

He took fifty dollars out of his pocket. "That should replace what was taken and have her watch repaired. If it can't be fixed, purchase a new one. Expense is not an issue."

Todd added another fifty dollars. "Please add fresh flowers every day for her room--roses, crocuses, and lilacs."

Ensign Keith examined the list. "This will be expensive."

"She deserves it."

Buzz directed her attention to the back of the sheet. "Those are contact numbers and names. Just tell them what you need and they'll see that it gets taken care of."

Petty Office Watt took the list from Keith, "With your permission, Ma'am. I'll look after this."

"Thank you, Petty Officer. Carry on."

The Petty Officer looked at Todd and Buzz carefully. "Either of you been in the service of your country?"

Both men shook their heads in the negative.

He turned to Ensign Keith as he continued on his rounds, "Damned waste of manpower."

She raised her eyebrows. "Gentlemen, you are, indeed, in very rare company! Petty Officer Watt does not grant complements easily or often."

Todd and then Buzz each extended a hand. "It has been an honor to have met you."

She stepped out from behind the counter and returned the handshake. "The pleasure has been all mine."

Buzz spoke for the both of them. "Unfortunately, it was not the visit we had hoped for. We regret that there was no way to tell her how damned sorry we are that we didn't do enough then, and that we can't do anything, now."

"She knows, Gentlemen,… she knows."

As they walked out to the car, Todd Stiles and Buzz Murdoch didn't notice that they had regained something that they had lost in the thirty-three years they had spent sailing carpet. It was in the walk. The way a heel hits pavement. There are plenty of ways to describe it: purpose, drive, maybe mission. Back in the fifties, they called it stride. In the sixties, they called it strut. It had many names, but what it came down to was street-feel, the confidence that comes from the feel of pavement under your feet, and knowing that you can walk anyone's turf and own it. When they got to the car, Buzz looked at Todd over the roof. "Are you hungry?"

Todd opened his door and got in. "Later."

Two of the interesting and lesser known facts about the AMC Pacer were that when it was equipped with a V-8 engine, it was fast for its size and it was as tough as a tank. Todd and Buzz covered the distance between Vanderwagon and Dusty very rapidly. Todd barely slowed as they entered the town limits. Guided by memory, he maneuvered through traffic, looking for something, although if you asked him, he wouldn't be able to give you a specific answer.

He spoke as he drove. "Slezak was at the hospital with the doctor the day before she had the cardiac arrest."

Buzz had to yell over the sound of the engine. "It could be just a coincidence."

Todd wheeled the car left on to the next cross street. They could see the Ratepayers Building a block up on the right. A white Cadillac was parked in front of the entrance, in a "No Parking" area.

An old colored man raised his white cane and stopped a woman who was about to cross the street with her groceries. He extended an arm to indicate he was blind and needed assistance. "There's a fine old bench just behind, if you don't mind." The look on her face made it clear she was being put upon, but she agreed to help him to the bench.

When they got there, he didn't relax his grip. "You ought to come sit down and watch the show with me. It'll be safer, too."

The man's voice was strangely compelling. She put down her bags and joined him, just as an odd looking car accelerated across the road to the right. She suddenly realized that if the old man had not intercepted her, she would have been right in its path.

As they approached the Ratepayers Building, Buzz suddenly remembered the significance of the brand new white Cadillac. He reached down, retrieved his seat belt, and buckled it. The Pacer was passing forty-miles-per-hour, when it hit the left rear quarter panel of the Cadillac. The taillight exploded and Buzz ducked as chunks of plastic blew in the window. Todd held the wheel hard over to the right as the car slowed to twenty-five-miles-per-hour, after the first impact. He then jammed down on the accelerator. Paint and chrome came off the car in sheets. As the Pacer's front bumper crossed the gap between the rear quarter panel and the door, bending it out and peeling it back like a can of sardines. Buzz yelled to Todd that they didn't make them like they used to.

The Cadillac bucked and howled as the right front wheel jumped the curb and the car crushed the no parking sign. The rear bumper of the Pacer caught the edge of front fender and tore it off, taking the grill with it. The left headlight exploded in a shower of glass. As Todd wheeled the car smoothly around the corner to the right, he wondered aloud if he got the right car.

Buzz released his seat belt and looked back out his window. Two men had come running out of the building, pointing vigorously at their car as they drove away. They weren't waving "Welcome to Dusty."

"We got the right car, Todd."

"Let's eat."

Slezak was having trouble breathing. In fact, he looked like he was going to have a stroke. No one, absolutely no one in the town of Dusty, had ever "sassed" him like this before. Sure, every once in a while, someone would forget themselves, and talk back to him. They, of course, would get stomped for their mistake. But this! Slezak's car was a symbol in Dusty. Where ever it went, people and car drivers moved aside, and no one screwed with his car. It took a full five minutes for him to get his anger under control enough to say anything. "Perch! Get Peterson out here."

When Peterson made it to the sidewalk, he turned around to find that Perch had decided not to return to the street. Peterson was the treasurer for the Ratepayers. His clothes did a poor job disguising the fact that he was a weight lifter. He whistled softly. "Someone is going to pay big time for this."

Slezak spoke softly. "Not someone, *everyone*. Go get the keys to Perch's car. I'll use it to drive home."

"His car is crap on wheels. We can get you something better than that."

Slezak smiled. You're right and you'll pay for it with the Ratepayers money. Call it a donation. I want it parked out front in the morning."

Peterson pointed to what was left of his car. "What about your Caddy?"

"Have it towed over to the garage, and put it out of sight around back. I don't pay you enough to ask questions. Get Perch's keys."

Peterson was back in less than two minutes. Perch was terrified of him and couldn't give up the keys fast enough. Peterson reported back about Perch's question. "He asked me when he could have his car back. He lives a mile out of town and has no way to get home. What do you want me to tell him?"

"He isn't getting it back. He isn't going to need it, because we're going to kill him anyway. Besides, this works for us because we can keep him in town until we're ready to use him. Put him in the conductor's overnight room at the old train station. That will make it real easy to do him when the time comes." Slezak took the keys out of Johnson's hand and walked to the parking lot at the back of the building.

Peterson felt bile rise in the back of his throat, and not for what was going to happen to Perch. He didn't have a problem with that. The man was pretty much a waste of air, anyway, and it was for the cause. No, it was Slezak. It wasn't about the cause with him. What he wanted was a war, and he wanted it at any cost. He had been denied once, and not even hell was going to stop him from getting it the second time around. This time, everyone was going to come to the dance and pay the cover charge. In a way, he envied Perch. He was the lucky one because he'd be the first, and maybe it would be quick, but Peterson doubted it.

Slezak unbuttoned his collar and loosened his tie as he walked up the driveway. The kid next door had screwed up the lawn again. Ten bucks every two weeks and the moron couldn't push a lawn mower in a straight line. As he reached for his keys, he saw that the front door wasn't just unlocked, it was partially open.

He pushed it open with an elbow, stepped inside, and waited in the hall until his eyes adjusted, before he closed and locked the door. He could hear the TV on in the living room.

Terry Nevins was Walter Slezak's nephew. Tall and lanky, he was in surprisingly good shape, despite making every effort to be lazy and unkempt. It was impossible to find any resemblance in him to his uncle. His father Bill, in his short life, was a firefighter in Chicago. He had been tall, good looking, and something of a hero, everything his brother Walter wasn't. Terry's mother died when he was three months old. His father gave Terry her surname out of respect and had tried to pass on to him some of his better virtues. It still remained to be seen if any of them had stuck. Sprawled across the sofa with his feet up on the coffee table idly eating chips out of a bag, he ignored his uncle when he walked into the room.

Slezak stopped at the end of the sofa and briefly watched the game show on the TV. The volume was so low it was nearly impossible to hear what was being said, which indicated that his nephew wasn't paying much attention to what was actually on. He turned and looked down at his nephew, and for the second time in a day, his fury went white hot.

His foot lashed out with surprising speed and swept the legs off the coffee table. "You've got to show some manners and stop behaving like an immigrant."

Terry slowly put the bag down beside him and brushed off the crumbs, which landed on his shirt and floor. He picked up a chip that was worth saving, put it back in the bag, and closed it.

He stood up and faced his uncle. At 5' 8 he had a good three inch advantage in height. "Look who's talking! Have you looked in a mirror lately? You look like a thug, dress like one, and smell like one. Cheap suit and five o'clock shadow! You couldn't sell a used car to a blind man."

Slezak delivered a sharp powerful blow to the solar plexus that doubled Terry over. "So let's talk about how things went at school today."

About the same time that Walter Slezak was expressing his concern over his nephew's education, Todd Stiles stepped out of the trailer with a couple of drinks in his hand and stopped briefly to look at the setting sun. It was going to be a beautiful evening, at least in the night sky. He handed a drink to Buzz before sitting down in the other chair. "You feel it?"

"Yeah, a gust of hot wind, the calm before the storm."

Todd took a deep breath. "The air out there is like a drink of cold clean water. You figure we're safe out here?"

Buzz sniffed his drink in approval. "The Sioux believe this is hallowed ground and who are we to argue with that kind of wisdom?"

"I hope you're right."

"I am correct. Whoever treads this soil is safe from all manner of darkness. That has a nice mystical ring to it, doesn't it?"

Todd laughed quietly. "It does indeed and if I have learned anything in life, it is never wise to question Murdoch's wisdom or mysticism."

"Smart man, so how should we play this hand?"

Todd took a swallow to give himself time to think. "Well, we have certainly learned that it's not about who wins or loses. We are way past that, because all Slezak and the widow want now is a war."

"Agreed, but the only real player at the table is the widow. She has been stuck here for three decades and you can bet she is seriously annoyed. The only reason the place isn't a smoking hole in the ground is because everyone is terrified of her."

"That's the only thing everyone does agree on, Todd"

"So, how do you think it'll go down?"

Buzz looked at his drink and debated on whether to refill it. He decided to pass. "Back in the kitchen, everything was straight up and honest, even with the guy who was trying to stick a knife in you. There were rules to be followed. That was the only way to earn respect on the street. That's why you met in the center of the road. Things were quieter, no traffic, and the playing field was equal. It was different in Brooklyn and Bedford Stuyvesant. If you wanted to get rid of someone, you set them up and let his own people do it for you."

"That sounds pretty harsh."

Buzz shook his head in mock disapproval. "Your roots are showing, Todd. We're talking New York, not Connecticut. South of the bridge, you didn't drive on the asphalt. You lived on it. Slezak isn't very bright, but don't under estimate him. He knows his turf."

"Yeah, if you want to win a war, you have to start by pinning it on someone. Who do you think it's going to be?"

"That is the big question and I have no idea."

Todd finished his drink. "I've got a good idea who does. I think it's time we paid the widow a visit."

Why don't we just burn the place to the ground, ourselves, and call it a mercy killing? There isn't a jury in the country that would vote to convict. You want another drink?"

"No, tomorrow is going to be a long day."

Todd was up early. He made himself a cup of coffee and went out to watch the sun come up. He debated whether to wake Buzz, and then decided he could use the sleep that Todd didn't get last night.

As the sun started to lighten the horizon, his mind began a playback. Memories and faces moved slowly in the back of his mind. Occasionally, he would struggle for a name or significance to go with it, but it would fade before he could make any sense of it. His mind, then, moved on to something else. He didn't hear Buzz until Buzz joined him.

"You made the coffee."

"It's instant."

"Oh, that explains it."

"I can't remember the last time I saw a sunrise."

Buzz suddenly had a rush of memory. "It was in Hawaii, Oahu. Molly got us up at four in the morning to see it. When it was up, she said it didn't matter what we did for the rest of the holiday, because it was the only memory that was going to matter."

Todd stood up. "I'll get some breakfast together before we go into town, any preferences?"

Buzz stayed in his chair and held up his coffee cup. I'm good, thanks."

They took their time and it was close to nine by the time they were getting into the car. Buzz stopped as they passed the Corvette. A thin film of dust had settled on the car in the couple of days that it had been parked.

"It's hard to believe how much that thing has become a part of our lives."

"Did you ever drive another Corvette?'

He shook his head. "Not once. But I'd always react when I saw one. My oldest daughter took one out for a test drive when she was looking for her first car."

"How did you handle it?"

"Not well."

"We'd better get going."

Buzz pointed to a hardware store as they pulled into town. "How about we get the ball rolling here?"

He wheeled the car into a spot right out front. "Good call, Buzz. I am going to enjoy this."

"Me, too, I just hope he's still here."

"He's here. I can smell him from the street."

They stepped into the store and quietly closed the door.

Buzz pointed to the sign and the door. Todd turned the sign from OPEN to CLOSED and locked the door.

In the back of the store, a man in his late sixties was making coffee in a small kitchen. He pulled a bottle of rum down off a shelf, poured two full shots into the mug along with a tablespoon of Maxwell Instant Coffee, and added hot water from a pot on a hot plate. He stopped, not sure if he had heard someone come into the store. No, it was just his imagination.

Bob Sales, or Silly Bob as most people called him these days, had been a tall man in his youth. Now he was a sloppy, battered drunk who had trouble keeping his pants up, even with suspenders.

He also used to be the Sheriff, but his luck finally ran out along with the job, when the town got tired of him spending more time drinking and sleeping in his patrol car than actually driving it. At least, that was the story the town council used to fire him. The fact was he was dumped because he couldn't be trusted to keep his mouth shut. Fortunately for Silly Bob, he could fall back on the income from the store, which had been left to him by his father.

He put the bottle down, certain that someone had come in to the store. He picked up his coffee, shouldered the curtain aside which separated the kitchen from the store, and found him self staring down the barrel of the 44-caliber Eagle revolver from his display case. "The money's in the back."

Todd poked him in the face with the barrel. "I'm really disappointed, Buzz. Bob, here, thinks we're going to rob him!"

Out of the corner of his eye Sales could see a man appear from behind some shelves of tools. He was carrying a baseball bat. "That's a shame. A couple of old friends come all this way for a visit and Bob thinks they are couple of shoplifters, and after all they have been through together."

Sales turned his head enough to get a good look at Buzz and smirked as he remembered Buzz and Todd, "Words all over town that you two were back."

Todd pushed the gun harder into Salas's face. "That's good, because we sure as hell couldn't forget a man who strung up a thirteen-year-old girl."

Sales laughed. "It was sure as hell better than the alternative."

Todd cocked the gun. "You're a generous man, Sales."

"And you can't shoot someone with a gun that ain't got any bullets in it."

"You want to bet your life that there isn't one under the hammer?"

Sales choked back a chuckle. "I'll take that bet. I keep all the ammo in the back."

Todd turned to Buzz. "Well, how about that, Buzz? He called my bluff. The gun's empty."

In one swift movement, Buzz swung the bat in a vicious over-hand swing that brought it down on Sales right wrist. It shattered with the sound of a gunshot. The coffee cup, which Sales was holding, hit a display case and exploded in a shower of ceramics and coffee.

Sales grabbed the counter with his other hand to steady himself and gasped in agony. His right wrist looked like a blackened banana. A pool of blood was forming under it on the counter. "You son of a bitch, you had no right to do that!"

Todd looked at the wrist and then at Buzz in mock disapproval. "He's absolutely right, that was just wrong. Old Bob here is left handed."

Buzz did the same thing to Sales left wrist. The second blow was delivered with so much force that it broke the wood under the wrist. The force drove Sales back from the counter and against the back wall, before he hit the floor screaming.

"Take him in the back and finish the job, Buzz. I'll make the call and meet you out front."

After Buzz had dragged Sales into the back, Todd stepped behind the counter and looked at a list of numbers Silly Bob kept by the phone. From the back of the store, he could hear the bat going to work again. He found the telephone number he needed, and dialed.

The phone rang for quite a while before a gravelly voice answered, "Ratepayers."

"I got a message for Slezak."

"Who the hell is this?"

"He knows. Tell him he wanted a war and now he's going to get one. Tell him we're coming and hell is coming with us. Do you think you can remember that, you inbred retard?" Todd didn't even bother hanging up the phone. He just dropped it on the floor and walked away. He could still hear the screaming coming from the receiver ten feet away.

Buzz joined him in the car five minutes later. "Did we make the call?"

"We made the call."

"Were they happy to hear from us?'

Todd got in the passenger side "Delighted."

"Do you remember the way?"

"Are you kidding?"

As they approached the hill, it might have been perception, but the light seemed to dim and the air got colder. When they pulled up in front of the house, Todd looked past Buzz and out the window. "The place looks about the way I remember it."

"That's the problem. It looks exactly the way it did in 1963."

Todd opened his door "Like we never left."

As they stood in front of the house, Buzz examined the front carefully, comparing what he saw against his memory. He pointed to a board sticking up out of the porch floor. "Remember that?"

Todd nodded. "Yeah, it doesn't look like it has seen a day of weather."

Their attention was drawn to the front door, which was opening. It was impossible to make out the figure standing in the hallway darkness. "Gentlemen, if you would follow me. The widow is expecting you. Please step inside."

This was surprising, considering the role the widow had to play in what had happened. They had only been to the house once, for less than ten minutes, in the same room where they were now standing. Like the front of the house, there had been virtually no change to it.

The butler directed them to a couple of chairs and asked them to make themselves comfortable. He told them that the widow was not as young as she used to be. It would take a few minutes to find her way from the second floor to the living room.

Buzz told him abruptly that they weren't going anywhere.

The butler opened the sliding doors at the back of the room before answering. "That, Sir, is most decidedly so."

Todd walked over to a chair, examined it carefully, and gave the cushion a push with his hand.

He thrust a hand behind the cushion and wiggled his fingers.

"What are you doing? You should be ashamed of yourself, ripping off a nice old lady for her laundry money."

Todd stood up. "I'm not looking for money. I'm looking for the wiring.

"You needn't have bothered."

They turned in unison towards the voice. "My so called butler has been fishing in that pond for years."

"   How much has he got so far?

"Squat, I empty it before he can get his hands on anything!"

Buzz walked over to another chair and began to sit.

"I wouldn't. That one's plugged in."

The widow, who had come out of the shadows far enough to be seen, directed them to a couple of hard-back chairs next to the fireplace. They sat down and waited. For a full minute, nothing was said and nothing moved. The room was in total silence. She finally shifted her weight in the chair and it moved farther into the light coming through a window over the fireplace. Buzz was sure that the light was playing tricks on his eyes, on his mind, or on both.

Todd always considered his memory to be above average. The widow in 1963 had been in her mid-forties, which would make her well over seventy now. What he was seeing, at least from where he was sitting, was a woman who was still in her forties, maybe even less. Maybe he had the age wrong and she had aged well. It was possible.

She rolled the chair over to the coffee table and looked at two of them carefully. "You two look like you've seen a ghost. Maybe refreshment will help perk you up."

They declined.

"Tea!"

The butler appeared and returned with a pot of tea and three cups.

"Help yourselves and pour me a cup. I can assure you that it's very good."

Both men were long time coffee drinkers, but after taking a drink, they silently agreed that the tea was just as advertised, excellent. Besides, it was not a good idea to say no to someone who had made a career out of scaring the hell out of people.

She put her cup down and smiled. The temperature in the room went down ten degrees. "Let's recap, boys. It was 63. You were just passing through, a couple of drifters on the way to someplace else. We got a lot of drive throughs back then. But you two were different: road wise, experienced, and smarter, full of passion, commitment, and wanting to make things right."

Todd was angry. "You're damn right! We didn't start out that way, but we learned. We could have driven in one end and out the other and not even bothered to stop, but we didn't. There was no way to walk away from what was happening."

She looked at Buzz with contempt. "What about you, Mr. Strong and Silent."

"I agree with him."

"Of course you do. You were a couple do-gooders who were trying to make the world all bright and beautiful."

Her voice was suddenly low and menacing. "What did you two do when you screwed it up?"

Buzz looked her in the eye. "We weren't perfect, still aren't, but at least we tried."

She leaned forward and repeated the question. "What did you do?"

When neither of spoke she answered for them. "You did nothing, just got in that car of yours and drove away, satisfied that you tried. You didn't have to worry, no sir, because you didn't expect to ever be back here. It was easy to walk away in those days"

Buzz got up, stretched, and went over to the window. "No, it wasn't, and we paid a hell of a price for doing it."

The widow was briefly impressed. "You still are and so is this rotten town."

Todd tossed his cup on the table. "What the hell is it with you, anyway? We tried to save Parsons life. If we did anything wrong, it's that we didn't get there soon enough and she wouldn't have spent the rest of her life as a vegetable."

She laughed in his face. "It was better than the alternative. Parsons was just one piece on the board and you yanked it off before it could be played."

It was the first time in Todd's life that he actually wanted to hit a woman. No, he was going to beat her senseless.

"She's right, Todd."

He turned and looked at Buzz in shock, not being able to accept what he just heard.

Buzz, without turning from the window, went on. "You remember the fight we had in VanderWagon before we split up, how you wanted to go back and confront Sales? You argued that we shouldn't have abandoned Parsons in Dusty, that we should have taken her up to the state hospital. Do you remember what I said?"

Todd's voice hadn't taken his eyes off the widow as he replied. His voice was barely over a whisper. "You said she would be alright in the hospital in Dusty and that we should move on, rather than start a war."

Buzz joined him and the widow. "Just before I got on the bus, I said that if you wanted, you should feel free to go back and burn the town down."

He reached into his pocket and took out the coin and looked at the widow. "That's what you wanted. It's what you all wanted, an all-out war, winner take all. Looking at the widow, he condemned her in words. You're no better than Slezak."

The widow smiled. "Wrong! I'm exactly like Slezak, except for the tan. He actually believes he is going to survive it, but he won't."

Buzz considered Slezak and the widow. "The two of you have waited three decades to finish your own personal Armageddon.

"Well, it sure beats the hell out of the alternative, doesn't it boys?"

"Purgatory or hell, it's the same thing. You brought us back here to toss the coin, again."

She pointed to the both of them. "I didn't bring you back. The road was going to do that, anyway. I just put in the request to have you stop here."

Todd shook his head in amazement. "All those years staring across the street at each other, waiting for the moment when you two could kill each other."

She took the coin out of Buzz's hand, and turned it over carefully a couple of times before handing it back to him. "Very nice. It's going to be one hell of a toss."

Buzz handed the coin to Todd without taking his eyes off the widow. "Tails, yesterday, heads for tomorrow, and the hell that comes with it."

Todd held it up so that she could see clearly that both sides were the same. "Care to make a bet?"

"Tails will do just fine." She answered with a laugh.

He tossed it. In the silence, it was almost possible to hear the air passing over the faces as it spun. Sometimes, seconds can feel like an eternity. As the coin approached the table top, the widow slowly moved back in her chair.

The coin bounced once and then, a second time. She relaxed as the one side of the coin appeared on the second bounce. As the coin reached vertical, it halted and began to rotate slowly, dissipating the last of the energy from the fall. It wobbled slightly and came to a halt. A shaft of sunlight hit a coin face on the last turn and explosion of light went off in the room.

Buzz picked the coin up off the table and put it in his pocket. "We can see ourselves out."

Buzz stopped at the door and looked back at the widow. She was now back in the shadows and impossible to see. "There are 8,500 hundred people in Dusty."

From out of the shadows her voice sounded like death. "Who cares?"

The butler had returned to clear away the coffee table. The voice said, "get Slezak."

Slezak's phone rang. He looked at it steadily on the third ring. It was late, just the way he liked it. He did his best work at night and he liked the dark, a lot. It rang another four times before he leaned forward and retrieved the receiver. He was in no hurry. "Ratepayers."

"You got your people in position?"

It was the widow. "It's always a pleasure to talk to you."

You're being stupid, again. "Are your people ready?"

Slezak sat up in his chair. As much as he despised her and was going to make her pay personally, he also had a very healthy fear of her. "They know the plan and are ready. What about yours?"

"Our guests are turning out to be more dangerous than we thought."

"They are old and not up to it. We can handle them."

"Slezak! You're fat and stupid and they're smart and tough. Make sure they don't get off the chess board."

The blood in his face began to get hot along with his temper, and his mouth got away from him before he could stop. "We know what we're doing. Word is already getting around town that they are back and stirring up trouble. You understand?"

The widow's voice chuckled, went quiet, and then very cold. Slezak could almost feel the receiver turning to ice. "Let's clear up a few things here. You aren't in control, not now, or in the sixties. We literally set it up for you the first time, handed it to you on a silver platter, and you screwed it up. Now, here we are three decades later, back doing it again. Except this time, there won't be any foul ups because we're running both sides of the equation. Our people have been in position for as long as this town has been sucking down oxygen. Now, you have a nice evening, maybe even take a bath." The phone went dead.

The widow handed the phone over her shoulder. The butler stepped forward and took it from her hand. "You didn't tell him."

She grinned. "Tell him that he's a piece on the board himself? He knows now. What he doesn't know is that he's just a pawn."

"When the time comes, they'll be able to hear him screaming twenty miles away."

"Make sure he goes through the machine feet first."

Slezak didn't have anyone behind him to hand the phone. He slowly put the receiver back on the cradle. Anger and fear chased each other across his face. He finally took a deep breath. It helped. The widow is dead, she just doesn't know it yet, he thought to himself. He was going to enjoy being at her rope party. He looked up sharply as the door opened.

They had come in without even bothering to knock. They walked right up to his desk and stared down at him.

Christ, these guys are big, he thought to himself. So big, that he had to lean back in his chair to look them in the face. District had sent him eight men and these two weren't the largest. He handed one of them the instructions he'd written down. "You think you can follow them?"

The man with the paper read it carefully and handed it to his colleague, who pointed to the numerous spelling mistakes. "Sure, once I got passed the spelling and grammar mistakes. Is English your second language?"

There was intelligence in their eyes. These men could think for themselves and Slezak didn't like people who could think. "You understand what you got to do? I don't want any one dead, at least not yet. All I want is broken hands and teeth."

"We were sent down here to do your nephew and that kid he goes to school with."

Slezak exploded. "He doesn't go to school with coloreds. They go to the same school, which is what we are going to end. Thinking is my job. I'll tell you when and where to do them. Understand?"

The man dropped the instructions on the table and followed his associate to the door. Slezak picked up the paper and held it out to them. "Aren't you taking this with you?"

"No."

Barker and Gardiner had been working together for close to seven years. At a distance, they looked like a couple of guys who had gone to the same college. They worked well together and could anticipate each other's moves, a very good thing in their line of work. But in seven years they hadn't any knowledge or interest in each other's personal life. They were not even on a first name basis. Gardiner and Barker had no loyalty to each other, to Slezak's cause, or to anyone else. Their services were for hire and they weren't cheap.

Gardiner squeezed into the passenger seat and fumbled with the seat belt for a minute, before giving up. Even with the seat all the way back, the only way they would get him out of the car after a crash was with a can opener. Barker shook his head. "This shouldn't take long. Probably longer to watch you do up a seat belt."

Barker pulled his forty-five automatic out of the holster and removed the clip. He was three short of a full magazine, but it would be enough. Slezak didn't say anything about using a bullet to remove fingers. The plan was to arrive at least an hour before Todd and Buzz got back.

"That should be it on the right." Barker steered the sedan off the road slowly avoiding the occasional pothole.

The sun was still a couple of hours above the horizon when they pulled up in front of the trailer and stopped. Gardiner checked his watch. They should be back here in about forty-five minutes."

Barker got out and stretched. "This should be an easy bonus. Do you want to do it here or inside?"

"Let's do it out back. We can relax inside when we're done."

Barker agreed and turned back to the car to get his gloves and the ropes. "Damn!"

Gardiner wheeled and reached for his gun. Standing less than three feet away was a man silhouetted against the setting sun.

"Gentlemen, it's a beautiful evening,…isn't it?"

Todd opened his eyes and stared at the ceiling for a good twenty minutes. It didn't move and he didn't feel the need to chase it anywhere. No one could accuse him of being a morning person, at least that's what Al would say, although those wouldn't be his exact words. It took another half hour before he managed to get out of bed, get cleaned up, and make some coffee. Buzz still hadn't made an appearance. "Lazy sot!"

The alarm clock refused to stop, despite repeated applications of a fist. Buzz sat up and wondered what was so important, that it required being up at 7:30 in the morning. He lay down again and seriously considered going back to sleep, but he knew that wasn't going to happen.

Todd could hear Buzz moving around in his room. He looked down at the coffee in his hand. It was hot and black and it didn't get any better than that, good or bad. He pushed open the door and stepped out on to the porch. Even this early in the morning the wood was hot under his feet. He raised his cup and froze, finally putting the cup carefully down on the railing. A couple of minutes later, Buzz joined him. "Is the Corvette in the back?"

"Sure. It hasn't moved. Why?"

"You'd better go check, Buzz."

Buzz went inside for a moment, returning with his own cup of coffee and a confused look on his face. "It's right where we left it. You can see it from the kitchen window. What's going on?"

Todd pointed to the Pacer. "That's where we parked it last night and it hasn't moved either."

"Sure. Where are you going with this?"

Since we've been here, that is the only place we've parked the car." Todd pointed to the road behind the Pacer. It was crisscrossed with tracks in the dirt and dust, marking their coming and going. Buzz stared at him without saying anything.

Todd pointed slowly to the right. "Who are these guys?"

Buzz looked in the direction his arm was pointing. Clearly visible in the dirt and to the right of the stairs were a set of tire tracks that were definitely from a different vehicle. Buzz walked down the steps and walked in front of the porch. "Someone was here, yesterday."

Todd joined him. "They still are!"

"What?"

"There should be one set of tracks in and one set when they went out. But there aren't any."

Buzz pointed to footprints that went about a yard toward the trailer and then abruptly stopped. "The car isn't the only thing that made a one way trip."

Todd reached down and retrieved a spent shell casing out of the dirt. "I'm thinking we should go into to town for breakfast."

Slezak ate his breakfast slowly. The Wasteland was empty, just the way he liked it, a good thing because he wasn't enjoying anything else about the morning. Gardiner and Barker didn't show up for the meeting last night and there'd been no sign of them since they went out to deal with Stiles and Murdoch.

To add to his troubles, Terry had finally gotten into it with the mark he had been working so hard to set up.

Jason Tilbury wasn't from Dusty. A colored kid from Brooklyn, he had been sent to live with his grandparents by his parents so he wouldn't end up being ground down in a gang. He'd adapted well enough, made a few friends, and also some enemies. It wasn't like home. In Brooklyn, your enemies didn't get into a fist fight. They pulled a gun.

Jason and Terry were competing for the few remaining spots at State, but they barely knew each other. They didn't even have any classes together. The only real contact they had was a few words in the hall and couple of stare downs, including yesterday, typical high school stuff. By the time the both of them were home, they had forgotten about it. Neither of them saw Mrs. Potter, the technical science teacher; shove Terry into the back of Jason, who went head first into the lockers.

The results were fairly predictable. The books were dropped, and the crowd moved in for a better look. Mental wagers are exchanged; everyone takes sides, and then the screams for a fight. It didn't happen. They stood toe to toe for three minutes before Terry picked up his books and walked away muttering, "Screw this!"

Potter tried to reignite it by giving Terry a detention and letting Jason walk. But it didn't work. As soon as Terry walked away, the crowd lost interest and vanished. When Terry walked out of detention, she stopped him with a look of disgust. "You could have beaten him senseless. What's the matter with you?

"It wasn't worth getting wrapped around an axle."

She got right in his face and screamed. "You've got to start paying attention to what's important!"

He didn't even bother waiting for her to say anything else. He walked out of the room. "Maybe next time, try giving him the detention instead."

Slezak looked down at his plate. It was empty. He couldn't even remember eating his breakfast and he loved bacon and eggs. His blood pressure went up another notch. It wasn't even nine in the morning, and already people were jerking his chain. He didn't bother to look as the diner door open and closed.

Todd and Buzz stood at the door and watched Slezak as he sat with his back to them. Todd smiled to himself when he saw the look on Buzz's face. He hadn't seen that one in a long time. They made some mental calculations about those tire tracks at the trailer.

"Stupid man."

"That he is, Buzz."

Slezak looked up suddenly when he saw shadows cross the table. "Morning, Walter."

Slezak remained expressionless as he turned around to see Todd and Buzz standing behind him. Todd grabbed the back of his chair and yanked it out from under him. Slezak hit the floor hard, landing on his tail bone, and driving the air out of his lungs. Shelley ran out from the kitchen. "What the hell do you think you're doing? You can't treat my customers like that!"

"Mr. Stiles and I will have steak and eggs, toast and coffee."

She sneered, until she saw that the closed sign was on and the front door was locked. Buzz took a step toward her. "Give me an excuse."

Shelley beat a hasty retreat to the kitchen. When he was sure she was actually completing their order for breakfast, Buzz turned back to Slezak, who was sitting up on the floor. "Get up. You're getting the floor dirty."

Todd grabbed him and hauled him to his feet, as Slezak yelled. "You two think you're pretty tough!"

Todd answered him with a backhand across the face, causing Slezak to stagger back against the table. Buzz stepped up and delivered a blow to the stomach that doubled him over.

"You don't have to be tough in Dusty. You just have to have enough money to hire goons to be tough for you."

Buzz pulled him off the table, spun him around, and shoved him back again. Todd lashed out with a foot, which took the legs out from under him. This time, his head hit the plate, flipping it off the table on to the floor.

Slezak struggled to his feet and rubbed his sleeve under his nose. There was blood on his shirt, a lot of it. He held his arm up to show it to them. "Where are they?"

"Where is who?"

It was going to take more than what they'd dished out to slow down the kind of arrogance a man like Slezak had. "You know who I'm talking about! Gardiner and Barker."

"Never heard of them."

"I sent them out to deal with you two."

"I guess they skipped out on the hotel bill. What do you think, Todd?"

"It's tough to find good goons these days, Buzz."

Todd pulled Slezak off the table. "It's time we took out the trash."

They pushed him out of the diner on to the sidewalk. The street was busy with people and there was no way for Slezak to avoid being humiliated in public.

"Where's your car?"

Slezak pointed at Perch's car. Buzz burst out laughing. "Is your car in the shop?"

Todd started to push him to the car, but then stopped. "I've got a better idea."

Instead, Todd pushed him into the middle of the street so that everyone could see him. How about it? Are you ready? The whole town is watching. No more hiding in a basement or on a hill, Slezak, no more pulling strings. Now everyone is a player! *Tick, Tock*. Time's up!

Todd delivered a straight arm punch to Slezak's face that laid him out in the street in the cheap suit he was wearing. Todd reached into his pocket and dropped the spent shell casing he found in the driveway on the street next to Slezak.

Buzz tapped Todd on the shoulder. "Shame on you, that's littering."

A crowd was starting to gather on the sidewalk. There were few offers to help Slezak.

"It's only littering if someone runs over him."

"How about some breakfast, I'm buying?"

Todd looked at him in surprise. "Somebody drop dead and leave you money?"

"Now that is harsh, Mister Smarty Pants Rich Guy! Unlike you, I wasn't born with a soup spoon stuck up my nose."

"Are you saying I was spoiled?"

Buzz gave him an up and down look. "You had your butler ride your bike for you."

Todd responded with mock indignation. "I'll have you know my butler never rode anything for me."

Seriously?"

This time, Todd replied with a perfect snotty English accent. "The butler carried me to breakfast, lunch, and dinner, but never did he ride my bike for me."

Buzz thought that was pretty funny and turned back to The Wasteland. "Are you coming?"

"Aren't you going to carry me?"

By the time they finished eating and had returned to the street, Slezak and his car were gone.

Buzz walked over to where it had been parked. There was a lot of blood on the pavement. Todd stayed on the sidewalk and looked in the direction he'd gone. "This is it, Buzz."

"Yeah, it will be soon, even hours."

Todd could see the stain on the pavement from where he was standing. "Let's hope there isn't much more of that."

"I agree, and if we can figure out how it is going to play out, there won't be."

"Well, if you're going to start a fire, you need fuel, oxygen, and a match."

"Okay, what do you think?"

"It's going to take three people to get this thing going."

"That makes sense, Todd, but whom?"

"They'd have to be people he had control over. Someone at that place where he works, the Ratepayers, or friends, or relatives."

"Family, are you're joking?"

"I wish I was. The widow and Slezak have been waiting for decades to play the last hand. No one's safe."

"So, where do we start?"

Todd looked up the street again. "Whose car was he driving? That was definitely not his style."

"You trashed his car, remember?"

"True. But he could've easily gotten a better replacement, why that car?"

"I heard somebody say at the gas the station that he was driving the car belonging to someone who worked for him at the Ratepayers."

"Probably one of his heavy hitters?"

"No, someone small, that he doesn't need. I remember seeing a guy with him that looked like he couldn't lift a can of paint."

"That's got to be the fuel. Someone kills him and then pins on the oxygen."

"Then all you have to do is provide the match."

"How much time do we have?"

"I'm thinking forty-eight hours. He won't try anything in daylight. The roughing up we gave him will barely slow him down. I'm thinking it'll start the day after tomorrow in the late afternoon. What we have to do is eliminate one of the three parts to the fire."

"We could just go the police."

They both got a good laugh out of that one. "Okay, let's go get the guy who owns that car."

It was a long walk to the car and even longer drive for Slezak. He gave up trying to stop the flow of blood from his face and concentrated on getting home. There was no way he was going back to work until he got cleaned up. Considering the beating he had just received, he was surprisingly calm. Even the blood that was pooling on the car seat could be worked to his advantage. Then, he remembered that it didn't matter, because there wasn't going to be enough left of the town to make a difference when it was over. That was the beauty of it all. He was going to rebuild the place in his image.

There were two messages on his answering machine when he got home. The first was from the principal of Dusty Collegiate. His nephew was in trouble for fighting. The second was from Potter. Terry and Jason Tilbury had finally gotten into it and were in detention. This time, everyone saw it and took sides. Even better, Potter had gotten what she needed to set up Perch, Terry, and Tilbury. He listened for another for another thirty seconds, to make sure there wasn't anything else, before releasing the play button on the machine.

He had picked up one of Terry's electronic games and looked at it idly, turning it over a couple of times, trying to figure it out how to turn it on, while listening to the messages. It was beyond him, he could barely operate a toaster. Slezak dropped it on the floor, looked at it briefly before stepping on it hard, and grinding it into the carpet. It made a sound like a dying mouse as its casing collapsed under his weight. Terry wasn't going to need it a couple of days because he was going to be joining Jason Tilbury and Perch in the crusade. He went to the bathroom to clean up.

Two miles away in a small, windowless room at Dusty Collegiate, Sharon Potter's efforts were staring at each other across a table. Normally, detentions are spent in a class room doing homework. This, however, was a special case. She wanted it up close and personal with no distractions.

Jason and Terry stared at each other in silence, the hatred slowly building. The problem for Jason, however, was not the hate, although it was definitely there. What was really bugging him was that a lot of stuff didn't add up. There was no doubt that Potter was a racist. He could smell one blocks away.

Terry Nevins would agree with him that it wasn't clear how the whole thing got started. There was a fight, a couple of punches thrown, but that should have been it. He'd heard the words thrown at him, but he wasn't sure who'd said them.

On Jason's side of the table, his confusion was that this guy didn't make sense. He was smart, no question there. But this wasn't the kind of guy who started something every time he came across a homey. In Brooklyn, it would take less than a week and the police would be fishing him out of the river. One thing was for certain. After two hours, an hour longer than a regular detention, all they both wanted was to get out of that room and get away from each other.

When Potter returned to finally let them out, she was angry because they hadn't gotten into another fight. She would have to drive the harpoon in even deeper. She looked at Terry with mock concern. "Did he give you any sass?"

Jason and Terry gave her a look of disgust, which forced her to take a step back. When they got to the door, they looked at Potter and then at each other. "This isn't over, is it?"

Jason shook his head slowly. "Not even close!"

Slezak turned off the living room lights before leaving. He missed seeing his nephew by fifteen minutes. He looked in the rear view mirror before pulling out of the driveway. He had stopped the bleeding, but with a split lip and broken nose, he looked like hell.

The meeting got started promptly at seven as Slezak took his place at the head of the table. Nine sat down for the meeting, but there should have been eleven. "Did anyone find Barker and Gardiner?"

One of the remaining men from the district tapped the table to get Slezak's attention. "Not a trace and they haven't shown up back at district, either."

Slezak reached into his pocket and tossed the shell casing onto the table. One of the other men from district picked up. "That's Gardiner ammo."

"How the hell do you know that? You can buy that caliber anywhere."

"No way, he gets his stuff custom made! I recognize the stamping on the rim. Where'd you get this?"

Slezak shouted back. "It doesn't matter where I got it! The fact is he's gone."

Potter pushed the stuff she had gotten out of Jason Tilbury's locker on to the table. "What happened to you?"

He gave her a vicious response. "Mind your own damned business! This is my problem and I will deal with it."

"When are you going to tell us how this is going to happen?"

"Finally, a question that is not completely stupid! I'm moving the schedule up to the day after tomorrow. He reached into his briefcase and handed out envelopes to everyone, but the two men on his left.

"What are these?" Potter asked.

"They're called instructions."

"What about us?"

"The two of you will wait here. The rest of you go and get some sleep. You'll need it."

When everyone was gone, one of the two men leaned forward with menace. "Talk to us."

"Tomorrow night. Take that sleeping bag, and backpack that Potter brought, take some food that I left in the locker, and go out to the station. Make sure Perch doesn't get out of the room and that the door to the building and gate are unlocked when you leave. In the morning, call the police in VanderWagon and the local paper. Tell them there's been a homicide out at the old train station. When you're done, go back to the district."

"I thought we were going to do this guy."

"Things have changed. Our people are going to take care of that part and the widow. Your people are going to take care of that colored kid and my nephew. Everyone will think he killed the colored kid for doing Perch. They'll also dispose of Potter and our guests."

One of the men picked up Gardiner's shell casing. "You've already tried that and it cost two of our people."

Slezak jerked forward in his chair. ."Bullshit. They screwed up a simple beating."

The two men stood up. "Barker and Gardiner are professionals. When this is done, we are going to come back to find them. You had better hope that when we do, they aren't laying on your side of the fence."

Slezak worked late as usual. No else noticed the car sitting across the street when they left. It was getting dark and the Pacer was sitting well back in the shadows.

"You see him come out, Buzz?"

"No. I don't think he's there. The only one left inside is Slezak."

A half hour later, the lights went out and Slezak appeared in front of the building. He brushed some food off the front of his jacket and then rubbed his nose. He looked at his hand in anger. His nose was bleeding again. Buzz pointed from the passenger seat. "You do good work."

"Thanks. I've been getting a lot of practice lately."

They watched as he drove off, the tires screeching in protest.

"What do you think?"

Buzz continued to stare out the window. "The guy's name is Perch or something like that. He was Slezak's lackey, when he told him to jump, the guy asked how high on the way up."

"And now he's nowhere to be seen."

"Fuel?"

Todd started the car, "Fuel."

He did a U-turn in the middle of the street, his face illuminated by the dash lights. With the windows down, the still warm desert air poured into the car. Two miles before the turn off to Mickey John's place, Todd suddenly pulled off the road. He turned off the car and waited briefly before getting out. He could hear Buzz's footsteps on the gravel behind him. He raised a hand before Buzz had a chance to say anything. Buzz a waited patiently.

Todd pointed east at the now nearly dark horizon. "There!"

It only took Buzz a couple of seconds to find it, a star sitting right on the line between the earth and sky. Even in the stillness of the night air, with nothing around to make a sound, they had to strain to hear the whistle.

"It makes perfect sense, Buzz! That station has to be abandoned and isolated."

"Yeah, and if we find this guy, he should be able to complete the rest of the picture for us."

Buzz looked at his watch. "We had better get some sleep. Tomorrow is going to be a long day."

800 miles away in the office of the Chief of Atmospheric Physics at the National Oceanic and Atmospheric Administration--NOAA-- Randy Smothers had already had his long day and was getting in to bed. To be precise, he'd crawled onto the sofa in his office and pulled a blanket over himself. He had taken it out of one of the department's survival kits. Raiding the survival packs was one of the perks of being the Chief of Atmospheric Physics. He was sleeping in his office with one of his perks because he was experiencing the special joy of a no-holds-barred, winner-take-all, divorce.

In April, the comptroller had signed off on new furniture for his office: desk, chairs, credenza, "the whole enchilada." His staff, and almost everyone else who had an office within in the building, thought he had gone nuts because he'd passed on a total office rework, and elected to order a fold out sofa the size and cost of a Buick. They had to remove the office door to get it in, and it took up so much room, that anyone who came to do business with him felt like they were being watched by a large, inland alligator.

The only person who actually thought the sofa was a good idea was his lawyer, because, in his words, Smothers was going to be "Sleeping on the damn thing for years." Smothers was snoring loudly in less than a minute.

The door opened and a shaft of light poured into the room, hitting him in the face with a thud, "Boss?"

Smothers opened one eye and glared at the woman standing in the doorway. He briefly wished that the women in the office would stop waking him up, because it was a lot more fun with the guys. He could yell, scream, and say bad stuff to guys. "Get lost! You know how much I hate it when people interrupt me while I am in the middle of a divorce."

"You're going to need to see this."

"You'd better be dying."

"I'm not!"

"Go away and don't come back until you are!"

Despite her best efforts to get him to the forecasting room, he wasn't budging until he had some coffee.

"You should be drinking tea. It's better for you."

"That's about much fun as kissing your sister."

I'm just trying to be nice. It's not like you've got lot of friends these days."

"You're starting to sound like my wife."

"And that's why you don't have any friends. We're all routing for her."

Smothers finally joined a group clustered around a computer screen, and despite his threats to the contrary, he was wearing pants.

He was constantly amazed that such an intelligent group of people--two physicists and three PhD's, including the woman who had gotten him out of bed--lived such thankless, crummy lives. They all wore clothing that looked like they'd been slept in, had five o'clock shadows, except for the two women with doctorates. The one who'd interrupted his divorce looked like she'd brushed her hair with a weed whacker.

"What am I looking at?"

Someone pointed to a screen displaying what looked like a string of pearls strung across the state of Texas and into New Mexico.

Smothers groaned. "I can't see that. We've got four sixty-inch television screens in this place. Put in on the wall."

A screen lit up on the south wall. "Do you think you could get one farther away, schmuck?"

"Sorry, Boss." The screen went dark and the one directly behind them lit up

Smothers walked around the desk and looked up at the screen. "Up the resolution, give me a grid, and move it left 20. D2 to D8 and 107-108. Enhance."

The computer responded by bringing the pearls into the center of the screen. A series of small dots were now visible between the large ones.

A woman pointed to the left side of the string. "The small ones at the end are the down drafts. The ones in the center of the string are up drafts. Normally, all they would do is rip off some shingles and empty few garbage pails. But with the compression here, they are going to be at least F2. And, they're going to be supplying power to the large ones."

"Give me the data, including wind speed and direction.

The threat rating appeared. Tornadoes are rated F1-F5. Just as she said, the small pearls showed F1 on the end and increased to F2 in the center, while one at the far end was F3. On the big ones, there were only asterisks, because the software was only capable of reading to F5. These were very high and off scale.

Smothers turned and looked at the group over his glasses. "You clowns got me up in the middle of the night to show me this? The Cray isn't even designed to produce this kind of simulation. Stop screwing around with the algorithms in the software."

"It's not a simulation, Chief, it's a forecast."

He laughed at her. "It has to be. This stuff doesn't even occur in the movies. Run a diagnostic on the system and software. Get the gear heads to check their hardware and the radars. Have you got all that?"

"Is there anything else?" His instructions were going to generate work for a lot of people in the middle of the night.

"Yeah, call Los Alamos and see if this is another one of their ideas of a practical joke. They are still pissed off because we caught them putting in a ringer in last year's baseball game. Like no one is going to recognize Barry Bonds!"

"C'mon Randy! It's one in the morning."

"Well, that will teach you to wake me up in the middle of the night!" He stomped back into his office and slammed the door hard enough to rattle the windows. The blinds split open for a second and then closed with a snap.

The woman took a deep breath and stormed into his office. "We've got to talk about this."

He yelled back in frustration. "What is it with you women, anyway? Why do you all have to say that?"

"How the hell should I know? Anyway, this is not going to go away. We should run a crosscheck with NASA."

"Not a chance. They'll think we've spun a bearing. This doesn't get out of the house."

She got up to leave. "Okay, okay! What's our reliability on this?"

"No more than forty-eight hours. We will have confidence in thirty-two."

When she got to the door and opened it, he stopped her, asking her to close it for a moment. "I'm convinced the computers have screwed up, so it stays in the house, understand?"

She understood what he was saying and started to open the door. "You're right. If this got out, even if it is a mistake, it could cause a lot of grief. There's one other thing. You remember Bedard's work on low frequency acoustics in severe storms?"

"Sure. I was in Boulder when he presented the paper on it."

"No you weren't. You got wasted at the airport the night before and I had to replace you for the peer review."

"Okay, I read it on the plane back,... so what?"

"If Bernard is right, the acoustic signatures on these things will be less than 1Hz and infrasonic."

"Again, so what?"

She put a hand on the door frame to steady herself. "An F5 could touch down, less than ten feet away, and you wouldn't know it was there until it was all over."

He stopped her one more time. "You'd better start the clock on this."

The air, Randy Smothers wanted out of his office so he could get some sleep, blew in the Widow Weeks living room window and gave the curtains a good flapping. She looked up with a knowing smile.

Smith went over to the window, leaned out, and took a deep breath. He started to close the window. "The air smells bad."

She barked back. "Leave it open! As a matter of fact, it's such a nice breeze, that I'm feeling the need to share it. Get Slezak up here and tell the hired help to put on some of that tea of his."

That stuff tastes like crap and goes through you like grease in a chicken!"

She grinned. "Why do you think I keep him, and you, around?"

Slezak showed up an hour later. This time, he didn't wait to be shown in. He just pushed the front door open and walked into the living room, unannounced. He felt something brush past him. When he looked back, there wasn't anything there.

"Over here!"

He followed the voice into the shadows. A light came on. The widow was sitting in her chair with the butler behind her, with a pot of tea and a large cup. She pointed to a chair. "Sit down."

Slezak sneered. "I don't sit down with your kind, and I'm sure as hell not doing it here."

Smith grabbed him from behind and slammed him down in the chair with enough force to knock the wind out of him, as the butler filled the cup and put the pot the down on the table. When Slezak tried to get out of the chair, Smith came from behind and put a choke hold on him.

The widow leaned forward to inspect Smiths work. "Are we comfy Walter?"

He answered with a string of profanity.

She clucked in concern. "You should have some tea, calms the nerves."

Smith tightened his arm around Slezak's neck, pulling him up in the chair. With the other hand, he grabbed his nose, cutting off his air forcing his mouth open. The butler grabbed Slezak's mouth, held it open, and poured the tea down his throat. He emptied the entire pot into Slezak's mouth. When it was over, Smith let him go. Slezak rocketed forward in the chair, gagging and coughing up what was still in his throat.

The widow rolled her chair forward to get a closer look at Slezak. "Now, isn't that better? You already look more relaxed."

He tried to get up, but he choked again, and fell back into the chair.

The widow shook her head and looked at Smith. She told the butler to stand at the fireplace. "The hired help we get these days. Now Walter, what am I going to do with you? You were told to dispose of our visitors. It was so simple and yet you managed to screw it up."

He rubbed his throat. "The guys they sent me went yellow and took off!"

She laughed in his face. "They aren't yellow, Walter, they're dead."

"What are you talking about?"

"It's simple. One moron sends two morons to kill two people who aren't morons on hallowed ground."

Slezak spat at her. "I don't believe in that Voodoo crap!"

"Neither do I. But what I do believe in is much worse, and just to make sure you understand that, I am going to have to give you a small demonstration. But first, let's go over the details.

"Have you put the weasel in the bag the way I told you?"

"It's getting done tomorrow."

"What about the school?'

"We've got the colored kid set up for Perch's murder."

"And what about that nephew of yours?"

"No problem. He kills the colored kid, who killed Perch, and that sets it off."

She shook her head. "Walter, I can't decide if you are ignorant, stupid, or both. Probably both, so I am going to help you out."

The widow reached down in her chair and retrieved a silver plated 45-automatic that had, until Walter had arrived, been in his shoulder holster. She aimed it at the butler and continued pulling the trigger until the gun was empty.

The first three rounds drove the man back against the fireplace mantle. He stumbled to his knees and tried to get up. Two more rounds drove him backwards into the fireplace, leaving the legs sticking out. With the man now dead, the rest of the bullets were just for effect. Smith jammed the legs inside and dropped a couple of large logs on the butler's body.

She tossed the gun on the coffee table. "Now, wasn't that easy? We can pin that one on your nephew as well, and if you foul up one more time on me, you get to ride the log the next. Forty-eight hours, Walter, or I'll replace you and do it myself. Show our friend to the door, Jonathon."

Slezak stumbled down the stairs to the car. Now he had a bruised neck to go with his face. He was also, for the first time in his life, terrified. He had never experienced something so violent and primordial. Slezak was now well-motivated to get the job done, and if for no other reason, to see the world rid of the widow and the rest of her monsters.

As he got into the car, a terrible smell stopped him. He looked up and gagged. The fireplace had been lit.

Another dawn had come as Todd and Buzz stood in the backyard and watched. Sunlight exploded off the Corvette's chrome. I hate sitting here looking at it, Buzz."

"Our time will come soon enough, and we'll be on our way."

Todd stiffened at what sounded like gunshots in the distance. No worries, that's the sound rocks make when they break from thermal shock."

"That's not what's bothering me, Buzz." Todd said, pointing at the morning sky.

"I'm not sure what you're getting at."

"You see those clouds just above that range of mountains?"

"Yeah, they call them Cirrus, high and cold, really cold. That indicates high pressure, if I recall correctly."

"That's pretty good, Buzz! Now, that high pressure is going to run right over that warm wet chunk of air over there in the East."

"The air coming off the Gulf."

"Right, it's been getting hotter and more humid every day since we got here."

"Not good?"

"It's not good Buzz, not good at all."

"We may be running out of time faster than we thought. Let's get our kit together and get started."

"It was thirty minutes to the road leading off to the station. As they approached, they could see that the gate on the road had been forced. Buzz pulled over. "Let's get the car out of sight behind that shed and walk the rest of the way in."

It took longer than they thought because the road was over-grown with grass and debris, but they could see that there had been recent traffic. Buzz pointed to the back of the building. "The people we're dealing with don't use the front door.

The station had two doors at the back, one for the train master, and one for passengers. Both had hasps and locks on them which hadn't been touched in years. The same applied to the windows which were locked and tightly sealed.

"This looks like a dead end, Buzz."

"Yeah, you'd think that.

Buzz looked up at the roof line and then walked slowly back to the train master's door. "Todd, have a look at the other door and tell me what you see."

"This door has been secured for a long time. No surprise there."

Buzz asked him if the handle moved. Todd told him that it did and that the door could be opened a quarter of an inch, until the hasp stopped it. Todd turned the handle on the door where he was. It was frozen solid and it didn't move at all when he pushed on it. He stepped back a foot and looked at it carefully. "Your door says I'm old and locked, but I would open if I could. This door screams, *go away*!"

Todd grabbed the lock and hasp and pulled on it quickly. The whole assembly came off the door in his hand. "Hang on to this; we'll need to put it back when we leave."

When Todd pushed on the door, it moved with a wheeze, because it was being held in place with expensive weather stripping designed to keep it shut. "These are guys are good."

The station was dark and the air was stale from years of dust and neglect. It was also deadly quiet. Todd took a flashlight out of his pocket and shone it around the room. The place was a time capsule. He stopped at sign over a drinking fountain, "Whites Only."

A board in the floor squeaked. "Was that you?

Todd shook his head, pointing the flashlight at the ceiling, and then at a set of stairs on the far side of the room.

There's nothing like climbing a set of darkened stairs to keep a person motivated. They stopped periodically and listened for anyone waiting for them the top. There were no surprises. The only unusual item was a chair sitting on the landing. The hallway on the second floor led to the right and ran the length of the building. At the end of the hall was a door painted bright red. A sign identified it as the switch room and this time, it was legitimately locked. On the right, there was a small office and storage room, both open. On the left, there was a washroom and what was identified as the station master's quarters. They had no doubt that the room would be locked. Buzz reached up and ran a hand across the top of the door sill. He opened his hand to show a key.

He pushed the key into the lock and waited. No sound came from the other side of the door. Whatever was in there was either smart or scared. When he reached for the doorknob, Todd turned off the flash light. Buzz waited for a couple of seconds and then swung the door open quickly. This time, there was no one standing behind it. Todd turned on the flashlight and swung it around the room. In the corner was a sleeping bag and backpack, other than that, the room was empty.

In the darkness, another floor board squeaked. Todd moved the light quickly, illuminating someone hiding on the floor between the bed and a chair. He moved quickly and dragged the man to his feet. "I'd say we found the fuel, Buzz."

"Indeed, we have."

The look on Perch's face slowly changed from fear to recognition. "I know who you guys are. You are the one's Mr. Slezak has been waiting for. I'm surprised you two are still walking around. He was going to have you two taken care of."

"You hear that, Buzz?"

"The tire tracks?"

Todd nodded and shoved Perch violently against the wall. "The tire tracks too bad they didn't stay for a drink."

Buzz looked at Perch. "We don't like being stood up."

Perch was getting his arrogance back, brushing some dust off his shirt. "It doesn't matter none, anyway. He'll deal with you personally when he finds out you two had me locked up in here."

Buzz sat down on the chair and made himself comfortable. "We didn't have anything to do with your being here, although, I like the idea."

"You're a liar. I was told to come out here and wait for instructions. They told me to watch out because you guys were hiding out here. Someone jumped me from behind. When I woke up, I was locked in here."

Buzz asked how he got out here in the first place. "I walked. Mr. Slezak needed my car for important business."

"How long did it take you?'

"About three hours."

Buzz and Todd looked at each other, amazed at the man's stupidity.

"Tell you what. We're going to help you out."

Perch laughed. You're going to help *me*, a couple of dead guys."

"My friend, Todd, is making you a generous offer. This is the deal. You tell us everything we need to know or we will beat you senseless, which is a better deal than you are going to get from the next people who come through the door."

Perch told them to go to hell.

Buzz got up, walked over to Perch, and hit him in the stomach with an old table leg, which he had found on the floor. Perch folded like a card table. Todd looked down at Perch.

"That wasn't up to your usual standards."

Buzz was contrite. "Sorry. My work has been getting a little sloppy lately."

They hauled Perch up off the floor and tossed him on the chair. Buzz raised the table leg to hit him again. This time, Perch raised his arms and screamed for him to stop. For the next half hour, he sang like a bird.

Todd looked at his watch. "We've got everything we need. Let's get out of here."

Perch screamed. "You're not going to leave me here?"

Buzz tossed him the table leg. "Don't stand behind the door and hit the second person that comes through."

"Why hit the second person?"

"Because that's the one who's going to kill you, the first one is bait. Say hi to Walter. He should be along in a couple of hours."

"How do you know that?"

Todd laughed, because he'll be the second one through the door."

They could still hear him screaming when they got to the back door.

"Have you got the hasp?" Todd retrieved it from his pocket and handed it to Buzz. He slipped the hasp back into the place, locking the door, and securing it so it didn't look like it had been touched. "What is it with you? Where did you learn to do that, anyway?"

"Sent away."

They stopped as they came around the front of the station. In the distance, they could see a car pull onto the road to the station.

"We'd better take cover. It might be coming here and we won't make it back to the car in time."

They watched as the car went by and disappeared around the corner. "By my count, there were four in the car.

"We'd better get to those kids before Slezak finds out we have been out here."

They didn't have to worry. Perch screwed up, stood behind the door, and took it right in the face when Potter decided to kick it in, because she couldn't find the key in the dark. "It's ladies night, Perch!"

They had him the bag before he had a chance to scream a single word. They took their time. It was close to three in the afternoon before they packed up to leave. One of Potter's friends stopped and looked at what was left of the door frame. "Where did you learn to do that anyway?"

"Sent away."

She heard a moan come from the sleeping bag hanging from the ceiling. She walked back into the room and took a blackjack out of her purse, which Slezak kept in his desk drawer. They'd hung Perch in the bag by his feet. She swung it like a baseball bat against his head. There was a loud crack, the bag stiffened, and was still. She tossed the blackjack on the table and walked to the door. "Everyone is going to think Tilbury did him. But Slezak is going to wear it at district."

"I suppose you sent away for that, too?"

Todd and Buzz were long gone by the time the car reappeared from behind the station.

"Where do we start looking for them? We are running out of time."

"Damned if I know. Let's try the high school."

The place was deserted. They had to go from one end of the building to the other, before they found a teenage girl at her locker. "What the hell do you want? I'll scream if you touch me!"

"We just want to know where everyone is."

"Schools closed. It's staff development day. If you ask me, they don't develop anything. They just use it as an excuse to go party somewhere. Besides, what's it to you?"

"We need to know where Jason Tilbury and Terry Nevins are."

She yelled. "I don't know anything about that!"

Buzz and Todd looked at each other. "We didn't ask you about what was happening."

She immediately realized her mistake. "Just leave me alone! I don't want to get involved in that stuff. I'm not prejudiced like Potter and her Nazi friends. I like Tilbury and Nevins."

Todd spoke quietly and firmly to her. "You're already involved, and we are not going to go away until you to tell us what you know."

"Look, I don't know who is setting them up and I don't want to know, either, it's mostly rumor anyway. You know how it is in high school. But the plan is for them to get in to a fight on the old bypass road. That's why it's probably all a load of air, because it doesn't make any sense to do it out there where no one can see it."

"Who's setting it up?" Buzz demanded to know.

"I told you! I don't know. They were told where to meet and that is all I can tell you."

As they drove back downtown, Buzz spoke first. "Now it makes sense. Jason Tilbury kills Perch. Terry kills Jason during a fight, for the cause, and Slezak's nephew dies from his injuries. He's a martyr. The town goes boom."

Buzz pulled over at a store on Main Street. "What's going on, Buzz?"

"Directions, we can't afford to get lost."

Todd agreed and then suddenly stopped him, as he started to get out of the car. He pointed across the street at the black sedan. "That doesn't match the scenery."

Buzz looked carefully at the car. Todd was right. The car definitely didn't belong in Dusty, New Mexico. Two men got out and started across the street. They were wearing the full outfit, including dark suits, glasses, and coms in the right ear. Buzz put the car in gear, but Todd stopped him before he took his foot off the brake. "We couldn't outrun a car like that anyway, not even with the Corvette. These guys are pros. They won't do it in broad daylight."

Buzz looked at him. "You want to bet my life on that?"

The men split up, each taking up a position on both sides of the car. The man on the driver's side leaned in the window. "Good afternoon, Gentlemen. Can you give us a few minutes of your time? We'd like to speak to you about an important matter. Would you mind stepping out of the car, please?"

Todd told them they were in a bit of hurry.

"We are aware of that, Sir. But if you could give us a couple of minutes, maybe we can help each other out." Buzz had to admit they were certainly polite paid killers.

The conversation lasted less than four minutes. Buzz had his directions and was on his way to the bypass, alone. It was only a question of time, now.

Terry had been standing out on the road for over an hour, after his uncle had ordered him out of the car, without an explanation as to why they were here, or why he was being left on the road. In the distance, he saw a car approaching. What he didn't see was one of the men from the district standing on the bridge, and with a rifle in his hands.

The car slowed down and turned around in the road. A door opened on the passenger side and someone was pushed out onto the road from the back seat. As the car drove off, someone yelled, "For the cause!

The man thrown from the car got up unsteadily, and walked toward Terry, there was a fresh bruise under the right eye. Terry muttered, "Tilbury."

Jason Tillbury stopped ten feet away. "What do you think of your cross-burning buddy's handiwork? Not bad for amateurs!"

"What are you talking about? I didn't have anything to do with that! That's my uncle's hobby."

Jason delivered an upper cut that lifted Terry off his feet. Terry was slow to recover, but he returned with a well-executed jab that was so fast, Jason didn't even see it coming. It went back and forth between them until Terry started to get the upper hand, even though they were still evenly matched. Terry suddenly froze in the middle of a swing.

Jason screamed at him. "Come on jerk, throw your punch!"

Terry continued to stand there like a statue with his arm in the air, as though he was half way through a salute. He croaked out "My God!"

Jason turned slowly. They had been so wrapped up in their small personal war that they hadn't seen it coming. Although just a precursor of the main event, Randy Smother's string of pearls had arrived. A mere ten yards across and almost 300 feet away the tornado was close to a F3. It had formed so quickly that it was like it had popped out of the ground, and then waited for the two of them to notice it.

They just stood there terrified, their fight now completely forgotten. It had waited long enough. It tore off a chunk of pavement and shattered it. Jason grabbed Terry and started to run, dragging him to the bridge. For a second, Terry didn't budge. Jason screamed at him to move. Terry looked at him and nodded in slow motion, still not believing what he was experiencing. "Okay."

Fifty feet from the cover of the bridge, Jason stumbled, twisting an ankle, which slowed him down. The monster was almost on top of them. It almost seemed like it sensed victory. It appeared to slow down to a walk, ready to collect its prize. "No worries."

Jason got up and limped a few steps. He wasn't going to make it. Terry ran back, lifted him over his shoulder in a fireman's carry, and sprinted the distance to the bridge. They heard an unbelievable scream of agony as they passed under the bridge. The tornado howled and tore at the bridge as they climbed up the wing wall for safety.

Terry yelled over the noise and pointed. "Look at the bearing seats. They're moving!"

The tornado had grown in strength, to the point that it was able to lift the bridge deck. It was the longest twenty minutes of their lives, as the wind pulled on the bridge, trying to get at the two men hiding under it.

By the time Buzz arrived, the storm was spent, but it had left Terry and Jason bruised and scratched by flying debris. Buzz looked the both of them over carefully. "You two were lucky."

"Yeah, but I think there was someone on the bridge."

Terry looked at the top of the bridge. "I heard it too."

Buzz didn't have to look. "He already knew. Let's go."

As they got into the car Jason said he was glad that it was over. Buzz looked at the both of them. "Not even close."

He pushed the car as fast as it would move, but it still felt like a lifetime getting back. In the distance, they could see a building on fire. The war had already started. The volunteer fire department was trying to put out a fire at the clothing store. The battle had already been lost and they were trying to prevent it from spreading.

"Spunky's. That place has been here as long as the town. I got my first pair of runners there. The guy who owned it was right decent to me."

Yeah, and they are going to blame us for it." Jason's voice had menace in it.

' Terry looked at Jason with disapproval. "He was colored."

Jason was briefly at a loss for words and then looked up. "Pull over!"

He pulled on Terry's arm. "C'mon, let's see if they need any help putting that fire out."

Buzz pushed them out of the car. "Go! But don't leave this site. Either Todd or I will come back for you. You got that?"

There was a massive explosion on the far end of town. "Absolutely, we'll stay here!"

As Buzz drove back into Dusty, the place was starting to look like a war zone. People stalked the streets with whatever they could carry, not even sure where they were going or what they were looking for. Where there was a fire, they were either trying to fight it or light it. Things were getting ugly.

Buzz located Todd a block from where he had left him, still in the company of the men in black suits. Todd was glad to see that Buzz was back in one piece. "Did you miss me?"

"Very funny, Murdoch."

Buzz got serious. "A twister hit the bridge at the bypass. It was strong enough to move the decking."

"Terry,...Jason?"

"They're all right, but it was close. If they hadn't looked after each other, it would've been a different story."

Todd smiled. "Good. Where are they?"

"They're helping put out a fire at a clothing store."

One of the suits looked at the other. "I'll get them."

"One of us should go. They aren't going to trust anyone around here."

"Don't worry. I understand where they're coming from, and I can work around that."

They watched him leave for a moment. "Todd, that tornado was just the leading edge. It's going to get a lot worse. The warning covers nearly 200 square miles and Dusty is going to be ground zero. We're going to have to get those two out of here."

"Yeah, I know. That's why the suits are here, Buzz. I'm needed in Texas. My company is involved in a serious project that's hit a snag. They went to a lot of trouble to find me."

Buzz turned to the suit. "Do you mind?"

The man politely walked away, out of hearing.

Buzz turned back to Todd, and there was anger on his face. "This is the second time we've been here."

"You're right. After all we've been through, we get back here, and it's the same damn thing all over again. I'm staying."

Buzz signed. "No, it's not the same. The last time it was about choice and we made a bad one. This time it's about the rules of professional conduct and they are non-negotiable. You have to go."

"You're right. Thanks for reminding me."

"Just make sure you get back here so I don't have to hot wire the car."

"You're not coming?"

"No. I'm going to stay and help get these people get out of the way of what's coming. But what you can do is take Terry and Jason with you. Maybe work some of that magic of yours."

In the distance, they could see the car returning with Terry and Jason. "Sir, we're going to have to go before the weather grounds us."

"Ok, I'm coming. But a couple of you stay back and look after my friend."

One of the men looked over his glasses. "You're kidding?"

"I wish I was."

He walked away and had a brief conversation with his colleague and then returned to escort them to the car. "This is the deal. We're going to take the three of you to the plane to make sure it gets away safe, and then come back with the rest of our agents. Mr. Murdoch, we're going to ask you to wait here."

Buzz looked at his watch. "I hadn't planned on going anywhere, anyway."

"It's a fifteen-minute drive to the airport from downtown. Just outside of town." The man in the passenger seat put his hand to the com set in his ear. "Davios says he can see a car on the side of the road a mile from the turn off. There are a couple of guys on the pavement."

The driver grinned. "How about we run them down?"

The man stared at him. "Those anger management classes didn't help it all, did they?"

The two men were right where Davios said they were, blocking the entrance to the airport. The agent behind the wheel stopped the car in the middle of the road. "I'm seeing an M-16 and a sawed off 12-gauge jack and a frack Winchester with a choke,...are you sure I can't just run them over?"

"Will you, just once, try to be nice to people?"

The agent looked over the back seat at Terry and Jason. "We'll be back in a couple of minutes. Do not get out of the car."

Jason croaked. "Okay."

The agents walked out in front of the car and looked at the two men from the district, carefully. "Well, at least they look like they know what they're doing. So let's try to remember that we're all professionals here, okay?"

"All right,… I'll try."

He spoke politely to the district men. "Can I help you Gentlemen, are you having car trouble?"

The man holding the twelve-gauge roared with laughter. "Did you hear that, Starks? He wants to know if we have trouble."

Starks raised the machine gun. "No, we don't, but you sure as hell do!"

The driver reached into his pocket, pulled out a handkerchief, and blew his nose.

"You should take something for that."

When he had cleared his nose, he yelled back. "Are you the bad guys?"

Starks was getting angry because this was not going down the way he wanted. "Just think of us as a couple of white knights!"

"Well, you can't say I didn't try."

"You know how much I hate paperwork, so try not to kill anyone."

The agent took off his jacket and handed it to his colleague. "Can I use your gun? Mine only has three rounds in it."

When he slowly reached into his jacket, Starks yelled. "You're gonna die, anyway, so don't do it looking stupid."

The agent was comfortable, now. "Relax, you're forty yards away. With my gun, I couldn't hit a barn at that distance."

His partner grinned, as he handed his gun to him. "Stop being such a mooch and buy your own bullets from now on." He stopped him after a couple of steps. This time he was serious. "Make it quick. We don't have a lot of time."

The driver walked ahead of the car about ten feet with the gun relaxed at his side. "Who did you say you guys were?"

"White knights."

"Well, I'm the Easter Bunny."

Starks barely had time to say "What the,…?" before the Easter Bunny put a bullet through the magazine of his rifle. The gun exploded, blowing off his hand and putting two pieces of shrapnel in his face. The blast blew him backward onto the pavement. Stark's screams were deafening.

The driver waved a finger at the other man, indicating that he shouldn't be stupid either. However, the other man obviously didn't understand the message and raised his shotgun. His right knee exploded in a red mist.

The other agent walked up to his colleague, and retrieved his gun. "We're really going to have to work on your people skills."

"We'd better get the first aid kit out of the car."

He had maimed both men. They tied off the wounded limbs, so that they wouldn't bleed to death, and then dragged them over to their car.

As they walked away, the man with the shotgun yelled. "I thought you said you couldn't hit anything at that distance with your gun.

The agent took his out his handkerchief again and gave his nose another good blow. "That wasn't my gun."

Buzz was sitting on a bench in front of a variety store, watching the town of Dusty incinerate itself. It was like watching a disaster movie, and all that was missing was a coke, a bag of popcorn, and an intermission, so he could go to the bathroom. The car had returned. This time, six men got out and these guys were even bigger than the ones from district. As a group, they blocked the sun when they stopped in front of him, "Buzz Murdoch?"

"That all depends on whether you are the good guys or the bad ones."

"Oh we're the good ones, all right. But we haven't had any field work in six months, so we may be a little cranky."

As they walked back to their cars, Buzz asked which one of them was called Tiny."

"We all are."

"You guys work for Todd's company?"

"No, we work for Beachler-Carlyle."

"Isn't that a software company?"

"Hardware actually."

As Buzz got into the Pacer, along with one of the agents, he wondered what kind of computers needed that kind of security.

The agent with him pointed east. Mr. Stiles suggested that we start at the train station.

On the way there, Buzz pulled over. "That's where they park the school buses. We can use them to get people out of town."

One of them consulted a map. There's an abandoned Titan missile base twenty miles northeast of here. That will work great as a shelter. Those things are designed to take an atom bomb."

Buzz looked at the station. "There may be a man in there."

"Is he worth it?"

Buzz shook his head. "No, but leaving someone behind is not my style."

"I'll go with you. The rest of us will get the buses moving."

When Buzz pulled around the corner of the station and looked at the door, he knew no one was going to be rescued. "It looks like we're too late."

The agent got out. "Where is he?"

"Second floor, second door on the left."

"Wait here."

The agent returned fifteen minutes later with Jason's backpack and Slezak's 45. He got into the car. "We're too late."

When they got into town, they pulled over across from the center parking lot, which was jammed with the buses, cars, vans, and anything else which would move. The agents had all ditched their suit jackets, revealing Walther P38's, equipped with flash suppressors. Buzz was going to make a comment, when one of the men smiled and waved a finger at him.

"You guys are good. I didn't think there were that many sets of wheels in the town."

"It's amazing how tolerant people can get when they are all looking hell in the face."

"How bad is it going to get?" Buzz asked.

A couple of women overheard him and detached themselves from a group, "The perfect storm, a weather bomb. NOAA reports that the cells are so far off the scale, they can't even measure them. I strongly suggest you find yourselves a seat. They are giving us less than five hours and that is with zero reliability, which means they could already be here."

"Don't worry. I'll make it out. My car is here and I don't want to leave it behind.

The agent looked at him like he was nuts. "Murdoch, your life is in danger and you're worried about a car?"

"It's a 1962 Corvette and I'm kind of attached to it."

He looked at one of the other agents. "A 1962 Vet? Well, that's a different matter, all together."

The agent warned Buzz. "If I don't see you at the silo when this thing hits, I am going to come looking for you. I am going to come and get you and that will make me very cranky."

Buzz smirked. "You can come with me and be unhappy now."

The agent turned, and looked at the man next to him. "Go get the funny man the spare kit, a box of ammo, and three clips."

He returned with the kit and a shoulder holster. "It's cleared and ready to go."

"Isn't that the one they used?" He didn't finish the sentence.

"Yes, it is, but these actually work and are very accurate. You have any experience with small arms?"

"Once, back in New York."

"Terrific! See this? It's the safety. Move it this way, point and shoot. When you stop, put the safety back on. Please don't point it at me, okay?"

As they got into the car, the agent asked Buzz where his car was.

"We're going to the Ratepayers."

"Is it parked in the back?"

"No."

"Then why are we going there?"

"Because I'm going to take a short cut."

"I'm going to regret this, aren't I?"

As they pulled up, across from the Ratepayers, the man put his hand to his com set. "They're on the last trip. The head count is 1,489 out of 1,500. One of our people says one of the warhead sheds is still survivable and you can park your car in there. I assume the last eleven are your problem children."

Todd nodded and pointed to the building. "They're in there. Do you think you can start that car over there?"

"I'm assuming that you don't have the keys, and that it isn't your car."

"That is correct. Can you do it?"

The agent got out of the car. "I work for Beachler-Carlyle."

Three minutes later, Perch's car was across the street facing the front door of the Ratepayers, all set up, and ready to go. Buzz needed some money. "You got any change on you?"

The agent reached into his pocket and produced a dollar and a half. Buzz took seventy- five cents. "Thanks. I'll be right back."

He walked across the street to a pay phone, made a short phone call, returned to the car, and looked at his watch briefly. He held a rope, which was tied to a board holding down the brake.

Slezak's face appeared at the front door, just as Perch's car jumped the curb doing thirty-miles-per-hour. Slezak just made it back down the stairs as the car went through the front doors. The front of the building exploded in a shower of glass. Perch's car made it all the way to the back of the building, blocking the stairwell.

The agent looked at Buzz. "You've done this before?"

"You think he's dead?"

The agent shook his head. "I doubt it. Bigots are like cock roaches, really stupid, but man they're hard to kill."

"Where are we going next?

Buzz pointed to a hill in the distance. "There."

They repeated the process at the widow's place, using her car.

"How many more of those things have you got?" asked the agent, pointing to the rope and board.

"This is my last one."

You'd better make it a good one, because they know you're here and this time, you aren't going to have time to make a phone call."

Buzz yanked out the board and the 1966 Ford Torino went after the house like a dog after a bone. It was too big and heavy to make it up the stairs to the front door, but it demolished the porch and was halfway through the basement wall, before it finally came to a stop.

"We'd better go."

Buzz said to wait. "We're not done, yet."

"You could have fooled me."

The widow appeared from the back of the house, accompanied by John Smith.

When he saw Buzz had company, Smith reached into his jacket.

"Not yet!" The widow rolled to a stop in front of the agent. "Do I know you?"

"No."

She turned in her chair and examined the house and the car embedded in the wall. It was starting to smoke. She then turned back to Buzz. "You've become quite a pest!"

"I like to think that I'm remembered for my contribution."

"Robert. I've thought about nothing but you, every day, for the last thirty-three years."

She sniffed the air. "The weather's almost here,…good. It'll do the job these mistakes", she pointed to Smith and then in the direction of the Ratepayers building, "couldn't finish."

The widow turned in her chair and motioned Smith around so she could see him. "Robert, have you figured out why I wanted you back here?"

"So we'd have to watch everything that these people built destroyed."

She shouted at him. "Don't pretend to be stupid. Answer my question!"

"So you two could finish your vendetta we put on hold."

Her voice softened. For the first time in decades, there was compassion. "Penance, Robert. It had nothing to do with us. We're just garbage. It's about these people, who you condemned to a life in purgatory. That's why you're here."

"You didn't need us. You could have finished it anytime!"

"Yes, but it was our hatred of you and the war you deprived us of, that kept everyone in this town waiting. Along with us, we produced Mr. Smith here and the folks at the Ratepayers. We kept Walter alive just to make sure that it happened. That's our crime."

She snapped her fingers and Smith started to push her wheelchair. "Let's take a drive over to the Ratepayers and pay Walter a visit. Robert, we'll have to take your car, mine appears to have developed mechanical problems."

As they approached the Ratepayers, they could see a crowd gathered in front of what was left of the building. She instructed him to pullover to the curb. "My, my, my, you've been a busy little beaver, Robert.

Smith got out and set up her wheelchair. When she sat down, she told him she didn't need him anymore. She wheeled herself out into the street, pleased that Walter, Sharon Potter, and the remaining men from district were there. "Walter! Good to see you. I get out so seldom these days. Where are the rioting mobs, lynchings, and burned out buildings that you promised me?"

Slezak licked his lips in anticipation. He finally had the Widow out of her hole, where he could get his hands on her. "They've gone to shelters. When they get back, we'll finish it.

"That is quite a plan. They hide in the basement, and then you kill them when it stops raining."

Slezak raised a gun and rope in his left hand. "Don't you worry; we'll make out just fine without you."

She laughed. "And you brought your toys."

She reached down in her seat. "Now, where did I put that? Ah, here we are. This is a very nice gun, and Robert, you have the safety on, Smart man."

Buzz reached for the gun in his shoulder holster. It was empty. The widow was full of surprises today. Everyone stepped back in fear, because in less than a second, several feet separated her from her chair. She effortlessly kicked it out into the street. She turned, raised the gun in one swift movement, and put a hole in John Smith's head. He hit her wheelchair landing dead center and sitting upright, as though he had always been there. She pulled the trigger again, spinning Smith and the chair around. It rolled slowly away and down the street. "This is a really nice piece, Robert."

She turned and looked at Slezak. "Walter! I'm having splendid day,… how about you?"

One of the men from the district made the mistake of raising his arm. She cut him down before he taken a breath, and proceeded to take the other three men out, as though they were bowling pins. Only Slezak and Potter were left.

She stood there, without moving a muscle, and then spoke quietly to the agent behind her. "Young man, I wouldn't if I were you." The agent slowly moved his hand away from his shoulder holster.

Potter took advantage of what she thought was a moment of distraction and raised her gun to fire. "You bitch!"

"Potter, I love what you've done with your hair." She put two bullets in her face.

Slezak look down at Potter deciding that she'd be easy enough to replace. He looked at the widow and waved his gun. "That's an eight shot clip and you're out of bullets."

She just stood there without saying a word, the gun at her side, as Slezak walked towards her with his gun raised. *Tick, Tock*, the Widow's time is up!"

It happened so fast that it caught him in mid-step. The 9-mm shell ripped a hole in his shoulder and spun him around with so much force it tore the gun out of his hand.

The agent looked at the widow, 'And one in the breech."

She sighed. "Walter is not a very bright man."

Turning to Buzz, she handed him back the gun. "Your Penance is paid, the both of you, because you two came back for the right reason. It wasn't to soothe your own conscience. You made the trip for the town's sake, even knowing they didn't deserve saving."

.She looked up. A tornado was starting to form directly over them. "You don't have a lot of time. Get out while you can, and make sure you have everyone with you. Try not to shoot yourself."

Slezak had managed to get back to his gun and tried to rush the widow from behind. "Excuse me for a moment, Gentlemen."

She pulled Slezak's chrome-plated 45 from her jacket pocket, and shot him again, through the same shoulder. This time, he wasn't going to be picking anything up. As she walked to Slezak, she askcd Buzz to say good-bye to Todd for her. "Walter! Look what you've down. You've gone and spoiled the moment."

She pulled him up off the pavement and he spat in her face. "You will pay!"

"I've already paid more than you can possibly imagine. I paid when Arthur Slezak came to my house, burned it down, and killed my sister. I paid when he drove my husband and what was left of our family out of New Mexico, at the end of a rope. I paid when my husband went to Buffalo to hide for the rest of his life and I stayed back to make them pay for what they done. And did I make them pay,... I made them all pay! I could have ended it all in a day, but hate is just like Heroin. It's a gift that just keeps on giving. I became addicted to it, the same hate, that vermin like you have survived on for centuries. Every day in Dusty, I vowed to share my agony. The best part of it all was that I made Arthur watch, right up to his last breath."

Slezak screamed. "You are insane! That happened 100 years ago."

She started dragging him into the wind. "It's amazing what a good anti-aging cream can do for the complexion."

As they drove away, the last thing Buzz saw was the widow pulling Slezak to his feet and dragging him into the approaching tornado. They vanished in an explosion of blood and fragments. Slezak screamed, right up to the minute the winds blew him apart.

Todd sat silently in his seat as the winds buffeted the aircraft. In the cockpit, the pilot was trying to get through his checklist as fast as possible. Terry and Jason were amazed at how calm Todd was. Buzz had told Todd to go with the young men. Todd understood why Buzz insisted, but that didn't make it any easier to leave.

He looked over at the two boys. "You guys okay?"

Terry wanted to know why the pilot just didn't take off.

Todd reassured them. "This is a complex machine. If you don't follow the procedures, you'll end up crashing. Don't worry. Bill is the best pilot in the business."

Bill stepped out of the cockpit, made sure the cabin door was locked and secured, and then took a fast look around the cabin to make sure nothing was loose which could injure his passengers.
"We're ready, Sir."

"How long have we known each other, Bill?"

"Eight years."

"Then, why are you still calling me Sir?"

"It comes from chauffeuring around nagging, over-paid prima donna's!"

One of the agents in the back burst out laughing. Todd yelled back at him. "I'm telling on you!"

"Sorry, Sir."

Bill turned to Jason and Terry. "Have you ever been in one of these before?"

They said they hadn't.

"Make sure you tighten your seat belts." He then turned to Todd and the men in the back, "You too."

The Lear bounced and rolled as it moved slowly off the ramp towards the runway. Bill turned the jet suddenly to the left and stopped it, just as a dust-devil the size of a bus crossed twenty feet in front of the plane. When Bill was sure the winds were safe, he straightened the plane and continued to the runway. Out of his window, the sky was dark and overcast, but almost still. His radar, set to 200 miles, told another story. There were at least four storm cells forming in the middle of his flight path, and all were less than thirty miles out. Bill whistled through his teeth and considered his options. The Lear accelerated like a rocket, and as soon as the weight was off the wheels, Bill could feel the storm.

With less than 200 feet under the jet, he executed a rate three turn, 180 degrees to the right at 200 knots. From where Todd was sitting, the right-hand wing tip fuel tank looked like a lawn mower. When Bill got to the heading he needed, he put the jet into a 4,500 feet-per-minute climb. They just made it out of the storm's path.

After fifteen tense minutes, the Lear reached altitude and leveled off. Bill let everyone know that the flight time to NASA would be an hour and forty-five minutes. That would give Todd time to get up to speed on the problem. Todd picked through the report for a while, and got up to stretch. It had been a long day. He wasn't even sure what time it was.

He walked to the back of the plane. "How do you guys like your first flight?"

Jason's thoughts were somewhere else and he didn't answer. Terry looked up from a brochure. "I thought it would be different."

"How so?"

"There is a lot more movement than I thought there would be, and you can't hear the engines." Todd told him not to worry, that the engines were still back there. They were just quieter, because the plane didn't need as much power in level flight.

"You must fly on these a lot."

"When I have to, but normally, I buy a ticket and get on the plane, just like everyone else."

Later, Bill called Todd up to the cockpit. "We're thirty minutes from touchdown, Todd. I thought it would be better if you heard it from me."

"Thanks."

"It's even worse than the meteorologists were predicting. The storm line is close to 500 miles in length. The cells, which have touched down, were all off scale. Fortunately, ninety-percent of the storm is coming down in the desert. There is going to a shortage of cactus for a while. The rest of the storm will hit built up areas, such as Globe, Arizona; Big Spring, Texas, and Dusty. Globe and Big Spring have reported 150 killed and 300 missing. Fifty percent of the housing was destroyed."

"Dusty?

"Nothing. EBS reports no signal, no shortwave. The town isn't even generating a repeater signal. I'm sorry, Todd."

Todd was obviously distressed, but hopeful. "I appreciate you telling me. I'm sure they're all right down there."

"If I hear anything else, I'll let you know."

"Do me a favor. There's a Navy hospital in VanderWagon. See if you can find out if it survived the storm."

"You got a friend there?"

"A couple of good friends."

"I'll see what I can do. You'd better get back and buckle up. We're going to be descending through the tail end of this thing and it might get a bit bumpy."

The man had a gift for understatement. Descending past 11,000 feet, there was a loud bang and a shudder. "We lost the fuel access door on the left side" He turned and grinned out the cockpit door. "But hey, no worries, we still have the wings!"

A tail wind hit the plane fifty feet from touch down causing the jet to go long on the runway. As Bill yelled that they had passed the 8,000 feet marker, one of the agents leaned forward and asked Todd how much was left.

When Todd told him, the agent asked what it cost to fix one of these things.

There was final rumble and the plane finally came to a stop. In the cabin, the passengers could hear the engines idling and Bill talking to the tower. He finally turned and told everyone it was okay to take off their seat belts.

Todd leaned out of his seat. "You okay up there, Bill?"

Bill looked at his co-pilot. "Do I have to tell him that I've never been this far up the runway before?"

Todd got out of his seat and went up to cockpit. The runway threshold lights were just under the jet's nose. "It doesn't get any closer than that!"

"And only one casualty!"

Todd frowned. "Everyone's okay in the back and you look okay."

Bill shook his head. "The casualty is my wits, as in scared out of!"

Todd patted his shoulder and went back into the cabin. "You're the man, Bill, you're the man."

Bill muttered to himself. "Wait till he gets the bill for my underwear."

In a couple of minutes, a tow vehicle arrived to take them to the terminal. A NASA vehicle was waiting for them. They weren't expecting five people, so it was a tight fit getting everyone into the car.

"We're having the meeting about the weather in the flight director's board room. We'll drop your friends off at accommodations."

Todd pointed to Terry and Jason. "My associates will be coming to the meeting."

The hallway at the Flight Control Center were jammed with people, most of them from atmospheric and meteorology.

Someone yelled. "Make a hole people, we're going to a meeting!"

Someone yelled back. "We all are!"

The room was so crowded, that they had to drag in chairs from another room. The flight director, Shawn Spano, stepped out of the crowd with his hand extended. He looked carefully at Terry and Jason, and then he spoke to Todd. "Good to have you back."

"Well, I've been out of town on business."

Shawn grinned from ear to ear. Christ! You're still the worst liar I've ever met. There isn't a guy in here, including me, who doesn't wish they were out there with you guys."

Todd looked shocked. "You knew where we were!"

"Everybody does! We're taking bets on the make and model of your next rental car. If it survived, we were going to send it to the moon."

Someone handed him a couple of sheets of paper, "The payloads not healthy, Shawn?"

"We're lucky there's even anyone here to talk to. The main event missed us by 150 miles, but it tore a hell of a hole in our Ultra High Frequency relays. There was nothing left but the anchors. And it's not over yet."

"There's more?"

Shawn nodded. "Our resident wind bags can explain it better than I can. But it has gone in to a loop or a spinning top. As the cells unload water, they get lighter and accelerate. Who're these guys?"

"They are my guests. I'll vouch for them."

"Swell. There are lots of guests here today, so they'll have someone to talk to." He pointed to someone across the room.

"Eddie! Eddie Gluck?"

"You know him?"

"I do."

"Do me a favor. Bring four people next time, so we'll have enough people for a hand of Bridge."

"You bet."

Spano looked at Terry and Jason and then his watch. "We'd better get started. Stay out of the way, fella's."

Todd got Eddie's attention and shook his hand. "Mr. Stiles."

"It's Todd, Eddie. I'm surprised, but glad to see you. How did you get here?"

A familiar voice from behind them spoke. "I arranged it."

Everyone turned to see Doctor Carlyle standing ten feet away. "I took the liberty of bringing him along. He wasn't going to learn anything carrying bags at the Wilshire Hotel."

Todd laughed at the thought of the manager trying to argue with her. "How did you manage to convince the manager?"

"It seems that of the few abilities I possess, one of them is the art of persuasion."

No one said a word.

"And he sends his regards."

Todd muttered to himself. "I'll bet he does."

She looked carefully at Terry and Jason. "It's a pleasure to meet you, Gentlemen."

Jason managed to mumble a response. "The pleasure is all ours, Ma'am."

She looked at Todd with approval. "Very good."

Shawn was ready to start. "Okay, people, let's get to work."

Terry, Eddie, and Jason were seated between the Doctor and Todd.

"Okay. There's a problem in the payload clocks. As you know, they have to synchronize at 10 to 16th seconds. We started to see it during the stacking, but it wasn't significant. We could compensate for the discrepancy. But, in the last three days of the count down, the problem has gotten worse and we're now outside of the limits. Numbers came to a complete stop at T-minus three days fifteen hours, and we had to do a restart. Any data we get back now is useless. Our launch window closes at 2320 hours. Let's break for dinner. Eat light and only take thirty minutes, people! I don't want anyone taking a nap on my watch. We'll meet back in mission control at 1800 hours."

Todd and Carlyle passed on dinner and went straight to mission control with the flight director and his people.

Jason, Eddie, and Terry couldn't remember when they had their last meal. They mugged a couple of vending machines for sandwiches and drinks. They found a table in the viewing room. It was the first time any of them had a chance to relax. Jason took a sandwich out of the wrapper and tapped it on the table. Eddie and Terry did the same.

"What's in yours?"

Eddie took a bite and chewed carefully, "Brown."

Jason opened the top of his sandwich. "I got green."

Terry proceeded to eat his sandwich. "I much prefer the mystery. Bon Appetit."

"NASA really knows how to show a guy a good time."

"So, what exactly is the thing so supposed to do, anyway? "Terry wanted to know.

Eddie brushed some crumbs off his shirt. "The only thing I can tell you is that it is supposed to fly really fast."

"How fast is that?"

"I think Mr. Stiles said 10% of the velocity of light."

Terry coughed on a mouthful of food. "That's not possible,… is it?"

Jason did some mental gymnastics. "I think that's about 18,000 miles per second."

"How are they going to do that?"

Eddie shook his head. "They said something about using a gravity well. But it's way over my head. All I know is that those clocks have to be very accurate with each other, or it won't work."

Jason looked at the monitor on the wall. The rocket was dead center in the middle of the screen. "One thing's for sure, that has to be a really big rocket!"

"What's that coming out of the side of it?"

"I think its fuel."

Eddie frowned for a moment. "I read something about that in a science magazine, that's liquid oxygen. As it heats up, it turns into a gas and vents overboard.

"It has to be pretty cold."

Terry got up tossing his empty cup and sandwich wrapper in the trash. "It's seriously cold. You see people in horror movies falling into it and breaking into pieces."

Eddie wondered if that was causing the problem.

"I can't see it. These guys are pretty smart. If it was an issue, they would've solved it by now."

Jason got up and walked over to a phone on the wall. "Let's find out."

"Are sure you should be doing that?"

He laughed. "What are they going to do, fire us?"

About ten minutes later, a NASA public relations representative stepped into the room and introduced himself as Carl Soles. "What can I do for you, fellows? You must be getting hungry."

"No, thanks, we ate already."

"Where?"

When they explained it was sandwiches from the machine, Carl rubbed his eyes in frustration. "That's just swell! I'll see that you're reimbursed for the cost. If you start to feel bad, we'll get the flight surgeon!"

Jason asked him if the oxygen coming off the rocket would affect the clocks.

"I'm sure they designed the machinery to account for that."

"So, you don't know?"

Carl whistled between his teeth for as the answer. "I'm not real familiar with this payload."

Terry and Eddie walked over to the monitor. "Was it hot when you got here, Ed?"

"Very hot, in the high 90's"

"I've lived out here almost my entire life. That's the way tornadoes work. They're heat engines, really hot in the front and cold in the back. The temperature inside that thing could have changed as much as 100 degrees since noon."

They didn't hear Carl come up behind them. "It can't be that simple."

Carl went to the phone and dialed a number. From the viewing room, the group could see Shawn Spano pick up his phone. Carl spoke briefly to him, and put the phone down.

A group of people suddenly gathered around a console. For the next hour, they poured over data on the screens and through technical manuals.

Suddenly, Eddie yelled to everyone to come over to the monitor. Liquid oxygen was suddenly pouring out of the side of the second stage. It was nearly impossible to see the rocket. An alarm went off and someone announced that the countdown had resumed.

The phone rang. Carl picked it up on the second ring. "Viewing room."

He put the phone down. "Follow me."

He led them down a long hall to a set of secure double door. "Listen up. You are not to talk to anyone, or touch anything. You do what you are told and you do not leave your seats. Are we clear?"

They all nodded silently.

As they stepped into the rooms, all of the controllers stood and gave them a standing ovation. Spano waited about twenty seconds, before telling everyone to sit down. Spano did not approve of that sort of thing in his control room. Before he took his seat, he gave Eddie, Jason, and Terry a brief nod of approval.

Carl directed them to chairs off to the side and gave them headsets without microphones. At 2020 hours, ERF 404 left the pad at Cape Canaveral. It was a spectacular launch against the setting sun. When it cleared the tower and was safely on its way, Carlyle took off her headset.
"Our people did good work today."
"Indeed."

When the rocket reached stable orbit, Spano escorted them out. "These people still have a lot of work to do and you have had a long day. I understand you've an early departure tomorrow, with wheels up at 0730. Accommodation has been arranged for you in the astronaut quarters. Someone will be along to collect you in a couple of minutes. Have you had anything to eat?"

They all agreed they could use a break and that they weren't hungry.

It was the first good night that Terry and Jason'd had in years. They didn't see any astronauts, but they spent the night thinking about a future that was still years away. They all agreed on one thing that night, that they'd built a friendship they were going to look after.

They were up early and had a breakfast that wasn't dispensed out of a machine, thanks to Carl Soles, and were at the airfield 0700. They arrived as NASA's research facility B-52 taxied past.

That is a big airplane!" Eddie yelled over the noise.

There were two Lear jets parked at the hanger, one for Eddie and Dr. Carlyle, to take them back, and the other for Todd and his party.

Bill was doing an inspection when they arrived. "You guys have a good time?"

"Yeah, it was seriously impressive."

"Did you learn anything?"

Jason laughed. "Don't eat anything out of the vending machines."

Bill laughed. "You guys are going to go a long way on the road of life."

"Where's Mr. Stiles?"

"He'll be along in a minute. Eddie, I'm afraid you'll be delayed. Dr. Carlyle will be about an hour late. Carl has arranged a tour of the simulators until she arrives. I'll give you guys a minute to say the good-byes."

They took a couple of minutes to talk, and then shook hands. Terry yelled to Eddie as he walked away, "In a year!"

Eddie waved and gave him a thumbs up.

Todd's car pulled up. He got out and thanked the driver. "Sorry I'm late. Where's Ed?"

Jason told him that Dr. Carlyle was delayed so he was getting a simulator tour while he was waiting.

"I was looking forward to saying good-bye to him. Bill, did you get the panel replaced?"

Bill answered with sarcasm. "No, I just bought you a new airplane."

"I hope you're kidding."

Bill stood there and grinned. "And I sprung for the all the options including a newer model co-pilot."

A short wiry man with a shock of red hair stepped out of the plane. "I've checked the cabin oxygen. We're good to go."

"Todd, this is my right seat on the flight.

"Hi, I'm Andy Mangle."

Todd slowly shook his hand, trying not to react to the name. "Well, good to have you along. We appreciate you volunteering for this."

"I'm being blackmailed. Nobody volunteers to fly with Wild Bill."

Bill still hadn't stopped grinning. "It's a hobby of mine."

Andy turned and looked at Bill. "You're a mean little man and I hate you."

Bill patted him on both shoulders. "Come on now; let's not have any more sniveling."

As they prepared to board, another NASA car pulled up and Shawn Spano got out.

Todd was surprised to see him. "You didn't have to come all the way out here to say good-bye, Shawn."

Shawn looked Todd up and down with mock distaste. "Why would I come out here to see you?"

He waved Terry and Jason over. "I came out here because I failed to complete one of my duties as a flight director. "Gentlemen, you are steely-eyed missile men.

Without another word, he turned and headed back to his car and drove off. They looked at each other as Spano drove away, "Was that a compliment, Jason?"

Todd whistled. "Was it ever!"

Bill yelled at them and tapped his watch. Twenty minutes later, they were on their way back to Dusty.

When the plane was at altitude, Bill called Todd up to the cockpit. He had folded down the jump seat behind them. "We've got to stop meeting like this."

"I'm in trouble. You're the only one who laughs at my jokes."

"I wish this was funny. Andy, hand me that last update"

He leafed through it. "Okay, you wanted to know about the Navy hospital in Waggoner. It got hit, more like a side swipe. Broken windows, roof gone, and one wing was damaged. The good news is that the place was built in the 50's. It had been a civil defense shelter. No casualties. I spoke to that Lieutenant personally. She has a message for you."

Bill handed Todd a piece of paper off the clip board. "Winifred says thank you."

Bill looked at Todd, with concern. "You okay?"

Todd put the paper in his pocket. "Thanks Bill."

He looked down at the clipboard. "Do you want to read it?"

He shook his head. "You can tell me."

"There were four touch downs, two in the south end of town, one in the north. That would be the one your friends saw."

"And the fourth one?"

"It came down right in the center of town. The data is on the second sheet."

Todd looked through the numbers. Everything for a mile on either side of it would have been destroyed. He handed the clipboard back to Andy.

"Seventy percent of the town was destroyed. No one has been on the ground yet and there's no signal out of there. The good news is that there have been flights over the area, and they've seen a few people moving around down there. The airfield was on the north side. The navigation system was hit and we don't even know if there's even a serviceable runway. I can't promise I'll even be able to get us in there. Sorry, Todd, but I'm the Pilot in Command. It's my call."

"No problem, Bill. I wouldn't even ask."

"I know, but I still have to say it. It comes with the job."

An hour later, Andy was on the intercom. "We'll be over Dusty in two minutes. You'll be able to see it on the right side."

They made three passes over the town. The damage was impossible to describe. "Okay, Andy, we've seen enough. Let's plow the road with this thing."

Two passes over the airfield said it all. The tower was gone and the airfield was obliterated. "How's our fuel?"

Andy checked his gauges and the logs. "We've got twenty minutes and then we'd better be going to the alternate."

Heading is 202 at 15,000 which will get us there in thirty minutes. El Poro reports the wind is steady at 180, and the ceiling is 10,000."

"It means they are expecting weather."

"Looks like it."

"All right, let's make two passes over 16 and then 28. If we can't do it, we go to the alternate."

"That will work."

Bill put the Lear in a slow turn and started to descend.

"How low are you going?"

"About fifty feet."

Andy looked at him over his glasses. "Are you going to look at it or sweep it?"

Bill yelled into the back. "Buckle up!"

The Lear was low enough to move debris. When they completed the passes, Bill took them south back over the town. 8 is shot full of holes but 16 looks good enough. It looks like the winds blew everything away from the runway."

Andy checked the approach plates for Dusty. "Runway 16 is 4,800 feet. That's minimum under ideal conditions for this aircraft. Even with no passengers, we'd barely be inside envelope."

Bill laughed. "I flew Corsairs off the Kennedy. This should be a walk in the park."

When they completed the landing checklist, set the flaps and lowered the gear, Bill put the plane into a terrifying rate of descent to the runway. "Is this what a carrier approach looks like?"

Bill was very focused. "No, the runway moves up and down a lot more."

It was a perfect landing and Bill brought the plane to a stop 100 feet short of the taxiway. "How did you like your first carrier landing?"

Andy looked at him, expressionless. "You're paying for my underwear."

They couldn't get onto the taxiway because of debris. Bill turned the plane around on the runway to prevent Foreign Object Debris from getting into the engines.

Stepping out of the plane, the only sound they could hear was the wind rattling broken sheet metal in the distance, and the engine's ticking as they slowly came to a stop.

Now what happens?" Andy wanted to know.

"We'd better do a pre-flight check, just in case we need to get out of here in a hurry."

Jason joined Terry as he looked at the devastation. "You okay?"

"He was a monster and I hated him. But no one deserved this, Jason."

"Hey! Has anybody seen Todd?"

Terry pointed to something in the distance. "What the hell is that?"

"It's a towing tractor."

Todd drove up in a bright yellow vehicle. "It's not pretty, but there is lots of room. It's got a full tank of gas, and it's a convertible."

"Is this all there is?"

"Unfortunately, yes, everything else is gone. Maybe that's good news. Maybe they took everything to get out."

Everyone was quiet as they passed the spot where Terry, Jason and Todd had been stopped by the men from the district. "There was nothing there.

It was hard to tell when they had actually gotten into the town, because all of the landmarks were gone. In some places, even the foundations were missing, leaving only scars in the ground. Todd pulled over and got out. "The rest of you go on and see if you can find anyone. I'll be all right."

Bill looked at the hill in the distance. "We'll come back for you in a couple of hours."

Todd didn't watch them depart as he walked slowly up the road to the top of what was once a hill. It had been scraped absolutely clean. Not even the grass had been spared.

Thirty years of hatred, bigotry, had been wiped clean by a few seconds of wind. He took a deep breath, the air felt fresh. It was wonderful.

He didn't hear the car approaching or the driver getting out and walking up the hill. Buzz Murdoch stood there with his hands in his pockets, and allowed Todd time to take it all in, just as he had. "Todd Stiles!"

He turned as soon as he heard the voice. Buzz;... you're a sight for sore eyes!"

Buzz raised his arms. "I'm not just a pretty face."

They stayed for another hour without a word being said, looking at the space once occupied by the house owned by the Widow Weeks. In the end, before they left the hill for the last time, Buzz summed it up. "It's hard to believe we have come all this way for this."

"It was never been about the destination, Buzz. It was the journey."

They had to pick their way back into town because the road was full of holes. "Pull over for a moment, Todd."

They didn't bother getting out to look at the hole where the Ratepayers used to be.

The residents of Dusty were slowly starting to return from the missile silo. Jason had found his aunt and uncle, and introduced them to Buzz and Todd. They had nothing but praise for Buzz and the agents from Beachler-Carlyle, on how they organized everything. When a twister hit the top of the silo, Buzz and the agents were able to get everyone into the secure area before anyone was hurt."

Todd laughed. "The man does know concrete."

Jason's aunt looked at Todd, Buzz, and Jason. "You people are coming to our house for dinner."

His uncle looked at her like she had suddenly gone nuts. "Woman! We don't even know if we've even got a house."

` "Well, you had better find one, because I'm not eating on the lawn."

Terry looked in the distance. "I guess I'd better go home."

"I'll go with him Buzz."

"That's a good idea. I'll go help Jason's people and then drive out to the trailer."

"The Corvette?'"

"We didn't have time to get it." Buzz answered with regret.

"It's all right, there'll be other cars."

It was a slow walk the ten blocks to Walter Slezak's house, and the walk was even harder without reference points.

Nature, when it needs to, can send a message. "My wrath is often indiscriminate, but make no mistake; I can find time for those who are most deserving."

Every house on the block was obliterated, *except* Slezak's. Every piece of it was still there, but it looked like it had been stomped on by a giant foot. It had been flattened, right down to the foundation.

Todd stood back as Terry picked through the rubble. He looked down and picked up what looked like several papers from a memo that had been in a file cabinet. Slezak's last situation report to the district that was never sent, he had written it in advance, because he was that sure of success. It was not a good read. He looked up. Terry was on his way back. Todd tore up the documents and let the wind scatter the pieces.

He showed Todd a broken electronic game that he'd in his hand. The young man started to cry. "He stepped on it. What did I do to him that would make him want to do this?"

Todd looked at what was left of the house. He remembered the widow's place and the Ratepayers. "You can remember your uncle anyway you wish. That's your right. But trust me Terry, none of this was your fault."

After a minute, he asked the young man a question. Do you think you can get us to Jason's place?"

He rubbed his eyes. "I think so. He lives on the south side. It'll take about an hour."

"Good. It will give us time to talk."

As they started to walk, Todd stopped him. "Do you want to have a last look?"

"No, we'd better keep going."

It was a long walk. It was relief to see that the area where Jason's aunt and uncle lived had been spared.

"Welcome to Hotel FEMA." Jason's aunt shouted when they finally got to the door.

Jason's uncle rolled his eyes. "The taxpayer, if my wife has anything to do with it, is going to be screwed. By the time she's finished, there's going to be a mansion standing here."

Jason came out of the kitchen. "You okay?'

Todd reflected. "It's turning out to be a long day."

Jason's aunt stepped forward. "Call me Ann. I've got a room made up for you in what's left of the place. That miserable old fart of a husband of mine won't say it, but we'd be honored if you'd call this home."

Jason's uncle stepped forward and extended a hand. "Hi, I'm the miserable old fart!"

"Todd Stiles."

Todd looked around. When he was sure they were alone, Jason's uncle fished a bottle of scotch out of his jacket pocket. "I think we've earned this."

Todd took the bottle and looked at it. "I think we have."

"And the name is Gil."

Buzz appeared in the back yard an hour later, just as Ann was serving a late lunch. "I hope you like canned food. We will be eating it for a while."

"Todd, I have news," said Buzz. Do you want the good news, or the bad news, first?"

"I'll take the good first."

The Corvette is parked out front. "Not a scratch on it."

Todd was ecstatic. "That is great and that means we don't have to replace the luggage, either!"

"Oh, yes we will."

"What are you talking about? You said the car was all right."

"It is. It's the trailer. It's gone."

Todd put his drink down without saying anything, trying to understand.

"It's the damnedest thing. There was nothing left, not a trace, just the pole and the car."

"That is bad news. That was Mickey John's home."

Buzz shook his head, reached into a bag, and pulled out Todd's pajamas. "This is the bad news!"

"My pajamas, you saved them!"

Everyone was getting a good laugh, when Buzz responded vehemently and without humor. "No, I did not, and you can't prove it! They were stuck to the pole. I am not taking the wrap for this."

Gil stood up and introduced himself. "What was the name of the guy who owned the trailer?"

"Mickey John."

Ann put drinks down on the table. "Wasn't that the guy who ran the weigh scale?"

"Did you know him?" Todd asked.

Gil looked at his wife who shrugged. "Mickey John passed away ten years ago."

The next four days in Dusty, New Mexico, was a time of rebuilding and reconciliation. For Terry, it was a difficult time apologizing to people who understood, and who reminded him that they all had things to regret.

It finally fell to Ann, who took Terry aside. She told him that it was time to put the past behind him. It was the future that mattered. "I'm concerned about Jason and I'm counting on you to get past your prejudice, so that you two can work together on your journey."

"He promised that he would try.

She did something that four years ago, neither of them could have imagined. Ann pulled Terry forward and kissed him on the forehead. "I know you will."

It was seven in the evening when Todd Stiles and Buzz Murdoch pulled the Corvette off the road and came to a stop. Buzz turned the engine off. Farther down the road, they could see a road sign move in the breeze.

They got out and stretched. In the distance, heat rose off the pavement, making it difficult to see anything coming. "They'll be along, Todd."

He looked at his watch. "We've got a few minutes before they get here. Have you got the coin?"

"I'd forgotten all about that."

As usual, it took couple of minutes of searching to find it.

"It's your turn to toss, Todd."

"No, this is kind of a special moment, you should do it."

Buzz stood next to the car and tossed the coin.

This time, it seemed to take an unusually long time to fall to the car. The reflections from the coin made it seem as though it was falling in slow motion.

It hit the hood, bounced uncertainly, standing up right. They were about to start breathing again, when the coin wobbled briefly. It then slowly toppled over, landing heads up. Neither of them moved. Then, from far off, they could hear the sound of a car.

Todd reached out and picked up the coin, turning it over in his hand, sadly. "I guess every journey has to come to an end, someday."

He handed the coin to Buzz as a car pulled up behind them and two young men got out.

Todd walked over to their car and gave it the once over, as the old guard is wont to do.

Buzz nodded with approval. "It's a 1973 Corvette, big block, right?'

"That it is."

"Where did you guys get it?"

"Remember Barney's garage?"

"Wasn't that on the south side as you come into town, Buzz?"

"I think so."

"Well, we thought having a Vette was such a great idea we went and talked to Barney. He had been hanging on to this one for years and we made him an offer."

"What did you do? Mug him?"

Jason pretended to be shocked. "Sir,…we are professionals!"

"We traded your car for it."

Todd looked at them in amazement. "You traded a Pacer for a Corvette!"

"Well, that and a thousand dollars that Jason's aunt and uncle gave us to get us started.

Buzz burst out laughing. "It's a new generation."

"The Pacer was a good car."

"That it was, Todd."

Buzz pulled the coin out of his pocket and handed it to Jason. "It's been a good guide for us. When you are in a bind, let the coin decide for you."

Terry thanked them. "We'll look after it."

In the distance, they could hear and feel a ground thumping thunder. The car was past them, giving them less than a second to see long blond hair and the tell-tale cat's eye taillights in the distance, as the brakes came on. "Buzz, Corvettes are definitely getting faster."

He looked into the distance, "and better looking."

THE
LAST MILE

"All good journeys end at sunset."
—anonymous

They watched until the Corvette disappeared on the horizon.

"So, have you got a plan?"

Jason nodded. "Terry and I were accepted to Michigan State, but we're going to wait a year and drift around a bit, so that Eddie can catch up."

They were surprised. "Eddie Gluck?"

"Yeah, his grades are good enough to get into college. But, he wants to improve his math and science.

Todd was impressed. "Good for him!"

"It's pretty cool. He's decided to major in engineering."

Buzz whistled. "Awesome!"

Terry spoke for the both of them. "We sure appreciate everything you've done for us and for Eddie."

There was a silence for a minute before Buzz spoke. "We can't take any of the credit. It was a decision that you two made together and both of you followed it through to the end."

Buzz reached into his pocket, took out an envelope and handed it to Todd.

Todd opened it and examined the contents. He removed a short letter. He read it carefully, before putting it back in the envelope. "That looks good, Buzz."

He handed the envelope to Terry. "That's for the both of you. The amount is comparable to what we had in our pockets on our first day."

Buzz offered some advice on some places they could consider. "We started heading south towards Missouri."

Jason shook his head, politely. "Actually, Jason and I have decided to head north and see what's up there."

Buzz nodded, understanding.   There wasn't much left to say. Terry looked up at the sky and wondered about its color.

Buzz told him the color was indigo.

"Jason, we'd better get going."

All four, two young men and two older shook hands and split up.
They could hear the sound of the warm pavement under their feet, on a summer evening. It was Todd's turn to drive.

Buzz looked back to see Jason getting behind the wheel, before he climbed into the car. He slowly pulled the door shut until he could hear the latch catch.

Neither Buzz nor Todd said a word. They sat staring silently through the windshield. Behind them, they could hear Jason start the car.

A moment later, Jason and Terry pulled out onto the highway. As they passed Todd and Buzz they could see Terry with a map in his hand, making a suggestion to Jason.

Todd and Buzz were, once more, alone on the road to Route 66.

Buzz blew out a deep breath and looked at the sign a couple hundred yards up the road, "Interstate 93, Right 10 miles. Old Route 66, 10 miles Right, via 16."

He looked at Todd. "You all right?"

Todd had to think about that one for a moment. Yeah, I'm okay; I was just remembering something Andrea said to me."

Todd reached down, turned the key, and the Corvette came to life. As he was watching the gauges, the tach settled at 500 RPM. They waited another three or four minutes, trying to take it all in, one last time.

"It's time, Todd."

He nodded. "It's time."

Four miles southwest, an NOAA helicopter was doing ground radar surveys to assess the tornado damage.

The co-pilot tapped the pilot on the shoulder and pointed down and to the right at the road. "What kind of cars are those?"

The pilot leaned forward to get a better look and smiled,"Shame on you, young man! Those are Corvettes."

"You're sure?"

"I know my sports cars. The one out in front is a mid-seventies Corvette, and the one farther back is an early sixties."

A voice from the back of the helicopter came through the intercom. "We're here to do a ground survey, not a traffic report."

The pilot looked over at the co-pilot, shook his head, and laughed. He'd already moved on, and was back to looking at his instruments.

The pilot turned back to the road below him. There was an overpass in the distance, and two cars-- a newer one in the lead and the older one following.

The voice in the back called for a heading change and the pilot slowly rolled the helicopter to the left. Two cars: one young, one old. He smiled to himself,…passing the torch."

The first car went under the overpass, slowed briefly, and then, dropped off the highway on to Route 93 going north. The second car exited the highway, turned right, and went over the overpass.

The pilot let the helicopter drift slowly, keeping the second car in the lower left corner of the windshield, until it made the turn onto Old Route 66. There was a call for another course change for the helicopter, which would take it north and away from the receding car.

As the pilot made the course correction, he took one last look. It was an image he would remember for the rest of his life.

Two men in a sports car, crossing an old iron bridge at sunset.